A Salty Piece
of Land

Also by Jimmy Buffett

Tales from Margaritaville

Where Is Joe Merchant?

A Pirate Looks at Fifty

(and for young readers)

The Jolly Mon

Trouble Dolls

A Salty Piece of Land

JIMMY BUFFETT

LITTLE, BROWN AND COMPANY

New York Boston

The author is grateful for permission to include the following: "If I Had a Boat," written by Lyle Lovett. © 1987 Michael H. Goldsen, Inc./Lyle Lovett (ASCAP). All rights reserved. Used by permission; "Lawyers, Guns and Money," written by Warren Zevon, ©1978, Zevon Music. All rights reserved. Used by permission; "The Wind Cries Mary," written by Jimi Hendrix, © Experience Hendrix, L.L.C. Used by permission. All rights reserved; excerpt from *The Little Prince* by Antoine de Saint-Exupéry, English translation copyright © 1943 by Harcourt Inc. and renewed 1971 by Consuelo de Saint-Exupéry, English translation copyright © 2002 by Richard Howard, reprinted by permission of Harcourt Inc.

Fish illustration by Peter Bernard

Little, Brown and Company
Hachette Book Group USA
1271 Avenue of the Americas
New York, NY 10020
Visit our Web site at www.HachetteBookGroupUSA.com.

Printed in the United States of America

Originally published in hardcover by Little, Brown and Company, November 2004
First Little, Brown and Company mass market edition, November 2006

10 9 8 7 6 5 4 3 2 1

For Peetsy, Jay, and Groovy

To forget a friend is sad. Not everyone has had a friend, and if I forget him, I may become like the grown-ups who are no longer interested in anything but figures.

— *Antoine de Saint-Exupéry,*
The Little Prince

We sail within a vast sphere,
Ever drifting in uncertainty
Driven from end to end
— Pascal

contents

Author's Note   xv

Contents   xiii

author's note

November 30, 2001
Coconut Grove, Florida

George Harrison died yesterday. I found out as I
checked my e-mail this morning before waking
Cameron early, which I "pinky" swore to do last
night. I walked out onto the balcony of this hotel
and looked out to the east over the rusty Pan Am
hangars and the decaying wooden markers that
framed the once-active runways for the Clippers as
they came and went on their pioneering routes
from Biscayne Bay. They are gone as well.

Everything leaves eventually in the physical
form, but the memories of good people and good
work are timeless. So instead of saying a prayer, I
just visualized George Harrison boarding a Pan
Am Clipper, guitar case in hand, greeted by
Captain Gardner McKay and entertainment
director Fred Neil.

The plane lifts off the silky surface of the bay and heads toward the rising sun out over Elliot Key and the distant shimmering waters of the Gulf Stream — I would call a flight like that one hell of a joyride on the way to the ultimate adventure. Have fun, boys.

Mortality marches on — today, George Harrison; last week, Gardner McKay; and in July, Fred Neil. I'd better get to work.

December 24, 2003
Palm Beach, Florida

Unfortunately the manifest for this flight has grown. Please make a note that added to the crew is Gordon Larimore Gray III, copilot; and James Delaney Buffett and Mary Loraine Peets Buffett — newly arrived honeymooners bound for eternity.

— JB

1

The Soul of the Light

tully mars, checking in

It all simply comes down to good guys and bad guys. As a kid, I wanted to be like Roy Rogers, the good-guy cowboy of all time. Roy and his horse, Trigger, would go riding through the movies, helping those in peril while never seeming to sweat, get a scratch, or wrinkle a pair of perfectly creased blue jeans. When the day was over, they would join the Sons of Pioneers by the campfire and sing the sun to sleep. Now that is what I called the perfect job.

One day, long ago in another place and another time, I was playing out my fantasy of being Roy with my childhood pals in the rolling hills above Heartache, Wyoming, where I was raised. We were racing our horses, bat-out-of-hell style, through the aspen grove that led to our little ranch. Like a true daredevil, I passed my friends in a wild sprint to the finish line, and once I had the lead, I turned around to admire my move as the leader of the pack. The next thing I remembered was waking up on the ground, my head covered with blood, my left arm pointing in the wrong direction, and pain — lots of pain — shooting through my young body. That's when I knew that life wasn't a movie.

During my mending process, I discovered a new role model in Butch Cassidy, who took me through my teenage years. He wasn't perfect. He made mistakes, and that seemed more in tune with the way my life was working out in the real world. He thumbed his nose at authority. To put it in today's terms, Butch Cassidy didn't work for The Man. He was his own man. He ran away to Patagonia.

The West was changing, and so was I. Now, looking back, I have to thank old Roy for teaching me that when you fall from your horse, you climb back in the saddle and plow ahead. From Butch, I figured out that what I wanted to be was my own man — just a good guy with a few bad habits. This is Tully Mars reporting in.

When I left Wyoming some years ago and made a not-so-difficult choice between becoming a poodle-ranch foreman or a tropical expatriate, I tossed a massage table through the giant plate-glass window of the ranch house owned by my former boss and modern-day witch, Thelma Barston. That day, heading off to freedom, I made myself a promise. As I fled across America, I swore I would never again work for anybody but me. I pretty much kept that promise until I met Cleopatra Highbourne.

Cleopatra Highbourne is my present boss and the woman who brought me here to this salty piece of land in the southern Bahamas. She hired me to restore a 150-year-old lighthouse on Cayo Loco, which she owns, having swapped for it with the Bahamian government for some property on Bay Street in Nassau.

To begin with, Cleopatra is 101 years old, but she doesn't look a day over 80. She is the captain of her beautiful schooner, the *Lucretia,* which was a present from her father on her eighteenth birthday.

Cleopatra has simply defied the aging process. Her eyes are a piercing green, and her speech is lilted with an island accent that is somewhere between Jamaican and Cuban. There isn't a romance language or Caribbean patois she doesn't speak like a native, and there isn't an island she hasn't set foot on between Bimini and Bonaire. Her skeleton is erect, which she attributes to being a practitioner of yoga for eighty years, having been taught the craft by Gandhi himself. She wears no hearing aids or glasses. Her skin is void of the weathered, leatherlike appearance caused by age, ocean, and ultraviolet exposure. She never smoked cigarettes, but she has her daily ration of rum and occasionally will puff a little opium if she is feeling ill. She also has a taste for Cuban cigars.

She dines on fish, rice, and tropical fruits, and a collection of potions, teas, and elixirs keep her biorhythms, brain, and sense of humor humming. She cusses like the sailor that she is, and she is rabidly addicted to Cuban baseball.

Though she says she has a few good years left in her, Cleopatra is on a most urgent mission, and that is where I come in. I am here to rebuild the lighthouse as her final resting place while she continues her search for an original Fresnel lens, which was the light source for this and many other old lighthouses.

So how does a cowboy wind up as a lighthouse keeper? Well, I didn't fill out any job application. How I went from the saddle, to the deck of a schooner, to the tower of this lighthouse, still baffles me. But I believe in the aboriginal line of thinking that life's adventures are the verses and choruses of your unique song, and when it is over, you are dead. So far, I am still singing, but I would point out that adventures don't come calling like unexpected cousins visiting from out of town. You have to go looking for them, and that is exactly how I wound up on Cayo Loco.

I saw Cayo Loco for the first time from the deck of the *Lucretia*. All I knew about lighthouses up until that point was that they were warning lights, and they marked some kind of trouble. I'd heard a few stories, and I'd met a guy who had some theories about them, but that was it. I sat in a dinghy next to Cleopatra as the crew pulled for the shore, and the lighthouse loomed so huge that I had to lean my entire head back just to see the top.

"This is it," Cleopatra said to me as we made our way toward the beach. "I traded those bumbling bureaucrats in Nassau a building they needed for a Junkanoo museum on Bay Street for her. I think we both came out okay. All we have to do is fix her up and get the light back in shape."

"No problem," I said, shrugging. After what I had recently been through, fixing up an old lighthouse sounded like a piece of cake.

As the bottom of the dinghy brushed against the shallow sand, Cleopatra sprang to the beach like a teenager. I had to laugh. Three months earlier, my life was rolling by at a snail's pace, and I was sitting on the beach in Mexico, wondering if the day would ever end. Then, all of a sudden, a ship carries me to a completely foreign place that would now become my home.

Solomon, Cleopatra's first mate, buried the anchor in the sand. All you had to do was look at his huge body, his kind eyes, and his weathered hands to know that he was the kind of person you wanted running your crew and your ship. "I'll stay with da boat, Cap'n," he said.

"Then I'll be the tour guide," Cleopatra said. She nodded at a narrow path up through the dunes. "Welcome to Cayo Loco, Tully Mars."

The well-worn path from the beach snaked up through the small dunes and then disappeared up the hill into a cluster of sea oats. We stopped at the top of the hill and looked down on the wreckage of time. With the exception of the light tower itself, the place looked as if someone had dropped a bomb on it. The concrete walls of what had been the compound of the lighthouse keeper came into view. The windows had been blown out, and the roof had been partially burned off.

We made our way through the overgrown paths, pushing back thorny bougainvillea bushes, sea grapes, and hibiscus blooms that camouflaged more destruction.

"This is the old cistern," Cleopatra said as we walked across a large rectangle. "This place was one of the first spots on earth where they made freshwater out of salt water. Those damn limeys have a strange fascination for remote and desolate places, but you got to hand it to them — they knew how to bring creature comforts to the boondocks. When Solomon's father was the light keeper here, this place was a little piece of paradise. There was a vegetable garden, flowered paths, and even a manicured green lawn."

At close range, even the tower showed the ravages of

salt and sea. I stared up at the peeling paint and the cracks in the outer wall.

"Good morning, St. Peter," Cleopatra said as she stopped before a large, thick spiderweb strung across our path. Its weaver, a nasty-looking purple-and-yellow spider the size of my hand, hung suspended across the path. He seemed ready to defend his territory. There was no doubt that this was a web you could not just brush away without consequences.

"You know this spider?" I asked Cleopatra.

"He's perfectly harmless, if you don't piss him off," she replied.

We detoured around St. Peter and walked in the brush between two small buildings. A raccoon exploded out of the underbrush and scurried off toward the beach.

"I thought you said this island was uninhabited," I said.

Cleopatra didn't answer.

While I stood in the rubble looking around, I began to have serious doubts. Then a banging noise caught my attention, and I turned around to see Cleopatra hammering away at a padlock with the butt end of her machete. It was chained to a large iron door at the base of the lighthouse. Walking over, I waded through a toxic dump of decaying lead acid batteries that encircled the light tower. The people who'd been in charge of maintaining the automated light had simply tossed the dead batteries from the tower when they replaced them, adding to the bombed-out look of the cottages and grounds of the keeper's residence.

I looked from the rubble up to the lines of the giant lighthouse and the blue sky above it. On the voyage over to the Bahamas, Cleopatra had told me the story of where the lighthouse came from and how it had gotten here.

Even though the lighthouse had seen better days, the sheer strength of it was still very much apparent. I just stood there and stared up, wondering how in the hell they'd built it.

"This goddamn salt air will eat anything. I just put this lock on here last month."

I went over to lend a hand. After a few more direct hits with a big rock, the padlock sprang, and I pried the iron door open. It creaked and squeaked and let out a thud as it banged against the wall.

Inside, it was dark and hot and smelled like shit.

"Here," Cleopatra said, handing me a flashlight.

I followed her with the beam of my flashlight, trying to keep pace as she bounced ahead of me like Becky Thatcher while I cautiously navigated the winding staircase.

Our movements echoed off the iron cylindrical walls as we climbed through musty, humid air that had been trapped inside the lighthouse for God knows how long. Several furry little fruit bats scanned us with their radar as they fluttered around my head.

"Don't worry," Cleopatra called out. "I know a way to get the bats out of here when you move in."

Up and up we circled, until small beams of light appeared at the top. Cleopatra stopped on the stairs below the source of the light — a rusty hatch cover just above us. "I always like this part," she said. "It reminds me of the time I met Thomas Edison — the night he threw the switch that lit up the Brooklyn Bridge at the three hundredth celebration of the founding of the city of New York."

"You knew Thomas Edison?" I asked.

"No, my father did. We were in New York on our way

to France and boarding school, and we just happened to be at the right place at the right time."

I followed the beam of Cleopatra's flashlight as we inched up slowly.

"Electricity ain't a bad contribution to the betterment of mankind in general, but it sure as hell wreaked havoc on the lighthouse keepers of the world. The record player would have to go on the top of my list of Edison inventions, way ahead of movies and lightbulbs."

Cleopatra took a marlinespike out of the case on her belt and jabbed away at the hinges of the hatch. The hatch gave way with a creak.

"Ready?" Cleopatra asked.

Sunlight flooded down around us. We lifted ourselves through the hole in the sky, and I stood there bathed in the morning light of the glass room. Below us, the *Lucretia* looked like a toy boat sitting at anchor on the smooth surface of crystal clear water that seemed to be only inches deep. But in fact it was in nearly thirty feet of water.

I could see several members of the crew diving up conch from the bottom. The view from the light tower encompassed the whole island, against a backdrop of turquoise shallows and the deep blue ocean beyond. Cleopatra pointed out the landmarks of Whale Cut, Boo Hoo Hill, and Osprey Point that I would come to know as well as my horse.

"Unbelievable" was all I could muster.

"And well worth saving, don't you think?"

"I get the picture."

"Except for that," she added, pointing to the bizarre tangle of frayed wires, makeshift junction boxes, and a strobe light resting atop a long, skinny shaft. "That has to go. The original lens that came with this light was not only a piece of engineering genius but a work of art. The lenses, circular prisms, and source that created the beam of light is called the bull's-eye because it looks like a clear glass target. A French physicist named Augustin Fresnel designed it in the early eighteen hundreds."

"How did it work?" I asked her.

"The prisms concentrated the burner's light into a piercing beam that shot out to the horizon. The crystal lenses were held together by brass plates, and the whole thing weighed about four tons and floated in a circular tub containing about twelve hundred pounds of quicksilver. That allowed it to spin in a near frictionless environment. It was rotated by a clockwork assembly of ropes and weights that hung down the shaft of the lighthouse, and it had to be wound every two hours by the lighthouse keeper on duty. The sword of light it stabbed out into the darkness could be seen for twenty miles." Cleopatra paused as if remembering specific images. "Seen from the deck of a ship, it radiates its presence like nothing else on earth. Sailors call it the soul of the light."

"I guess all that beauty and precision seemed way too complicated for the twentieth century," I said.

"You would have thought that such a thing of beauty would wind up in a museum, but not here. They severed the base with a blowtorch, shoved it out the window, and just let gravity finish the job. Thus, the soul of the light was ripped out, smashed on the rocks, and the brass frame that once held the intricate Fresnel-lens system in place was sold for scrap." Cleopatra let out a big sigh. "That is what replaced it," she said, pointing at the present light source. "In a modern world, there is just no time for hand-pumping kerosene or winding a clock. In the name of progress, they turned the Cayo Loco Light into a giant toaster."

As we wound our way down the steps and finally out of the dark interior of the lighthouse, Cleopatra also wound me around her finger. Her mission was to find a bull's-eye lens before she died.

"You can't just order one up from the True Value hardware man," she told me. "It's a needle-in-a-haystack thing, but I'll find one. In the meantime, we have to rebuild this place and make it look like it did in its heyday, and that is where you come in."

Back out in the fresh breeze at the base of the tower, Cleopatra reached into the pocket of her pants and pulled out a key. "Tully, I've been around long enough to know that the bullshit people heap on one another is more toxic than all the oil refineries in Texas, so I will come straight to the point. I know it all must sound wacko, coming from a batshit crazy old woman like me who you met on the beach in Mexico, but I think fate has somehow thrown us together. It seems that I bailed your ass out of trouble back there, so the way the karma thing works, I think you owe me one."

"I couldn't agree more."

"Well, it occurred to me that maybe you could hang around here and fix the place up while I go find us a light," she continued.

"I have no problem with that," I told her. A hideaway in the middle of nowhere was something I could use at the time.

"This job ain't gonna be no little fixer-upper, you know, but I just somehow know that you can do it."

"Well, I think I can."

With that, Cleopatra gave me a big, long hug, which was witnessed by St. Peter, hanging down from the branch of a sea grape. "I just want to show you one more thing before we go, and then we *will* go."

We walked past a battered radio antenna and then around the back of the light tower. Cleopatra started to laugh. "You know, when I was a lot younger, I had me a cowboy once. They weren't much on huggin', but they got the job done," she said. "There," she added and pointed at a corroded, half-moon-shaped object near the base of the tower. The sea grape branches had snaked their way through what looked like bolt-holes, and the piece of iron had become a part of the tree.

"What is that?" I asked.

"That is the old collar of the bull's-eye that they threw out of the light tower." Cleopatra gazed up at the tower and the indigo sky above. "At first, I wanted to cut it down and hang it on the door as a reminder of what I needed to accomplish, but then I decided it meant more where it was."

"I like that approach, boss," I said. "I'll clean up this mess. You go and find us a bull's-eye lens. We are going to rekindle the soul of the light."

She didn't say anything but stood there with tears in her big green eyes. St. Peter suddenly appeared on one of the branches of the sea grape as if he were bearing witness to a historic event. Then she handed me the key to the lighthouse door.

That was the day I became the keeper of the Cayo Loco Light.

2

The Song of the Ocean

Back when I lived in Heartache, Wyoming, before Thelma Barston took over the ranch, my home was a little Airstream trailer decorated with palm trees and pink flamingos and situated up on the side of a half-frozen mountain. The location of my trailer was a direct result of needing a spot free of trees and power lines, where I could receive a clear signal from the heavens.

The signal came in through a radio that had belonged to my father. It was a Hallicrafter S-40B shortwave model that he had bought in San Francisco the day he was discharged from the Navy. He came back to Wyoming wearing a flower-covered Hawaiian shirt and a cowboy hat and returned to civilian life as a forest ranger. A year later, he married my mother, whom he had first seen at the rodeo. She was a champion barrel racer. It was my mother who ran the ranch while my father managed a local state park from a cabin in a thick grove of fir trees just off the main road.

The Hallicrafter was my father's most prized possession. Not only could that amazing radio broadcast the local country music station from Jackson Hole but it could also, with the flick of the large green dial on the left side and a small knob labeled "sensitivity," produce Polynesian melodies from his beloved Hawaii.

He taught me at a young age how to tune in the world, from the fire tower at the top of the mountain to the BBC from Hong Kong. I would watch the light in the tubes grow brighter as the signal meter rose and the music got louder.

When I wasn't doing my chores around the ranch, I was listening to the radio and reading stories in *Popular Science* about people who could pick up radio signals with the gold fillings in their teeth. I wanted to be one of those people — a radio head. Well, it never happened. My molars remained silent, but I still had my father's radio. It was over that radio that I heard the report of the avalanche that buried him while he was trying to rescue survivors of a plane crash in the Bitterroot Mountains.

In the numbing days that followed, all I had were questions that adults couldn't or wouldn't answer. What had happened? Where was he? What do I do now?

With no help given to me, it made perfect sense to try and call my father on the radio. All I needed was a tower tall enough to send a signal to heaven. If I just had a tower tall enough, I kept thinking, I could reach him. That was the only time I ran away from home. I was eight years old, and though I was terribly sad about losing my father, I wasn't angry; I was just trying to stay in touch.

I took my father's radio and hitchhiked, walked, and paddled my way to every tall structure in the state of Wyoming that I could use as an antenna to call my dad. I was finally captured by the military police at a secret Strategic Air Command radio tower near Sheridan, and when they finally realized that I wasn't an alien or a Communist infiltrator, just a boy missing his dad, they sent me home.

My mother had no choice but to tell me the real truth about my father — that he wasn't coming back. I cried my eyes out for weeks, but then one day, as I lay in my room listening to the steel guitars on the airwaves from Honolulu, I realized that though my father was gone, my radio was my window to the world — and maybe still to him. Life is unpredictable, but there is a lot out there to do and see if you just tune in to the radio.

The tubes of the old Hallicrafter hummed and glowed a good number of years before I finally pulled the plug and told myself it was time to transmit instead of receive.

I was working as a wrangler and living in my little Airstream trailer when a blinding snowstorm rumbled down from Alberta one weekend. When the storm finally moved on the next morning, I was busy digging a path from my trailer to the corral, not paying much attention to the task at hand. That's when I saw the conch shell fly out of the shovel blade and back into the snowbank.

I dropped the shovel and immediately began to dig carefully with my fingers for what I knew to be a delicate and rare find.

"I'll be damned," I said as I pulled the little conch shell out. I held it up to the sun, then held it to my ear, the way the old medicine man who had given it to me had showed me when I was a kid, and a smile replaced the scowl on my face.

The shell was a special good-luck charm, but it had disappeared a month earlier, during a surprise attack by a pack of raccoons who had pillaged my trailer and had made off with a string of rainbow trout from my kitchen sink. When I examined the scene of the crime, I sadly discovered that somehow, along with the fish, my conch shell was missing from its usual resting place on the windowsill in the kitchen. I was pissed. It was a bad sign.

Johnny Red Dust was the man who had given me the shell. He was an old war buddy of my dad's. They had fought together against the Japanese up in Alaska in what became known as the "Forgotten War." They had survived bullets and frostbite and were rewarded for their efforts by being assigned to a unit in Hawaii, where they finished out the war years together.

After the war, my dad came home to Wyoming. Johnny went back to the reservation in eastern Montana, where he took up his old job as a medicine man. My dad and I would go and visit Johnny every fall when the tribes gathered for the annual Crow Fair at Little Bighorn. My daddy believed in the magic of the Indians and passed it on to me.

"Tully, city folks go to the doctor for a checkup every year, but the Mars boys prefer to charge up our good-luck streak with Johnny Red Dust."

What I remember most was the last visit with my dad, when I had just turned eight. It was a few weeks before the accident.

Usually our visit consisted of eating, fishing, and watching the dances, but that year, Johnny Red Dust sat at a smoldering campfire late one night after the drums had stopped beating, looked at my dad, and said, "It's time."

The next thing I knew, I was smack-dab in the middle of a full-blown ceremony of some kind, with Johnny and Dad smoking a long pipe. Johnny was speaking in tongues, and then he rattled a bag around my head and dropped the contents in front of me on the ground.

What rolled out was a wooden gecko, rattlesnake tails, bear claws, arrowheads, wolves' teeth, moonstones, and a purple-and-white-striped conch shell. The conch shell had fallen between my boots. Johnny looked at me and smiled. Then he said, "Pick it up."

I followed his command.

"What you are holding in your hand is called a *Strombus listeri,* better known as a Lister's conch."

I looked at the beautiful little shell, with its purple-and-white bands wrapping around the body all the way up to the high, conical spire.

"That shell comes from deep in the Indian Ocean, and how it got to Wyoming is still a mystery that even I can't explain. What I do know is that if you hold it to your ear, something magical happens."

I didn't need to be prodded further. I held the shell to my ear and listened in silence for more than a minute.

"What do you hear?"

"I think I hear music."

"I think you do too," Johnny Red Dust said. "It's the song of the ocean."

"What's that?" I asked.

Johnny Red Dust took the conch shell from my ear and put it in the pocket of my shirt. "When the time is right, you will understand," he said.

Dad and I headed back to the ranch, and I certainly didn't have a clue then what he was talking about. Still, I held that shell to my ear every night and fell asleep listening for the song, as if it were a life jacket and I was lost at sea.

I'd kept the conch shell all the way into adulthood and had only lost track of it that one time. The morning I'd found it in the snow, the sun seemed to shine with an intensity that I could feel in my bones and my heart. The shell was a sign.

That evening, one of the other wranglers rode up to my trailer with a message from Johnny Red Dust's daughter. If I wanted to see Johnny again, I'd better get moving.

The last time I had seen him was nearly five years earlier, when I had been hunting in eastern Montana and stopped by the reservation to check in on him. I didn't find him in his double-wide on the reservation this time, but at a veterans' hospital in Butte, where his shriveled body was stretched out in a bed, hidden from the evening sun by dingy sheets and dark curtains. It didn't take a brain surgeon to figure out that the demise of Johnny Red Dust was due to the pack of Marlboros that sat on the bed stand next to the oxygen hose that snaked to the clear mask covering his face.

He sprang awake at the creaking of the opening door, jerked off the mask, and greeted me with that old familiar smile. "You found it" was all he said.

I looked down at the shell in the palm of my hand.

"Well, let's visit," he growled. "I ain't got much time, and let some goddamn light into this cubicle." He pulled out a cigarette, took a puff, and started a coughing spasm that would tear any normal man in two. The coughing finally subsided, and he sat up. He held the Marlboro between his tobacco-stained fingers. "Nails in your coffin," he gasped, staring at the cigarette. "That's all these sons of bitches are, Tully. Nails in your coffin. But hell, I'm ready to go anyway."

I placed the conch shell on the table beside his bed. "I lost it and thought I would never find it again. Then early this morning —"

"I know," he wheezed. "Well, I guess I better tell you the rest of the story." And with that, Johnny Red Dust rekindled the magic my father had taught me to believe in. He stubbed out the cigarette and then took several deep breaths from the oxygen tank. He sat up in his bed and took my hand.

"Tully, there are no words to the song of the ocean, but the message is and always has been simple: not to forget where we came from. The melody is locked in the water that composes much of what we are. Most humans tend to ignore the song, but not all. You are one of the lucky ones who hold the melody in your heart. But be warned: it is a wandering song carried by the winds and the currents. It can turn you into a piece of driftwood that washes up on shore after shore, but one day, when you find the place that is meant to be, you will take root. Send me a postcard when you get there."

Before I left, he told me to fetch his old duffel bag from the corner of the room. As I did, he started to laugh and wheeze at the same time. The coughing fit lasted about ten seconds, and then Johnny caught his breath.

Out of the depths of the weather-beaten canvas he produced the worn leather pouch from which he had given me my conch shell as a kid. He reached his trembling hand into the bag and produced a small carved gecko lizard that hung from a leather strand.

"Put it on," he said. "He is your traveling companion."

I took the pendant from Johnny and tied it around my neck.

"It may not seem like it now, but you are heading

home. The conch shell reminds you of where you are going, and the gecko is your traveling companion so you will never be alone."

"Something tells me there is a journey in my future," I said.

"Most people's jobs suck. You just need to find one that sucks less. Fuck what is going to happen to your ranch," he said, "and get on with your life."

After I hugged him and left, I stood on the steps of the entrance to the hospital and looked up at the window of Johnny's room. I waved to an empty pane, knowing I would never see him again in this life. I held the conch shell to my ear and knew that it was time.

Johnny was right. Things were about to change. A week later, the fine Wyoming ranch where I'd worked for most of my life was bought by Californians and was being turned into a poodle-breeding operation. It hit me like a bomb. The new owner, Thelma Barston, brought a fresh meaning to the title "Wicked Witch of the West." It was only a matter of time before we clashed. The battle of the Heartache poodle ranch certainly would not make the history books, but it was definitely a life-altering day in my world. Before I even knew what was happening, I had smashed Thelma's massage table through her window. An hour later, I put the conch shell on the dash of my pickup; crammed my saddle, two-piece art collection, clothes, and radio into the tack compartment of my horse trailer; loaded in Mr. Twain; rubbed the wooden gecko around my neck for good luck; and never looked back. I was taking my pony to the shore.

3

The Patron Saint
of Lightning

One of the many pearls of wisdom I have picked up from Captain Cleopatra Highbourne goes like this: "There's a strange sense of pleasure being beat to hell by a storm when you're on a ship that is not going to sink."

The only problem with that thought is, I had not met Cleopatra before I went out on the ocean for the first time in a boat. So back then, all I had were my good-luck charms — the gecko Johnny Red Dust had given me, my conch shell, and a painting that Captain Kirk Patterson had let me hang on the bulkhead of the pilothouse for good luck on our journey to paradise, after he heard the story of how I had found it.

I know it sounds weird, but I am a cowboy with an art collection — all two pieces, which traveled with me from Wyoming across the country to Alabama. That is where I hooked up with Clark Gable, the cutting-horse trainer, who introduced me to Captain Kirk, the owner of a shrimp boat. Kirk had agreed to take my horse, Mr. Twain, and me across the Gulf of Mexico to Key West and the Yucatán Peninsula.

One of the pieces of art I brought along is a very valuable engraving that I packed away in a long tube inside a waterproof bag under my bunk. It belonged to my almost great-grandmother, who had run away from home to Ecuador from Tennessee. Her story and how the picture found its way into my hands will be addressed later. The other piece of art is called *The Patron Saint of Lightning*.

My art appreciation began at a flea market outside Cheyenne, Wyoming, one spring morning. I had gone there to attend the annual cowboy version of Mardi Gras called Frontier Days. Like most tribal celebrations, the myths, cultures, and historical events that originally sparked them still present a slight attraction to the attendees, but it is more of an excuse to throw a wild party, during which time the local chambers of commerce and religious leaders tend to cast a blind eye toward the debauchery because of the business it brings to town. I admit I did go to Cheyenne in hopes of getting laid, but I also did it to hook up annually with friends.

I had staked out my rally point for the week in the drive-in theater on the outskirts of town, which had been turned into a temporary RV haven. In the process of taking my horse for a morning walk around the property before heading off to the parade, I wound up in the middle of a giant flea market near the entrance to the drive-in.

I am not a great shopper, and flea markets are not what I would consider exciting entertainment, but for some strange reason, that day I found myself stopping at a booth after a painting caught my eye.

If the saintly woman in the painting was crying out to be rescued, then her prayers had been answered. She was resting on a puffy white cloud with beams of light extending from her bare feet down to a stormy horizon lined with jagged bolts of lightning. On the surface of the ocean, the light beam from her feet met a beam of light that came from a lighthouse. Where the two beams met, a tiny sailboat was following a safe path through the storm toward a patch of calmer water in a little harbor behind the lighthouse.

The painting was in a big cardboard box that had HARTZ MOUNTAIN printed on the side, atop a pile of typical flea market junk: Tupperware containers, old Merle Haggard eight-track tapes, a battered Scrabble board, and about a dozen pairs of roller skates.

As I made my way over to the cardboard box for a closer look, a bald-headed biker dude dressed in leather pants and a leather vest cut me off at the pass. Tattoos covered every epidermal cell from his wrists to his shoulders. He lifted the painting out of the pile and held it up to compare it with a tattoo of what looked to be the Blessed Virgin Mary that was spread across his right deltoid.

"Hey, Spike. Check this shit out, babe!" he yelled to his soul mate, also adorned in cowhide, who stood at the end of the table holding an Army-issue .45 automatic that she was examining as if she were a Marine drill sergeant. "She looks just like Sally Field in that TV show I loved when I was an altar boy. I must be having a goddamn senior moment. What was the name of that show?"

The woman with the gun glanced over at the painting. "*The Flying Nun,* and you are totally not even fucking close, Bart. You better start looking through this shit for a pair of bifocals."

She released the breech on the pistol and turned her

gaze to the old woman running the rummage booth. The old woman sat in an electric wheelchair, sucking hard on a Camel.

"How much for the gun?"

"Make you a deal. The pistol and the painting for your boyfriend for fifty bucks."

"Just the gun," Spike snarled.

"Forty-five bucks," the woman told her.

"Sold."

Bart dropped the painting back into the Hartz box, Spike paid for the .45 and tucked it in her belt, and they climbed onto their motorcycles and roared out of sight.

"So that painting is five bucks?" I said to the woman in the wheelchair.

"No, it's ten bucks," she said.

"But I just heard you offer it for five to that woman who bought the gun."

"That's right, Cowboy. I offered it to her as a package, you know, like when you get french fries with a cheeseburger, and it don't cost more than a nickel or a dime more than the burger itself. That gun and that painting were a combo platter."

"Well, ma'am, I can see an obvious connection between a cheeseburger and a plate of fries, but I'll be damned if I can find a common thread between a .45 automatic and a religious piece of art."

"Oh, so we are a big businessman now, are we? I'll tell you what, Mr. Home on the Range meets Harvard Business School," the old lady said, "give me six bucks for the damn thing, and I will throw in a pair of roller skates."

"Tell you what. I will give you five bucks, and you keep the skates."

"Deal." The old lady mashed a steering button on the

wheelchair arm and pivoted in place. "I'm telling you, with a belt buckle like you got cinched around your waist and the business head you're hiding under that hat, you could be fucking president of these United States one day, sonny. I'll get you some bubble wrap for your painting," she said and wove her way through the obstacle course of hanging racks, cardboard boxes, and bargain hunters like an F-14 pilot, leaving her own vapor trail of cigarette smoke.

While I was waiting for her to return, I picked up my painting to get a closer look. As I was examining the picture, I felt a card glued to the back of the frame. I flipped it over and began to read.

The faded yellow card described the lady in the painting to be St. Barbara, the patron saint of those besieged by lightning. The short, handwritten description of her sainthood said that she had earned her title when her mean stepfather was struck dead by lightning after he had lopped off her head for some minor offense.

My painting of St. Barbara went home in a blanket of bubble wrap. Little did I know that she would lead me into a world where lighthouses not only still existed but still guided the lost souls loose on this earth.

My travels with Mr. Twain had taken me all the way from Heartache to the Alabama beach town of Heat Wave. As Mr. Twain and I boarded the *Caribbean Soul,* Captain Kirk's shrimp boat, I rubbed the wooden gecko I wore for luck.

St. Barbara was looking over our collective shoulders as we ventured forth across the Gulf of Mexico. The surface was as flat as a pancake, and the sun melted away over the horizon to the west. I'd had an unexpected encounter with some unpleasant business from my past just before we left town, so I could not have been more relieved to be getting the hell out of Dodge. I was tasting the first bite of a new world that was to become a steady diet in time.

With Alabama behind me and the Yucatán Peninsula of Mexico off the starboard bow, I was doing my turn at the wheel, daydreaming about the stories I'd read of the explorer John Lloyd Stephens, the first American traveler to the Yucatán. He'd discovered the ancient Mayan cities that once composed a mighty empire — which were now my destination as well.

As we traveled on, Captain Kirk stood at the open wheelhouse door, looking up at the boundless display of stars in the dark sky. I was too nervous to sleep. Captain Kirk said it was no big deal, just what happens when you leave land behind for the first time and start to feel your gills again. He told me I would get used to it.

I tried to be as nonchalant as Kirk, but to no avail. In my mind I had dreamed, imagined, and willed myself onto the deep ocean for such a long time. I admit that the wheelhouse of a shrimp boat isn't the rolling deck of a blue nose schooner like the one that had captivated me in my youth in the movie version of *Captains Courageous*. But the *Caribbean Soul* was exciting nonetheless.

Captain Kirk seemed to come alive out in the middle of the ocean, obviously more comfortable on a rolling deck than on solid land. We amused ourselves recalling my odd way of coming aboard for this trip. I told him about my travels from the mountains to the ocean and my complicated feelings for a woman I'd met in Arkansas,

Donna Kay Dunbar. I also mustered the courage to include the fact that though my journey had been a lifelong dream, it had been hastened by a crime I had committed back in Wyoming. I assured him I was no ax murderer, and he assured me that I would not be on his boat if I were. He told me he had actually gone to sea with an ax murderer once, and he knew how they behaved. Finally I asked him why he had let me on the boat with my horse in the first place.

"I have a friend from Wyoming, and he's a pretty square fellow. You reminded me a little of him." That was all he said.

When I was finished telling Kirk about Thelma Barston and how there was a warrant out for my arrest because of it, Kirk told me a little about his own path. He had grown up in a fishing family, having worked the family charter boat as a deckhand, then a mate for his father, combing the clear waters beyond the barrier islands off of Alabama, Mississippi, and Louisiana for billfish and big sharks. When he went off to Vietnam in his late teens, he had wound up in the Mekong Delta as a boatswain's mate on a "swift boat." One day, his squadron was caught in an ambush, and Kirk had literally been blown out of the water. He had lived, but after that, he swore to himself that he would avoid rivers in the future and spend the rest of his life on the open ocean. And that is what he had done.

As the boat moved steadily along on its southwesterly heading, the stars that had only been twinkles started to come alive as heavenly creatures and road signs of the universe. I couldn't sleep even after my turn at the wheel, and I just stayed in the wheelhouse, reading a book about Mayans and waiting for sunrise. It was ushered in by a school of dolphins that crisscrossed our bow.

When finally, after seeing my third sunrise at sea, the buildings of the Key West waterfront popped up on the horizon, I could think only of what it must have been like for Columbus that day on a similar island in the Bahamas. Though my two and a half days at sea would never come close to equaling the feat of the Admiral of the Oceans, I still felt that kindred spirit and a certain sense of accomplishment at having made it across a large body of salt water for the first time. Tully Mars and his trusty horse had crossed the Gulf of Mexico.

Key West nearly got me, like one of those collapsing galaxies out in the universe sucking everything in. My day started with a cop chasing me off the beach where I had taken Mr. Twain to run in the morning. I must confess that after riding the Conch Train and hearing all the stories of the wild things that had happened on that island and seeing the splendid old houses built by the wealthy wreckers and sea captains, I did have a momentary thought about leaving Captain Kirk and the *Caribbean Soul* to seek my fortune in that pirate town. But I had signed on for Mexico. I had a feeling that Key West would be popping up on my horizons for a while.

Two days later, we were anchored off of Fort Jefferson, the old Civil War relic in the Dry Tortugas, getting ready for the big jump across the Gulf of Mexico to the Yucatán Peninsula.

Needless to say, with a horse roaming the foredeck of a shrimp boat in the middle of the ocean, we had some curious visits from the local fishermen. I was getting used to the routine when this guy rowed over in a dinghy from a big powerboat and came alongside. "You look like that Lyle Lovett song personified," he said.

I immediately recognized Willie Singer. He was one of

my favorite music stars and had gotten me through some pretty rough winters in Wyoming with his songs.

Unlike most entertainers, Willie Singer became more popular the older he got, but he didn't care that much for fame. Though he was still making great music, it was his other exploits that kept him in the headlines and also made him a fortune.

He had taken up surfing late — in his early forties — but now he was hooked on it and spent most of his time on a long board looking for waves. As a by-product of his search for waves, Willie Singer had wound up investing and participating in a treasure-hunting expedition. In the Philippines, they had found a Spanish galleon that had traveled the ancient Pearl Road from Manila to Peru. The ship had contained the largest cache of ancient black pearls and Chinese porcelain ever discovered — along with a vast quantity of gold bars, emeralds, and the usual swords, cannons, medallions, and jewel-encrusted crucifixes.

The story had made world headlines, and I vividly remembered the photos of Willie in *Life* magazine, sitting on the deck of a salvage ship with his guitar, singing to the crew. He was standing on a stage that they had built out of the gold bars from the wreck, and he had been surrounded by men in bathing suits who were shouldering M16s.

If I'd ever had a modern-day hero, Willie Singer fit the bill. And that is why I was completely shocked when I found him bobbing alone in a small boat, tossing a line in my direction. He was quite curious about Mr. Twain on deck, and he asked me what a horse was doing on a shrimp boat.

At first I couldn't speak, but eventually a few dumb

words came out. Meanwhile, Willie told me that he was out there shooting an album cover and that he was dying for some fresh shrimp.

I told him that we weren't rigged for shrimping, but I did have a large strawberry grouper that I had speared earlier in the day. We worked out a deal, swapping the grouper for some autographs on the half dozen cassettes we had on board.

The next thing I knew, we were all eating on the beach with him and the photo crew. Willie played the guitar and sang and told amazing stories of his treasure discovery. Then, to validate his tales, he pulled a pearl the size of a gum ball out of his shirt pocket and passed it around for us to see and hold.

I could have stayed up until dawn listening to Willie, but Captain Kirk called it a night. We had a tide to catch and a five-hundred-mile trip ahead of us.

I tried to sleep, but it was pretty useless. I lay awake thinking about Spanish ships that had plied the very waters in which we were anchored and had spilled vast amounts of treasure on the reefs of the Florida Keys. I started to think that "treasure hunter" sounded like a good job description. I finally fell asleep thinking of the thousand questions I wished I had asked Willie Singer.

The next morning, as we hoisted the anchor and fired up the diesel, we slipped a Willie tape into the cassette deck for good luck and were on our way. We were heading across the Gulf of Mexico, but I was still daydreaming about the Pearl Road and put it down on my list of eventual destinations.

I first saw Punta Margarita on a chart under Captain Kirk's pointed cedar pencil as he was teaching me how to plot a course and turn minutes of latitude and longitude into miles. With his guiding eye, I worked the ruler parallel along the weathered course line that ran from our present position at Fort Jefferson to Cape San Antonio Light at the western end of Cuba. Beyond that, the line continued to the southern end of the Yucatán, then fifty miles south of Tulum, around the tiny Punta Allen Peninsula, ending at a small island shaped like a crocodile, with its tail pointed northeast toward the high-rises and hotels of Cancún and with its jaws on the south end opened wide to enclose a deep channel lined with mangroves and shallow flats. The island was named *la piedra del cocodrilo,* or Crocodile Rock. Punta Margarita was the nose of the crocodile.

According to Captain Kirk, the Mayans had originally named the place, and the Spanish kept it, varying from their normal habit of reanointing and renaming every spot in the New World after Catholic saints and martyrs. On the surface, Crocodile Rock was a picture of beautiful jungle splendor. Palm tree groves, crystal clear waters, and sand beaches collectively conjured up visions of paradise to the first Europeans. But as the conquerors quickly found out, hidden in the beautiful facade of the island were a variety of poisonous reptiles, freshwater alligators, saltwater crocodiles, big cats, fire ants, and clouds of mosquitoes. Add to that the natural-disaster wing of nature that resided in these latitudes — hurricanes, earthquakes, and the occasional meteor collision — and this little slice of heaven could quickly turn into hell.

The Mayans had used their magic and cunning to carve out a civilization in the midst of all this beauty and danger, but the Spanish had tried to burn and blast their way through it. They had only temporary success, and the pirates and shipwrecked sailors who eventually founded and named the village of Punta Margarita took a more practical approach — they forged a coexistence with the perils of the jungle.

Through tribal wars, European conquests, independence uprisings, and the like, Crocodile Rock was pretty much forgotten territory, left to those who dared to live there. Nobody came looking for anybody on Crocodile Rock.

Punta Margarita had always been a pirate outpost, dating back to the days of Blackbeard, who had hidden out in these waters in the eighteenth century, when the Indians had taught him how to navigate a secret channel where he hid his ship for many years. If they had issued travel advisories back then, the story on Punta Margarita would have probably read something like this: STAY AWAY!!!!! CROCODILES, PIRATES, POISONOUS SNAKES, AND HOSTILE NATIVES!!!!!

Blackbeard left these waters and met his fate in the James River on the coast of America, where he was killed and beheaded, but it was another pirate named Jean Lafitte who established the village of Punta Margarita. After being pronounced the hero of the Battle of New Orleans, he had tried to go straight but failed miserably at being a businessman. It wasn't long before he had moved to Galveston and was back to the profitable and familiar job of pillaging and plundering ships in the Gulf of Mexico. When he ran out of Spaniards to harass, he started preying on U.S. ships, which roused the U.S. Navy to pursuit, but he fled south just in time to get to the Yucatán.

Though his headquarters were on the Gulf Coast near Dzilam de Bravo, he had plenty of hideouts stretching all the way down to Ascension Bay. But Crocodile Rock was Lafitte's favorite hideout. The small bay lay between two promontory points and was guarded by a treacherous series of offshore reefs that he had learned to navigate with the help of the local Mayan fishermen.

The village of Punta Margarita had its beginnings as the by-product of a Mardi Gras celebration. Lafitte had been forced to seek shelter in the bay from a vicious winter storm and could not return north to his headquarters in time to celebrate the time-honored ritual of Fat Tuesday. Not to be deterred, Lafitte instructed his crew to erect shelters on the beach and to build a large stage and floats.

Mardi Gras came to the village, and it never left. After the bacchanal on the beach, the weather broke, and Lafitte limped home on Ash Wednesday. But in the fog of the Mardi Gras hangover, he had left about a half dozen revelers on the beach by mistake. The storms that winter prevented a return to Punta Margarita, and the abandoned celebrants took an immediate liking to their harsh surroundings. They sent word to Lafitte that they were quite happy to stay where they were.

Lafitte had no problem with their request. It wasn't long before Mayan fishermen, who used the beach to dry their fish, took a liking to the new arrivals and the supplies that now came their way from the pirate trade.

Jean Lafitte spent his final years as an old, rich, and happy pirate, roaming the magical beaches of the Yucatán. When he died, he was buried in the sand under a mound of conch shells and a palm tree overlooking the Bay of Campeche, but he was mourned just as much in Punta Margarita.

Life went on, but the heydays of pirating faded away. Adjusting their sense of survival, the Margaritians combined forces with the Indians and took up the time-honored trade of wrecking, which was the economic artery of any town or village located within shouting distance of coral reefs. It was a simple trade: wait for ships to hit the reef, which they seemed to do with amazing regularity for nearly a hundred years, and then pillage them.

Wrecking provided quite an income to the locals, who spent it as fast as they made it. They knew the value of living well. There was even an opera house built, which was frequented by the great singers of the world. Fast, beautiful boats raced back and forth to the reef when the cry of "Wreck offshore!" was heard from the lookout tower.

Since there was no proper laundry service in the village, some of the more prosperous wreckers sent their linen to New Orleans on a regularly scheduled boat.

But all good things come to an end eventually. As improved navigation made sea disasters less common along this coast, the rich days of wrecking went with the channel markers. The opera house burned down and the laundry ship sank. Punta Margarita became a simple fishing village again, and the villagers returned to the less glamorous life of the sea, gathering the lobsters, grouper, and snapper that lived beneath the reef as opposed to the ships that hit it.

That is how Captain Kirk had found Punta Margarita on his first trip up the tricky channel. He was fighting his way south to the shrimping grounds of Honduras, rounding the western tip of Cuba in a gale, when he came across a couple of fishermen in a small boat being tossed about by the storm. Somehow he managed to get a line to them before their boat sank, and he dragged them aboard the *Caribbean Soul*.

Once he got enough coffee and chocolate into the near-frozen fishermen, they told him that they were from the village of Punta Margarita. Kirk said he had heard of the place, but he had never visited because of the treacherous waters and reefs that surrounded it. The fishermen told him they could take him through the channel if he would take them home.

As they were finally about to tie up at the town dock of Punta Margarita, a funeral procession was filing down the sand street of the waterfront. When the priest looked up and saw the fishermen on the shrimp boat, he began pointing and going loco about a miracle. It seems the fishermen had arrived home in the middle of their own funeral mass.

Well, to the residents of the village, Captain Kirk had brought the men back from the dead. He was declared a hero by the villagers, and he simply fell in love with the place and began to base his southern shrimping operations from the island. Soon he found that he could make more money servicing the island with goods from America than by the backbreaking work of hauling shrimp out of the ocean. He converted his boat to a cargo carrier and began a regular route between Alabama and Punta Margarita.

As the tourism boom lit up the beach towns to the north, the good road ended at Tulum, and Punta Margarita was again left to its own resources, which was fine with the locals. They preferred the village to be what it always had been, an outpost manned by an odd mix of pirate children, Indian fishermen, and the occasional gringo shrimp boat captain who splashed ashore and liked what he saw.

It sounded like just the place for a cowboy–deckhand–art collector on the run.

4

Dreaming of Columbus

It was later that night, back on the boat, as I lay in my bunk reading, that Captain Kirk asked me to come to the pilothouse. There, in the red glow of the compass light, he explained a few things to me about the voyage. He said he had done the run hundreds of times, but it was never quite the same trip. He explained that at the western end of Cuba, the land drops steeply into a mammoth trench more than six thousand feet deep. In this trench, the old Gulf Stream cranks into warp drive and pushes one of the most powerful currents on the face of the earth around Florida, up the eastern seaboard, and across the Atlantic, finally running out of steam off the coast of Ireland, where the last of the warm tropical water can still cause palm trees to grow.

Along the edges of the stream, the force of the moving water, eddies, and countercurrents, along with the dramatic underwater reef close to shore, can turn calm waters into a nightmare in a heartbeat. With a good forecast, Captain Kirk said, we would cross at night, but even with the weather in our favor, he gave me the warning of a wise mariner. "All that said, just remember, Tully, that we are at sea, and it could all go to hell in a moment's notice."

That night, I dreamed of Columbus. He was in his cabin on the *Santa Maria* with his beautiful charts laid out on the mahogany captain's table in front of him. He looked up at me and said, "Remember, Tully, just don't panic, and it will be all right."

The rising sun brought a day made-to-order for our crossing, and after a quick breakfast of scrambled eggs and fried grunts, Captain Kirk plugged in a homemade tape he called *The Greatest Hits of the Lesser Antilles,* hoisted the anchor, and as James Taylor sang to us of Captain Jim's drunken dream, pointed our boat toward the Yucatán Peninsula. When the old fort disappeared behind us, my anxieties of being out of sight of land seemed to vanish.

It was a glorious day at sea. I got to try my hand at rope splicing and started to learn more about navigation and how to read a chart. I did my turn at the wheel with a lot more confidence than I had the first day out of Alabama.

Around lunchtime, we hooked a big wahoo, pulled it aboard, sliced it into steaks, and dined on grilled fish sandwiches made with Cuban rolls from the *panaderia* in Key West.

I climbed out of my hammock just before sunset and doused myself with the freshwater hose, then washed the salt off Mr. Twain. I had the six-to-midnight watch and was raring to go. That is when I saw Captain Kirk staring south at a faint little flash off the port bow.

"Got to keep an eye on that," he said, his eyes still glued to the south.

"What?" I asked.

"You might get your first taste of real weather tonight, Tully."

"But I thought you said it was going to be fine."

"I did, but it seems the gods have changed their minds."

"Well, what do I do?" I asked.

"Live and learn."

I think darkness is the thing humans fear the most, for it takes away our advantage. In the dark, we have to rely on our instincts to survive, and as a species, those feelings haven't been around the track in a while. You put all that fear onto the deck of a rolling ship in mountainous seas on a pitch-black night, and you can begin to understand why it was a sailor who probably painted the image of the patron saint of lightning.

The first time I had put my hands around the worn wooden spokes of the wheel, Captain Kirk had given me a simple piece of advice: "The helmsman may steer, but the boat usually knows where she needs to go. She's more like a horse than a pickup. Just give her her head."

I loved steering the boat. It is a unique pleasure that combines all the sensory perceptions sparked by wind and waves and the way a boat deals with those elements. During the preceding days of sunshine and gentle swells, all she needed to keep her course was a gentle nudge — but everything changed that night off the Cuban coast.

I was no longer in the mind-set of loping along on Mr. Twain, giving him a gentle feel of the rein on his neck to make him turn. I was riding atop a four-ton Brahma bull, keeping a death grip on the riding rope, holding on for dear life.

The little flickers of light that had appeared on the southern horizon had turned into long, defined shafts of lightning. In a split second, they connected to the vast amount of raw energy contained in a giant, anvil-like cloud that hung over most of the horizon.

By sunset, the storm had caught up with us. Captain Kirk had quickly set about securing the boat for a blow. He told me to stay at the wheel while he and the rest of the crew set about their routine procedure for handling bad weather, with one exception — dealing with a horse on deck.

They moved Mr. Twain back to the stern and found him a safe place away from the booms and rigging where he could ride out the storm. He took it all in stride and seemed much better equipped to deal with bad weather than I was.

In the wheelhouse, I kept my eyes constantly moving from the compass heading in front of me to the flashes of lightning off the port beam to the painting of St. Barbara on the pilothouse bulkhead behind me.

When the storm finally hit us, it was both terrifying and exhilarating. I had ridden through blizzards and run from tornadoes back home, but out on the ocean, the weather is a whole new ball of wax. To my amazement, Captain Kirk simply sat behind me and let me drive the boat. "Just keep her head into the seas, Tully, and you will be fine."

"You sure you don't want to take her?" I repeated several times.

"No, you're doing just fine. This will blow over in about half an hour. It's just a little line of squalls moving through."

Though he let me steer, he was constantly checking

the chart, our GPS coordinates, and the radar. He didn't have to remind me that our primary concern was, of course, the safety of our ship, but almost equally as important was the fact that we did not want to drift into Cuban waters. Despite Captain Kirk's calming manner in the wheelhouse, my brain was flooding with visions of the boat on a reef, a collision with a speeding whale, and a midnight encounter with Cuban gunboats.

Suddenly, all of those scenarios didn't mean shit. I am not sure whether I heard the explosion first or saw the sizzling arc of electricity that shot from the dark sky toward the outriggers, but it sure as hell got my attention.

There was a split second of blinding light, and then I was in the world of Ray Charles. I still had my hands on the wheel, and before I could get the thought from my brain to my vocal cords to yell "HELP!" the beam of a flashlight popped on and lit the compass.

"That was close," Captain Kirk said calmly. He quickly fit the elastic band of the light around my head and aimed the angle of the beam at the compass. "Ten degrees to port, and then hold that course until I get back. I need to check on a few things," he added. "Hey, what do you feed that horse? Never heard of a horse that wasn't scared of lightning. Whatever you feed him, I want some of that."

As usual, Mr. Twain was way ahead of me in the calm, cool, and collected department. Finally I spoke. "The GPS isn't working."

"That's what I'm going to check on, but in the meantime, all we have is our compass. But that's all anybody had before electricity. Funny, isn't it, that electricity is the thing that can help you the most out here, but it's also the thing that can hurt you the most. Just steer that course until I get back, and a little prayer to the patron saint of lightning might not be a bad idea, either."

With that, the door to the wheelhouse opened and let a moment of the storm in and Captain Kirk out. I was alone on the bridge. I reached for my good-luck charm.

In my dream, Columbus had told me, "Tully, just don't panic," and I tried to remind myself of that, repeating the phrase under my breath as I wrestled with the wheel and prayed to St. Barbara at the same time. The roller-coaster ride through ten-foot seas and the tropical downpour continued for longer than I wanted it to, and the duration was not helped by the fact that I kept glancing between the compass card and the big hand on the fluorescent dial of my watch. Ten eternal minutes later, the lightning barrage erupted again, but it was definitely moving away from us to the north — just as the captain had said it would. "Thank you, ma'am," I whispered under my breath.

In my pitch-black surroundings in the pilothouse, I could feel the seas subside a bit, and I was able to relax my grip on the wheel and catch my breath. The stars had disappeared long ago in the curtain of the storm, and I didn't know if I was hallucinating from the long absence of light or not. At first I thought it was one of those spots that moves across your eyes when somebody pops a flash camera in your face, but it seemed to be staying in one place. I turned off my headlamp for a minute and then saw it flash for real. I counted to four, and then the light flashed again.

That was the first time I experienced the uncanny sense of relief that the soul of the light brings. "God-damn," I cried, "it's the San Antonio light, right smack-dab where she's supposed to be! The compass worked!"

And just like that, the power in the pilothouse came

back on; screens started flashing, bells sounded, and the whir of the autopilot gyro spooling up was music to my ears.

A few seconds later, Captain Kirk came back through the pilothouse door like an actor coming out for his curtain call. "We're fine. It wasn't a direct hit. Just popped all the breakers. This old lady may look a little long in the tooth on the outside, but she's got the guts of the Terminator. The guy I bought her from was an ex-CO on a Trident who, along with a fondness for catching shrimp, liked the survivability components of an attack submarine. How you doin'?"

"Fine, I think. I've got the lighthouse in sight."

"No shit!" Kirk exclaimed. "Well, damn, Mr. Chekov, you've turned into a fine helmsman."

Kirk stared down at the green glow of the radar screen and fiddled with the knobs a bit. Like Merlin weaving a magic spell, he brought the coastline of Cuba into view right where it was supposed to be.

Half an hour later, what I thought was a camera flashbulb had turned into a huge beam brighter than the stars, sweeping across the tormented sea. It was like an angel riding on my windward shoulder.

The light did its job, and we put Cuba behind us. When I finally looked at my watch, it was four in the morning. Overhead a break in the sky appeared, allowing the reflected light of the stars to accompany the still-strong beam emanating from the direction of Cape San Antonio. It may have been my first look at a lighthouse in action, but it would surely not be my last. The storm let up, and the tension on the boat naturally eased.

"Nice job, Tully," Captain Kirk said and gave me a pat on the back. "I am going to buy you a drink when we hit town. Take a break, and you might want to check on your horse."

I relaxed my hands, and they ached as I stretched my fingers out. As I zipped up my foul-weather jacket and turned toward the pilothouse door, I noticed that the painting of St. Barbara was hanging crooked on the bulkhead. I straightened her out.

In the dim red glow of the compass light and the green wash of the radar screen, I thought I saw her smiling back at me.

The storm had tested us, and then it went off like a bully to bother its next victims somewhere up the Cuban coast. It had rousted all hands to the pilothouse. I was so full of adrenaline that I never even realized I had stayed up all night until the sky began to lighten behind us and Captain Kirk ordered me off the wheel. It was as if someone had turned off my power switch. I was out of juice. I dropped in my bunk and slept until a little after noon.

When I woke up to the smell of grilled onions, the crew was busy getting ready for our arrival. We ate our cheeseburgers out on the stern. The wind had dropped off to a light breeze, and the swells had subsided to a gentle roll. I finished my lunch and gave Mr. Twain a bath with the freshwater hose, which he seemed to enjoy immensely. Around four in the afternoon, the land clouds rolled up over the horizon like a list of movie credits and were followed by a tree line, a beach, and finally houses and people on the shore.

"Take the wheel," Captain Kirk said.

I responded instantly to the invitation to take the ship

up the channel to the end of the voyage, but there was only one problem. I couldn't find the channel. The declining angle of the sun had turned the clear green waters into a doughnutlike glaze, which made shallow water indistinguishable from deep water. On top of that, a cluster of fish traps, lobster pots, and skinny wooden stakes that seemed to serve as perches for a variety of shorebirds suddenly appeared off the bow like a minefield.

I checked the Fathometer, and we still had ten feet under the hull. I took a quick glance at the chart and grew concerned when all I saw around Punta Margarita were shallow-water depth indicators and lots of little skulls and crossbones, which were the icons for reefs and wrecks. Captain Kirk was casually standing in the doorway.

"Skipper, I am having a little trouble making out the channel here."

"Let me see if I can help your vision, there," he said as he made his way inside the wheelhouse, opened a cabinet under the radar unit, and extracted a miniature brass cannon from a wooden box. "It was old Jean Lafitte who secretly marked the channel back when hiding places really were hiding places."

"Well, he did a damn good job," I said as I reached for the throttle to slow the boat as the water depth had dropped to six feet.

Captain Kirk cradled the little cannon in his arms like a baby and walked out the door. Then he dropped the stem of the gun into a fitting on the port rail.

"You can keep your speed up, Tully," he said calmly. "See all those birds out there?"

"Sure do."

"Well, watch them carefully."

I did as commanded and focused all my attention on

the birds. Suddenly I realized that some were real, and some were just decoys. Kirk had cracked the breech of the gun and was inserting a large, fat shotgun shell into the magazine. "When Lafitte had been shown the secret channel from the Gulf of Mexico to Crocodile Rock by the local Indians with whom he traded, he devised a rather ingenious way of marking, and then disguising, the waterway.

"He created a collection of painted wooden decoys: pelicans, egrets, herons, flamingos, and rosette spoonbills, and he set them along the outer edges of the channel, among the local population of shorebirds who gingerly scour these flats and reefs in search of food. When he needed to enter the harbor, he would do this." Kirk pulled a knotted piece of twine that dangled from the little cannon, and a deafening roar erupted from the barrel of the gun.

The crew let out a cheer and began laughing up on the bow. Even Mr. Twain seemed to have enjoyed it, but the suddenness of the explosion had sent my heart leaping into my throat.

"There's your channel," Captain Kirk said, and as I looked to where he pointed, I saw that the live birds had taken flight from their perches, and the decoys that remained were a set of channel markers that laid out a path to Punta Margarita.

As I weaved along the channel, there were secondary explosions from the cannon when birds started to make landing approaches to the poles. At first, the little island sat suspended in time off the bow like a distant planet, but then it materialized into palm trees, Norfolk pines, docks, faded Creole cottages, funky Caribbean clapboard homes, and traditional Mayan beach huts that lined a pink-sand beach. I felt strange, as if I had either been there before or simply belonged there all along. A gathering of well-wishers stood at the dock, watching and waving as Captain Kirk instructed me in the art of docking. Somehow I nudged her gently to the pilings, and the crew secured her with lines and fenders.

"Welcome to Punta Margarita, Tully," Captain Kirk said with a smile.

The first thing we did was get Mr. Twain ashore. Dockside at Punta Margarita during the extremely low tide left a gap of about five feet between the deck of the boat and the pier. Mr. Twain was a great horse, but he was no jumper.

However, we had an instant solution. Back off at the Dry Tortugas, before the beginning of our crossing, the crew had jury-rigged one of the big wooden stabilizers into a makeshift platform we could use to lower Mr. Twain into the water for a swim and a quick run on the beach.

We used it again at the dock in Punta Margarita, but this time we drew a rather large crowd. Mr. Twain kept a watchful eye on the whole process. He was an instant celebrity. Nearly the entire village had gathered at the dock as we hoisted him aloft. Suspended between sky and sea, he simply seemed to enjoy the brief flight.

There is something odd and unnatural about seeing a horse suspended in midair, and when he touched down on the dock, the children were referring to him in Spanish as the angel horse, which is a name that he still goes by among the locals in Punta Margarita.

Once Mr. Twain was safely ashore and tied to a palm tree, an adoring crowd of young fans gathered to keep him company. We hosed down the decks, and cleaned up the boat, and Kirk inspected our work. Then he turned to us with a smile and said, "I think it's cocktail hour."

5

Land of the Lost Boys

Johnny Red Dust had told me that people who nurture and love animals are better humans. So although Captain Kirk's words about cocktails were of supreme importance to a person like me, who finds it very easy to reward one's accomplishments, my first concern after steering through the storm and making landfall was for my horse.

Captain Kirk understood. He and the boys headed to the bar, but before going, he made a call on the VHF radio and told me that he had made arrangements with a friend of his named Bucky Norman to pasture Mr. Twain at his fishing lodge. That is when he revealed to me that Bucky was the other cowboy from Wyoming who had, in a way, been responsible for my coming aboard the *Caribbean Soul* with Mr. Twain.

When you're on the run, which I was, and you've put a couple thousand miles between you and your past, it is a little disconcerting when you run into someone from your neck of the woods. Captain Kirk had mentioned a "fellow Wyomingite" several times on the voyage, but he had failed to mention that the guy was in Punta Margarita.

If you subscribe to the theory that there are only about two hundred people in the world, and, everywhere you travel, you're bound to run into somebody you know or somebody who knows somebody you know — well, in my case, with Thelma Barston's warrant still on my tail, that could spell trouble. It immediately raised some bothersome questions. Is this guy's brother a cop? Did he fish with Thelma Barston's ex-husband? Is he an opportunist who could use the reward money I'd heard had been offered for my return?

"What are you thinking about?" Kirk asked.

"Oh, nothing," I replied.

Kirk then instructed me to just ride down the main street of town, which dead-ended at the beach. Then I would take the path south along the shore as far as I could, until I came to a green dock with a half dozen pretty little skiffs alongside. I was to look for a large mahogany log that had been carved into the likeness of a giant crocodile with a clock in its mouth. On it was a sign that read LOST BOYS FISHING LODGE. Bucky would meet me there.

I started my journey with thoughts of turning and riding out of town the other way and not stopping until I found a village with no gringos anywhere. Somewhere out there I felt the presence of Captain Hook in the form of a pissed-off poodle rancher. Paranoia was taking hold, but fortunately it was held at bay and driven from my thoughts by the little island as she revealed her beauty to me as I rode along. Step by step, I fell instantly in love with the place. It was neither the history that I had heard from Kirk nor the obvious charm of the town but rather a feeling of belonging that swept over me as I made my way to the lodge.

I thought I would be viewed as a one-man Mardi Gras parade, drawing a crowd of curious stragglers who would fall in behind me as I trotted along the sand streets of downtown Punta Margarita for the first time. But though I was the only man mounted on a horse, cruising down a street occupied by golf carts, mopeds, and an array of island cruiser bicycles, I did not seem to attract any sense of astonishment from the locals. I was simply the guy riding the angel horse through town.

It was obvious that old Jean Lafitte not only had a taste for stolen treasures of gold, silver, and jewels but was also a pirate with a green thumb. Kirk told me that, like many sea captains before him, Lafitte had studied and collected plantings in his journeys around the Caribbean and had brought them home. Here they grew and prospered and turned into a lasting monument to his vision of a tropical paradise. He was also a kind of conservationist, growing pine forests for firewood so that the hardwoods would never have to be sacrificed for fuel.

Lafitte had traded with the Indian tribes in South Florida, and he had learned from them about natural hammocks and the healing and nutritional value of the wild citrus that grew in the swamp. Using this information, he had supplemented the native flora and fauna with orange, grapefruit, and tangerine trees. Added to that was a collection of guava, pomegranate, breadfruit, and ackee trees from neighboring islands.

As a result of Lafitte's green thumb, despite the ravages of two centuries of hurricanes, Punta Margarita was still shaded from the intense tropical sun by the ancient branches of rosewood, mahogany, cedar, lignum vitae, and dogwood.

There was a delicious scent of barbecue on the wind that first ride. I could smell it, mixed with the wood smoke, citrus, and jasmine. I made the turn at the beach and felt Mr. Twain start to twitch. He wanted to run, and I let him. He wasn't called a quarter horse just because it sounded good. He sensed the distance that he had been born to feel, and I just held the reins loose and let him go.

As he galloped down the beach, my apprehensions about meeting a fellow Wyomingite flew away like the landscape we were passing at a fair clip. We splashed along the flats that had been uncovered by the falling tide until the green dock came into view around the right, where it was supposed to be.

Mr. Twain lunged sharply when he caught sight of the giant carved crocodile under the Lost Boys sign. There were no *Federales* at the end of the trail — just another gringo.

"You must be Tully. I'm Bucky Norman," he said.

I slipped off of my horse and went to shake hands. I had been expecting to meet some lanky, bleached-blond, bronze-skinned expatriate in cutoffs and flip-flops, but Bucky stood there under a large straw hat that sat upon a collection of strawberry blond curls. Across the front of the hat the words NEVER GROW UP were painted in bright red letters. His long fishing pants and long-sleeved shirt buttoned at the collar covered nearly every inch of his six-foot-four-inch frame — except for his hands and neck, which were dotted with freckles. "Welcome to Lost Boys," he said.

Mr. Twain scanned the surroundings and seemed to approve. I tied his halter to a coconut tree.

"Pleasure to make your acquaintance," I said.

"Pleasure's all mine. What took you so long?" Bucky asked.

"Sightseeing," I told him.

"That is a fine-looking animal," Bucky added. "Most four-legged creatures we see on this island climb trees and have forked tongues. Anyway, we aren't officially open yet, so there aren't any guests to complain about a little horseshit lying around."

"I really appreciate you takin' us in like this."

"Well, it ain't brotherly love," Bucky said. "Kirk tells me you are not only a sailor but a Wyoming fisherman. Where you from?"

"Heartache."

"I'm from Simmons Creek," Bucky said.

"I've fished it!" I blurted out, knowing there were fly fishermen from all over the West who would gladly pay any amount of money, donate a kidney, or give up their firstborn child to get a spot on that stretch of cold, clear water when the caddis hatch was on.

"An amazing piece of water, but you are in the salt world now. Let me show you around."

The Island of the Lost Boys was my favorite part of *Peter Pan,* and now as Bucky showed me his camp, I was seeing life imitate art. From the beach, we took a path through a small patch of dunes speckled with sea oats. This led past a cave that had been carved out of the rocky shore by the sea.

The camp itself sat on a tiny peninsula and consisted of a group of small thatched cottages all painted in bright

Caribbean colors. The smell of fresh paint and turpentine hung in the afternoon air, and sawhorses and stacks of lumber were piled near an unfinished cottage with a red thatched roof. A main clubhouse with a large screen porch had been built at the far end of the enclave facing the water. In the middle of the camp stood a colossal banyan tree with giant, thick limbs that sagged just a few feet from the ground, from which hung a cluster of rope hammocks. The tree was covered with vines, climbing nets, rope ladders, and a set of wooden stairs that ascended to the top. Up in the high branches perched a sprawling driftwood tree house. At the base of the tree, a weathered bamboo fence encircled a patch of thick green grass.

Bucky pulled back the unhinged gate to the corral, and Mr. Twain strolled out of my grip and immediately began munching the grass.

"How did you find this place?" I asked.

"Kirk found it for me."

"How did you guys meet?"

"That's better discussed up there," he said, pointing to the top of the tree. "You game?"

"I'm game."

"Going up," Bucky said as he grabbed a vine and swung over to a low limb where the ladder rungs began. Like Cheetah following Tarzan, I mimicked his movements.

As I measured the distance to the ground, I realized that I was already as high as a tall ship's mast, and there was nearly the same distance left to the top of the tree. The huge orange sun hung motionless out over the water as if it were waiting for us to get to the top before it traveled beyond the horizon.

Bucky narrated as we climbed the wooden ladders and

branches to the tree house. "It started out as just a look-out platform. Ix-Nay says that this tree has been used for centuries to scan the horizon for enemies and storms. We use it to check the wind conditions, watch the sunset, and point the telescope at the stars."

"Who's Ix-Nay?"

"He's my head guide — and the only guide at the moment. He's off island right now, but you'll meet him soon enough."

When we reached the deck of the tree house, I was puffing hard. The view from the top of the tree was incredible. I could see all the way to town. There was an enclosed area with a guardrail and a ship's ladder that led up to another level. Bucky led the way up the last steps, and we popped through a hatch into a makeshift observatory where a big brass telescope rested under a viscuine cover.

"Have a look," Bucky said.

I shut my right eye, put my left eye to the lens, and turned the big wheel at the base until the blurry circle transformed into sharp images of the world below. I could make out the birds on the channel markers and the waves crashing on the distant reef. Directly below us, I spotted Captain Kirk out on one of the flats, stalking a school of mullet with a cast net, silhouetted by the falling sun.

"He'll be out there till dark," Bucky said. "How about a boat drink?"

Bucky slipped behind a little bar area and produced a bottle of Haitian rum, limes, and ice. He punched a button on a cassette deck lashed to a tree branch, and a familiar melody filled the air. I sipped my drink and gorged on the view, listening to the perfect background music. Joni Mitchell sang of beach tar and the Mermaid Café.

"I love that song," I said.

"You heard that a lot on the boat, right?"

"Yeah."

"Joni is the reason Kirk and I met."

"How so?" I asked.

"Well, this ex-girlfriend of mine from Denver took me to New Orleans to Jazz Fest. You ever been?"

"To New Orleans, yes, but not Jazz Fest."

"That was seven years ago, and I haven't missed one since. Anyway, it was in this place called Café Brazil. My girlfriend had dragged me downtown, after a full day at the fairgrounds, to a bar called the El Morocco, where it was rumored that Boz Scaggs was going to jam with the Neville Brothers. Well, we weren't the only ones who heard the jungle drums. The street outside the club was packed with people and stalled cars.

"Georgia, that was her name, tells me she is going to get in to see Boz or die trying. I told her that I love Boz as much as anybody, but I was no good with crowds. She headed through the door into the insanity, and I wandered down the street to Café Brazil, which was much less crowded and where Joni Mitchell sat in a wicker chair on the stage with just a conga drummer backing her. It was magical. Joni had slipped up on the stage in between sets, completely unannounced, and was singing away.

"Captain Kirk was standing next to me at the bar. As she finished her set, we both broke into roaring applause and coaxed an encore out of her. She headed from the stage to where we were standing and introduced herself. Then, when she learned we didn't know each other, she introduced us. A salsa band came on, and we found ourselves dancing with Joni, sandwiched between members of an Italian wedding party and a pack of Air Force pilots on weekend leave from Biloxi. The crowd had discovered

Joni's presence, and she sensed it. She kissed us both good night and jumped in —"

"A big yellow taxi," I interrupted.

"It was actually a Checker cab," Bucky said. "Well, I checked back by the El Morocco and saw that Boz was indeed onstage, and the place was going nuts. I told Kirk I had about two hours to kill before I would attempt to reconnect with Georgia across the street, and he told me about a restaurant on the corner. It was there in the Port of Call, over a bowl of gumbo and red beans, that we discovered we both love fishing."

There was a loud splash in the distance. Bucky and I looked up, and down below was Captain Kirk with a net full of kicking mullet. A small sand shark was on his heels, observing the catch.

"That shark would be better off finding a dead whale to gnaw on than trying to get fresh mullet out of that man."

I laughed out loud recalling my own experiences with mullet back in Alabama.

Bucky continued, "Anyway, Kirk and I talked about the Yucatán, and that is when he told me he came down here on a regular basis. He also said there were great, undiscovered flats for bonefish and tarpon in the bays along the southern edge of Crocodile Rock. If I ever did get down here, he told me, he'd take me out to the flats."

"Obviously you made it," I said.

"My family owns a very successful fly-fishing guide service and tackle shop back in Wyoming, and they groomed me to run it for the rest of my life and pass it on to my children, when I had them. That was before I ran into Kirk. I'll never forget our first meeting. It fueled my curiosity. I read everything I could about fishing in the southern Yucatán. Finally, when I was guiding up on the Snake River, I met a guy who had actually been here. He told whopping stories about the place. He said that the waters of Ascension Bay and Espíritu Santo were jam-packed with bonefish and, even more exciting, with permit. But he said you had to fish with a gun strapped to your side to ward off aggressive crocodiles. It all sounded way too amazing. I don't know if you know, but in the fly-fishing world, discovering tropical waters that hold large schools of permit is like finding gold."

Along with the fishing stories, Bucky ran across a few important facts. The Mexican government, he said, had declared the bays and nearly 2 million acres of tropical forest, marshes, mangroves, lagoons, and coral reefs surrounding them a protected biosphere. They had given it the Mayan name of Sian Ka'an. There was little development in the area, and the purpose of the biosphere was to make sure it stayed that way — which to a fisherman meant very little pressure on the fish. Bucky had counted the days until his next vacation, and then he'd hopped a plane to Mexico to meet up with his ex–dancing partner.

Kirk met Bucky at the airport in Cancún, and they drove south, bouncing along the dirt road on a roller-coaster ride through world-class Mexican potholes until they came to an isolated ferry terminal in the middle of nowhere.

"We caught the ferry to town, and Kirk drove me out here and told me the place was available. As they say, the rest is history. I was snagged just like a permit. I quit the family business and moved to Punta Margarita to fish."

"It didn't look like this, did it?" I asked.

"Oh, hell, no. That's my own damn fault," Bucky said with a laugh. "The guy I leased this from was a country-

and-western star from Nashville who planned to move here and raise horses and start an offshore religion. It didn't work out for him. To my recollection, this is the first time a horse has ever been in that corral, but that is the beauty of bamboo. It lasts forever."

"Unlike country pop stars," I said.

"Ever heard of Shawn Spurl?" Bucky asked.

"Not really," I said, fishing for recognition.

"How about Tex Sex?"

"Tex Sex. Of course. I saw him once at Frontier Days down in Cheyenne. That guy can draw the women. I have never seen as many good-looking chicks anywhere. They were stacked up like spawning salmon in front of the stage."

"Shawn Spurl is Tex Sex's real name."

"No shit. Tex Sex lived in Punta Margarita?"

"Well, I would say he more like visited for a spell . . . but that is another whole story."

"I got nowhere to go," I said.

6

How Nightmares Turn into Dreams

Like everything and everybody in the tropics, the Lost Boys Fishing Lodge had a history of its own, and Tex Sex was certainly a big part of it. It had been another gringo folly, an alcohol-soaked, sunstroke vision of paradise driven by ego and lack of any geographical knowledge whatsoever of the region.

Several years back, Tex Sex had shocked the music world by announcing his early retirement at the peak of his short but very successful singing career — which was like dropping a hydrogen bomb on the millions of thirty-five- to forty-five-year-old female devotees who comprised his very lucrative fan base.

Tex Sex had skyrocketed from obscurity to being voted the Country Music Entertainer of the Year. He claimed Lubbock, Texas, as his home, though his parents had moved two weeks after his birth to Chicago, where Shawn's father had gone to work for Kraft Foods, the inventors of his favorite source of nutrition, Velveeta processed cheese.

Shawn was much more of a "cheese head" than a "longhorn." He dropped out of high school his sophomore year and moved to Fond du Lac, Wisconsin, where he went to work in a video arcade and did what any oversexed American male child of the entitled generation did — he started a band.

The Rectal Thermometers never made it out of the garage that the bass player's grandmother had let them use. They broke up a week before their first gig when the lead guitarist discovered his girlfriend and Shawn fucking in the hedges.

The Marshall amps were repossessed, and Shawn went to work delivering pizza for Domino's. Then one night, he rediscovered his Texas roots at a local shit-kicker karaoke bar, when, after several shots of tequila and Jägermeister and the urgings of his coworkers, he drooled the words on the screen to Garth Brooks's "Friends in Low Places" into the handheld microphone. His performance not only won the evening's competition and a bottle of cheap champagne but was also witnessed by a local funeral parlor / limo service operator from Milwaukee named Aaron Segal. When he introduced himself to Shawn that first evening and handed him a card, Aaron said, "I have contacts in the music business."

The funeral business, as dreary as one might imagine, did have one useful asset — a supply of long black limousines, which also filled the bill for celebrities who passed through town on concert tours. Aaron Segal wanted to get into show business almost as much as Shawn Spurl did, and the limos were his "contacts."

It didn't matter to Aaron that Shawn couldn't carry a tune or play the guitar very well. He didn't have to, due to his amazing resemblance to the film star Brad Pitt, which Aaron Segal planned to exploit to the max. Shawn's journey down the road to success started behind the wheel of a stretch limo, which paid the bills while Aaron devised his plan. He signed him to a long-term contract, got his teeth capped, paid him a weekly salary, and got him laid on a regular basis.

Then one night, the magic that is show business smiled on Shawn Spurl. He was driving a middle-aged woman named Darcy Trumbo to a country concert that had been booked to follow the Brewers game in Milwaukee. Darcy Trumbo was from the Jersey Shore and had graduated from Princeton with a degree in journalism, but she opted for a job offer to follow the Eagles around the country on tour. After a show in Nashville, she somehow got separated from the caravan, which moved on, and when she came to, she liked what she saw and decided to stay in Nashville. She went from cocktail waitress to Music Row secretary to becoming the host of a country line-dance show on the Nashville Network. She too was just waiting for the right thing to come along at the right time, and somehow she recognized it in her limo driver in Milwaukee.

Darcy Trumbo sat in the back of the long stretch limo, stealing glimpses of Shawn in the rearview mirror and asking her driver polite questions that did not require complicated answers. When Shawn opened the door for her at the press gate of the ballpark, she paused, took one full-body look at him, and said, "Care to join me?" Well, their relationship bloomed, and so did Shawn's new career. It was Darcy who bought out Aaron Segal and became Shawn's manager, signing him to Rhinestone Records. Then she went to work on making him a star.

It didn't take long. She groomed him, dressed him, fucked him, and got him voice and guitar lessons. She changed his name to Tex Sex. Then she made a country video that combined the highlights of Roman orgies with a Las Vegas rodeo championship, and it brought out the Christian coalition in droves across America to protest the sexually charged video at record stores and the offices of Rhinestone in Nashville.

It was like throwing gasoline on a fire. The first Tex Sex album sold 4 million copies. They were off to the races, and Darcy Trumbo was driving the lead car.

In less than a year, Tex Sex was *it* in the country field. He skipped along atop a kaleidoscopic existence filled with beautiful women, fast cars, jet planes, and Hollywood mansions, and just when everything was going gangbusters, Shawn Spurl, aka Tex Sex, made that amazing but often repeated mistake that so many shallow performers do. He went looking for depth in his life and his career. Frustrated to discover that there was none, he called a news conference in Nashville and announced his retirement. Darcy was in London, setting up his first European tour, when Tex Sex got on his private jet and told the pilot to head south to Machu Picchu. He had seen a program on a National Geographic TV special about the lost city of the Incas, and he was heading there to find the answers to his questions.

The plane had a pressurization problem over the Gulf of Mexico, and the pilot made an emergency landing in Cancún. While the plane waited for parts, Tex Sex went to the bar. There he was recognized by a Jet Ski dealer from Houston who told him that they had lost cities in Mexico as well, and pointed to Tulum on the tourist guide map. Tex Sex bought a case of Dos Equis, rented a Jeep, and headed south on Mexico Route 403, following the signs to Tulum. He was trying to read a road map when he went right past the turn to Tulum. Lost on the Yucatán Peninsula, he drove until he ran out of beer and gas about a half mile from the Punta Margarita ferry dock, where he was directed to the only pay phone in the area. He accidentally stumbled onto the ferryboat and landed at the Fat Iguana a short while later.

Tex Sex never made it to the pay phone, but he did find a bar stool at the Fat Iguana. There, after ordering a variety of local rum drinks, he fell over backward off the bar stool, carving an eight-inch gash in the shape of a half-moon around his left ear. Shawn Spurl, aka Tex Sex, proclaimed his immediate infatuation with Machu Picchu and his revelation that he was a reincarnated child of the sun.

"You are a drunk gringo in a beach bar in Mexico," one of the locals told him.

"What's your name, amigo?" Tex Sex asked the man.

"Ix-Nay is my given name. What's yours?" asked the small Indian at the end of the bar.

Tex Sex was receiving no input from his liquor-logged brain. All he heard was the sound of his own voice. "My Incan brothers and sisters, you have found me, and for this I plan to reward you. It is my desire to live among you on this beach forever," he announced.

"I'll alert the media," Ix-Nay replied dryly as he tended to Tex Sex's bleeding scalp.

Tex Sex's proclamation of self-discovery was not met with much enthusiasm by the fishermen in the bar who were watching the Cubs game, but they broke into a dance of their own when Sammy Sosa knocked a ball over the center-field bleachers, beating the Mets in the bottom of the ninth. At that point, Captain Kirk happened to walk in, and he recognized the bloody figure leaning on Ix-Nay's shoulders.

While Sammy circled the bases, Ix-Nay and Captain Kirk carried Tex Sex back to the boat, stitched up his head, and deposited him in a bunk to sleep off his hangover. Captain Kirk had his crew keep an eye on their guest while he went fishing.

When he returned, he was greeted by a contingency of Mexican and U.S. military and immigration officals who stood in front of an unmarked Huey helicopter that had landed in the tiny square in the center of the village. A man in plain clothes, sporting a crew cut and telltale sunglasses, spoke to Captain Kirk. "We are here to investigate a possible kidnapping of a very prominent American."

"You mean Tex Sex?" Kirk asked.

"If you have any information about the abduction of Shawn Spurl, then I'd suggest you share that with us right now." The Mexican police moved forward.

"I don't know anything about a kidnapping, but I do know that a drunk asshole who claims to be Tex Sex fell off a bar stool at the Fat Iguana and sliced his head open. I stitched him up and put him on my boat. I figured someone would come looking for him, but I didn't figure it would be this fast."

Kirk led the assault team to the shrimp boat. Tex Sex was still out, snoring loudly in the bunk.

Tex Sex's identity was verified by a bartender from the Fat Iguana who appeared with a pile of CD jewel-box covers with the singer's picture on all of them, and the assembled entourage agreed that the barfly in the bunk was the balladeer on the CD covers.

In a matter of hours, film crews from Fox affiliates in Mexico City, Dallas, and Hollywood were on the scene to film the "rescue and evacuation of Tex Sex from the snake-infested jungles of the Yucatán Peninsula" as the uninformed reporters described it. The *Caribbean Soul* was encircled with a defense line of Mexican Navy personnel.

While Darcy Trumbo was winging her way south of the border on her quarter-share jet, she received updates from her office as the wire services lit up with several different versions of the story. They were all blown totally out of proportion. Darcy smiled and asked the flight attendant for a margarita.

Tex Sex slept through the whole clusterfuck in the air-conditioned crew quarters on the *Caribbean Soul*. When he finally came to, he saw a soldier standing over him. The man rushed from the room, and then Tex Sex suddenly found himself staring into the stern eyes of Darcy Trumbo. "Read this," she said as she handed him a one-page script.

With the help of a Special Forces squad that had been training in the nearby jungle, Tex Sex was carried past a row of cameras, microphones, and popping flashbulbs to a waiting medevac helicopter. At the entrance to the chopper, Tex Sex struggled to sit up. With Darcy at his side, he read his statement of thanks to the people of Punta Margarita and plugged his upcoming TV special on Fox.

"I will return," he said, and from the door of the chopper he screamed, *"Mi casa es su casa, amigos!"* The helicopter engines spooled up, the whirling blades created an instant sandstorm on the beach, and then the chopper rose vertically and headed north out over the water. Moments later, silence returned to Punta Margarita.

Tex Sex never did return, but to everyone's surprise, a month later an architect from Santa Fe arrived on the mailboat, laden with a dozen containers filled with the pieces of a prefab wooden beach house — Tex Sex's dream come true. The land for the house had been purchased from an art dealer in Mexico City by Far Horizon Limited, an offshore real estate holding company. In reality, it was Darcy Trumbo who had bought the property and had built the house to keep Tex Sex happy and simply dreaming of his return. She knew full well that Shawn Spurl would never set foot on the Yucatán Peninsula again.

Six months after his fall from the bar stool, things were back to normal. Tex Sex came out of retirement and announced his comeback tour. He also wrote a song based on his short stay in Punta Margarita entitled "I Have the Scars to Prove It," which was his biggest-selling single to date. Neither his voice nor his guitar playing had gotten any better as a result of his inward search, but he sported a new, short hairdo that accentuated the scar around his left ear, and he began to refer to himself onstage as being one-third Native American. This surprised the hell out of Darcy Trumbo, but she could care less, as long as the money kept rolling in.

Construction was stopped on the compound, and the pieces were left for the jungle to reclaim. It damn near did until Bucky Norman floated ashore with his dream of running a fishing camp and picked up the bamboo baton. By then Tex Sex had discovered Cabo San Lucas, which suited Darcy's idea of an island much better than Punta Margarita. Bucky leased the property from Darcy with an option to buy at a later date, and island history repeated itself for the millionth time as one man attempted to build his dreams out of another man's nightmare.

7

Pancakes Make the World Go Round

I could have stayed up in the tree house listening to Bucky for the entire evening, and I probably should have, but the gods of ocean crossings and celebrations would have no part of it.

We were ordered out of the tree by Captain Kirk, and after checking on Mr. Twain, who could have cared less about our concern as he snoozed on his side, we all jumped into Bucky's Jeep and headed to town and the Fat Iguana.

With salsa and rock 'n' roll blaring from the weather-worn speakers lashed to palm trees, I was introduced to the good citizens of Punta Margarita by Captain Kirk and Bucky. One drink led to another, and then came the multiple toasts and tequila shots. The story of our encounter with the storm was told and retold, the size of the waves growing with each rendition, until the wee hours of the morning.

I have a dim recollection of making my way back to the *Caribbean Soul,* but in the morning I woke up in pain. I carefully climbed out of my bunk on the boat with the visible signs of a penitent sweat streaming from my pores, and I tried to focus on the hands of my watch, with no luck. I opened the crew quarters door to a bright, hot sun that sent me scurrying back inside in seach of sunglasses. The boat was deserted, but the waterfront was humming with morning activity.

"Great party last night," a short man with a smile called out as he passed the boat.

"Thanks," I said, having no idea who he was.

Several fishing Pangas moved down the channel to the Gulf in seach of lobster and grouper. I certainly hadn't seen those guys at the party. They were on their way to work, which reminded me that I had no intention of making a repeat performance of the night before. I walked down the waterfront toward the beach with the foggy remnants of blue agave still in my bloodstream and a line from a John Hiatt song looped in my cerebral jukebox as I tried to sing my pain away.

> *Oh it breaks my heart to see those stars*
> *Smashing a perfectly good guitar.*

I walked the shoreline to Lost Boys and found Mr. Twain munching away happily on his oats. One of the workmen thankfully stopped hammering on an unfinished cottage and told me that Bucky had fed my horse and had gone to the town for breakfast and had asked me to join him.

The breeze blew in from the water, and I suddenly caught a whiff of myself. I needed an immediate and total immersion in salt water to wash away the smell of cigarettes from my clothes, the dead brain cells from my head, and the sins from my soul. I took off my shirt, tossed it up into the shallow waves, and then I walked out into the clear, calm water up to my knees. I just fell face-first, like some villainous victim of a gunfight with Clint Eastwood, and I stayed submerged for as long as I could hold my breath. While under the water, I once again vowed never to get that drunk.

It is probably safe to say that in these parts, liquor in a never-ending stream has probably killed more expatriates than have hostile encounters with pirates, Indians, or disease-carrying insects. If I were actually going to stay here for a while, I would want to act more like the fisher-men I had seen that morning than the barfly I had been the previous night. I had not come all this way to wind up as just another pickled gringo.

I swam away to the deep, cool water. Half an hour later, my heart was pounding, the blood was flowing, and I sensed that though I had a few more payments to make to the bank of bad habits for last night's fun tickets, I would survive the self-inflicted assault.

I floated on my back with my arms stretched out and stared up at the morning sky. Silently I made my second resolution. There weren't a lot of cattle to herd or fences to mend in these parts, and if I were going to stay and be productive and live a contented life in the tropics, I would have to find some new kind of work. I waded out of the shallow water, walked back to the boat, showered, and got into a fresh T-shirt and a pair of shorts. I was going job hunting, but first I needed pancakes.

Captain Kirk and Bucky sat eating breakfast at a plas-tic table under a faded green awning in front of the Fish-erman's Café, which was across the street from the Fat Iguana. The tranquil little hacienda was alive with activ-ity and the smell of hot coffee. I recognized a few refugees from the bacchanal and started my Spanish lessons with an *"Hola"* to them. Captain Kirk finished his eggs, grabbed his coffee mug, and then went to talk to a tableful of folks on the porch. Bucky and I sat in the shade of a giant Norfolk pine that was an oasis from the already rising temperature.

"You should try the banana pancakes with coconut syrup. It helps," he said.

"Thanks. I just wanted you to know that I don't behave like that on a regular basis," I said apologetically.

"It's what sailors do after a long and perilous voyage," Bucky told me.

"Oh, I'm no sailor."

"That's not what Kirk told me," he said. "Hell, I was much worse my first night here. I got bulletproof drunk and then did this." He pulled open his shirt to expose his left shoulder and turned around. Running from his shoulder blade down to the small of his back was what appeared to be a naked Mayan princess lying in the missionary position, being penetrated by an alligator with a bird face as she was strangling a large snake with each of her hands.

"Jesus!" I shouted, startled by the hideous sight. "Who thought that one up?"

"I don't recall. I was told later that I told Hilo, the tattoo artist, to just use his imagination." Bucky smiled.

Somehow I avoided having someone carve up my body last night, but that was about all I missed.

Bucky rebuttoned his shirt and said, "It's those permanent reminders of a temporary feeling that you have to watch out for in these parts." He signaled for the waitress, who brought a pot of coffee and refilled his mug. He took a sip and said, "I've got a problem that just might be a piece of luck for you. Are you planning to stay on with Kirk on the boat?"

I was surprised by the question. It had never occurred to me that working for Kirk was even an option. "He hasn't asked me."

"He's going to. That is, unless you want to go to work for us at the lodge."

I couldn't believe what he was saying. An hour earlier, mangled by the jaws of guilt, I was wrestling with my future and what I would do. Now I had not one, but two job offers.

My pancakes arrived, and I went to work on them immediately, shellacking them with butter and drowning the plate in syrup.

"Have you ever read a book called *Don't Stop the Carnival*?" Bucky asked.

As I gulped down the large glass of ice-cold milk that I had ordered, I nodded. "Of course."

"It is the bible for expats. Kirk and I read it three times together before we leased the lodge from Tex Sex — trying to convince ourselves that the perils of Norman Paperman would never be the perils of Lost Boys."

"Kirk owns part of the lodge?"

"He does. Can you think of a better partner?"

"You're right about that. So what happened when you read the book?"

"We were wrong, like everybody else who thought they could lick the Caribbean."

"But the place looks great, and you're about to open for business," I said.

"Exactly. And just when you think you've turned the corner, and there is light at the end of the tunnel — BAM, something else happens." Bucky held up his left hand. A large bandage covered his index finger.

"What happened?"

"Norman Paperman referred to it as Kinja Rules."

"Meaning?"

Bucky removed the bandage from the tip. I saw a dark, jagged thread of stitches that zigzagged around the end of his finger. "Last night, or should I say early this morning, I left you party animals because I had to get up early. I had promised to take a couple of American guys out fishing. One of them was a client of mine back in Wyoming, and he was down with his buddy, who — thank God — was a surgeon at Harvard. They had stopped in for a day to see the lodge on their way to Ascension Bay, and I wanted to drum up some future business. We caught a few bonefish, and he was happy, and we were about to call it a morning when this giant barracuda cruised up the flat. I urged the guy to make a final cast, and the fish crashed the fly, and the fight was on. Ten minutes later, the big fish was at the side of the boat, and in what would be the normal method of removing the hook and releasing the fish, the barracuda got pissed, flipped his head around, and *wham*. Next thing I saw was blood gushing everywhere. The fucking barracuda chomped off the tip of my finger, which was hanging like a Chicken McNugget by just the skin.

"Well, my old client's friend happened to be a top-notch plastic surgeon. I got on the radio and called Kirk, who rushed down with his first-aid kit, and the doctor laid me down on the Ping-Pong table in the lodge and re-attached the end of my finger. That's the good news."

"And the bad?"

"I'm left-handed. I got my finger back, but I can't hold a fork, much less tie a knot or cast a fly. And I need to train my guides before the season." Bucky looked at his mangled finger, and he winced slightly in pain. "How much fly-fishing have you really done?"

"I fished the creeks and streams in Wyoming since I was a kid, but I'd never dropped a line in salt water until I was on the *Caribbean Soul*. We anchored off the Tortugas, and I played around for a few hours on the flats by the fort."

"The wind is the only difference," Bucky said. "That and the size and speed of the fish, of course." I was listening to Bucky, but my mind wandered back to an ad I had read in the classified section of a fishing magazine back when I was about to go crazy at the poodle ranch. It simply read: "Flats guide needed — no previous experience necessary. Contact Vaughn: Last Mango Lodge, Isla Mujeres." I had almost answered that ad.

Bucky took a sip of his coffee and leaned over the table and looked me in the eye. "I won't bullshit you — we can't afford to miss this opening season. We have clients due to arrive in two weeks. My plan was to train Ix-Nay and another guide, and we could handle the traffic this year. Then I'd train a few more local guides. But with this fucking finger, I can't cast or pole the boat. I talked it over with Kirk. He was going to offer you a job on the boat, but it would really help us out if you would consider staying on at the lodge for a while.

"I can take care of your work papers," Bucky continued. "I've got a good friend who works for the government, so that's no problem. I can teach you enough in about a week on the water to be a flats guide, which is just about all the time I have. I've also got the books you need to study, and Kirk just brought me down a VHS player and instructional tapes that I was going to set up for the lodge guests. I can only pay you a couple of hundred bucks a week, but there's an old cottage from the Tex Sex days that you can have. It needs a little fixin' up, and there's a nice little field behind it where we can make a spot for Mr. Twain. After this season, we can just see what happens."

I was stunned. "You're offering me a job?" I tried not to look shocked. "When do we start?"

"Yesterday," Bucky said.

I don't know what it is about all that sugar, flour, and melted butter, but after my cowboy nights in Wyoming, a breakfast like that was a necessity and referred to as a "soaker." That's because of its ability to absorb the abundance of alcohol that's left in the body of a party monster. Those pancakes and the fact that I had plans for the immediate future were the medicine I needed to cure my hangover.

We went down to the boat to tell Captain Kirk, and he seemed very happy about my decision to work for Bucky. He was doing a turnaround trip back to Heat Wave and was leaving on the rising tide at ten.

I did my final chores as a crew member of the *Caribbean Soul,* loading handmade furniture that was bound for a beachfront home on Perdido Bay. With the cargo secure, I off-loaded my few belongings into Bucky's beat-up old Jeep. The Tully Mars art collection rode shotgun with me. I propped the painting of St. Barbara up so she had a good view of the ride, and I tucked the other, rolled-up picture snugly behind her for safekeeping. Then we drove to the Lost Boys lodge — my new home.

I unpacked my stuff and took Mr. Twain for a ride back to town to see the *Caribbean Soul* off. When we got there, Kirk was all loaded up and about to cast off the lines. As I watched him I thought about what to say. There was so much I had to thank him for, yet I knew he would be embarrassed if I started some litany about how he'd given my life new direction. Captain Kirk is a man of a few, always well-chosen, words. He is a wise leader — one of those rare individuals who places everybody else's well-being above his own. It earned him a medal in Vietnam, though he never speaks about it. He lives in the moment, not dwelling on what happened yesterday or what might happen tomorrow.

He came down the gangplank, scratched Mr. Twain's withers, and shook my hand. "I'll see you in a couple of weeks. Take care of my investment," he said with a smile. In the next breath, he was shouting orders to the crew, and the lines were hauled in.

As Captain Kirk spun the big boat on her axis and headed north, the crowd at the dock waved for a few seconds, watched as the boat made its first turn toward Bird Channel, and then went back to work and chores.

I nudged Mr. Twain's left shank, and he turned south. He seemed to know where we were going.

I returned to Lost Boys and the sound of chainsaws, hammers, and Tito Puente blaring from a paint-splattered blaster as the crew of workmen were putting final touches on the buildings at the lodge.

I steered Mr. Twain off the beach and through a small

grove of orange trees at the rear of the property while my mind tried to play catch-up and grasp the unlikely fact that this was where I would be living for a while. In the process of unpacking my clothes, hanging my pictures, and feeding my horse, I just had to stop and look out over the wide expanse of emerald water and pinch myself to make sure it wasn't a dream.

That evening, Bucky and I sat on the beach with a couple of local carpenters who had done a little work on my beachfront property. We roasted lobster tails and conch steaks over a fire of coconut husks.

We were playing a story game Bucky had invented called the Last Supper. It consisted of allowing those evil, avenging creatures of God — horseflies — to light on the exposed skin of your arm or leg and take a bite. At that point, you make up an epitaph, which you deliver to the horsefly as he eats his last meal, and then you flatten the little bastard. The speeches are voted on by those in attendance, and the best speech wins a bottle of wine.

"I am simply trying to make the eradication of biting insects into a sport. There is only so much backgammon and Scrabble you can play on any given day," Bucky explained.

We devoured the lobsters, which were coated with a Mayan home-brew hot sauce called *Agua del Infierno,* which I happily translated by myself to the delight of my professor.

"I think the Waters of Hell can give Tabasco a run for its money," I said to Bucky as we sipped cold Coronas to take the sting of the peppers from our lips. Then we toasted the lucky stars above our heads. My cheeks hurt from smiling all day. I had been so caught up in the fast-track course change of my life — moving off the boat in the morning to sitting on the porch of my beachfront house at sunset — that I had forgotten my most important task: studying the books and tapes Bucky had given me that were my crash course in flats fishing. This brought my part of the beach party to a close as I suddenly realized that there was work to be done.

"It's okay," Bucky said nonchalantly. "I told Ix-Nay you had never fished in salt water but that you could cast into the wind."

"Is Ix-Nay on his way back?" I asked. "What kind of name is that, anyway?"

"Mayan," Bucky told me. "But Ix-Nay is more than just a Mayan. He's a Hunan."

"A medicine man?" I asked.

"How did you know?"

"My father's best friend was one," I told him.

"Well, this should be interesting," Bucky said, shaking his head in amusement.

"When do we start?" I asked.

"As soon as he gets back."

"I know you said he was off island right now, but where is he?"

"Last week he was suddenly called by the gods to Xibalba."

"How far is that from here?"

Bucky started laughing. "Well, it ain't down Highway 307. Xibalba is the nine-layered netherworld where shamans seek the wisdom of the spirits. There is a steep and secret road through a series of caves that can be entered only by shamans. It is a very dangerous place, with lots of snakes and dragons down there; torrents and abysses flank the road, which is covered with thorns. In this place, the evil demons live who dare to challenge the gods to combat."

"I think I'll wait until he gets back," I said.

Ix-Nay, who was also supposed to be learning to be a guide, still hadn't shown by the middle of my first week of training for the job. I attacked the art of saltwater fly-fishing like a hungry fish myself, gobbling pages of information and local knowledge from Bucky. At the same time, I was falling in love with the natural beauty and tranquility of the whole process of stalking large fish through shallow water and connecting them to thin lines on small rods. I was hooked.

I would read the fishing books well into the night and fall asleep to the symphony of crickets and tree frogs with my book parked on my chest. One night, I had a fishing nightmare. I was surrounded by a group of pirates who were watching me cast badly and shouting things like, "He ain't no flats guide! Let's string him up!" The early-morning light saved me from the gallows, and I boiled a pot of hot water for tea. Then I took Mr. Twain for a ride and spent the next few hours outside, practicing casting at a Frisbee until Bucky arrived.

We spent about an hour on the beach, where Bucky adjusted my cast, polished up the absolutely necessary "double haul," and then pronounced me ready to fish.

At the brand-new dock behind the lodge, we loaded into one of his skiffs. The boat was something of a shock; it did not look anything like the sleek skiffs I had studied in Lefty Kreh's book, and I asked Bucky about it. He said he had just bought it from an old Mayan fisherman down in Punta Allen who had to give up the sea because he was going blind from years of squinting in the sun. Just before he lost the last of his sight, he painted the boat to represent a dream that had spoken to him.

The hull was covered with a multicolored chain of Mayan gods that were laid out down the port and starboard sides. At the stern, the chain was connected to a big green crocodile tail, and at the bow it was plugged into two giant, glaring eyeballs, which the old man said were the eyes of the fish god Chac Uayab Xoc, who provided a good catch but also devoured comrades. He told Bucky that he needed money for a cataract operation, but still he would only sell the boat under the condition that the paint job remained the same for the life of the boat. Bucky called it the *Bariellete*.

"What does *Bariellete* mean?" I asked.

"Skipjack," Bucky answered. "She is an all-purpose rig. There are no flats skiffs down here yet, and quite frankly, I like the local boats just as well. All we have to do is modify your boat a bit for the flats."

"My boat?" I asked.

"If you're going to be a guide, Tully," Bucky said, "you need a boat. It's the least I could do."

I didn't know what to say.

That day, we spent the rest of the daylight hours on the shallow waters of Ascension Bay and the lagoons amid incredible natural beauty unlike anything I had ever seen before. This was to be my "office," but that day, I never even made a cast. I just observed Bucky and listened to his instructions.

I learned the tides; poled the boat; adjusted my eyes to nervous water, mud, and tailing fish; and started picking up the words of the trade in Spanish. All these lessons took place in a classroom shared by crocodiles, monkeys, manatees, and countless species of waterfowl that seemed to be watching my progress. A particularly large colony of blue herons found us and circled, squawking loudly as they returned to their nests in the mangroves. I was like Alice falling through the looking glass. I had never seen such beautiful shallow water.

The next morning, there was still no sign of Ix-Nay. After our early practice run, I joined Bucky for lunch in the dining room, and we tested the new chef's menu selections. Ix-Nay had helped to hire one of his cousins, who had cooked at the Four Seasons Hotel in Toronto. His cousin would be the camp chef, and we dined that day on lobster club sandwiches and potato leek soup, with a bottle of rosé to wash it all down as Bucky practiced eating with his one good hand.

He was called away to the office as I sipped my espresso and prepared to retire to my hammock for a siesta, but I overheard the gist of Bucky's phone conversations. He was speaking with his first clients, who were due in a week, and he was assuring them that everything was fine — which it wasn't. He said good-bye, came out of the office, thanked the chef, and said, "Come on! It's time to solo, Tully."

At the dock, he handed me a portable VHF radio and a box of flies. "Try these on the permit, and see if any work. I have some fires to put out here. You'll do fine. I'll be standing by on channel seventy-one."

I stared at the big eyes on the bow of the *Bariellete,* hopped on board, and gave the starter rope a tug. The outboard coughed to life and engulfed me in two-cycle exhaust, thick with the smell of oil. I untied the boat from the dock and headed out the narrow channel into the lagoon, feeling as if I were the only human on the planet.

Twenty minutes later, I found the spot I was looking for — after running aground only once on the way. I anchored the boat, put on my wading shoes, lathered myself with sunblock, and checked the fly line. Then the fly and I slipped over the side into the knee-deep water.

For the next four hours of the incoming tide, I eased my way along the shore, scanning the surface for the incriminating mud cloud of a bonefish or a feeding permit's forked tail pointing skyward. I had no luck at all, but I didn't care. I was literally walking on water, and I was soaking in the whole experience like the sponges that lay scattered in the bottom of the lagoon. Near the apex of the tide, I climbed back in the *Bariellete* and found an indentation in the mangrove trees along the bank that provided a patch of shade from the overhead sun. There I took a short nap and a swim, where I just floated on the end of the tide, watching the food chain drift along from behind the lens of my mask. As I treated myself to an ice-cold Ting and enjoyed the silence of my new office, I saw the current shift. It was time to fish.

I took the skiff farther into the biosphere than Bucky had taken me. I simply sat in silence in the boat, drifting along and listening to nothing and seeing everything.

The speed nap was unexpected. I was supposed to be fishing. I woke to a thumping against the hull. I had drifted onto a flat. I had run aground. I sat up immediately, searching the bottom of the boat for holes, but saw none. Looking over the side, I realized I was hung up on an underwater hill at the edge of a long flat that I didn't recognize.

I got out to push the boat off the bottom, and two small lemon sharks buzzed by at lightning speed. Like a gymnast, I launched myself back into the boat. The sharks were not after me; they were hunting a school of shad that moved like one gray shadow over the bottom.

I discovered the source of the loud knocking on the bottom — it was the hard, pointed top of a conch shell, which I managed to dislodge and set myself free to float again.

I looked around and did not recognize a single landmark that Bucky had shown me. I was lost. The sun was listing to the west, and the water was being sucked off the flat by the waning moon. I sat there pondering my situation. Though I really didn't want to, I had no choice but to use the radio Bucky had given me to call for help.

I was just about to reach in my fishing bag when the setting sun came out from behind a drifting cumulus cloud. In the shadows moving rapidly across the water, a ray of light reflected like a Boy Scout signal mirror off the forked tail of a giant permit. It was a hundred yards above the boat, cruising down the flat, dining on small crustaceans, and heading right for me. I dropped the radio and picked up my fly rod. I might be spending the night donating blood to a squadron of mosquitoes, but a shot at a fish that size was well worth the consequences.

Stepping like a shorebird to reduce the noise of my feet, I eased myself out of the boat and maneuvered my body and rod to within casting distance of the big fish. I was already hyperventilating and made myself stop and take several deep breaths. The fish was just zigzagging up the flat, enjoying his appetizers.

I suddenly had a complete lack of confidence in my casting ability and thought about chucking the rod and just diving on the fish and wrestling it into the boat, but I managed to gather my wits, and the next thing I knew, the rod was moving back and forth above my right shoulder, and the line was feeding out.

Somehow I dropped the fly right where Bucky had told me. "You want to bring out the jack in a permit."

The crab fly plopped into the water right on the nose of the fish, and it swirled on the fly and tracked it across the bottom. I quickly ran my fingers over the gecko charm hanging around my neck and then began to strip, like Bucky had taught me. I somehow resisted the temptation to set the hook, and my patience and luck paid off when I suddenly felt the tension on the line in my left hand.

I gently raised my rod toward the sky, holding the line tight, and then I set the hook.

Immediately, the fish headed instinctively for deep water, which lay around the mangrove-covered point to the south. I held the pressure on the rapidly departing line and could only hold the rod and feel the surge of the powerful fish in my arms and my heart. The first run took nearly all three hundred yards of backing from my reel before I got a turn.

Thirty minutes and six more runs later, I was finally able to steer the exhausted fish to within reaching distance. The big eye of the fish stayed glued on me as I unhooked the creature and began to resuscitate him by holding on to his black tail and moving him back and forth over the bottom until he regained his strength and swam away from my grip. As I watched him depart, I was grinning like a Cheshire cat. At that moment I just let out a howl so big that I know Johnny Red Dust and my dad could hear it up in heaven.

I listened for the echo of my voice over the water and almost had a heart attack when not an echo but a blood-curdling howl came from right behind me. I turned around, and I was ten feet from an Indian who was wearing only Nike shorts and a leather belt with a .45 automatic strapped to it. I immediately dropped my fly rod and reached for the sky.

The Indian burst out laughing. "That is not the way to treat an expensive fly rod," he said. "Put your hands down, my friend. The gun is for protection only. You must be the cowboy." He stuck the bamboo spear he was holding into the sandy bottom and walked through the shallows toward me. "Bucky sent me out here to find you."

"Are you Ix-Nay?" I asked.

"I am Ix-Nay."

"Tully Mars," I said, extending my hand.

"I know." He grabbed it. "That was a nice fish you caught there. I think you'll be a good teacher."

Ix-Nay had one of those natural smiles that revealed a large gap between his front teeth. He was five foot four inches of lean muscle that had never seen a gym, and he moved through the water like a bird. "You know," he said, "what amazes me about fly-fishing is how you can fool such cautious creatures with just hair, glue, and feathers. It is like magic."

"That it is," I said. I seemed to have gathered my composure back and was relaxing a little. I picked up my fly rod from the bottom and was reeling in the line, wondering if Johnny Red Dust had sent Ix-Nay, but my newfound serenity was instantly extinguished when I looked up to see Ix-Nay now standing at point-blank range with the .45 in his hand.

The gun exploded. Seconds later, I felt my chest for a bullet hole and waited for the pain to set in, but nothing happened.

I saw Ix-Nay looking to the right of where I had just been standing. I followed his gaze to the ten-foot crocodile scurrying toward the shore. It was obvious by the wake behind him that the big croc had been cruising up the trail of muddy footprints I had made while fighting my fish.

"Time to go home, Cowboy," Ix-Nay said and hopped in the skiff. "You drive, and I'll point."

For the next week, Ix-Nay and I lived up to mutual promises we made on that first day we met. I taught him to fly-fish, and he taught me about Crocodile Rock. I learned just about as much from him about the land where I had chosen to live as he did about casting and tying knots. At the end of the week, we did a review with Bucky, and he pronounced us flats guides. It was one day before our first customers were due to arrive, and we celebrated our phony-baloney jobs at the Fat Iguana.

The lodge opened up on time, the fishermen arrived, and we went right to work. It was obvious from the start that we had overtrained. Most of our first clients hailed from the Rocky Mountains and had come south to escape the cold as much as to catch fish. There is a big difference between the streams of Wyoming, Idaho, and Montana and the flats of Ascension Bay. Fortunately, both Ix-Nay and I had become quick learners in the art of casting into the wind, and the fishing gods smiled on the lodge itself, for when the biosphere came into existence, net fishing was banned, and as a result, the large concentration of bonefish gave us plenty of targets within the range of thirty feet.

Most of our clients caught fish. That pleasure, along with the cocktail hour in the tree house, our incredible Mayan chef, and a night or two in town at the Fat Iguana, made Lost Boys an instant hit. Our first clients went back to the Rockies with snapshots of themselves with sunburned faces and big bonefish in their hands. Business boomed.

Bucky's finger healed up, and he came back to work. He immediately started training two more local guides.

When Ix-Nay and I weren't fishing or exploring the inner sanctum of the biosphere, Ix-Nay was teaching me about the world of the Mayans. Bucky Norman may have taught me to fish the flats, but it was Ix-Nay who would show me the road to Xibalba.

Mr. Twain was quite happy in his bamboo corral, and things couldn't have been better. But that was all about to change.

8

One Man's Cathedral

Flats fishermen are an odd bunch. They have to be because the location of their catch is so remote.

Fishing to most folks is as simple as a can of worms and a pole, or dropping a baited hook over the side of a bridge, but to the flats fanatic, it usually means traveling. The creatures they seek are difficult to catch because they live in such hard-to-find places. One of our customers, a very successful businessman from the Midwest who owns a major-league baseball team and an airplane-manufacturing plant in Kansas, summed it up. "Tully," he told me, "when I was younger, I would travel like Indiana Jones to find fishing spots. I lived in sleeping bags, ate lizards, drank Skin-So-Soft, and would wade into a pool of sulfuric acid if you told me bonefish were in it. Now, when I go fishing, I don't want to be more than an hour away from lemon veal, and I want to sleep on cotton sheets in an air-conditioned room. That's why I came to Lost Boys."

Bucky understood the idea of marketing creature

comforts in the boondocks better than anyone, and that is why Lost Boys was an instant success. In addition to offering four-star-caliber lodging and food, Bucky taught Ix-Nay and me that our job was not only to train our guides as mere guides but also to turn them into teachers and pals.

It didn't take long for the story of the Lost Boys lodge to go spinning off the Yucatán Coast like an advancing hurricane. It churned its way quickly and effectively through the marinas, cocktail parties, boardrooms, and tackle shops of the world of saltwater anglers. That first winter, not only was the lodge full, but guests began arriving on large yachts and in private planes and helicopters.

Mr. Twain had to start sharing his favorite little open grazing pasture with a makeshift landing pad in the barley field. So it didn't come as that much of a shock when Bucky informed us that a party of fishermen from Birmingham, Alabama, would be arriving by seaplane. What was odd was that they had booked the entire lodge for a full week, and there were just three anglers. So, at five p.m. on the appointed arrival date, I was perched in the tree house with my binoculars, scanning the horizon. I heard the distant rumble of engines and pointed my lenses in the direction of the sound.

At first, I couldn't believe my eyes. The seaplane was pink. The color immediately reminded me of Thelma Barston and her pink poodle assault on the Wild West, but it wasn't like Thelma to announce her arrival in such a manner. If she was still after me, she would come in the night when I was least expecting it.

The closer the plane got, the more clearly I could make out the fuselage. The bright coloring was in fact a painting of a giant flamingo running the entire length of the fuselage and spreading out on the underside of the wings.

If you choose to fly in a pink plane, you are either crazy or have a deep-seated desire to be noticed. The plane was now clearly visible to the staff of the camp, and they were all headed to the dock with cameras. As pink as she was, it was still remarkably graceful when the craft glided to a landing in the channel, framed in the rays of the sun over Crocodile Rock. It reminded me of one of those old travel posters that I had seen in a shop in Key West.

As the plane idled over to the dock, I scurried down from the tree house and joined the crowd. Ix-Nay was trying out his new Nikon camera to capture this Kodak moment.

"What do you know about these people?" I asked Bucky as we stood by to grab the lines and aid with the docking of the seaplane.

"There are three guests and two pilots. They registered under the name Smith, and they wired a cashier's check from a New York bank and paid in advance for a full week for the whole lodge."

"Maybe they're movie stars," Ix-Nay said.

"Pot dealers are more likely to be flats fanatics than movie stars," I told him. "Do you know any movie stars who fish?" I asked Bucky.

"Does Tom Brokaw count?" Bucky said. "He came down here right before you got here, and I fished with him for a day. It's a real treat when you meet somebody you've heard about, and he's a nice guy."

"But Tom Brokaw would *never* arrive in a pink plane," Ix-Nay added.

"You've got that right," Bucky said.

The pilot skillfully used the wind to nudge the nose of the plane toward the dock as the copilot disappeared from his seat, then hopped out of the forward hatch with a dock line that he tossed my way. The pilot cut the engines, and the plane drifted over to the dock. Bucky held the tail off, and I secured the bowline to a cleat.

The copilot was already on the dock, hustling back to open the cabin door, and we followed. When it popped open, a beautiful woman appeared and said, "Hello, Cowboy." It was like being hit in the face with a hand grenade. For there, framed by the sea and the sky, was not a movie star, Tom Brokaw, or Thelma Barston. It was Donna Kay Dunbar.

I had not laid eyes on Donna Kay in more than a year, since before the ill-fated weekend when I had stood her up in Belize City. Three months later I had sent her a lame excuse note, but she had never answered me, and she had good reason. More than twelve months ago, I had invited her to rendezvous with me by sending her a winning lottery ticket worth ten grand and the closest thing to a love letter I've ever written. But the nearer I came to meeting up with her, the colder my cowboy feet became. Like any warm-blooded American male terrified of commitment, I'd conveniently stumbled into a mishap that had made it impossible for me to show up. After I sent the note, I never followed up on it, and although I had mixed emotions because I truly did care about her, it was easiest to shove the whole experience into a black hole at the back of my mind labeled CLOSE ENCOUNTERS OF THE INTIMACY KIND. I figured I had blown it big-time with Donna Kay, and I had never expected to hear from her again, much less see her. Now she was standing two feet from me, pointing a video camera at my face.

All I could do was wave like a football player on the sidelines, uncomfortably introduce her to Bucky and Ix-Nay, and ask myself why she was here. Bucky raised his eyebrows and gave me a curious look, while Ix-Nay just grinned.

Donna Kay was radiant and seemed more as if she were returning from a vacation than embarking on one. She wore a pair of exotic drawstring pants covered with African animals. Her sleeveless shirt matched the Caribbean blue of the waters behind her and revealed her lean, tan arms. She had a canvas bag draped over one shoulder, and her blond ponytail poked out the back of a St. Louis Cardinals baseball cap. As her feet hit the dock, her hands cupped my face, and she gave me a soft, sweet kiss on the lips. She smelled of orange blossoms, and I closed my eyes and just enjoyed the taste of her lipstick and the citrus aroma.

When I opened my eyes, two men were standing next to her. The older of the two was twice Donna Kay's age and was a walking outfitter mail-order catalog ad. He was dressed in bright green fishing pants and a pink outfitter shirt, and his island attire was topped off with a pair of dark sunglasses in a turtle-shell frame. A white silk bandanna was tied snugly around his head.

The other man was half his size and age and wore one of those long muslin shirts over a pair of white pants. He handed a silk handkerchief to the larger man, who was sweating profusely. It was not hard to figure out who the couple was.

"Tully, I would like you to meet Sammy Raye Co-conuts . . . my boss. And this is his chief of staff, Del Mundo."

Sammy Raye shook my hand and gave me an

immigration-officer scan. "I've heard a lot about you, Cowboy," he said in a thick southern drawl with a slight lisp.

I didn't have a clue how to reply.

Bucky walked over to Sammy. "Hello, Mr. Coconuts. I'm Bucky Norman, the owner. Welcome to Lost Boys." He extended his hand.

Sammy shook it, and a big smile lit up his sweaty face. "The pleasure's all mine," Sammy said, clearly excited. "This place looks incredible — just like your brochure. How's the fishing and the air conditioners?"

"They are humming like a temple full of Buddhist monks," I said.

Del Mundo shot me a glance.

"It should be a great fishing week," Bucky said. "The wind is down, and no storms on the horizon. Will your pilots be joining us for dinner?"

"Yes, sir. This here is the copilot, Drake."

The man now standing next to Del Mundo tipped his hat.

"And Will is in the plane somewhere," Sammy added nonchalantly.

A voice echoed from the front of the plane through the pink aluminum hull. "Nice to meet y'all," he drawled as a hand appeared in the hatch and waved. "Sammy, I'll be a little while. I need to check the fuel pump," Will said, and his hand disappeared back into the forward compartment.

Drake, Ix-Nay, and I loaded ourselves up with duffel bags and fly-rod cases and headed up the dock.

"Well, let me show you around," Bucky said.

"Donna Kay tells me you are quite the fisherman," Sammy said to me.

"I think she might have me confused with my boss," I said.

"Sammy Raye just started taking up the sport," Donna Kay added.

I did my best attempt at hospitable talk. "Well, you've come to the right place."

"Mr. Twain!" Donna Kay yelled out as she spotted him in the pasture. She ran down the dock.

"Del Mundo will tell you where the bags go," Sammy Raye said to us. Then he stepped quicker to keep up with Bucky. "So, let's talk fish, Bucky," he said, and they left us behind and headed to the lodge.

I directed Del Mundo to Sammy's cottage and stopped to watch Donna Kay petting Mr. Twain. She seemed a hell of a lot happier to see my horse than me. I had a sick, nervous feeling in the pit of my stomach, like the way you feel when you're a kid and you've just been caught lying to the nuns. I figured it was going to be an interesting week at the Lost Boys lodge, but I had no idea just how interesting it would get.

The landing of the pink plane and the arrival of Sammy Raye Coconuts had caused about as much excitement to the staff and locals who had gathered at the shore as does that infamous Mexican celebration the Day of the Dead, but soon the plane melted into the backdrop of life in the tropics. Sammy Raye had gone to his cottage, and Bucky was working on the outboard on his skiff. The delicious scent of dinner preparation drifted out of the kitchen, and on the porch, Sammy Raye and Ix-Nay were busy tying permit flies for the morning run. Del Mundo was practicing yoga on the beach, and I was trying to figure out what they were all doing here. I was nervous.

I had agreed to Donna Kay's request to take Mr. Twain for a quick ride before dinner. I was in the process of saddling my horse for her when I heard the screen door slam on her cottage, and I turned around to see Donna Kay coming toward me.

I don't know what it is about a good-looking woman in riding clothes, but it gets my immediate attention. Donna Kay sashayed up to the corral wearing a white sleeveless shirt knotted above her tanned belly button and a pair of tight hip-hugger jeans. Her hair was still tied in a ponytail at the back of her head, and she already had her sunglasses on. She smelled like Coppertone.

"When's the last time you rode a horse?" I asked.

"Yesterday," she said with authority. "Sammy Raye has a string of polo ponies and cutting horses up in Alabama, and he gave me one a few months ago as a present."

"Well, there ain't much you can hurt yourself on if you stay on the beach. I keep the overhanging limbs trimmed back since I nearly decapitated myself once. Mr. Twain knows that beach by heart, so have fun."

"Thank you, Cowboy," she said. She took the reins from my hand and grabbed the saddle horn but couldn't quite reach the stirrup. "Could you give me a hand, Tully?"

I lifted her at the waist, and as she swung up into the saddle, I felt her hips press against my shoulders, and I went primal.

It was impossible not to think about Donna Kay naked in a French Quarter bed, which is exactly what was running through my mind as I adjusted her stirrups.

"See you later," she called out and galloped off to the beach.

I headed down the path that led to the end of the pier.

I needed a swim to get some endorphins in my system to battle with my testosterone. I dove in and did several laps around the pink plane. Next came work as a deterrent. One job led to another, and I washed the hull of my skiff, cleaned out the live wells, and removed the buildup at the waterline. Then I climbed up on the dock and went to work on a freshwater pipe that had sprung a leak.

I was hanging over the side of the dock, wrapping the leaking pipe with duct tape, when I looked up and saw Donna Kay walking down the dock. She stopped in front of the spigot.

"That was a wonderful ride. Mr. Twain still has his stuff," she said. She scanned the half dozen guide boats moored to the dock. "Now let me guess which one is yours," she said in a slightly mocking tone. She stopped next to the yellow-and-green hull with the blazing eyes of the Mayan fish god.

"How did you guess?" I asked.

"I don't know, Tully. It just looked like your boat." She studied the large pink letters scripted on the hull and then asked, "What does *Bariellete* mean?"

"It's skipjack, in Spanish. You know, the fish?"

"And who picked the paint job?"

"Well, that's a long story, but she's a seaworthy craft."

"Well, you certainly can't miss her," Donna Kay said.

"She's all ready to go for tomorrow. Looks like the weather's gonna hold. I was about to take her out for a little test run. Want to come along?"

"A cruise before dinner? Why not? It will take me a second to change."

"Bring a bathing suit!" I yelled as she ran down the dock.

She returned in a couple of minutes wearing shorts, and

I helped her into the boat and gave the rope start a crank, and the engine came to life. I cast off the bowline, and we steered away from the dock.

Donna Kay dropped into one of the turquoise Adirondack porch chairs that sat in the middle of the boat, sighed, and took in the evening light. "Now this is the way to end a day," she said.

I brought the *Bariellete* up on a plane and headed south out of the channel. Now we were creating our own wind, and a cool breeze washed over us as we paralleled the shoreline.

"I try to do it as often as I can," I said.

"Where are we headed, captain?"

"Off the beaten path. There's a pretty neat little Mayan ruin not far from here. We'll be back before dark."

"Sounds per—. Shit!" Donna Kay shouted as she sprang straight up in the boat. A large crocodile was lazily crossing the channel in front of us.

"Tully, that is an alligator! And so close to the lodge."

"It's actually a saltwater crocodile."

"Jesus!"

"Don't worry, we haven't lost anybody yet."

"They look so . . . so ancient," Donna Kay said.

"The Mayans believe that the earth in its flat form is the back of a giant crocodile, resting in a pool of water lilies."

The crocodile gulped a breath of air and submerged, leaving a trail of bubbles as he set off for the deep water of the channel.

Donna Kay cautiously sat back in her seat. "Tully, I trust you with my life, but I would prefer to put a little bit of distance between us and the crocodiles before I jump off the face of the earth."

I headed out of the channel and then turned north. We

ran in silence for about twenty minutes along the deserted shoreline until I spotted the landmark I was looking for. I steered for the beach and pulled into a sheltered little cove that Ix-Nay had shown me a few weeks earlier.

I slowed the *Bariellete* and spotted the cluster of coral heads that marked the way in. I handed Donna Kay a bucket with a clear bottom and showed her how to hold it over the side and see what was under her. "This is an amazing reef. I've never seen so many fish."

"And you probably never will. Ix-Nay and Bucky made this reef, and almost nobody knows it's here."

"Jesus, look at the size of that barracuda." She gasped. "How do people make such a thing?"

"They worked last winter on a project up in Isla Mujeres to create man-made reefs with hundreds of wrecked boats from the last hurricane. Not all the wrecks made it to their destination off of Isla. Several of them lost their way here. It's not even known by local lobster fishermen, and it's too far south and too dangerous for the fishing boats from Cozumel and Playa del Carmen. We call it the 'snack bar.' Want to see it up close?"

"Shit, I forgot my bathing suit," she said.

"This might be your only chance to see it. If the wind comes up, we can't get back in here. Besides, I've seen it all before."

"Not lately," Donna Kay instantly retorted. "You stay in the boat."

"I'll do better than that. I'll move the boat over to the beach, anchor it, and get a towel and your clothes ready for your return from the sea."

"How far away is that?"

"Just over there, twenty yards. You can wade in from the reef."

"Okay. Turn your head," she said.

I followed her orders, and in a few seconds I heard a splash.

"Can you hand me a mask and snorkle, please?" She was in the water, hanging on to the side of the boat, and I slipped the dive gear over the side, into her waiting hands. She donned them like a pro and propelled herself along the surface toward the reef as the sun illuminated her naked body.

I headed for the beach, slipped the anchor over the side, cut the engine, then stepped off the boat. I got a towel out of my bag and arranged her clothes on the chair.

She stayed in the water about fifteen minutes, and just as I was about to call her to come in, she was already swimming back. I did my about-face as she toweled off and dressed in the boat.

"I have never seen so many fish. It's like a personal aquarium."

"We can come back if the weather's right and make a day of it, but I just wanted to have time to show you the altar."

The word seemed to freeze her for a moment. "What altar?"

"Follow me," I said and walked over to the collection of giant limestone boulders that marked the end of the beach. Donna Kay, with her wet ponytail swinging in the breeze, waded in and followed.

At the edge of the beach, two of the large boulders formed an opening, and a path led under them.

"Ladies first," I said.

We squatted down and duckwalked through the opening for about twenty yards in the dark toward the rays of evening light that lit the exit of the crawl space. We came out into what appeared to be a dead end of solid rock beside a patch of sand the size of a beach blanket.

"Now, Tully, wait just a minute," Donna Kay said.

"We're not there yet," I told her and walked to the opposite side of the sand patch. I squeezed my body through a space about the size of a porthole and dropped down from a ledge to a worn path. "If I can do it, I know you can."

I had hardly gotten the words out before Donna Kay hit the ground beside me. We could hear the waves crashing against the boulders in the natural echo chamber they formed.

"What is this place?" Donna Kay asked.

"Come on," I said.

We tiptoed along the carved edge of one of the biggest boulders, then carefully stepped down a rock staircase toward the ocean. We were standing at the base of a tiny Mayan temple no larger than a phone booth. A series of steps descended into a small blue hole where a single ray of sunlight lit up the deep water.

"Legend has it that Mayan navigators came here to chant prayers and make offerings to the gods, who then sent them visions of their impending journeys."

"I thought you were allergic to religion for most of your adult life," Donna Kay said.

She walked slowly down the steps of the altar, watching the water in the blue hole rise and fall as the ocean surged and then ricocheted off the rocks.

"I always had a problem with blind faith and stories from the Bible," I said.

"They do seem to have been created more to terrify people than to help us understand what we're doing here," she added.

"Exactly," I said. "I prefer this spot to any church I've

ever been in. I am more amazed by lobsters turning a car hood into an underwater condo than Moses parting the Red Sea."

"One man's cathedral is another man's fishing hole," Donna Kay said and smiled.

"Amen," I added.

At that point, without warning or notice, Donna Kay did a graceful swan dive from the altar steps into the blue hole. I instinctively followed. We broke the surface about ten feet apart and kicked our way to each other. All I could think about was making love to Donna Kay in the sacred pool under the navigator's altar. I pulled her to me. She didn't resist as I pushed the hair out of her eyes and kissed her firmly on her salty lips. I slid my hands up under her shirt and cupped them around her breasts and lifted her slightly out of the water. I felt her body tense as if someone had flipped a switch.

"Donna Kay! Donna Kay!" a shrill voice screamed. We sprang away from each other immediately. Above us on the steps, two gray-haired women with cameras strung around their necks stood beside a guide. How they got there I had no idea, but all we could do was wave.

"Can you believe it?" one of the women said. "We come a thousand miles away from Alabama on a ship, and we run into the owner of our favorite restaurant. Y'all have fun."

Donna Kay swam to the steps, and I just floated for a moment, wondering what other surprises lay in store for me.

The aperture for a passionate moment without discussion, questions, or explanations had closed. All those things were now on the back burner. We rode home in silence with our wet clothes drying in the wind. I steered the boat, and Donna Kay sat in one of the chairs, twisting her ponytail in her fingers. The furrow above her brow told me she was thinking hard about something. I tried not to dwell on the inevitable moment when I would be held accountable by this woman for the wrong I had done her, but I knew it was coming. There were things we needed to talk about, things I had to explain, and issues that had to be addressed. But as Venus drew the curtain of the night sky up over the eastern edge of the horizon, we were simply jockeys straddling the back of that giant, unpredictable crocodile called life.

9

Fish Tales

There was just enough twilight left in the day to illuminate the channel markers back to Lost Boys, and when I got there, Donna Kay jumped up on the dock before I even got the bowline tied. She thanked me in a nervous voice, suddenly as distant as a paying guest, and hurried down the path to her cottage. It was then, as I washed off my fishing tackle and cleaned up my boat, that I asked myself the big question of whether or not I really wanted something as complicated as a woman back in my life.

I know it sounds odd, but from the time I arrived at Punta Margarita up until the moment that seaplane hatch opened, I had been so involved in covering my tracks, changing my life, and learning to be a fishing guide that women had somehow gone out of the picture.

I guess one of those fancy radio psychologists would have said that since I'd come to Lost Boys, I had been running away from some deep-seated fear of relationships, but I just saw it as being really busy. Now I felt guilty that I hadn't even been thinking about Donna Kay, at least not since I blew her off by not showing up in Belize City. Besides, I reasoned, she'd kept the rest of the $10,000 from the lottery ticket I'd sent her. Wasn't that enough payment for my sins?

I'd kind of become a monk in the sexual department, and the scary thing is that it really hadn't bothered me up until the moment I saw Donna Kay again. It didn't help matters much when Donna Kay appeared on the porch for dinner that evening looking like a forties movie star. She wore an almost see-through print sarong and no shoes. Her hair was now brushed out of the ponytail and fell across her shoulders, and she wore a choker with a single pearl that matched her earrings.

Bucky was up in a flash, attending her chair at the table. Donna Kay folded into her seat, trailed by a scent of citrus perfume. Bucky slid in next to her, thank God. I took a seat at the far end next to Sammy Raye and reached for the wine, asking myself this: What the fuck is she doing here?

When I first saw her on the dock, my initial instinct was to recoil and run. I figured that she had come seeking revenge and that she would whack me over the head with a rolling pin or worse for leaving her stranded in Belize. But here we were, having dinner in the tropics. It might have looked like a party, but I felt like the piñata. It was only a matter of time before I got hit with a stick, but I wasn't sure what would come out when I cracked open.

To my great relief, the gay, rich, rookie fly fisherman from Alabama could have also made a living doing stand-up. He had the whole table in stitches that evening, telling us stories of his exploits in the less traveled but heavily exotic parts of the world. It was welcome comic relief for me after my failed love moment with Donna Kay and the long, silent ride home. Drake came into the bar, but the other pilot hadn't shown up yet when the bell rang for dinner, and we were seated at our table.

Food immediately appeared from the kitchen, and the stories and conversations were fueled by several bottles of Romanee Conti La Tâche 1985, which were poured by Del Mundo. He had dressed for dinner in a tuxedo. I am no wine connoisseur — or let's just say I wasn't until I tasted that stuff. It's a long way up the vine from Mateus to La Tâche.

The subject of the evening pretty much stayed on fishing until Bucky mentioned that Tex Sex had been the previous owner of the property.

"I knew Tex Sex in another life," Sammy Raye said. "Did you know he was gay?"

"Sammy Raye thinks everybody's gay," Del Mundo chimed in.

"Well, it's sort of like fishing, in a way," Sammy Raye said.

"What is?" Ix-Nay asked.

"Being gay," Sammy Raye replied in a bored voice. "Everybody's got their pole in the water, and you just never know what you are going to catch."

"There are a lot of sharp teeth in the ocean, Sammy," Donna Kay said.

Sammy Raye flinched at her words, squealed, and cupped his hands over his crotch.

"Not where we are going tomorrow," Bucky told him.

"I try. I really do," Del Mundo said. "I've insisted on charm school and etiquette class, and I still get this big fruit from Alabama." Del Mundo shook his head.

"Well, beat me, fuck me, and make me write big checks," Sammy Raye responded. "Any way you sliced him, Tex Sex was still light in his loafers — which is not a big career enhancer in the country-music business. Take it from one who knows. Pass the La Tâche, please."

The table was collectively cracking up. From behind the kitchen door, one of the waiters was translating for the cooks, and this was followed by roaring laughter.

"Will we see sharks?" Sammy Raye asked.

"Big ones," Ix-Nay said, "but they only gum you."

"Well, hell, boys, let's go right now," Sammy Raye guffawed.

The wine was working, and I made the nearly fatal mistake of laughing as I chewed on a carrot stick.

The next thing I knew, I couldn't breathe. I couldn't talk. Everyone was still laughing at Sammy Raye, who had begun to imitate a shark. Nobody noticed that I was choking to death on a vegetable.

I rose out of my chair in what seemed like stiff Frankenstein movements. They thought I was doing an imitation as well. Spots appeared before my eyes, and I was on the verge of passing out when suddenly somebody turned me around and looked me directly in the eye. I knew the face from somewhere, but I couldn't put two and two together in my panicked state.

"Can you talk?" the man asked calmly.

I just wheezed. The next thing I knew, he had his arms around my waist, then jerked his clenched fists into my abdomen.

The carrot popped out of my throat and shot across the table, dropping like an Apollo capsule into Sammy Raye's wineglass.

I gasped for air and felt my way back to the chair. Now people had finally figured out that something was wrong with me.

"Can you talk to me now?" the familiar voice asked.

"Yes," I said hoarsely.

My breathing began to get back to normal, and my head started to clear. I looked up at the man and was about to thank him when all the lights came back on in my mind. "Willie Singer," I said in disbelief.

"Hello, Cowboy. How's that horse of yours?"

Del Mundo offered me first aid in the form of a full glass of wine. I had made an unbelievable trip back from death's door to dinner, and to my wild surprise, I was sitting right next to Willie Singer.

Willie vividly remembered our first meeting back in the Tortugas when we traded grouper for autographs. He told me he had actually written a song about the evening and had recorded it for his new CD, which he had made with a host of old-school calypso singers in Trinidad.

Willie, it turns out, was from Mississippi originally, and he was a distant cousin of Sammy Raye Coconuts. They had actually written songs together back when Sammy Raye was still actively involved in the music business. One of Sammy's regular pilots had gotten sick, so Sammy had called Willie to see if he wanted to go fishing and help out in the cockpit. Willie, it turned out, was planning a trip to the Yucatán himself. So it had worked out perfectly for both of them. Willie would crew for Sammy Raye and use the plane to go up to Mérida, where he had some business to handle while Sammy Raye and Donna Kay fished.

I needed more wine. I had nearly died, and the woman I had jilted had shown up along with one of my all-time heroes, not to mention Sammy Raye. Storytelling seemed to be a family tradition with these cousins, and Sammy Raye and Willie traded hilarious, outrageous stories back and forth at lightning speed until all of us were laughing so hard our faces were wet with tears.

Of course Sammy Raye had been an investor in the Pearl Road treasure hunt. When Bucky asked what it was worth, Willie just shrugged his shoulders and said, "Enough to keep looking," but Sammy Raye interrupted, saying it had been a $30 million take between them. It was too amazing, and we all wanted to hear more. Sammy egged Willie on to tell about his latest adventure, and he did.

Willie had bought a new plane. Actually, it was quite an old one and, like all old planes, came with quite a story. He was working in a recording studio in Sausalito when he had taken a day off and gone driving up to the wine country. The ever-present fog that enshrouds San Francisco Bay had retreated away from the coast. Meanwhile, Willie had gotten lost and had wound up way off on the Tiburon Peninsula. While trying to figure out where he was, like most men, he refused to ask directions. After about a half hour of winding around the roads and seeing the same old abandoned lighthouse again and again, Willie finally pulled up to try to find help. A huge, rusty fisherman's anchor was planted at the head of the lighthouse driveway. The sign on the chain read EQUATOR AIRLINES — KEEP OUT.

Willie slipped under the barricade. The place had an abandoned and haunted look to it, but music was coming from the building behind the old lighthouse. It was Glenn Miller's "String of Pearls," and as Willie rounded the corner of the building, he was not ready for what greeted him. In a deserted boatyard, he came face-to-face with an airplane.

At a table next to the plane, an old man was busy working on what appeared to be a model plane. He was shirtless in the hot sun, and his skin looked like a tanned hide. He was covered with faded tattoos. He wore a pair of tiny wire spectacles and a faded military beret, and a cigarette drooped from the corner of his mouth.

Willie called out to him, but the old man didn't look up. He was entirely focused on the tiny pieces of model plane.

As he moved closer, Willie saw that the model was made of bamboo and matchsticks, and it was a replica of the antique seaplane that sat in the field.

Finally the old man looked up. "You lost?" he asked Willie.

"You got that right."

"Most people are," the old man said. "Have a seat."

It turned out that the old man, Burt Brown, was the owner of the plane and the property, which he had turned into a flight museum. He told Willie his story, how he had flown for Pan Am across the Pacific in the Clippers and had retired after the war to Sonoma and had become a winemaker.

"I was looking for glamour, but wine making is just farming. It wasn't as much fun as flying," he told Willie. So he had bought an old DeHavilland Beaver seaplane in Alaska, and he'd gone into business operating out of a boathouse just north of Sausalito.

About this time, the whole wine craze hit Sonoma, and he sold his vineyard for a small fortune. He had no idea what he wanted to do with this newfound money, but the first thing he did was fly to Hawaii. While there, he read in the paper that a local island-hopping seaplane service was ending its flying-boat operation and switching to land planes. The retiring seaplane was a civilian S-43, smaller than the four-engine S-42 flying boats the old man had flown across the Pacific. He said they called them Baby Clippers.

He then went on to say that Howard Hughes had originally bought the plane for a proposed flight around the world. He had modified it for the trip, installing larger engines and more fuel tanks and a luxury interior, but then the seaplane nearly crashed during a test at Lake Mead in Nevada, and Hughes opted for a land plane instead. The S-43 was then sold to the airline in Honolulu. Eventually the plane would be auctioned off.

Burt Brown bought her for "chump change," then hired the crew to fly him home to Sausalito. His dream had been to complete the trip Howard Hughes had built her for. He bought the antiquated lighthouse station at a government auction on the condition that he would maintain the light. He hauled the plane up the old ramp and turned the boatyard into his base of operations for the trip. Twenty years later, Equator Airlines Flight One still sat on the ramp.

"Shit happens," Burt said. "I kind of got sidetracked."

The story immediately infected Willie, and he told Burt about his recent adventures and good fortune. A few beers later, Willie offered to buy the plane. Burt said he would sell it to him only if he would do the trip around the world. They shook hands.

That was a year ago, and now the trip was going to happen. Once Willie flew Sammy Raye home to Alabama, he was heading to San Francisco for the final test flight and to wait for a weather window for the return flight of Equator Airlines Flight One to Honolulu. He had named her *The Flying Pearl*. He was going to fly and surf his way around the world.

I was so caught up in Willie's descriptions of his adventures that I never noticed Donna Kay get up and leave the table.

Dinner evolved into dessert and after-dinner drinks and more fishing tales. Sammy Raye was busy showing Ix-Nay and the other guides the new underwater video camera he had brought along, and Bucky was getting out the cigars and fly-tying gear. Del Mundo said good night and went to his cottage to paint. I excused myself from the fishing fest and stepped outside to take a leak. I was feeling the effects of the wine, standing alone pissing downwind and staring up at the moon that had risen above the big banyan tree, lost in thoughts of stars and galaxies and spaceships.

"I still want to see that tree house."

I nearly jumped out of my skin.

"Did I startle you?" Donna Kay asked.

"I think it borders more on cardiac arrest," I said with a sudden tinge of anger.

Donna Kay then noticed me zipping up my pants. "Oh, my God. I am so sorry," she said.

"Apology accepted," I told her. I turned around to see Donna Kay in shorts, a halter top, and hiking shoes. While I had been spellbound by Willie, she had obviously gone back to her cottage and changed. She had wanted to climb the tree house the minute she saw it. Back in the boat, I had told her that I would take her up after dinner when the no-see-ums finished feasting on human flesh and the breeze picked up.

"I thought we could finish up our dessert with a view.

The chef wrapped up some cake and the last of the La Tâche," Donna Kay said as she hoisted a backpack on her shoulders. "Besides, the dinner table was piling up with bullshit. Listen, before you run off to find your fortune with Willie or Sammy, I think there are a few things we need to discuss." She adjusted the pack and looked up to the top of the banyan.

I began to climb in silence. My fantasy about a treasure-hunting ship had just been torpedoed by a sentence uttered by a woman with a purpose. Paybacks are hell.

There was an unpredictable wind howling through the branches of the big banyan tree, and I could see small whitecaps splashing against the dock, rocking the string of skiffs at their mooring. Loose leaves swirled about my head, and for some reason goose bumps started to run down my spine.

The Mayans liked to attach stories or characters to anything unpredictable. Ix-Nay said that the appearance of a land breeze that shouldered no visible weather carried spirits instead. The journey up the banyan tree that night confirmed his theory.

I told Donna Kay I wanted to check the climb and put some lights up for her, so, armed with a string of small lanterns, I took my sweet time in making the familiar but still potentially dangerous ascent. I wasn't Sir Edmund Hillary climbing Mount Everest, but it was adventure enough for the tropics on a dark night with a head full of burgundy and spirits on the wind.

While she waited, Donna Kay wandered over to Mr. Twain's corral and chatted with him as I headed up. When

I made it to the first big horizontal branch, I had the feeling that I wasn't alone in the tree.

I hung the first lantern and called down to Donna Kay to ask if she could see it.

"Just fine," she answered.

At that moment, a sudden, violent gust of wind rushed through the branches of the tree, shaking the huge limb I was standing on. I grabbed for the first thing I could reach, which was a swaying vine, and hung on. That is when the familiar, gravelly voice of Johnny Red Dust rang out amid the rustling limbs and leaves: *"I taught you to use your brain and connect it to your heart, but teachers can only teach so much."*

"What do you mean?" I asked as I relaxed my stranglehold on the vine.

"I didn't say anything," Donna Kay called out from below.

"Here's what I mean," Johnny replied. *"One morning you are shoveling the snow away from the door of your trailer in Wyoming. You discover your lost conch shell, and it sends you off to see me for some answers to questions that are bothering you. I give you a gecko, and you get the picture and set out on a life-altering journey. On your way to the ocean, an invisible cloud of grilled-onion aroma ambushes your pickup truck outside of Blytheville, Arkansas, and you are steered by an unknown force into the parking lot of the Chat 'n' Chew, where you follow the scent to its source — a hot grill being attended to by a beautiful waitress."*

"Tully, who are you talking to?" Donna Kay shouted from below.

"It's just the wind," I answered.

"How much farther to the top?"

In true island fashion, I answered, "Not much farther."

Johnny continued. *"Less than one week later, after a cheeseburger at the Camellia Grill and some slow dancing at Storyville in New Orleans, you are making love to the waitress in a four-poster bed in the French Quarter. Later that week, you stop for a chili dog in Alabama, where you meet a cowboy named Clark Gable, who introduces you to a shrimp-boat captain named Kirk Patterson in the village of Heat Wave on Snakebite Key. Captain Kirk needs a man to lend a hand on his next trip. You take the job. He agrees to bring Mr. Twain as well. It's all going like you had planned, and then the shit hits the fan. You bail on the waitress, leaving her emotionally stranded. Then you run away and land in Punta Margarita, where everybody seems to have an unspoken past, which suits you well since you have conveniently avoided mentioning yours to Donna Kay, Kirk, or your new employer at Lost Boys."*

"That's not fair. I told Kirk," I retorted as the wind picked up again.

"Life is not fair. You should have told her first. Your brain is not connecting with your heart. You are cruising along, and then the waitress, Donna Kay, pops back into your life like a piece of toast. You try to jump her bones in a sacred pool, but she has come for answers. Get ready."

"I'm confused," I said.

"What did you say about my shoes?" Donna Kay called out.

"I said you won't believe the views," I called back. "This is not easy, having a multifaceted conversation with a spirit and a woman," I whispered to the ghost.

"Mixed emotions can be as confusing as a Sunday buffet at Shoney's," Johnny added, *"but unrest of spirit is a mark of life."*

I had reached the top of the branches where the ladder to the tree house began. I hung the last lantern and called down to Donna Kay. "See it?"

"Clear as a bell. I'm coming up," I heard her say.

"Well, I can see that there is only room for two up here."

"But I need more info," I said.

"Just remember that contentment is a quality best suited for cows — not cowboys. You are searching for truth. Who knows? There may be a little to be found this very night in the top of this tree."

The wind was suddenly gone, pulled from the branches of the tree as if it had been a gimmick in a magic show. The night was again still as I heard the rustling below me and saw Donna Kay coming my way. "How far to the next rest stop?" she asked.

"One floor up."

10

Into Everyone's Life a
Coconut Man Should Fall

Donna Kay stood next to the telescope and stared out into the tropical darkness as she ate her chocolate cake with a plastic fork. There was no moon, so the dusty halo of the Milky Way filled the sky. The planets and stars above us shone with a piercing light upon our lookout spot above the jungle canopy. It was a long way from the Chat 'n' Chew Café in Blytheville, Arkansas, where we had met. She was a country girl who could turn leftovers into gourmet meals and who loved to go to the city and dance. I was a cowboy who craved the seashore. It was New Orleans, with its strange sense of place and time, that worked its magic by throwing us together like the ingredients in a large pot of gumbo. In our case it had brought us together, pulled us apart, and dropped us in a big tree in the middle of Mexico, where I knew that something in my life was about to change.

"This is an amazing perch," Donna Kay said and sighed.

I sat at the bar, eating my cake. I had seen this view

many times before, and though I never tired of it, I wanted Donna Kay to have the room to take it all in.

"It makes me want to be a pirate," I added.

"Still haven't gotten over that pirate thing, huh?"

"No, I don't think so."

That sick, nervous feeling I'd had at dinner had vanished with the voice of Johnny Red Dust, but it hadn't taken long to return once the climbing had stopped. I knew Donna Kay had something else on her mind but had not yet brought it up, which was odd for her. She was a very direct person, and small talk was not her style. There was obviously a lot that needed to be said, starting with why she had surprised me by popping out of the seaplane in my backyard, to my no-show at Belize City, to the very big question of what exactly our relationship was now. I felt very unsettled in the top of the tree that evening. I didn't know if catching up was the topic of conversation, but I did know that I wasn't the one who would start it.

You see, I am a very bad communicator. I don't blame anybody for that, but I spent most of my life with cows and horses, and they are a lot less complicated than women. I was well aware that I'd had a full year to get in touch with Donna Kay, and I couldn't even really explain to myself why I hadn't tried to do it, since I knew all along that she mattered to me. I guess I'd just been scared. And, judging by my sweaty palms, I was really scared tonight. Default questions such as "So, what have you been doing?" or "What brings you down here?" or "What did all that mean back at the blue hole?" didn't quite seem to have the right words. All I could come up with was "So, what's the story with Sammy Raye?"

"He's my partner," Donna Kay told me.

"I thought he was your boss," I said.

"He's both." Donna Kay put her plate on the bar and slipped past me to the hammock, where she eased herself in and curled up. With her left leg, she pushed at the wooden deck and began to rock slowly back and forth.

From her freshly made nest in the hammock, Donna Kay told me the story of Sammy Raye Coconuts, the man who had deposited her here on the shore of Lost Boys lodge.

According to Donna Kay, Sammy Raye Coconuts had made a wrong turn that had been the right turn for her. It happened one afternoon after his annual Elvis Presley pilgrimage. He had left Graceland, made a wrong turn on the interstate, and the next thing he knew, he was crossing the Mississippi River. Lost in Arkansas, he had pulled into the parking lot of the Chat 'n' Chew in a pink Cadillac El Dorado, looking for a cheeseburger and directions home to Alabama.

After her disappointing return from Belize City, Donna Kay had thrown herself into her work. She had moved quickly up the ladder of success at the Chat 'n' Chew from waitress to cook, and her culinary talents were striking flavorful chords with the local population and diners from Memphis to Mobile. Under Donna Kay's tenure, the Chat 'n' Chew had been crowned the best "meat, tea, and three" restaurant in the state of Arkansas. Donna Kay was no ordinary short-order cook, and Sammy Raye Coconuts was not just another hungry customer.

His real name was Simon Cohen Jr., son of Si and Dolly Cohen. They had fled Europe before the war, eventually winding up in Pensacola, Florida, where Si's brother had trained as a pilot in the U.S. Navy. Si was no flier. He was a farmer by trade and eventually found the potato fields, watermelon patches, and pecan orchards of Baldwin County more alluring. He and Dolly moved to Fairhope, Alabama, where Si opened a grocery store and Dolly taught piano lessons.

Si's grocery store eventually became the local farmer's market, which he supplied with fresh produce from the dirt cheap farmland he started buying in small parcels. Little farms became big farms, and farmland became golf courses and residential, affluent neighborhoods when the snowbird migration from northern cities discovered the quality of life on the temperate shores of Mobile Bay. Si Cohen made a fortune, and they lived well. He and his wife and Simon Jr. visited New York several times a year to see the shows on Broadway and summered on the Mediterranean coast of Italy.

But all that came to an end on a foggy night in July of 1956, when the family was returning from Europe on the luxury liner *Andrea Doria.* Off Nantucket Island, the ocean liner *Stockholm* sliced into the *Andrea Doria* and sank her. Si and Dolly Cohen were killed instantly, and young Simon was discovered miraculously alive in the twisted foredeck wreckage of the *Stockholm,* clutching his teddy bear.

The traumatized Simon Jr. — and the teddy bear he keeps with him to this day — returned to Alabama, where his Orthodox aunt Shirley and uncle Merv raised him. "He was such a nice Jewish boy before the accident," his aunt used to repeat like a parrot to anyone who would listen.

It may have been the trauma of losing his parents in a ship collision or just growing up Jewish in Alabama, but whatever it was, Simon Jr. found his own path in this world.

It didn't hurt that his journey was probably made a bit easier by the fact that at age eighteen, he inherited $17 million from his parents' estate. So, in the fall of 1966, the young multimillionaire from Fairhope bought Uncle Merv and Aunt Shirley a nice house on a kibbutz in Israel and saw them off at the dock in New York. A day later, he legally changed his name to Sammy Raye Coconuts, bought a flat in Greenwich Village, and charged out of the closet and into the world to pursue the thing he really loved most — music.

Having inherited the Midas touch of his father and the nimble fingers of his mother, Sammy Raye Coconuts became one of the biggest songwriters of first the folk, then the folk rock, then the disco era in New York. Luckily his flamboyance, along with his flatfeet and fat wallet, kept him out of Vietnam. He was an investor in clubs, musicals, Key West and Fire Island real estate, computers, and the development of liposuction technology. He kept an array of boy-toy models busy waiting on him hand and foot and even bought a yacht, on which he circled the island of Manhattan partying until dawn, though foggy nights at sea still gave him the creeps. You would think all the fame and fortune would have been enough for Sammy Raye, but by age forty, he had burned a gross of candles at both ends. He was still alone, and he was ready to go home.

Sammy Raye returned to Alabama, bought a sprawling cattle ranch and pecan orchard on the Magnolia River south of Fairhope, and named his estate Pinkland. For the next ten years, he used Alabama as a base for his sojourns, which started in the Caribbean but eventually took him to the far side of the world.

He bought a big private jet that flew across oceans, and

that is what he did for several years, buying plush get-away hotels. During all those years of travel, he never missed his annual pilgrimage to Graceland to pay homage to Elvis and gather ideas for his own mansion on the shores of the Magnolia River.

It was the most recent run to Memphis, and a drive through the Arkansas countryside, that placed Sammy Raye on a counter stool at the Chat 'n' Chew. After tasting Donna Kay's chicken and dumplings and coconut banana cream pie, Sammy Raye Coconuts dropped to one knee and began quoting Thoreau. "He who distinguishes the true savor of his food can never be a glutton; he who does not cannot be otherwise," Sammy Raye passionately recited to the startled Donna Kay, who was flipping burgers behind a counter full of customers.

Sammy Raye Coconuts turned his soliloquy into a generous job offer as his private chef at Pinkland. The left-over cash from my lottery-ticket money had felt tainted, so Donna Kay had used it to improve her karma by donating the whole thing to a battered women's shelter. She had just about given up her dream of owning her own place when Sammy Raye made her the offer.

The next thing Donna Kay knew, she was on Sammy's Falcon jet that he had sent to Blytheville to pick her up. "It's called a Falcon Fifty. It's French, and it's fast," the well-dressed pilot had told her.

"There I was, tucked into a rolled leather seat on a rocket ship at forty-one thousand feet going five hundred fifty miles per hour, sipping a glass of fresh-squeezed orange juice and nibbling a hot croissant. Something told me my life was about to change for the better."

Forty minutes later, the plane descended over the shoreline of Mobile Bay. Donna Kay stepped off the plane into the invisible but identifiable smell and feel of the Gulf Coast that she remembered from her days in New Orleans.

"I'm afraid I could get used to that kind of travel very fast," she said to the pilot.

"They say it's a worse habit than heroin," the pilot replied with a smile and a tip of his hat. "Welcome to Alabama."

A stretch limousine pulled out into the parking area next to the plane. She was greeted by a polite chauffeur named Bransford, who quickly put her one suitcase in the trunk and whisked her into the backseat of the car. Fifteen minutes later, Bransford slowed the limo and turned off on a red dirt road past a sign that read WELCOME TO WEEKS BAY MARINA. There, she was handed over to the crew of a dazzling speedboat that looked more like a varnished piano than a watercraft.

Donna Kay stretched out on the seat in the back of the piano boat and took in the view. Pelicans cruised by overhead, and small mullet sprang from the water in front. As they made the turn from the bay up the channel of the river, the dorsal fin of a dolphin effortlessly broke the surface of the water.

They moved slowly upstream past cottages, mansions, and piers, then around a long, narrow bend in the river where a man stood at the end of a wooden dock beneath a pair of matching flagpoles. On one, the American flag rode on the morning breeze. On the other was a large pink flag with the single letter P.

Del Mundo met her at the dock and introduced himself as Mr. Coconuts's chief of staff. A pair of large golden retrievers, whom he introduced as Si and Dolly, roamed the dock and the beach, chasing fiddler crabs. A waiter in a starched linen jacket appeared, holding two matching glasses of iced tea, garnished with mint and pineapple. "Sweet or unsweet?" he asked.

"Sweet," Donna Kay replied. As she sipped her tea in the rapidly accelerating heat of the early morning, Del Mundo told her that Sammy Raye was in a meeting and would see her soon, but he had instructed Del Mundo to take her on a tour of the property. Waiting at the end of the dock was a horse-drawn carriage. "I felt like I was in a movie," Donna Kay told me. "I only hoped Sammy Raye would be more like Cary Grant than Vincent Price."

The carriage rolled slowly along the grass roads with Si and Dolly trailing behind. Del Mundo pointed out the sculptures and manicured gardens of azaleas, camellias, and dogwoods that covered the landscape and what they meant to Mr. Coconuts. They toured the guest cottages, then the chef's living quarters, which, Del Mundo pointed out, came with a Jeep, bicycle, and the Boston Whaler, which was tied to a small crabbing pier behind the cottage.

"What exactly does a chief of staff do?" Donna Kay asked without thinking. She instantly wished she hadn't said it, but it was too late.

However, Del Mundo just stifled a laugh. "Everything, honey," he said. Then he continued the tour without missing a beat.

Donna Kay got out of the buggy and walked around the lovely little cottage that could be her home. She was picturing herself swinging in the rope hammock that hung in the shade of two magnolia trees that faced the river when she heard a muffled transmission from the radio Del Mundo carried. Del Mundo responded to the voice, then turned to her and said, "Mr. Coconuts is ready for you now."

Sammy Raye Coconuts stood on the giant veranda of the main house at Pinkland, dressed in white linen Polo shorts and a flowery Hawaiian shirt that sported coconut trees and guitars. He was not as big as Marlon Brando, but he was getting close. He personally escorted Donna Kay on a tour of the main house, ending at a glassed-in, air-conditioned porch that offered a view of the Magnolia River all the way to Weeks Bay.

Sammy Raye got down to business. He told Donna Kay that he really loved her cooking, but the sad fact was that no chef had ever stayed at Pinkland for more than three months because he was basically an aging old queen who suffered from menopausal depression and was a pain in the ass. He had seen several therapists, hypnotists, and yogis over in Pensacola, but nothing had worked to make him more agreeable, other than traveling around the world on his jet. He ate out when he was on the road, and therein lay the problem with Donna Kay's predecessors at Pinkland. It was not too much work that drove them crazy. It was the lack of it.

Donna Kay just asked Sammy when she could start.

Donna Kay broke the endurance record for Pinkland chefs by two months, at which time Sammy Raye was once again on his knees. He had flown all the way back to Fairhope from Thailand to beg her to stay on.

She told him that she had fallen in love with life on Weeks Bay and knew it was where she was meant to be. She thanked Sammy Raye for giving her the opportunity to work at Pinkland, but she really wanted to move on and was hoping to open a little restaurant of her own in Fairhope.

They were sitting in the air-conditioned porch where she had first talked business with Sammy Raye, and it was there that he moved their relationship to another level with the words "How about the bait shop?"

Sammy Raye told her that he owned a fleet of shrimp boats and a processing plant down in Bon Secour, and there had been a restaurant and a bait shop that had a not-so-successful history as a honky-tonk, health-food restaurant, and biker bar. At the present time it was sitting empty due to damage from the last hurricane along with complaints from his neighbors about the heavy-metal bands. Sammy Raye Coconuts told Donna Kay that if she stayed three months longer at Pinkland and found him the right replacement when her time was up, he would give her the bait shop and restaurant property and back her in the restaurant business.

Sitting in the banyan tree, Donna Kay took a sip of wine and continued. "So that is why I never wrote back to you . . . after that . . . letter and everything." Off on the invisible horizon, a telltale cluster of bright lights moved slowly along. "What is that?" Donna Kay asked.

"I would like to say we have visitors from another planet, but it's just a floating casino bound for Cozumel."

"It could be one of Sammy Raye's," Donna Kay said.

"He owns cruise ships in the Caribbean?"

"Honey, Sammy Raye Coconuts is a living Monopoly game. He started on Baltic and Mediterranean and ended up on Boardwalk and Park Place. I can't keep up with all the stuff he owns. All I know is that he is good at what he does, and he is a fair partner." She paused. "Sammy Raye is a man of his word and did what he had promised me. In turn, I trained the replacement chef and taught him dishes that Sammy Raye liked to eat, and everybody was happy. As for me, there wasn't a happier resident last fall on the eastern shore of Mobile Bay than Donna Kay Dunbar, the proud new owner and operator of the Pickled Oyster. We've been open for five months, and in that time, we've been featured in *Southern Living* magazine and on the *Today Show.* Even the Allman Brothers Band stopped their tour bus and had lunch one afternoon."

"You're famous?" I asked.

"Well, I have a cooking show on the local channel in Pensacola. Remember the ladies at your secret swimming hole?"

"How could I forget?" I answered.

"Well, I guess you could say that I've had my fifteen minutes and people do ask me to sign menus and aprons."

"I'm happy for you," I said. "So that's what all the fuss was about in the swimming hole — those two ladies taking pictures and everything."

Donna Kay laughed. She climbed out of the hammock and walked over to the rail and leaned out, watching the cruise-ship lights disappear behind a cloud. There was a very long moment of silence, and then she said, "Tully, I am not just here for a vacation. I needed to come talk to you."

"Uh-oh," I muttered.

"No, no, it's not about that lame excuse for standing me up in Belize. I mean, boy, was I pissed at the time, but then because of that, things took a different turn in my life, and I was able to forgive you. Well, actually I figured out that you were just that way, and I doubted that you would change. I didn't think I wanted the job of trying to change you, no matter how much I was attracted to you." Donna Kay could get a lot of information into a short speech. She came over to the bar and took a big gulp of her wine.

I stayed frozen to the bar stool as I felt my legs start to become rubbery, and my palms began to sweat. I braced myself for what was coming.

"Tully, things are about to change in my life."

A preview of what she was about to say flashed across my mind. Donna Kay was about to utter the big C word. She was going to ask me to come back to Alabama with her, give up my life down here, and commit to a relationship. I was going to have to finally face that dragon that I had brought down to Punta Margarita with me.

So when I heard the words "Tully, I'm getting married," at first it didn't register. Then I felt Donna Kay squeeze my arm. "Did you hear me?" she asked.

"Yes. You said you wanted to get married," I whispered. "Donna Kay, I can't. There is something I have to tell you. . . . It's about that trip to Belize. And, well . . . it's about everything. It's about why I couldn't come back —"

"Tully, *stop!*" she ordered, taking my other arm. She turned me so my eyes looked directly into hers. "Listen carefully," she said slowly. "*I* am getting married. *You* are staying here."

I felt like such an asshole.

Donna Kay sat down on the bar stool next to me.

"So that's why you swam away from me before we left the altar?"

"It was tempting, believe me, but I just couldn't."

"Of course not," I muttered in defeated agreement. "So who's the lucky guy?" I asked.

"Remember Clark Gable?"

11

Tree House of the Mayan Moon

The world is full of victims and habitual whiners these days, and I try not to be one of them, though it is hard not to go there. Donna Kay was getting married, and I hadn't even been a long-shot choice as the groom.

I liked Clark Gable — he was a cutting-horse trainer I met back in Alabama. He was the one who hooked me up with Captain Kirk, and Kirk had introduced him to Donna Kay. But the news was confusing to my sense of self-worth. It hit me like one of those giant rogue waves, crashing in avalanche fashion over the bow of a ship in a storm, and my reflexes sent me immediately to that self-centered preservation zone known as survival mode.

I avoided my initial impulse to fall to my knees, let go of a flood of tears, and scream to Donna Kay, "What about me?" Somehow I managed to keep one hand on my ship as the rogue wave engulfed me, then washed astern. Already my thoughts of having some kind of a romantic relationship with Donna Kay were turning into storm debris and scattering.

I poured the last of the La Tâche, and Donna Kay took a sip of wine. Then, in her matter-of-fact style, she relayed the story of her engagement in a concise, three-act melodrama. The first was "Tully stands me up in Belize City and takes off for Punta Margarita." I listened as she described that scenario as a selfish, unconscious, typically male, nearly unforgivable event.

Though it had been a year since it had happened, it was still very fresh in her mind. She also reminded me that in the year since I stood her up, other than one lame excuse note, she hadn't heard one word from me. Act two could have been titled "Get Even," but knowing Clark as an honest and thoughtful guy, I knew that Donna Kay's description of him helping her remodel the restaurant, helping her train her horse, taking her to Horn Island and New Orleans for weekends, and finally popping the question were genuine expressions of his feelings for her. I was just pissed off at myself that the guy Donna Kay was describing wasn't me.

She told me that Clark had really wanted to come with her, but he felt uncomfortable, given that he believed he had stolen Donna Kay away. She had told him that the past was between her and me, and she felt she could better explain the situation alone.

Donna Kay seemed her old self as we climbed down from the banyan tree. Back on the ground, her usual confidence and candor surrounded her like a bouquet. Coming down in the dark had taken all my concentration, but when my feet touched the ground, I realized my knees were shaking, and it wasn't from too much exercise.

"It's really simple," Donna Kay told me. "We both had dreams, but my dreams were different than yours, and I had to chase them. I wound up in Alabama, and you made it to Lost Boys. I don't think I have to —"

"You don't know the whole story," I said, interrupting.

"Tully, I wasn't finished," she retorted.

Something had come over me. I could not let her go without telling her what I had fully intended to do when I had stepped on the dock of that shrimp boat a year earlier. "You don't know the whole story," I said again.

"Of course I do. You ran out on me for whatever reason, and now that I am getting married, you want another chance."

"No, you're wrong. You think you know the whole story, but you don't," I said. I was angry now because she wasn't listening, and it showed in my voice.

"What story?" she asked.

"In your version, it just sounds like the self-centered ex-boyfriend ran off and got what he deserved. Donna Kay, you haven't even asked me what happened."

"Well, for God's sake, let's hear it," she said. "Tully, I've never heard you talk like this," she added quietly.

"It's because I have to. I know all of this is my own damn fault, and I accept the blame. I know I should have told you sooner, but I didn't, and I can't change that. I want you to marry Clark. Clark is rooted, and I can't be. Not now for sure, and maybe never. You have chosen the right man for you."

Donna Kay didn't say anything. She just turned around, headed back to the tree, and started to climb. I followed her back up and, finally, that night in the tree house under the Mayan moon, I was about to make the speech of my life to an audience of one.

"I know it looks suspect that I hightailed it across the Gulf on a shrimp boat to Mexico and disappeared on you, but there was a reason."

"I'm listening," Donna Kay replied. "How long will depend on your sincerity and honesty."

I took a deep breath, looked up at the moon, and then began. "My memories of our time together are some of the happiest of my life."

"They call that the honeymoon stage," Donna Kay said.

I was taken aback a little by her crisp response, but I gathered my thoughts and stayed focused.

"That's a good name for it," I replied, "because it felt like a honeymoon. I enjoyed every single minute that we spent together, but I knew it couldn't last, even before I was kidnapped."

"*Kidnapped?* Now, Tully . . . ," Donna Kay began, with a doubt in her voice like a teacher who had heard too many excuses.

"It's true. I swear," I pleaded. "Please. This is important to me, but I have to start at the beginning. My original intention after leaving Wyoming was to keep going and never look back, just like Butch Cassidy did. I'd had it with my life the way it had been. I needed a break. I'd never seen the ocean. I had wanderlust, but there was something else. Then, I walked into the Chat 'n' Chew, and there you were." I pulled my chair closer to the hammock where she was slowly rocking. "Donna Kay, I have been in love with you right up until the moment you told me you were marrying Clark."

Donna Kay made no sudden reaction to stop me, and once the dam broke, the river of words just kept coming.

It was almost as if someone else was saying them. "So in my mind, I just assumed that you would want to do what I did. It was naive of me, but I just envisioned the whole thing working out perfectly."

"That is a common mistake that most men make," Donna Kay said.

"I know. My idea was for you to come down to Mexico and visit me and fall in love with me and the tropics at the same time. My problems in Wyoming would be far behind me. We would live happily ever after. You would open your restaurant on the beach. I would help in the kitchen and learn to make omelets when I wasn't tending my fishing business, which I would start. We'd spend our days growing old together under the tropical sun and shady palms of Mexico."

"Sounds like *The Swiss Family Robinson*," Donna Kay said dryly.

"Not quite." I got out of my chair and walked to the rail so Donna Kay couldn't see the tears that were welling up in my eyes. "I wasn't really free to pursue my dream life with you because I was hiding something. A lie."

"What lie?" Donna Kay still sounded skeptical.

"I wasn't really a carefree cowboy loping along, taking his pony to the shore. Back in Wyoming, I committed a crime."

"What kind of crime?" Donna Kay wanted to know. She suddenly sounded nervous. "Did you murder somebody?"

"No, nothing like that. It was back at the ranch. I got in a big fight with the boss lady, a real control freak named Thelma Barston, and I ended up throwing a table through her plate-glass window. She reported it to the cops and made up a lot of other stuff about assault, and pretty soon I was all over the Wyoming papers with a warrant for my arrest and a big fat reward for my capture. I ran."

"You have got to be kidding," Donna Kay said.

"I wish I were."

"Go on," Donna Kay told me.

She was listening.

"Thelma isn't a woman to be scorned by an out-of-work cowboy. She also hired two bounty hunters to track me down."

"Oh, God. Bounty hunters. I thought they only existed in old movies," Donna Kay said.

"Horror movies," I replied. "Within a week, with her political connections in Wyoming, they had trumped up the charges against me, increased the reward money to twenty grand. That certainly got the villagers fired up to find Frankenstein, and the newspapers painted me to be Charles Manson on horseback. All this happened while I was cruising across the country towing Mr. Twain to the beach. I wasn't watching the news, I hadn't read any papers, and I was all the way to Alabama before I even heard about it. Meanwhile the two bounty hunters were on their way — I kid you not, their names were Waldo and Wilton Stilton."

Donna Kay shook her head and laughed. "Tell me this is just a tall tale, Tully. It's too weird to be true."

"How could I make up names like Waldo and Wilton Stilton?" I asked.

"I don't think you could," she said.

"It gets a lot weirder," I continued. "I had a client last

month who was a writer for *The New Yorker.* We were having a sunset cocktail at the Fat Iguana when the rumor of my Wyoming background came up, and the Stiltons returned to haunt me. This guy had written a piece on modern-day bounty hunters, and guess who his subjects were?"

"Waldo and Wilton," Donna Kay said, on cue.

"Exactly. The guy said that their great-grandfather was an Irish immigrant who changed his name to Park Stilton because when he got off the boat, he had to sleep in Battery Park, and he got through his first week ashore by eating a huge wheel of Stilton Cheese that he stole. I kid you not, it was all in the article — he showed it to me."

"Tully, how do you remember all this stuff?"

"They were hunting me — for money. The Stilton brothers were third-generation ne'er-do-wells of a family that had made the classic transition from robbing people with guns to robbing them with fountain pens. Great-Grandpa Stilton had pillaged, stolen, and murdered his way across the Rockies until he was hung outside of Livingston, Montana. His son, Park Jr., was the one who figured out that he could make more money catching outlaws than being one. He got religion and a badge and hunted down his friends for the rewards.

"Providing protection and intimidation for railroad barons had made the family a fortune, and money bought the family respectability. It was only a matter of time before they entered politics, and when a few Stiltons had law and accounting degrees, they became pillars of Western society.

"But not all of them were criminal geniuses, and that's what brought Waldo and Wilton Stilton into my life, and vicariously into yours. It took every connection their fa-

ther had with the local politicians, law enforcement officials, and school board members in Missoula just to keep
them in high school and out of jail.

"After finally graduating, the Stilton twins celebrated
their achievement by following the Metallica tour around
America. It was on the road that they decided not to follow in the family footsteps but to enroll in chauffeur
school in Salt Lake and become limo drivers for rock
stars. That summer, they also set a personal goal of putting folded two-dollar bills into the thongs of one thousand strippers. They were at number eight ninety-six
when Daddy ordered them home to Montana to get real
jobs or lose their inheritance.

"He had already planned their future. In order to keep
them out of the real family business but actually working,
he had created a company of their very own. In one fun-
filled week, Waldo and Wilton bought new guns and
handcuffs, and with the help of their answer booklets,
they passed the one-page written exam that provided
them with diplomas to hang on the wall of their new offices — along with laminated ID cards and free BEA in-
signia caps. After that, they went to work in a three-state
area, chasing deadbeat dads and repossessing pickup
trucks. The lofty, new age term used to describe their job
was 'Bail Enforcement Agents,' which really meant they
were bounty hunters.

"At first, having left the state, I managed to stay pretty
well off the radar screen of the Stiltons."

"This is beginning to sound like the plot of a bad
movie," Donna Kay said.

"It gets even worse," I told her. "Thelma had been
upset with their inability to find me, so she put some pressure on their father. I heard about the whole thing and

couldn't believe it. I was not going back to Wyoming to a jail cell and the smug satisfaction of that ranch Nazi. I was heading to Mexico, and I wanted to tell you why."

I took a half-filled bottle of rum from the shelf of the bar. "I could use a drink. How about you?" I asked.

"Sure, but I'm not so sure about the end of your story." Donna Kay held out her hand and took the glass.

"Don't worry. Nothing really bad happens."

We touched glasses and sipped the rum, and then I continued. "You ever heard of the Galactic Wrestling Federation?"

"The GWF?" Donna Kay said it as if it were as common to her as IBM. "Sammy Raye is part owner of that circus."

"You are shitting me." I took another sip of rum. "You ever heard of Kelly Brewster?"

"Of course. He's the world champion — or was the world champion, until Ric Flair cracked him over the head with a pogo stick and then proceeded to literally tap-dance on his skull."

"Well, along with their job of chasing me around the country, the Stiltons also wound up in show business as bodyguards for Kelly Brewster."

"So how did you get tangled up with that bunch?"

"At the Mullet Toss."

"Oh, Jesus, how did you wind up there?"

"By mistake, of course. I went for a fish sandwich. How was I to know that there was a place on the planet where people throw dead mullet across a state line as an excuse to have a party and a beauty contest?"

"This country is going to hell." Donna Kay sighed. "It's a wet T-shirt contest, Tully, not Miss Fucking America."

"Whatever," I replied. "The point was that I didn't

know Kelly Brewster from Kelly McGillis, but he was the honorary judge for the Mullet Toss, and that is how he and the Stiltons wound up in Alabama."

"Seems like everybody in this soap opera wound up in Alabama," Donna Kay said. She motioned with her hand for me to continue. "I guess I want to hear the rest."

"It was the day before my departure for Key West. Kirk had suggested that I go over to the Flora-Bama for a sandwich and a beer, and to take a walk on the beach. When I got there, the Flora-Bama was more like a rock concert than a bar. My first instinct was the right one, to get out of there, but I was hungry, so I tried to hang out inconspicuously at the end of the oyster bar, which was away from all the action. I was eating a fish sandwich with my head buried in *Islands* magazine, thinking about my future and my rendezvous with you — really.

"I didn't notice the crowd of large, loud men at the end of the bar, huddled around a three-foot-high mound of oyster shells and a mountain of empty Dixie beer bottles. I never recognized the blond mullet cut or the tattooed biceps of the two hundred sixty pounds of twisted steel and sex appeal in the form of Kelly Brewster — as he chewed a beer can in two with his gold teeth. Two local girls in skimpy bikini bottoms and flimsy, tie-dyed T-shirts with holes in them were going wild. I never saw Waldo and Wilton standing behind them, but they sure as hell saw me.

"I left the Flora-Bama to head back to the boat in Heat Wave, but the Stiltons blindsided me in the parking lot. I fought like hell to get away, but they maced me and the lights went out.

"They stuffed me in the back of their rented station wagon, and I came to with a splitting headache and a singed feeling in my lungs when I inhaled.

"Somehow I had clicked into survival mode and had begun to think quite clearly. The first thing that came to mind was that we were not moving. Then I heard Wilton's voice.

"I opened my eyes to see Wilton Stilton sitting in the driver's seat. The winner of the Miss Mullet Wet T-shirt Contest was sitting in his lap. Wilton was bragging into his cell phone to Thelma Barston about what a dumb fuck I was. He held the phone with one hand, and the other hand was fondling the knot of Miss Mullet's bikini top. Wilton told Thelma that Waldo had gone ahead to the airport in Gulf Shores and that I'd be in the Heartache jail by morning.

"My idea was to launch my escape plan as soon as Wilton cranked up the car. I would pry my way out from behind a pile of suitcases and onto the backseat, and I hoped that the engine noise would cover my escape when I made a dash for the beach and ran like hell.

"I waited for the car to start. It didn't, but the music on the radio suddenly got louder. As Jerry Garcia sang about scarlet begonias and a late-night card game, I made my move. I couldn't believe my luck. Wilton was now sprawled out behind the steering wheel, moaning as his head rested on the top of the seat, and he stared out the sunroof. He was singing along with the Dead as Miss Mullet's blond hair bobbed up and down in his lap.

"When Wilton started to scream, 'Oh baby!' again and again, and the car began to rock back and forth, I took off. I don't know who that Deadhead chick was, but in my book, she is a mullet-tossing guardian angel. I just ran like hell for the boat dock and the *Caribbean Soul,* where I tried to act casual and took refuge belowdecks. Captain Kirk calmed me down, and we set sail for the tropics on schedule.

"Looking back, I know I should have just returned to Wyoming and faced the music, but at the time, it didn't seem like a real option to me. I figured the best way to avoid trouble was to just disappear for a while. The Stiltons went back to being ringside bodyguards for wrestlers, and I heard through my sources out west that Thelma Barston was more determined than ever to find me and drag me back to Wyoming. That woman is completely crazy. I saw no choice but to stay out of the country until the statute of limitations ran out or Thelma spontaneously combusted. When I won that lottery, I wrote to you and sent you the winning ticket."

I paused.

Donna Kay said nothing.

I looked around. No ghosts were hanging in the tree branches — just the evening breeze. "That's it," I added.

Donna Kay climbed out of the hammock and silently strolled across the deck and looked out at the moonlit ocean. "Jesus, I don't know what I think right now. Either you've had one hell of a run of back luck, or you've made up this whole story and you are the most pathetic man on the face of the earth for trying to get me to believe such a pile of horseshit." She turned and looked at me, hard. "Tully, you have never struck me as the kind of man who would lie your way out of your responsibilities. So I am going to have to think good and hard about that one."

"I know it's bizarre, but it's true, Donna Kay. I swear it."

"Tully, I came down here because I had a score to settle. I wanted to start my marriage clean and clear, with no unfinished business left from my past. Plus, I didn't think it was fair that you could just sail in and out of my life like I was some kind of port of call. I wanted to tell you that, face-to-face. Falling in love with Clark sure helped, but I guess I couldn't take this big step in my life without making sure it was the right one. I came down here to vent my anger at you, but now *you* — the man of so few words — are the one who got to make the big speech."

"At least now you know the whole story. That's the reason I disappeared, and I'm sorry for the trouble I caused you."

I was through talking. There were no more words to say. I was exhausted, but I felt as if something had been accomplished.

"I guess that means you won't be coming to the wedding?" Donna Kay asked.

I smiled and shook my head. "Stranger things have happened, Donna Kay. If that is an invitation, then I am going to work on an RSVP."

Once again we descended from the heights of the tree, and I walked the bride-to-be to her cottage. The final act of the play starring Tully Mars and Donna Kay Dunbar was now completed, and even though it had not worked out as I had originally planned, I knew that Donna Kay was still my friend.

At the door of her cottage, she quietly said good night and gave me one of those friendly pecks on the cheek. It was no movie love-scene kiss, but it worked just as well, because I felt forgiven. Then, as any great departing love interest should do, she disappeared behind the bamboo curtain.

12

If I Were Like Lightning

Once again it was Mr. Twain who showed me the path out of the swamp. After a restless night of twisted dreams, I was awakened before dawn by that familiar and predictable sound of my horse in the nearby corral. It was again time to take my pony to the shore.

Donna Kay had not only brought the news of her marriage to Lost Boys lodge — she had also brought the weather. That morning, as I pulled myself up aboard Mr. Twain by his withers and turned him to the east, we were greeted by a perfect tropical day. The ghostly winds of the previous night had dissipated, replaced by a gentle breeze that made itself visible in the small waves that carpeted the bay. Mr. Twain was ready to run, and I was full of cobwebs.

We were scheduled to meet up at the dock at nine, which would put Bucky and Sammy Raye right on the incoming tide at the south end of the bay. Willie was taking off for Mérida, and I was left to entertain Donna Kay. I had no idea what she might want to do. Despite our past relationship and our revelations in the tree house, she was still a paying customer, and I was the guide.

I galloped through the spray, trying to put a little distance between me and Johnny Red Dust, Alabama wedding bells, and that nagging question about what I was really doing with my life.

"Just me upon my pony on my boat," I sang to the motionless orange starfish camped on the flats who had no idea who Lyle Lovett was. I repeated the line like a broken record as we headed along the shore toward town. At the end of the beach, I nudged Mr. Twain into a right turn, and we ran headlong into the crashing waves until we were both swimming. I ended up where I had always been with regard to Donna Kay — over my head.

A short while later, Mr. Twain and I were sprawled out, lying on our respective sides in six inches of clear Caribbean water, looking at each other. Mr. Twain had that "What's next?" look in his big brown eyes, and I had no answer.

As we headed back to our waiting world, I noticed a small thunderstorm had darkened a portion of the sky and momentarily blocked the sun's rays from the beach where we were walking. I stopped my gait, and Mr. Twain stood still. As we gazed at the gray mist of rain below the dark cloud, a searing bolt of lightning arced over to a random spot on the surface of the ocean, sending a cloud of water skyward. The sun came back out, and something had changed. I looked at my watch. I still had an hour before I had to be at the dock. I had no idea what the day had in store for me, but I knew that it was going to start with breakfast.

I turned Mr. Twain toward town, the land of cheese grits and huevos rancheros. I scratched at my good-luck charm and began to sing to my horse as we rode:

And if I were like lightning
I wouldn't need no sneakers
I'd come and go wherever I would please
And I'd scare 'em by the shade tree
And I'd scare 'em by the light pole
But I would not scare my pony on my boat out on the sea

13

Grandma Ghost

I headed up Main Street to La Cocina Café. As I sat finishing my breakfast on the tiny round plaza at the end of the main street of Punta Margarita, an old woman strolled to the far side of the circle. She carried a small canvas stool and an easel. She made several trips around the fountain and finally settled on a view of the church. Then she unfolded her gear, sat, and pulled a large sketch pad from her canvas bag.

She was obviously American, but she was no tourist. She had that weathered look of a real traveler, and of course the fact that she was painting caught my eye. She wore a long khaki skirt and a blue work shirt with a bleached-out, wide-brim hat that hid her face.

I sipped the final wash of coffee in my mug and watched her hands as she turned the parchment in her grip from a blank page into a work of art. She moved almost in slow motion as she stopped sketching, turned to look at me, and smiled, connecting through my eyes to the tropical soul that lived inside me.

If the visit the night before from Johnny Red Dust hadn't been enough, the old lady painting in the square had reminded me that I was not the first Mars family member to run away to the tropics. That title went to my almost great-grandmother — Sarah Sawyer Mars — better known to her great-grandchildren as "Grandma Ghost."

I think what connects some people to the art they like is not wishing they could paint it but rather wanting to be *in* the scene that the artist has painted. I know that traditionally cowboys are not known as collectors of art, but I can't help it; it runs in my family, and it started with Grandma Ghost.

Art had connected me to the tropics long before I bought St. Barbara at the flea market or took off my cowboy boots and sank my bare feet into a sandy beach for the first time. I might have sold my truck, my trailer, and most of the keepsakes I had accumulated over the years after my exodus from Wyoming, but my pony and my two paintings came with me.

I have already told the story of *The Patron Saint of Lightning*. This is the story of the other piece of the Tully Mars art collection. The painting is called *Heart of the Andes,* and it was created by the great American landscape artist Frederic Edwin Church. Church was a member of what they call the Hudson River School, and when he was not traveling to the ends of the earth for inspiration, he made his home along the river. Although I call it a painting, my Church is actually a black-and-white engraving. The original hangs in the Metropolitan Museum of Art in New York, where I saw it as a teenager on a high school graduation field trip. Its beauty simply wore out my brain and my body as I stood and drank it in until they closed the museum.

Besides being a painter, Frederic E. Church was kind of like the George Strait or the Dale Earnhardt of his day. Back before the Civil War, when visual art and books and live music was *it* for entertainment, people actually followed the careers of painters like they do NASCAR drivers and country music stars today. Church was not only a painter but an explorer. He had been drawn from the comfort of his home and studio along the banks of the Hudson River to the jungles of South America after reading the book *Cosmos,* written by the legendary German explorer Alexander von Humboldt.

Church was bowled over by von Humboldt's description of the tropics and wrote to the explorer, offering his services as an illustrator. That is how Mr. Church went to South America with von Humboldt.

Now remember, this was before cameras and Photoshop, when only painters and sculptors could record striking visual images. Church set up his easel in the jungle and started to paint those mysterious landscapes of South America, attempting to capture the beauty of the tropics and acquaint people with parts of the world they would never see. He succeeded beyond his wildest dreams. Waterfalls, volcanoes, and dense jungle scenes came to life on his stretched canvas, and when he brought these visions home, the art critics in New York City had to give Mr. Church's works a new name. They called them "heroic landscape paintings," and that is just what they were.

Heart of the Andes had inspired my lust for the tropics long before I ever came here. I know cowboys are supposed to be into Western art like those sculptures by Frederic Remington and that picture of Custer being scalped at the Battle of Little Bighorn that hangs in bars all over the West with the Budweiser logo on the bottom, but it didn't work out that way for me. Grandma Ghost had seen to that.

Heart of the Andes was completed in 1859 and put on exhibition in Church's Greenwich Village gallery on the island of Manhattan. Crowds flocked to the gallery. It was art and entertainment all rolled up into one.

Among the visitors to the Tenth Street Studio Building in April of 1859 were Jubal and Sarah Sawyer Mars, my great-grandparents.

The way the story goes, the newlyweds had journeyed from East Tennessee to New York on business. Jubal ran a successful fleet of steamboats on the Tennessee River and had many business connections in New York. Sarah had willingly left the coast for the Cumberland Mountains as part of her marital obligations, and she assumed she would, like most wives of the day, make the geographic transition that often accompanied marriage. But Sarah Sawyer Mars was no mountain woman. She was a belle from the coastal metropolis of Charleston, and her roots were firmly attached to the low-country lifestyle. She soon became very depressed with her new surroundings.

Jubal had thought that the trip to New York would "do her good," and he had a surprise for her. The talk of the town that spring was a painting by the famous artist Frederic Church, and Jubal had put aside his business meetings to take his wife to view it. Afterward, they would have dinner at one of New York's finest restaurants.

They set out that evening for the one-picture, paid-admission special exhibition and eventually found the studio. Nailed to a tree out front was a sign with these words in big red letters: HEART OF THE ANDES. Jubal and Sarah dropped two quarters into the till, signed up to purchase a black-and-white engraving of the painting, joined a line of nearly a thousand interested New Yorkers, and waited patiently, as Southerners would, to view the painting.

Finally they got to the benches arranged in front of the painting and took a seat. The picture was encased in a dark wooden structure and adorned with draperies, and it looked like a window that opened to reveal not just a landscape but a complete condensation of South America in a single image. The painting was brightly lit by gaslights while the rest of the room was left dark. Dried palm fronds that Church had actually brought back from South America hung overhead and transformed the room into a tropical setting.

Well, it sure as hell worked on my almost great-grandmother, for when the usher motioned for her and my great-grandfather to vacate the bench, Sarah Sawyer Mars wouldn't leave. She refused all requests, overtures, and finally commands to leave by my great-grandfather, the gallery manager, and even the artist himself, and she had to be physically carried out on the bench by the police. During this whole ordeal, she said not a word but just stared at the painting.

Jubal Mars accompanied his wife in the police wagon and sat beside her on the bench on the way back to the hotel. When they arrived, Sarah shocked them all again by calmly rising from the bench, taking my great-grandfather's arm, and stepping out of the paddy wagon. Then she asked if they might have a cup of tea.

They went to bed that night, and the next morning, my almost great-grandmother was gone. She had left a note describing her feelings about what the painting had done to her, and she couldn't help it, but she was going to the tropics, where she felt her destiny was calling her. She said that the painting had not only captured a scene but also shown her a window into the world where she felt she belonged. Sarah Sawyer Mars had walked into that painting, and she never came back.

My great-grandfather was in shock for a while, but he returned home to Tennessee, went off to war, survived, went west to Wyoming when the Civil War finally ended, and remarried. My almost great-grandmother disappeared into the jungles of South America.

Stories of her adventures and exploits were whispered at family reunions. She had run off with a painter to Paris. She had gone crazy and died of a fever in the Amazon. She had been murdered by pirates. My memories of my real great-grandmother were of a kind and loving woman who took care of her family and had never left the county in which she was born. "Grandma Ghost" was a forbidden subject in our house, but of course tales were told and retold by children and adults alike in the corners of parlors or around campfires in the mountains, but it was me who really discovered her secret.

One summer at a family reunion at my great-grandfather's ranch, my hellion cousins and I were rummaging through his attic when my cousin Baxter accidentally spilled the contents of an old cedar box out onto the floor. As we scrambled to clean up the mess, I picked up a faded yellow envelope with the words SARAH SAWYER MARS — DO NOT OPEN written across the front. I jammed the letter into my pocket.

Later that night, I snuck back into the attic by myself and unsealed the envelope. Out dropped a stack of ancient sepia photos. I quickly unbound them. The top one was of a young woman standing on a beach with a letter in her hand. She was about to drop it into a wooden mailbox. Two giant tortoises watched her from a distance. On the back of the photo were scrawled these words: SARAH SAWYER MARS, POST OFFICE BAY, GALÁPAGOS ISLANDS, 1859. The rest of the photos told the story. She had sailed from New York to Panama, crossed the isthmus by train, and continued on by ship to Ecuador. She had disembarked at Guayaquil and then made her way up the river to Quito, following the path of Frederic Church to the Valley of the Volcanoes. In the last photo, she is painting next to a mountain trail with the volcano behind her.

Grandma Ghost was a ghost no more. Along with the photos was an envelope, wrapped with a faded blue ribbon, which held a long-dead flower. It was addressed to THE DESCENDANTS OF JUBAL MARS. I slit open the envelope with my Swiss Army knife, pulled out the letter, sat back in an old rocking chair with my Boy Scout flashlight, and began reading.

The letter started with a quotation from Alexander von Humboldt. It read, "Why may we not be justified in hoping that landscape painting may hereafter bloom with new and yet unknown beauty, when highly gifted artists shall often pass the narrow bound of the Mediterranean, and shall seize, with the first freshness of a pure youthful mind, the living image of manifold beauty and grandeur in the humid mountain valleys of the tropical world?"

The letter continued:

Dear Family,
As I lie here in the cool of the late afternoon, staring for the millionth time at the conical summit of Urubamba aglow in the twilight, it seemed the fitting moment to write down those

words of von Humboldt that inspired me so long
ago. This is Sarah Mars Menendez, known to
some of you as "Grandma Ghost." I hope I haven't
haunted you too much. I promise not to do so in
the next life, either. I am about to leave this world,
and it is time to make amends. Oftentimes I have
wondered what might have been, if I had done the
proper thing and returned to Tennessee from New
York with Jubal and had only stared at this
wonderful engraving with regrets. But lying here
now, listening to the music of the birds out my
window and seeing the landscape that I have come
to love so much here in the Valley of the
Volcanoes, I know that I may not have done the
proper thing, but I did the right thing for me.

I apologize if I have caused you harm. I know
that Jubal was a fine father, and I heard wonderful
things about Bessie. They have honored the Mars
family name with great pride and lasting heritage.
I die with no family. Sadly, that was part of the
price of my ticket to freedom, but I have no
regrets. What I did learn in my leaving was that
there are far more roads on which you may
traverse life's paths than those that seem to have
been preordained for you by others. Of course
there are times when I wonder what could have
been. But I chose my path, and that is that. I have
found a home, and I will die happy here in the
jungle and be buried near the river, which gives
life to this region. In looking back, I know it was
the kindness of Jubal that led to what I am sure
was a much unforeseen outcome.

There will always be those who feel more

comfortable not venturing from the warmth of the hearth, but there are those who prefer to look out the window and wonder what is beyond the horizon. There is no beauty like that which overtakes us by accident. This picture was the accident that diverted me from the well-traveled path and onto a bumpier, but more interesting, route. Maybe up there in America, there is another Mars son or daughter who feels the urge to fly like I did, who sees life not as a flickering candle but as a torch that can illuminate an undiscovered world. If so, then take this gift and do with it what you will. Hang it up and dream of what it is, or use it as a map to take you there. And if you do decide to wander, please leave a tiny bit of room in your heart for me. For if I live in your hearts, I really have not died.

Love,
Sarah Mars Menendez
Otavalo, Ecuador
February 10, 1931

"What painting?" I whispered to myself. I tore that attic apart until I found what I was looking for. It was a wooden crate buried beneath a stack of storm shutters and baling wire with shipping labels still attached that indicated it had come from Otavalo, Ecuador. I had found the treasure.

I remember the exotic fragrances that still lingered as I pried the crate open and lifted out the mahogany frame. I don't know if it was the jungle view from Frederic Church's hand or the words of Sarah Sawyer Mars

Menendez, but I knew I was where I was now because of one or the other. The vision of Mr. Church had done its job. His work had ignited my senses and spoken to my heart. And as for Grandma Ghost, what is a picture without the story of how you came to love or acquire it? The same sentiments that had glued her to that bench in Greenwich Village nearly a hundred fifty years ago had led me to this plastic chair on a sandy street in the village of Punta Margarita.

The silence of the moment was shattered by the unmistakable sounds of radial airplane engines. Willie Singer was taking off for Mérida. A few seconds later, the pink plane zoomed over me at treetop level. I instinctively waved, as most people do when they see a low-flying plane going somewhere, but it wasn't Willie Singer who waved back. It was Donna Kay. I realized that she was heading off to her new life, just as Grandma Ghost had done.

I watched the plane disappear behind the coconut palms, figuring Willie Singer must be enjoying the view from the pilot's seat, and somehow I felt certain our paths would cross again. I finished my coffee, paid my bill, tucked my letter back into the safe confines of my waterproof pouch, and walked my horse to the little plaza, where the artist watched me approach and smiled. I looked down at the sketch, which had captured the church and the morning perfectly.

"That is a beautiful piece of work, ma'am," I said.

"Want to be in it?" she asked with a smile.

"I already am."

14

Everybody Out
of the Pool

The morning that Donna Kay flew away with Willie, it
so happened that the weather gods produced a fishing
day we hadn't seen in these parts in quite a while. The
tides coincided perfectly with the cooler part of the morning, and Ix-Nay had come back from the biosphere flats
with a report that the semiannual hatching of red-back
calico crabs, the favorite food of hungry permit, was
under way.

All these events were relayed to me by Bucky, and he
came down to the corral to meet me. That is when I told
him that Donna Kay had left on the seaplane and that I
wouldn't be fishing. He'd known Willie was going to
Mérida to look for something he needed for his trip
around the world, but he was stunned by the news about
Donna Kay. He seemed to want to stay and comfort me,
but I could tell he was also extremely excited about what
looked to be a great fishing day. I told him he should get
going.

"Why don't you take the Jeep and drive up to Cancún

and chill out for a few days?" he said. "Ix-Nay and I can handle Sammy Raye."

"You have customers. Don't worry about me. But I'll think about it," I said as I hosed Mr. Twain down with freshwater.

The silence of the morning was then suddenly broken by Sammy Raye as he bolted out the door of the lodge with Del Mundo right on his heels. "You have got to call that fabric guy in Morocco," Del Mundo hissed.

"I am going fishing, bitch," Sammy snarled back. Then they spotted us, and the catfight ended. Del Mundo went back inside, and Sammy Raye put on his happy face. He walked toward us and began to whistle the theme from *Gilligan's Island*. He was covered from head to toe in what looked to be a tailor-made muslin outfit with a fishing bag on one shoulder and his brand-spanking-new fly rods hanging over the other. He wore a long-billed fishing hat, and his nose, ears, and mouth were smeared with thick sunblock. He looked more like a circus clown than a fisherman as he stopped at the corral.

"You knew she was leaving?" I asked.

"Not until she woke me up this morning and asked if Willie could drop her in Cancún."

"Did she say anything else?"

"Only that she believed your story. Well, we have to catch the tide, you know."

"I know."

"See you this evening." He started to walk off, then turned and, in a very sincere tone, said, "Tully, it is the best thing for both of you."

"I suppose it is." I sighed.

Then Sammy Raye patted my shoulder and waddled on down to the end of the dock, reconnecting to the spirit of the morning and shouting, *"Que tal, amigos?"* to the smiling guides.

I watched them all load up from the vantage point of the tree house, as Bucky advanced the throttle on the skiff. The light hull zigzagged out the channel as the birds flew from their roosts on the markers. They disappeared around the end of the island, and I headed for the hammock. It had been an emotional night for this cowboy.

I woke up thirty minutes later and felt much better. I had decided to take Bucky up on his offer of the Jeep. It was a rust bucket held together with duct tape and baling wire. It would never make the trip to Cancún and stay in one piece, but it was time to drive somewhere. Tulum seemed the perfect answer.

Driving is one of those things that you get so used to in America, but it doesn't seem necessary on an island. My horse and my bicycle had served me well during my time here, and I really had no need for wheels. But that morning, I was ready for a road trip.

I went for a short swim to wake up, packed an overnight bag, then jumped in the Jeep. I buzzed through town and waved to everyone, then caught the ferry to the mainland and started up the sandy road that led north to Tulum.

I guess I wasn't watching where I was going, and being away from driving for so long proved to be my undoing. From a distance, the puddle that lay across the road looked just like that — a puddle. Plus, I was in a Jeep, the vehicle that had earned its stripes in World War II. So I didn't even bother to slow down; that is, until the puddle turned into a pothole the size of a swimming pool.

Well, when I finally cleared the mud from my face, eyes, and ears, I was literally up to my ass in water. Only the windshield of the Jeep was visible.

My first thought was a movie image of the dreaded quicksand pit that slowly swallowed people who panicked. Those who didn't panic or move were eventually rescued by the screenwriter, who would write in a convenient nearby vine that could be used by the human plum who was stuck in the pudding.

I was sitting in a half ton of steel, and there was no vine in sight. I sat movie-still for about three minutes and watched the level of water on the windshield. I was not sinking.

The only redeeming thing in this mess was that my waterproof fishing bag, which held my towel, a change of clothes, my lucky conch shell, and my book, floated from the backseat to the front. I grabbed it and hung it on the rearview mirror, then slowly squirmed from behind the wheel and floated out of the Jeep, feeling for the bottom. To my momentary delight, I found hard sand, not mud, beneath my feet. I walked out of the pothole and just looked at the mess I had made.

My day was not going very well so far. My ex-girlfriend had flown away, and I had drowned a Jeep.

I was rescued from a slide into depression by the sound of a badly running engine coming out of the jungle. I felt my luck changing as a beat-up pickup belching smoke came around the bend. I recognized the driver as a local fisherman named Chino, who sold us bait at the lodge. Unlike me, Chino had the good sense to steer around the pothole. He slowed to a stop.

"*Hola, hermano,*" he said with a sardonic smile. "Looks like another one of the giant iguana attacks to me,

Tully," he said as he examined the nearly submerged Jeep.

"No, it was aliens from the Pleiades who set this trap."

"Happens all the time," Chino said in a matter-of-fact voice as he groped around in the bed of his truck. He pulled out a thick piece of rope, which he tied to his bumper. "I got mine done," he added.

I waded back into the muddy water and was quickly up to my waist in muck.

Chino whistled and said, "Now that's a pothole."

I connected the Jeep, climbed back out, and watched as Chino fired up his truck, revved the engine, and dragged the Jeep free and moved it to the side of the road. Water poured from it as if it were some kind of giant sprinkler can. I knew it wouldn't be running anytime soon.

"I'm heading to Playa del Carmen, Tully, but I ain't in no hurry. I can take you back to the lodge if you want."

"That Jeep ain't goin' nowhere, Chino. I'll call Ix-Nay from Tulum. I have appointments there."

"I bet you do." He laughed.

Before I jumped in his truck, I grabbed my waterproof bag and dashed through the palmetto palms for the ocean. I peeled off my mud-soaked shorts and T-shirt, went for a quick rinse, and changed clothes. I was kind of feeling human again.

It may have been early morning, but Chino was already ahead of the day. From his shirt pocket, he produced and fired up a big fat joint and held it in my direction. "They call it *da kine*. I got it from that Rasta band that was playing down at the Iguana. It is so strong, it will take your mind off pussy for nearly ten seconds."

I burst out laughing. It was the first laugh I'd had since I left the dinner table last night — a very long evening.

"Ten seconds?" I asked as I took the joint from him.

After the abrupt departure of Donna Kay and now the Jeep mess, I was more than happy to help him turn his ganja into ashes. We traded the joint back and forth as we drove.

As the buzz came on, I settled into it, staring at the tops of the palm trees passing by and occasionally glimpsing the green ocean.

Chino turned up the radio, and Celia Cruz sang to us. "That shit working yet?" he asked.

I nodded my head and smiled. "I believe so. I am only thinking of coconuts, amigo."

My first view of the ruins had been from the back of my horse. Shortly after I arrived at Crocodile Rock, Ix-Nay had given me directions to a beach trail that led all the way up from the Punta Margarita ferry dock to Tulum. I had met an American geographer in the Fat Iguana who was working on the site and had offered to show it to me. I had decided to go up early and camp out on the little beach under the cliff, to get a look at the place as the sun rose out of the Caribbean.

That morning, I woke before dawn, took a swim, and then rode Mr. Twain up the bluff to the ancient city.

Just as we reached the top of the cliff and the entrance to the ruins, the sun rose over the eastern horizon. I expected to see a bunch of rock hunters and scientists taking measurements and chipping away at rocks, but there was nobody there. I sat on my horse, surrounded by silence and history.

For the moment, I was the king of Tulum. Staring at

my kingdom of ruins that morning, I found myself with a head full of cosmic questions, and I certainly had no answers — so I decided to survey my domain on foot. I tied Mr. Twain at the base of the tower they call El Castillo, and I ascended the stairs, heading to the top. The tiny stairs told of small occupants back in the old days.

On the way up, I passed what appeared to be an old altar and wondered if that was where they sacrificed the virgins. Reaching the summit, I scanned the panorama of my kingdom and declared all things to be well. I took a few pictures with my camera and then descended to my waiting steed.

The true spiritual essence of the morning and my rule over the ruins was brought to a swift conclusion in a split second as I transformed from the King of Dawn into a gringo trespasser. Standing next to Mr. Twain was an angry-looking guard in a soiled uniform, pointing an M16 carbine at me and shouting in Spanish. My reign was over. He looked as if he not only would shoot me but might eat me as well if I didn't do what he said.

As frightening as the situation was, I couldn't help but think that the guy with the gun looked very familiar to me.

Now I don't know if adrenaline is supposed to speed up your thought processes, but I can tell you that the sight of the gun pointed at me jump-started something. I *did* know the guy. Of course he didn't come to the Fat Iguana in his uniform, but I recognized his face.

His real name was Hector, and he was a Jimi Hendrix freak. He would regularly show up at the bar and repeatedly punch every Hendrix tune we had on the jukebox. I shared his love of Hendrix, and one night in the bar, as he was loading up the jukebox, I asked him how he had become such a fan.

It seems that as a teenager he had spent time in San Francisco and had worked for a caterer who did all the Bill Graham shows. I guess Hendrix liked Mexican food, and Hector had actually met him. Jimi had signed his Giants baseball cap, which he never took off his head.

"Hector!" I blurted out. "I'm Tully, the other Hendrix freak from the Fat Iguana."

Hector lowered the gun. The next thing I knew, I was having coffee in the guard shack, which was covered with Playmate cutouts, Hendrix posters, and pictures and brochures of Las Vegas.

It was there in the shack that I met Dr. Destin Walker for the first time. Dr. Walker was studying the windows in the tower, trying to figure out if there was any truth in the legend that the Mayans had used them as some kind of light system to guide their trading ships through the coral reef.

It was my long conversation that day with Dr. Walker that had put me under the spell of Tulum. It also got me thinking more seriously about the world of magic lights atop rocky shores that were meant to keep us from danger. I found myself heading up there quite often while the scientists were there. Dr. Walker had even hired me to help him with his research from time to time.

The day of Donna Kay's departure, I had gone to Tulum looking for that morning magic, but after the Jeep was attacked by travelers from another planet, I arrived at a different Tulum than the Spanish had first seen.

Back in 1518, a Spanish expedition led by Juan de Grijalva bobbed on the waters of the Caribbean. They set their gazes shoreward upon a high cliff wedged between the indigo sky and the turquoise sea. There, a city of red, white, and blue buildings stretched so far down the coast that Tulum appeared to them as large as the city of Seville back across the sea in the land of the Inquisition.

It took the Spaniards a while before they ever set foot in Tulum, due mainly to the fierce determination of the Mayans not to be conquered. But in the end, gunpowder trumped arrowheads, and that was that. The old "Excuse me, Great Nations of Europe coming through" machismo overpowered the Indians, and the gun-toting, armor-laden, overreligious, disease-ridden, gold-lusting, self-anointed crusaders from the civilized world finally managed to get ashore. Funny thing was, after all that bloodshed in the name of God and Country, it was the mosquitoes that sent them packing after three months.

*C*hino deposited me, my waterproof bag, and my buzz at the main entrance to the grounds, where a parking lot was filled with tour buses that made the daily trek down from the hotels in Cancún with loads of gringos. Unlike the Spanish before them, these gringos were armed not with metal helmets and muskets but with Instamatics and video cameras.

I paid my entrance fee and joined the throng of visitors who combed over the ruins like ants. Today the crowds were actually a welcome sight. It was as close to the real world as I had been in a while, and I was thoroughly entertained by their going about their vacation activities of taking pictures, posing for videos, eating ice cream, buying T-shirts, and yelling at their misbehaving children in four or five different languages. I looked for Hector, but another guard told me he had gone to town to get lunch.

I sidestepped the crowds at the base of El Castillo and headed down to the beach. It too was packed, but I managed to find an unoccupied spot in the shade of the bluff. I laid out my towel, took off my shirt, got out my book, bought a hot dog and a beer from the beach vendor, and went on vacation.

Several beers later, I took a walk down the beach past the altar at the north end of the city. I still had my Jamaican ganja buzz going, and I just sat on the rocks and watched a flock of pelicans dive-bomb a school of pilchers repeatedly, wondering how many times a pelican dives in his life.

I got tired of counting, and the Technicolor shimmer was no longer visible on the water because the angle of the sun had changed. A bank of gray clouds started to fill in.

I returned to my spot in the shade of the bluff and moved my belongings to the shelter of a thatched hut on the beach. The sand and sea were now becoming less occupied as the loudspeakers from the parking lot had begun to blare out the announcement that it was time for the buses to leave.

I waved to my fellow vacationers as they gathered their bags and souvenirs to take off. I used a creative combination of waves I had learned in my rodeo days in Heartache when I rode my horse around arenas, carrying the American flag. It was quite a trick to secure that flagpole with one hand and acknowledge the crowd with the other. I had learned to mix my waving up, starting with the "unscrewing the lightbulb" wave, followed by the "washing windows" wave, and finishing up with the ever-popular doublehanded, open-palmed "Pope" wave while

I secured the flagpole against the saddle with my knee. My waves in the rodeo arenas had drawn a big response. People waved back, whistled, and clapped. Here on the beach at Tulum, people looked at me like I needed to be locked up.

"The bus is leaving, sir," one overbearing American woman shouted at me. I waved at her and said, "I'm not on the bus, ma'am," and heard her say to her husband as she waddled by, "He should be under the damn bus."

All that waving had made me tired, and I still had no idea how in the hell I was going to get home. I had called the lodge from a pay phone outside the guard shack at the ruins, but I only got the machine. I knew they were all still out fishing. The look on Sammy Raye's face earlier that morning told me they would be fishing until the sun went down. I left a message about the Jeep and just said I would find a ride home.

My day in wonderland had been totally void of any thoughts of how that return trip might happen, so I decided it was time to think up a plan. I arranged my towel against my waterproof bag until the two items created a makeshift pillow, perfect for a thinking man to rest his head on.

An undetermined amount of time later, the thinking, sleeping man was awakened by strange sounds. I opened my eyes to Hector, who was playing air guitar on his M16 and singing the words to "All Along the Watchtower." Hector's wake-up call was accompanied by the sound and sting of rain. The sunny panorama of the day had quickly been displaced by a sudden squall that blocked the sun and erased the horizon. A nearby clap of thunder and a lightning flash sent me scrambling from the beach to the shelter of the overhang of the bluff.

Hector followed. "Have you seen the big boat?" he asked in Spanish.

"What boat?"

"That boat," he replied, pointing his gun at the beach. I looked out at the gray ocean. At first I saw nothing. Then I heard the sound of a bell ringing across the water. Seconds later, the huge bowsprit of a very large sailing vessel poked a hole through the rain and mist. It was followed by the graceful lines of a long green hull.

If the residue of ganja wasn't affecting my vision too badly, I could swear I saw a very old woman, dressed in a yellow foul-weather slicker, shouting orders to the crew. They all moved swiftly at her command along the decks of one of the most beautiful two-masted schooners I had ever seen.

"I see you later, Tully. I got to go to work," Hector called out as he ran through the rain along the path that led up the cliff.

I barely heard him. The bell rang again, and command was passed forward with a series of shouts. Then the large anchor dangling from the hawser beneath the bowsprit splashed into the water.

15

Schooner Fever

If meeting Cleopatra Highbourne for the first time that afternoon on the beach at Tulum was the beginning of an odyssey to the distant shore of Cayo Loco, then the boat that she commanded was the barb at the end of her hook that reeled me on board.

I had caught "schooner fever" at an early age back in Wyoming. The carriers of this infection included the movie version of *Captains Courageous,* Grandma Ghost, a songwriter named Fred Neil, a novelist named Patrick O'Brian, and Captain Adam Troy.

Captain Troy was neither a ghost from my past nor a skeleton in my closet. According to my mother, he was much worse than that. He was an actor. His real name was Gardner McKay, and as the skipper of the schooner *Tiki,* he was electronically transported from the back lot of the 20th Century Fox Studios in Hollywood to the screen on our television set as the star of a new series called *Adventures in Paradise.* I didn't have to go to the library to find out about Gardner McKay, because he came to the doorstep of my house in Heartache. He arrived on the cover of *Life* magazine, and I devoured every word about my new hero.

In real life, Gardner McKay was actually descended from a long line of shipbuilders and sailors. He had pet lions, played on the studio basketball team, and seemed from the magazine story not to be too caught up in his success.

The TV voyage of the *Tiki* lasted three years. I was on board for all thirty-one episodes as I grew up in a world of cows, ranches, and lots of snow. I remember clearly that the last episode of the show was entitled "Blueprint for Paradise." Captain Adam Troy and the schooner *Tiki* were exactly that to me.

Now, a decade or three later, I was standing in the rain on a tropical shore where a schooner had come back into my life again. The crew was launching a dinghy that was headed for the beach with what looked to be some kind of sea witch at the helm.

If you have spent much time around boats, and you see a small vessel heading for a dock or a beach, you just naturally stand by to offer a hand or tend a line. That, along with a strong sense of curiosity about the vessel that lay at anchor off the ruins, is what instinctively took me to the shoreline where the tender from the schooner was headed.

My assistance wasn't needed as two of the four sturdy black oarsmen leaped from their positions in the dinghy and held it in the knee-high surf until the remaining rowers disembarked, followed by the woman who would soon steer the course of my life. She waded nimbly ashore in my direction. She was wearing a green straw hat with a large brim, banded by a wilting pink hibiscus held in place by a blue ribbon. All this action was set to the backdrop of the green-hulled schooner, bobbing gently on the turquoise water behind the reef. Meanwhile, as the gray squall clouds tore apart like tissue paper, the setting sun re-appeared above the horizon. It was quite a sight for a cowboy from Wyoming.

"Hey, gringo!" she shouted as she walked toward me on the beach. The sound of her voice and the look in her eyes froze my feet in the sand. "I am looking for Destin Walker. Ever heard of him?"

"The lighthouse guy?" I asked.

"I know him as Dr. Walker of the National Geographic Society."

"Ahh, yes, ma'am, I do know him. I did some work for him awhile, actually right here at Tulum, about a month ago," I replied uncomfortably.

"Well, aren't you a bubblin' fountain of information this afternoon, junior? And who might you be?"

"Tully Mars."

"So, Tully Mars, are you one of those expat beach bums that found his way to Mexico and is just goofing off or trying to find himself?"

"No, ma'am. I live here."

"Well, you certainly aren't from here."

"Ah, no. I would originally be from Wyoming. I am a fishing guide."

"I thought you said you worked with Dr. Walker at Tulum."

I was getting more and more uneasy as one question unfolded into the next. Normally I would have told anybody else to mind their own fucking business, but there was something about Cleopatra that made me just keep delivering the information she was asking for. "That was just part-time, because I was interested in his lighthouse experiments. But my real job is —"

"Whoa, whoa, whoa," she interrupted. "Son, you just said the magic word. What kind of lighthouse experiments?"

I gave her a brief explanation of Dr. Walker's work with the windows and the lights.

"Do you live here in Tulum, son?"

"No. I'm a guide at the fishing lodge down in Punta Margarita," I answered.

"Oh, pirate country." She beamed. "And are you a pirate, son?"

"No, ma'am," I said rather nervously.

I must have been showing my extreme discomfort with her questions. Cleopatra stopped talking and just looked at me for a moment. Then she said with a slight laugh, "Relax, junior. I am not the law."

"Is that your boat?" I asked.

"She certainly is. She is called *Lucretia*," Cleopatra replied.

"That's a nice name," I said lamely.

"It was my mother's. So back to my original question," Cleopatra said. "Destin Walker?"

"Oh, yeah. They finished their work here about two weeks ago."

"So where did Dr. Walker go?"

"He told me that he was headed to Belize, to a little island out in the Turneffe archipelago called Half Moon Cay. There's an old lighthouse there that was banged up pretty bad in the hurricane, and he was helping a local conservation group repair it."

"Well, that is some valuable and interesting information that I could have gotten nowhere else on the planet today if I hadn't decided to pay a visit to this Mayan tourist town. It is a noble thing Dr. Walker is doing, but it don't help me one goddamn bit with my search."

"What are you looking for?" I asked.

"That, Tully Mars, is a long story better discussed over dinner. Would you care to join me aboard this evening?"

All I had ever hoped for that day was a Kodak moment with me on the beach and the schooner in the background, so Cleopatra's question hit me like a Jack Aubrey broadside. The thought of ever actually going on the schooner had never crossed my mind. "I . . . I'm not really dressed for dinner" was all I could muster up.

"You look fine. You will find us a rather informal bunch, and I would imagine that suits your style, sir. I think we are having freshly caught dorado tonight, and I have a few bottles of good Chilean wine."

I just stood there for a moment trying to figure out if all this was really happening.

"You have a previous engagement this evening?"

"No. Actually, my dance card is a clean slate these days," I told her. "I just don't know what to say."

"'I accept' would be a start," she said.

"I accept."

16

Dinner and a Show

I felt as if one of my dreams had come true as I sat in the immaculate white tender. The crew rowed toward the big boat. The man at the tiller had introduced himself as Roberto, the second mate, when he gave me a hand up into the dinghy. Captain Highbourne perched next to him, and he kept one hand on the tiller while he extended the other to her as she made herself comfortable. Roberto spoke that wonderful island English with clipped diphthongs and local metaphors.

His crew set about their tasks like a well-oiled machine, maneuvering the dinghy out of the surf break as Roberto called out commands and made course changes with the tiller.

Once in deep water, a young boy sitting in the bow produced a polished turtle shell. Roberto said, "Okay, Benjamin," and the boy began tapping out a rhythm on it with a small mallet. He was setting the cadence of the oars, and then Roberto broke out into a rhythmic tribal chant of some kind. It certainly was not Spanish, and I didn't think it was French. Roberto sang what sounded like a question, which was answered by the crew with a song. The music seemed to lighten the load, and the dinghy glided through the waves.

I just sat back and enjoyed the ride, realizing that with each stroke of the oars, the schooner ahead was becoming more three-dimensional and more real. I had the sense that my song line was about to move in another direction, and the *Lucretia* would somehow be a part of it.

A short time later, the large links of the anchor chain came into view as we crossed under her clipper bow. The sprit itself was a massive, varnished prow held in place by angles of chain and steel wire that seemed to guard the carved figurehead below. There was no maidenhead with her breasts pointed out at the oncoming seas; instead, a teak dolphin led this ship. A name board trailed down the bow rail, and black letters spelled out *Lucretia* in Old English script.

"How long is she?" I asked.

"A hundred and forty-two feet from stem to stern," Cleopatra answered proudly.

"She's so big, but she looks fast," I said quietly.

"She is both. She was originally built to race from Nova Scotia to the Grand Banks, have her hold filled up with codfish, and race home."

"Like in *Captains Courageous*?" I asked.

"She is one of the boats that was in *Captains Courageous*."

"No!" I gasped, thinking about how many times I had actually seen that schooner race back to Gloucester when the mast snapped and Manuel Fidello was fatally pinned in the wreckage.

"Son, I am one hundred and one years old. I don't have time to bullshit you."

I wanted to ask Cleopatra more about the Hollywood past of the *Lucretia* and a thousand other questions, but I was too overwhelmed by the physical presence of the schooner herself. She was a living, breathing work of art. At the waterline, the air was thick with the smells of a working ship. An invisible cloud of pungent tar, peppered with diesel exhaust, surrounded the *Lucretia.* I heard the low rumble of a generator midway down the hull and what sounded like tango music reverberating from somewhere within. As the dinghy moved slowly down the long, blue waterline, mechanical odors gave way to galley aromas. Something good was cooking on board the *Lucretia,* and my stomach started to growl, but my mind was transported skyward from hunger by the masts and rigging of the ship. I tilted my neck as far back as I could and followed the rigging to the top of the twin masts. I almost lost my balance and nearly tumbled out of the boat in the process, but I was quickly and firmly replanted on deck by Roberto, who kept pace with the other oarsmen with one hand and now held me with the other. It was my near catastrophe that made me aware that there was a strong current and ground swell ripping through the anchorage.

A pair of deckhands dressed in khaki shorts and blue shirts bobbed up and down on the gangway, waiting for our arrival.

"Solomon, we have a guest for dinner," Cleopatra called out to the large black man who stood at the top of the gangway.

One wrong move, and the tonnage of the hull could splinter the tender. The closer we got to the ladder, the more dramatic was the sway of the vessel, but there was no fearful shouting of orders by Cleopatra or anxious clambering by the crew at the oars or the men on the ladder. They quietly docked the little boat to the big boat and held her there.

"Beauty before age," Cleopatra said and gestured for me to step up.

A ship's bell sounded, and the ringing stayed in my ears as Solomon, the first mate, barked an order to assemble. He spoke in a deep voice accented with that beautiful Bahamian dialect, and the way he seemed to be an extension of the ship — like a mast or a rudder — immediately told me he knew what he was doing and was to be obeyed at all times. People climbed out of hatches, slid down rigging, and quickly and neatly gathered in the large oval in front of the wheel.

"That's everybody but the cook, Cap'n," Solomon reported to Cleopatra.

I counted sixteen young black faces and four "yachties," those lucky kids who had somehow landed the dream job of crewman on a schooner. As would be expected on a ship run by Cleopatra Highbourne, a third of the crew were women.

"Ladies and gentlemen, this is our guest, Mr. Mars, who will be joining us for dinner. He is also a lighthouse junkie like me."

That brought a laugh from the line as they looked at me. The crew all smiled. I probably seemed more like a beach bum than anything else in my Jams, tank top, and flip-flops, but I had the feeling they were used to some rather unusual guests being brought aboard by their captain.

"Enjoy the sunset. Mr. Solomon, please set the watch. That is all," Cleopatra said.

As the crew went back to their routines, I stood there, not knowing whether or not I should lend a hand.

"Looks like you want to go to work," Cleopatra said.

"I've never been a guest on a boat. I only worked on one."

"Me too," she said.

"They're all so young," I added as I watched the crew working efficiently along the deck and up in the rigging.

"No, you are just getting older," Cleopatra answered.

"How do you get a job like this? God, I would have *killed* to be their age and working on a ship."

"The white kids are on loan from a maritime college up in Maine. They come for three months, but the rest of the crew are actually from Belize — from a small town in the southern part called Dangriga," she added.

"That's where the Turtle Shell Band comes from, right?" I asked.

"How does a cowboy from Wyoming know about the Turtle Shell Band?"

"I saw them in New Orleans."

"They are all Garifuna," Cleopatra said.

"What's that?"

"It's not a that, it's a them. Here is a short history lesson, Mr. Mars. The Garifuna originally came from the Yellow Island Carib Indians, who occupied the Orinoco River Basin in Venezuela. From there, they conquered most of the Caribbean islands and intermarried with the Arawaks. That mixture gave birth to the island Caribs. In the late fourteen hundreds, they were waiting on the shore to meet, cook, and eat the arriving Europeans. A couple of hundred years later, a slave ship was wrecked on the island of Saint Vincent, and the survivors who didn't drown or weren't shot made it to shore and were taken in by Indians. They began to intermarry, and that gave birth to the Garifuna."

"How did they get from Saint Vincent to Belize?" I asked.

"Through the courtesy of the conquerors from Europe, Mr. Mars. The Garifuna strongly resisted the invasion of the whites and held on to their traditions. They fought and killed the Spanish, British, and French, but in the end they were conquered and had pissed off a lot of people. They were deported to the bay islands of Honduras, and from there they eventually settled on the coast near the Honduran border. Unlike so many other cultures that disappeared, the Garifuna, because of their remote habitat, were able to hold on to their traditions. They are great singers and sailors, and I have employed them as crew on the *Lucretia* for more years than you have been on this planet. My crew now mostly comes from Dangriga. It's the largest town in those parts. It's part African, part Indian, and, of course, it has a bit of a pirate past."

"Sounds like a place worth checking out," I said.

Solomon approached us, apologized for interrupting, and said to Cleopatra, "Captain, excuse me, but if you be goin' up, you should do it now."

"Thank you, Mr. Pinder," she replied.

"Mista Mars, will you follow me, please?" Solomon Pinder asked.

I said good-bye to Cleopatra and followed the first mate to the open companionway that led down into the ship. He spoke as he walked. "You evah been on a schooner before dis, sir?" he asked.

"No, I haven't, but I sure have dreamed of it," I told him.

"Well, I guess dat dream come true. Dis be da doghouse. Since we have da exposed steering station, dis offa da protection from da wedder for da watch."

Mind you, my seafaring experience up to this point had been on a fishing skiff and a shrimp boat, and with no criticism intended of Captain Kirk's old *Caribbean Soul,* it wasn't the neatest ship on the ocean. The *Lucretia,* on the other hand, seemed to be.

The inside of the doghouse was clean as a whistle. There were bunks on each side of the passageway, and sets of foul-weather gear, binoculars, and searchlights hung in order from polished brass hooks in the corner. I wanted to go slowly and take it all in, but it seemed Solomon was in a hurry. That meant I was too. We passed through the navigation station, where a chart of Tulum was laid on the table amid pencils, pointers, dividers, and other piloting tools. The shelves on the walls were jammed with navigation books. The other side of the room held a large radar screen and several very complicated-looking radios.

"Here we be," Solomon said. "Dis be da guest cabin. You be findin' an assortment of deck shoes in da closet along with shorts and crew shirts, but you be needin' to change quickly. And dat instant camera der? Dat's for you, if you be wantin' to take some pictures." With that, he left the cabin.

Alone in the cabin, I suddenly realized that I could happily live in this space forever and join this crew and go sailing around the world. The cabin smelled of polished wood, and the walls were covered with black-and-white photos of the *Lucretia* in a dozen different exotic ports. In the middle of all the photos was an oil-painted portrait of a beautiful woman walking on a beach in a long blue dress that spoke of the turn of the last century.

The bunks were covered with blue cotton blankets with white anchors stitched in, and the matching pillowcases were covered with stars. Little brass hurricane lanterns were gimballed above the bed for reading. A skylight ran the width of the cabin, and there was even a small fireplace in the corner. It was like a wooden womb, and I wanted to crawl in.

When I opened the door, the closet let out the fresh scent of cedar. I found my size in the selection of outfits hanging inside, and in a matter of seconds, I had transformed myself from beach bum to crew member. I slipped the camera into my pocket. Then I found a pair of deck shoes that fit and crammed them on my feet. I quickly opened my waterproof fishing bag and placed my lucky conch shell on the bookshelf.

"Mista Mars!" I heard Solomon shout down into the ship.

"Thank you, Johnny Red Dust," I whispered to the shell, rubbed it again for good luck, and raced back out of the cabin through the doghouse and up the companionway where Solomon was standing.

"Where am I going?" I asked.

"Up," he replied.

"Up where, Mr. Solomon?"

Solomon laughed. "First of all, Mista Mars, you can drop da mista. I appreciate it, but I simply be Solomon."

Solomon was holding a thick canvas belt with a large hook attached to it. He led me down the steps. "You put dis on, Mista Mars. Da captain be takin' you up."

"Up where?" I asked again.

Solomon smiled, lifted his thick index finger, and pointed to the top of the mast, where a long, triangular pennant blew in the breeze. "Up der," he said.

I thanked God for my climbing experience in the tree at Lost Boys, but that tree didn't move. I felt kind of bad trying to keep pace with a centenarian who was scampering up the ratlines of the schooner toward what I knew from my reading had to be an old-fashioned crow's nest perched near the top of the main mast. My instructions had been simple: Clip in where you're climbing, and don't ever put both feet on the same line. If you are afraid of heights, don't look down.

I stopped several times on the ascent just to stare at the boat below, but I was quickly ordered to keep climbing by Cleopatra until we reached the safety of the crow's nest.

Once you are in the rigging of a tall ship, the boat to which it is attached seems a separate world. Cleopatra told me that all her crew, even the cook and the dishwasher, were taught to set sails, steer the boat, and climb the rig. Some loved it and some hated it, but it was a necessity of life at sea.

"You seem to be at home in this cobweb," Cleopatra called down to me.

"That I am, Captain. That I am."

Once aloft, I understood all the hurry as I saw the bottom edge of the sun slide down from under a cloud. Minutes later, the whole orange ball of light began to melt away behind the Mayan ruins on the cliff.

"Takes you to another place, doesn't it?" Cleopatra said.

"It always has."

There was no green flash that night, but who needed one, given the vantage point from which we watched the day turn to night. The ship rocked gently in the swell behind the reef, and the first stars began to appear above our heads and back to the east.

"So what was Destin working on here?" she asked.

I pointed at El Castillo. "You see those windows at the top of the tower?"

"Yes," Cleopatra said.

"The Mayans called those the windows to the world. Destin's theory was that the Mayans used a light system to steer their ships through the offshore reefs, and that enabled them to go to sea and become world travelers as opposed to lagoon paddlers. He also thought that it might prove that ancient Mayan navigators logged a lot more mileage than anybody ever imagined."

"Like to Egypt," Cleopatra said in a dreamy voice. "Pharos Island."

"Where's that?" I asked.

"Pharos Island was situated at the mouth of the Nile River near Alexandria. It is said that the priests who lived there fueled beacon fires in a six-hundred-foot tower that could be seen thirty miles out into the Mediterranean. For fifteen hundred years, wood fire, smoking by day and glowing at night, guided ships from all over the world." She paused and looked at the tower. "Maybe even from here."

"I don't know about the theory, but I sure like the story."

"Me too. So what did you lighthouse detectives find out about the windows to the world?" Cleopatra asked.

"It's pretty amazing. When you put lanterns into the windows in a certain order, they deflect beams of light out across the water. The precise spot where both beams line up is the old natural opening to the reef — not the man-made channel that you entered through. The trick is knowing how to line the lights up. It's like one of those Rubik's Cubes. Dr. Walker figured that the knowledge of how to get through the channel was important stuff and was known only to certain priests."

"Like navigators on ships back in the old days."

"Exactly," I said. "It seems that they were the only ones who knew which lights in which windows would get you through the channel. A wrong light in a wrong window puts you high and dry."

"And I suppose now you possess this ancient information," Cleopatra said.

"Me and Ix-Nay."

"Who's Ix-Nay?"

"He's a shaman fishing guide I work with, and he's my best friend."

"And you ran this channel?"

"That we did. It was our job to follow the light beam and check the depth."

"So can you run this channel, even at night?"

"Dr. Walker believed that the system was designed to work at sunrise and that the bearing of the sun and the small temple over there on the north shore was involved in the calculation as well. But we ran it with just the lights lining up, and it seemed to work," I said with a sense of pride.

Cleopatra unhooked her clip and slowly climbed out of the crow's nest and into the rigging. "I'd like to do it," she said.

"Do what?"

"Run that channel," she said calmly. "We came in through the dull, old, well-marked, dredged-out ship channel that any one-eyed drunken shrimpin' boat captain could get through. I think we should do it like we did in the old days. Sail off the hook and trust in God and a good local pilot." She poked me in the chest with her bony finger. "That, Mr. Mars, would be you."

I nearly fell out of the rigging, laughing at what Cleopatra had said. I was sure she was joking. I also thought of the consequences of attempting to wake the heavily armed Hector in the wee hours from a tequila dream. "And I'd like to catch a twenty-pound bonefish on an eight-weight line, but that's impossible."

"Oh, is it?" Cleopatra said. "Well, since you possess a secret of the ancients, Tully Mars, let's have a little wager. You get me a light show at dawn, and I will give you a ride on my boat."

The words came out of my mouth before I had time to think about what I was saying. "My Jeep is stuck in the mud thirty miles from here, and I could use a lift home."

Cleopatra was silent for a few seconds, and then she laughed. "You've got balls, son," she said, "and you're on."

"What time would you like to leave?" I asked.

"We'll have a little dinner first, and then a show."

17

The Dance of Life and Death

Let's face it, you don't run into characters like Cleopatra Highbourne every day. I was so excited about the fact that I might possibly sleep in the guest cabin and be taken back to Punta Margarita on this ship that I couldn't really think about eating. I did manage a shower, a shave, and a fresh change of clothes, which I was told by Solomon was part of the drill when you had dinner with the captain.

I thought I looked kind of spiffy in my blue Bermudas and white Polo shirt until I headed down the companionway to the dining room. Solomon greeted me with a smile. He was dressed in khakis and had on a tie, as did the male half of a collegiate-looking couple whom Solomon introduced to me as the other guests. The Estrellas were a newlywed pair of Incan history professors from Costa Rica. They were traveling with Cleopatra to the Caribbean side of Panama, where they would leave the boat and return to San José.

Solomon hinted to me that dinner was never dull

aboard the *Lucretia*. It was Captain Highbourne's style to always have a collection of "young sprouts" on the ship. Her present mission kept a constant flow of scientists, students, and crackpots on board. It didn't take long to figure out which category I fit into.

I asked the Incan experts if they were surfers. They just stared at me strangely as I tried to enlighten them about the world-class surf breaks in their country, but I might as well have been talking about beach houses on the moon.

A waiter appeared next to me with a tray of carrot sticks. I recoiled as if it were a platter of vipers.

"Good for the old eyesight, Mr. Mars," Cleopatra said as she entered the cabin. She wore a flowered muumuu with a hibiscus behind her ear, and her gray hair was tied up in a bun on the top of her head. "I have heard that even condemned prisoners in the foulest dungeons dress for dinner every now and then. They say it keeps them sane and human. Be seated, everyone."

I was thinking how much different she looked from the old salt with whom I had just crawled up the rigging. I still could not believe that she was more than a hundred years old.

"You've met my other guests, Mr. Mars?" Cleopatra asked.

"That I have."

"Here, sit next to me. We have much to discuss this evening."

I dropped down in my chair and nervously adjusted my seat under her gaze, then looked down the long table at Solomon, who was taking his seat at the far end. He gave me a reassuring wink.

"I must say, you clean up pretty good, Mr. Mars."

"Thank you, ma'am," I answered as I unfolded the big linen napkin and dropped it across my lap.

On a normal night, I would have gobbled down the plate of avocados and fresh hearts of palm that were placed in front of me by the chef, but nothing about the last few days had been ordinary. I remembered to chew slowly as my brain sifted through several thoughts at once. I was wondering how to deal with Hector, the Hendrix-freak security guard. And then there was the idea of running the channel by myself without Ix-Nay and Dr. Walker. I did remember the basic elements of the set-up, but I'd also had Dr. Walker in the tower, not Hector. Could I keep her in the deep water? Would Hector get the lights in the right windows? Did Bucky get my message about the Jeep? I stopped chewing and swallowed. That went well. I took a sip of the Chilean wine. It wasn't Sammy Raye's La Tâche, but it wasn't bad. For a moment, all the questions went away, and I took another sip and tuned in to the music.

Like everything else on the *Lucretia*, the melody and the voice were old but stylish. It was the same tango that I had heard earlier, wafting through the hull as we approached the schooner. The source of the music was an antique record player, mounted on a gimballed device that kept the turntable balanced as the ship moved.

"Who is the singer?" I asked Cleopatra.

"That, my young friend, is Carlos Gardel, the songbird of Argentina." There was reverence in her voice.

"My mother loved the tango," I said.

"And you have never heard of Gardel?"

"I thought of it as my mother's music, which made it something I didn't want to listen to. Besides, there wasn't a big demand for the tango in Wyoming," I confessed.

The music set the mood for the evening, and the wine did its thing, slowing down the conniving part of my brain. Thoughts of Hector had been replaced by the voice of Carlos Gardel and the story Cleopatra told.

"I saw Carlos Gardel for the first time when I turned thirty. I had taken a shipment of polo ponies to a rich rancher outside of Buenos Aires. What a city that place was in those days. As a birthday present, my shipping agent took me to see Gardel at the Teatro Colón. Recordings are wonderful, but there is nothing like seeing a real performer work an audience live. The heat, the emotion in his voice, the miraculous fingers of the guitarist — and then there was the response of the audience, singing every word to every song. I tell you, that show was responsible for a long and serious visit to the confessional. This was back when I still believed all that dogmatic bullshit. I guess that might have been the start of my defection from Catholicism to the tango."

"Is the tango a dance, or is it music, or both?" the lady scientist asked.

"It is life and death played out in a few verses and a good hook chorus." There was a sad feeling in her voice as she spoke.

"What's this song called?" I asked.

"*'Tomo y Obligo,'*" Cleopatra answered promptly. "It was the last song Gardel sang before he was killed in a plane crash."

"When was that?" I asked.

"Oh, God, before you were born, son. He played his last concert in Medellín, Colombia. His final show ended shortly after midnight, and some time in the morning hours, he was killed in a plane crash. It was probably the longest and saddest funeral procession in history. They sent his body first from Colombia to New York on an ocean liner, and then to Argentina. I flew to Buenos Aires on the old Pan Am Clipper. I couldn't really enjoy the magic of the flight. It was a sad time, you know — Gardel dead, and war coming. But the music lives on. Even to this day, there is a fanatical group of fans who keep his legend blazing by playing his songs every day at the Cementerio de la Chacarita in Buenos Aires and placing a lit cigarette in the hand of the life-size statue in front of his tomb."

"Kind of like Graceland," I said.

"Better," Cleopatra responded. "I mean, I have nothing against Elvis. I really liked all his early work before the goddamn corporate creeps in America decided to cool his jets and ship him off overseas, but Gardel . . . well, there is a saying in Argentina about Gardel. *Cada día canta mejor.*"

"He sings better every day," I interpreted.

Cleopatra pointed her wineglass in the direction of the Victrola, and I joined her in a silent toast to this haunting voice from the past.

"Exactamente!"

Dinner aboard the *Lucretia* was like attending a fascinating lecture series. Cleopatra was the professor of living long and wise. The vast amount of knowledge she imparted was simply amazing. I now knew the nautical terminology for the mast and rigs of this schooner, having had them indelibly printed in my brain as I touched and climbed through the rigging. I had learned from the Costa Rican archaeologists that back in the heyday of Incan civilization, the big-cheese Inca himself had fresh fish delivered to him from the sea to his palace in Cuzco every day, and we are not talking about a Domino's truck as a delivery vehicle. They explained that a series of runners were stationed along a path that ran two hundred miles from the ocean to the palace — from sea level to eleven thousand feet. I had also heard the music of Gardel, which I would now be able to recognize as easily as that of Van Morrison when I heard it.

Well, you would have thought from those beginnings that the conversation would have naturally evolved toward universal theories and philosophies, but true to form, Cleopatra took an unexpected, extreme tack, and instead we began to talk about Cuban baseball.

"Did you know that when Fidel Castro marched out of the Sierra Maestra, headed for Havana and the life-and-death struggle with his oppressors, he stopped in a grocery store in the small town of Guisa to talk with local fans about the World Series up in Milwaukee?"

"No," the bewildered scientists answered in unison.

To say that Cleopatra Highbourne is a baseball fan is an extreme understatement. She is as shameless in her lust for baseball as a fundamentalist preacher is about selling prayers for money on television, and she is just as maniacal when it comes to converting the "unsaved" to the game of baseball as played by the Cubans — and in particular by a young pitcher who goes by the name of El Cohete. The Rocket.

The rest of dinner was spent discussing the career of El Cohete from the time he was a child up to his dramatic appearance in the Olympic Games. He attended them despite the death of his father, for whom he pitched a perfect game and led his team to a gold medal. All of this could have been Arabic to the other dinner guests, and over brandy Cleopatra pointed out a framed photo of herself beside a very tall, handsome young man wearing a baseball uniform with INDUSTRIALES stitched across the front in faded red letters. They were standing at home plate in the stadium in Havana.

"I guess it's because I'm really Cuban that baseball is in my blood," Cleopatra explained to the Estrellas. "Baseball came to Cuba from America shortly before the American Civil War, and it quickly became a symbol of being Cuban. The Spanish rulers, who had followed the conquistadors ashore and ran the colony, despised the game. They called it a rebel game.

"Baseball also came from the United States and was modern and progressive," she continued. "It was a way to denounce the Spanish traditions that bullfighting represented. Baseball eventually became the darling sport of the Spanish Creoles, but what began as a middle- and upper-class leisure activity was quickly absorbed by all social classes all over the island, and it has remained that way through conquests, hurricanes, and revolutions."

The scientists had had enough brandy and baseball and passed on coffee. They politely excused themselves with a perfectly good alibi about having to look at some research material.

That left me. I wasn't going anywhere. I spooned down the coconut sorbet and doubled up on coffee. My chance to win my trip home would start at three in the morning, and I decided to shoot on through the night.

Several crew members in white dinner jackets busied themselves with clearing the table, and Cleopatra guided me back up to the doghouse, where I sat on a daybed as she fooled with the dials on one of the big radios. She finally stopped on a station playing salsa music. She dropped down on the bunk across from me and put her feet up on a pillow. "Great reception tonight. It must be a station from the Isle of Pines. You want a cigar?"

"No, thanks," I said.

"They're Cuban," she told me with a smile.

"Somehow smoking is one of the few vices that I inadvertently avoided in my youth, but God knows how."

"I wasn't that lucky," Cleopatra said as she lit up a fat cigar shaped like a small torpedo. She held the cigar out of the doghouse hatch, and the thick smoke was carried off by the breeze.

"Tully the navigator. It has an ancient and very confident sound to it, don't you think?"

"Well, I'm not really a navigator, but I would like to be."

"That could be arranged," she said, leaving me with a questioning expression on my face. Cleopatra checked her watch. "So we have eight minutes until the baseball game starts. Would you like the short version of why a one-hundred-and-one-year-old woman is completely off her rocker about a baseball player from a Communist country who is young enough to be my grandson?"

"The question has entered my mind."

Cleopatra puffed on the cigar and blew a smoke ring. "If we're lucky, we can hang on to a piece of our childhood forever. The soft feel of a favorite blanket or teddy bear; the look on the face of your first puppy; the sound of the music played by the ice-cream truck. If we are lucky, these are the kinds of memories that keep us from growing old too fast. Chocolate — I would add that to the list. His grandfather was the great love of my life.

"His name was Luis Villa, and he was a switch-hitting first baseman for the Baltimore Orioles. All Cuban players have nicknames. Luis's was *Mantequilla*. The fans thought his swing was as smooth as butter. He came from the tiny fishing village of Chocolate, near the easternmost point of Cuba.

"Chocolate got its name because the village lay in the middle of a forest of cocoa trees protected by the Baracoa mountains. There are still no roads to Chocolate to this day. You can only reach it by boat. The winds of fortune blew me there on a voyage from Port Antonio, Jamaica, to Tampa with a hold full of Blue Mountain Coffee. We ran into a hell of a storm off Cabo Babo, and it took us the better part of two days to round the east end of Cuba. When the storm finally let up, there, sitting right off the port bow, was a tiny fishing boat. Its mast had been blown away, and the helpless little boat was barely afloat. On board was a very preoccupied young fisherman who was bailing the boat with his bare hands. When he saw us, he dove for the life ring we had thrown to him.

"We managed to get him on board and warmed up. He couldn't have been more than twelve years old, and he told us that he had gone fishing alone and had hooked a giant tuna that had pulled him from the waters of his native village of Chocolate out to sea. So we took him home.

"When we arrived, a double rainbow appeared, framing the *Lucretia* as she lay at anchor in the harbor.

"There was quite a celebration that night, and the next morning, as we prepared to leave and continue on to Florida, I walked out of my cabin and couldn't believe my eyes. Against the backdrop of the misty green jungle mountains, the rickety town pier had been painted the colors of the rainbow.

"It looked as if everyone in the whole village was standing on the dock to see us off. A lone fishing boat approached us from the shore, and a very tall, good-looking man was at the tiller. When he came alongside he spoke to me in perfect English. He said that the boy we had rescued was his little brother. He handed me a small box. Inside was a silver cross embedded with tiny emeralds. The man told me that according to legend, the crucifix came from one of Columbus's ships. He said the village wanted me to have it as a token of their appreciation for saving his little brother."

Cleopatra pointed to the companionway between the doghouse and the lower deck, where a cross exactly like the one she described now hung.

"That's it?" I asked. "Is it real?"

"I never checked. I took the man's word for it. He told me his name was Luis Villa. He said that he was from Chocolate but was now living most of the year in Baltimore, where he played professional baseball for the Orioles. He told me if I ever found myself on the Chesapeake Bay in the summer, he would be happy to take me to a game and out to eat boiled crabs. That was in November. The following May, I just happened to be hauling a load of pineapples to Baltimore, and I looked up Luis Villa, got my crab dinner, and went to a baseball game. I have been hooked ever since."

Cleopatra checked her watch again and poured us each

a small amount of brandy from a crystal bottle. "I should stop there."

"We still have three minutes till the game," I protested.

"You have work to do in the morning, you know?"

"Yes, Captain, and believe me, I plan to win the bet. But how does El Cohete fit into the story?"

"Luis and I had a torrid affair. He asked me to marry him and come ashore countless times, but I was afraid — of what, I don't know. Luis finally married a girl from home. They moved to Florida to be close to her relatives and had a son. Luis was killed in a car crash a year later. His wife took his body back to Cuba to be buried in Chocolate, and she stayed. I never met anybody else who came close to Mantequilla, so I just stopped looking and sailed on.

"Through the Batista years, the revolution, hurricanes, Russian missiles, and the embargo, the rainbow dock still glowed in the sun, and the sons and grandsons of Luis Villa played baseball. I kept up with the family in Cuba as best I could. I used to make excuses to stop in Cuba on most of my voyages to see two generations of Villa men play ball. El Cohete is, in a way, the grandson I should have had."

Cleopatra stopped talking and looked out the doghouse hatch at the moon coming up and then reached over and changed the channel.

"Well, sonny, it's past your bedtime. Good night."

"Good night?" I asked.

"Yes. I am going to listen to the game, and you are going to bed. I believe we have a wager that might be important to you, and I hate to admit it, but I would like to see you succeed."

I followed the captain's orders and walked back to the

guest cabin. The bed had been turned down, and the hurricane lights gave out a warm, amber glow. I undressed and slipped under the covers, not knowing whether I would be able to sleep or not. But I laughed again at the thought of where I was and how I got there — thinking to myself that it beat the hell out of sleeping on the beach.

The six-foot, six-inch, 220-pound El Cohete was perched like a pelican on top of a makeshift sandy mound on the beach. Ribbons of sweat rolled from under his cap, but he didn't appear nervous — just hot, as he stuffed a shiny white baseball into his well-worn leather glove.

He stepped off the pitcher's mound and checked the runners in jungle fatigues on third and second. It didn't seem to faze him that every position other than catcher was being played by barefoot Indian children dressed only in loincloths.

Ix-Nay was catching, dressed in fishing shorts with a .45 strapped to his side. The normally garrulous fishermen of the village watched the game from their boats and the beach in concentrated silence.

The near-naked infield was laughing and taunting the players in the opposing dugout, waiting for the next batter to take his turn. Out stepped Che Guevara in his familiar khakis and beret. Behind him in the umpire's box stood a young man in a tattered naval officer's uniform. "Play ball, and remember the Maine," he barked.

Che Guevara moved out of the batter's box. The silence of outer space enveloped the playing field as El Cohete served up a wicked curveball, which Che fouled off into the water.

The next pitch was a slider on the inside corner of the plate. Che never saw the pitch, but it hit the handle of his bat, shattering it into a thousand pieces. Che then strutted to the edge of the bay and walked to the end of the dock. A small hammerhead shark vaulted into the sky, and Che seized the shark by the tail, then walked back to the ball field and into the batter's box. Che stared at the pitcher and spat. "Let's have it, let's have it," he said, taunting El Cohete to throw the ball.

"You can't hit a baseball with a shark!" El Cohete yelled at the guerrilla.

"You can't lead a revolution or throw a split-fingered fastball past me!" Che shouted back.

The villagers reacted with a thunder of claps, whistles, and yells.

El Cohete responded with a fastball on the corner, and Che swung late again.

"Strike three!" shouted the umpire.

Che hurled the shark back into the sea, picked up a submachine gun from the nearby bench, and headed off for the mountains. "I have better things to do than play this silly, imperialistic, capitalistic, fucking game," he spat as he disappeared into the jungle to the boos of the crowd.

Out on the pitcher's mound, El Cohete had his eye on a longboat approaching the beach from the direction of three ships. The oarsmen and their leader landed and clambered out of the boat. They wore the iron helmets of fifteenth-century Spanish conquistadors, but gone were the bloomer pants and red stockings. Instead, the Spaniards were wearing pin-striped baseball uniforms. Stitched across their breasts were the words SANTA MARIA. Instead of swords, muskets, pikes, and lances, they all carried wooden bats.

They marched smartly up the dock in military fashion. When they got to the infield, their leader stepped forward. "I am Christopher Columbus, Admiral of the Oceans and servant of Isabella and Ferdinand, the Queen and King of Spain, and we have come to play ball."

"Baseball is not a Spanish game!" Ix-Nay shouted at Columbus from behind the plate. "You people kill bulls for sport! Baseball is a rebel game!" The crowd erupted in a huge cheer.

"We'll see about that," Columbus fired back at Ix-Nay.

A priest stepped forward and handed Columbus a wooden bat that was twice the size of the bats his crew held. Columbus dropped to one knee, bowed his head, leaned on the giant Louisville Slugger, made the sign of the cross, and whispered a prayer. Then he got up and walked to home plate.

"Play ball!" roared the ump.

"Excuse me, padre," Columbus said as he passed the priest, "but the Admiral of the Oceans is at the plate. Let's see what you got, serpenteria."

"We will play you for our country!" El Cohete shouted from the mound.

Columbus pounded the ground several times with the big bat, then took a couple of practice swings, spat, and said, "You're on."

"Vayamos, El Cohete!" the prepubescent infield shouted in unison.

"El Co-he-te," the fishermen and the rest of the crowd repeated from the shore.

Fish began to jump out of the sea, mouthing the chant.

On the mound, El Cohete was ready. He jerked his hat tight down on the crown of his clean-shaven head, inhaled a giant gulp of air, and began his windup. He coiled his whole body into a catapult capable of launching the ball at more than 107 miles an hour in the direction of the Admiral of the Oceans. He was going way inside, and he was going hard. As he kicked his leg to the sky and extended his long left arm behind him, he took one last look at Columbus, who stood ready at the plate. That was when El Cohete put the brakes on and released a changeup.

The ball seemed to move toward the plate in slow motion, and he could see the expression on the admiral's face at the revelation that the pitch he was looking for wasn't coming. Columbus started to make an adjustment, but he ended up sweeping the giant bat in a mighty swing that was completed before the ball ever got to the plate.

The crowd went crazy.

"I could have you burned at the stake by the Inquisitors!" Columbus yelled at El Cohete.

"What league do they play in?" El Cohete yelled back as he kicked at the mound and readied the next pitch.

"Strike two," called the ump.

"That was way outside!" Columbus protested.

"It might have been," said the ump.

A baseball player only knows one measurement of time. Regular clocks do not apply. Time to a baseball player is not calculated in days, minutes, or seconds. It is measured instead by innings, balls, and strikes. Columbus may have been thinking 1492, but to El Cohete it was the bottom of the ninth, runners on second and third, two outs, no balls, and two strikes.

Now everybody on the beach and the boats began to shout the familiar four-syllable chant that had rung out in ballparks all over the island for the last twelve years: "El Co-he-te, El Co-he-te!"

Villa started his windup. The ball tore a hole in the sky, and there was a tail behind it like a comet as it headed for the plate.

Columbus gripped the giant bat so tight that steam leaked out between his fingers.

"It's tree," a voice in my ear announced.

"Wait! The game's not over. They're playing for the independence of Cuba from Spain," I muttered.

"Mista Mars, it be tree in da morning. You are on da *Lucretia,* and it be time to go see da guard and light da channel. You must have been havin' a bad dream."

I now recognized the voice of Solomon as my eyes adjusted to the interior of the guest cabin.

"No, Solomon, it was a good dream. But the game wasn't over."

"It never is," Solomon said. "So let's go to work."

18

Leap, and the Net Will Appear

Once I had shaken myself awake, I was dressed and ready in no time. I put my lucky conch shell in my pocket and headed out. Solomon had the dinghy prepared, and the ride to the beach was a silent one.

The winds and the weather from yesterday had gone somewhere else. The night sky was crystal clear, and I could see the reflection of the stars on the water.

It felt as if we were mounting a predawn assault on an unsuspecting enemy, which in a way we were. Our mission was to storm ashore and surprise a sleeping army of one and brainwash him into doing something that he wasn't supposed to do.

Even with a cup of strong, hot coffee in me, I was still thinking about my dream and the unknown outcome of the game. Cleopatra seemed content, softly singing what I now recognized as a Carlos Gardel tune. Solomon held the boat in the shallow water as we unloaded and made our way up the cliff.

I fully expected to see Columbus and El Cohete

finishing the game as we reached the top of the cliff, but there were only the shadowy, deserted ruins of Tulum. I could see Solomon in the dinghy just offshore behind the phosphorescent foam of the breaking waves, and I signaled to him that we were okay — so far.

As we headed for the guard shack, Cleopatra broke the morning silence and provided a play-by-play of the game that the Industriales had won over their hated rivals from Santiago, 9–0. El Cohete had pitched a three-hit shutout. I told her about my dream.

"Oh, I have that dream all the time," she casually told me.

"Then who wins the game?" I asked.

"I think that was revealed to me when I was ninety-three."

"Great."

A morning mist hung in the mangroves and palms, and the probing beams of our flashlights guided us through the ruins to the guardhouse, which was up by the gate at the main entrance.

Cleopatra followed along behind me. I was thinking about what it would take to pull this off. I was going to need money that I did not have.

Earlier that day, which now seemed like ancient history, in the process of rinsing off all that mud, I had plunged into the ocean, forgetting about the spending money I had brought in my pocket for my big trip to town. It wasn't until I changed clothes in the guest cabin on board the *Lucretia* that I discovered the wet lump of twenty-dollar bills was missing. I searched my muddy clothes and my fishing bag frantically for the $500 I would have needed if I'd wound up in Cancún. I could only figure that while I was snoring away in my ganja-

and-beer-induced siesta, a beach urchin had locked on me as the perfect target and had hit the jackpot. All I had on me was $50 that I always kept stashed in my wallet. That wasn't nearly enough of an incentive to Hector to start his day before dawn. I had to think of something else.

It was obvious that Cleopatra had a little more in the bank than I did, but the bet had been for me to get the channel lit, and she was such a cagey old bird that I didn't want to be snagged on some kind of technicality and blow my ride home on the *Lucretia*. So I decided to go it alone and not even mention to her what I was thinking.

The guard shack appeared in the lantern beam a hundred yards ahead. I had no idea what I would offer Hector. I could stop, explain the situation to Cleopatra, and ask for advice, or I could just keep moving toward the shack as if I knew what I was doing, hoping something would come to me. Cleopatra said nothing. It was obvious that this was my play. I said a quick prayer to the gods of instant remedies and moved closer to the shack.

Twenty yards from the entrance, my prayer was answered. It traveled from the blaster in Hector's shack through the morning and was delivered to my welcoming ears by no one less than the king himself.

"Viva Las Vegas," Elvis sang as he repeated the chorus. Las Vegas was the answer to my problem. Hector's passion for everything Las Vegas — million-dollar slot machines, giant Belgian waffles, lap dances, and exploding water fountains — would be the carrot I would dangle in front of the rabbit. I would offer to make his dream come true. Viva Las Vegas. I would worry about how to pay for it later.

Hector looked more like a prisoner than a guard when he opened the door. The Elvis music had been turned off, and his gun was in his hand. It was obvious from his disheveled look that he had fallen asleep in his clothes with the music playing and had probably had a few nightcaps of the juice from the blue agave plant. He did not seem happy to see us.

I was about to make my apologies and introduce Cleopatra when Cleopatra engaged Hector in Spanish. She led with a barrage of compliments about Elvis.

"He's a Hendrix nut too," I whispered to Cleopatra.

"Who's Hendrix?" she whispered back.

Whatever she said to Hector changed his frown to a smile. I had never seen this man laugh that much. I had made good progress for a gringo since that first day when he nearly shot me, but I never saw anything like Cleopatra in action.

He motioned for us to sit. As we followed him past the pinups, brochures, and giant poster of Jimi Hendrix setting his guitar on fire, I pointed to the poster. "That's Hendrix," I whispered to Cleopatra.

"Why would you burn up a perfectly good guitar?" she asked.

"Remind me to tell you later. What did Hector say?"

"He says we are crazy, but he wants to know what is in it for him."

"I know," I said. "I will try to explain my plan to him. If it is not coming out right, I might need you to translate for me."

"I don't think that violates the original bet. I can do that," Cleopatra concluded.

In my best Spanish, I slowly explained my plan to Hector. When I was finished, he sat on the bunk and stroked his rifle. He looked pensive, and then he broke out into a big grin. "Las Vegas, *melones grandes allí*. I can do, but take dollars too. Me think twos hundred for lap dances."

What had happened to our civilization? At first I was ashamed. I thought for an instant of John Lloyd Stephens, a hero of mine and the man who had carved the Mayan ruins out from under the camouflage for the world to see. What would he think of me sitting at Tulum bargaining with a local for titty-bar favors? But then I think Mr. Stephens knew better than most that when you are on a mission, you must do what you have to do to succeed. I was almost there with Hector, but not quite. "How about fifty?" I tried to bargain as I reached for the lonely bill in my pocket.

"Not fifty. Two hundred," Hector said sternly. I was about to make my second offer, but it wasn't necessary. Cleopatra pulled her hand out of the pocket of her foul-weather jacket, and the light from the lantern in the shack reflected off of a small gold nugget that she held out to Hector. He grabbed it, examined it, and asked, *"Es oro?"*

"Si es oro."

He put it in his shirt pocket, said something to Cleopatra in Spanish, reached out, and shook both our hands. Then he stood up, opened the door, and motioned for us to follow.

"He says fifty now, two hundred in cash next week, and the gold nugget to cover expenses," Cleopatra whispered to me. "Not a bad deal at all, Mr. Mars."

Seconds later, we were standing in front of a shack behind the guardhouse. Hector came out with two giant torches on the ends of big poles and a gallon of kerosene. He went back into the shack and returned with his ghetto blaster hanging around his neck. As we followed him to the tower, I was feeling like a million bucks. I knew the channel was there, and now I had the means to find it in the dark.

"You had no idea how you were going to pull this off before you got to the shack, did you?"

"It worked out like I hoped it would." I said it like a politician.

"That doesn't answer my question. Solomon told me about your money being stolen on the beach."

I smiled. As I walked along, I looked up at the fuzzy glow of the Milky Way in the cloudless sky, thinking Johnny Red Dust would be up there having a good laugh.

"I was just following a piece of advice an old medicine man gave me back in Montana."

"Which is?"

I reached for the little wooden gecko around my neck, rubbed it, and said, "Leap, and the net will appear."

19

And the Wind Cries Mary

Inspired by thoughts of his Las Vegas weekend, Hector had made it up the steep steps to the tower at a triathlon pace. I had told him exactly where to hang the torches, and from the dinghy, they illuminated the windows and looked like perfect squares of light. Now all we had to do was line them up.

We had returned to the *Lucretia* and had roused the navigator and the third mate, who crowded into the small dinghy with us. Cleopatra had left Hector a two-way radio, and I was communicating with him.

Cleopatra stood next to Solomon, staring back and forth at the red glow of the boat compass and the lighted windows of the tower. Solomon was at the helm, following Cleopatra's instructions.

The young navigator sat on the rubber boat, sounding the depth of the invisible channel below us and calling out a number and the time to the third mate, who wrote the information in a waterproof journal.

We lined up the lights, one on top of the other, and

idled out toward the reef. At one point, the exposed portion of the reef was no more than ten feet to port of the dinghy, and we could see it clearly in the beam of our searchlight, but below us was still twenty feet of water.

"Mark that," Cleopatra called out to the mate.

In just under ten minutes, we had accomplished the run through the channel, and the sound of the surf crashing against the exposed coral heads came from behind us. We had found the deep water — just as the Mayans had laid it out.

"It worked. I'll be goddamned. It worked," Cleopatra said as she looked back at the lights in the tower, glowing against the dark morning sky.

"Dat it did," Solomon pronounced.

"Mr. Solomon, let's do it again."

"Why do we have to do it again?" I asked.

"Don't worry, son. You won the bet. We are taking you home, and we are going to run the channel with the *Lucretia.*"

"Holy shit!" was about the only way I could respond to Cleopatra's announcement. All along I had hoped to find the channel, but having accomplished that, I figured we would head back to the *Lucretia* and have breakfast. Then we would leisurely make our way inside the reef to the south and out the properly marked channel from which the schooner had entered the anchorage. Never did I dream that Cleopatra would sail the *Lucretia* through the Mayan cut.

As we approached the *Lucretia* at anchor, we were hardly noticed by the crew. They had sprung into action, and the deck was alive with preparations to get under way. It was all very exciting for me, and at the same time foreign and a bit scary.

To move the *Lucretia* — a 142-foot schooner with two masts more than 100 feet tall and 11,000 square feet of sails — from one place to another was a whole new ball game from anything I'd experienced. I was prepared to just stay out of everybody's way and watch.

As we tied the dinghy up alongside, Solomon and Cleopatra sprang up the ladder and headed for the cockpit as a pair of crew members descended and took control of the dinghy, preparing her to be hoisted up the davits that hung over the stern.

"Mr. Mars," Cleopatra called out, "your place is up here with us at the helm. Snap to."

I radioed Hector to keep the torches lit until he heard from me, and I made my way out of the dinghy and aft to the helm.

When I got there, the ship had become strangely silent. The main and the foresails had been unfurled and ready for hoisting; most of the crew stood by, manning the halyards that would raise these giant stretches of canvas. Forward, several crew members hovered around the captain, ready to break the anchor loose the instant the order came from the helm.

High up in the rigging, I could hear the creaks and moans of the ship about to come to life. The big American flag that flew from the end of the gaff of the mainsail signaled that the breeze was still from the southeast and beginning to freshen. A sliver of pink sky backlit the puffy gray clouds on the eastern horizon.

"Mr. Mars, may I offer you a ride home?" Cleopatra asked.

"Aye, aye, Captain," I said.

"Can I have your radio for a moment, please?" She took it and called Hector in the tower and explained what was about to happen. Hector replied excitedly that he was ready. "Mr. Solomon, send Roberto up the spreaders with the night-vision glasses. We will set the main, the jib, the foresail, and the forestaysail — in that order. Once that is done, we will tack inside the reef until first light, and then we will make our way out the cut."

"Aye, Captain," Mr. Solomon replied, and he repeated Cleopatra's command in a booming voice. Then he added, "Let's do it, Lucretians."

The boat came alive again. The anchor rose from the bottom, the boat pointed into the wind, and Roberto scampered up the rigging as the sails were hoisted, filling in the sky above the ship and blocking out the morning stars. The sails shuddered for a few seconds, and as Cleopatra ordered the wheel hard over to port, they began to fill and stiffen. Sheets and braces were adjusted, winches clicked, and a litany of strange words rang out all over the ship, but they were instantly interpreted and carried out by the crew. I could feel my body weight shifting as the ship heeled gently to port, and the ageless landscape of the shoreline began to change. We were moving.

As the sky lightened a bit more and we came around on a tack and headed back to the north, I could now see that when Cleopatra had told the third mate to mark something, he had literally done just that. Now bobbing in the chop were three pairs of fluorescent Styrofoam floats marking the path of the deep water out of the cut.

I guess I was staring at the markers, because Cleopatra smiled and said, "Just a little insurance, Mr. Mars, in case Hector has a sixties flashback or something."

Solomon drove the ship to within two hundred yards of the beach under the watchful eye of Cleopatra. "Bring her around to a heading of zero six five degrees, Mr. Solomon." The wheel spun, and the ship followed instantly. Once we picked up our heading, the wind speed increased ten knots almost instantly.

I watched Cleopatra as I rubbed the Lister's conch between my hands. All of her senses and instincts were plugged into her boat. She looked up at the sky, down at the sea, and back at the lights in the tower.

"We are at a slack high tide, Mr. Solomon. There is little current, and the wind is freshening. I think we can do with the fishermen and the jib topsail."

Orders were shouted, and the two sails went up, fitting into the high rigging like pieces of a puzzle. The ship heeled further, and I grabbed the post of the bench to my right for balance.

"Don't worry, Mr. Mars. She has the power to carry sail."

The ship seemed to contract like a giant muscle. She rose and fell on the approaching swells; the water rushed noisily down the hull and formed a smooth wake off our stern.

"Nine knots across da bottom," Mr. Solomon said.

"You have the wind on your beam, and she is slicing the channel in two. Your lights are lined up, and I can see blue water ahead. This is the way it should be for your first ride. Ease the main."

When I looked back at the tower, the lighted windows were lined up as they had been in the dinghy, but light was not the only thing coming from the tower. Out over the water, floating on the breeze, was music from Hector's blaster. As the water rushed under the hull, the *Lucretia* seemed to ride not only on the waves but on the music. The Garifuna crew sensed it immediately and began to tap out the rhythm with their hands on the deck, masts, and spars, and I started to sing along with Jimi Hendrix:

> Will the wind ever remember
> The names it has blown in the past,
> And with this crutch, its old age and its wisdom
> It whispers, "No, this will be the last."

The yachties from America joined us in the chorus, and a beat later, the Garifuna descendants of slaves, Indians, and pirates put their own icing on the psychedelic cake. As we all sang "The Wind Cries Mary" repeatedly, we steered down the path laid out by the Mayans, past the markers deposited by Cleopatra, on the guitar riff of Jimi Hendrix, out the cut into deep, deep water.

"Twelve knots," Mr. Solomon called out.

"Take her through, Mr. Mars. It's your channel," Cleopatra commanded.

I was startled, but this was not the time or place to politely decline. It had not been worded as an invitation, but as an order. Sometimes you just have to step up to the plate.

I handed Cleopatra my conch shell and took the wheel.

"Where'd you get this Lister's conch?" she asked. "I haven't seen one of these since the last time I was in Calcutta."

This was not the time for the Johnny Red Dust story as I looked at ninety feet of hauling-ass schooner in front of me, threading its way through a narrow channel lit up by a Mayan calculation that hopefully would guide us through a coral reef. "I'll tell you later," I said.

"I take it this is your good-luck charm?" she asked.

"Yes, ma'am," I answered.

Out of the corner of my eye, I saw Cleopatra rubbing the shell in her hands. "Well, let's hope to hell it hasn't run out of luck. Just watch the bowsprit against the horizon, and use a light hand."

I did as Cleopatra instructed. The wheel was amazingly light to the touch. The *Lucretia* knew where she was headed, and I was just along for the ride.

Holding on to the wheel of the *Lucretia* with the wind on the beam and all the sails aloft, curved and contoured to give us a forward speed of fourteen knots, I now knew why certain astronauts sometimes longed to stay in outer space forever.

Fourteen knots is just a little less than twenty miles an hour. In land terms, that is about the speed you are allowed to travel through a school zone in your car. It does not seem very fast, but at one time, it was as fast as any vehicle on earth traveled.

It seemed like the blink of an eye since Cleopatra had offered me the wheel. The lights in El Castillo had been extinguished by the rays of the rising sun, and the navigator announced that we were less than an hour from dropping anchor in the bay in front of Lost Boys.

My time aboard the *Lucretia* had not lasted long enough. It had been less than twenty-four hours since I had left Lost Boys, but it seemed as if I had been to the moon and back. Like the astronauts, I did not want to go home, but I knew I had no choice.

I stayed at the wheel as we paralleled the shore, running due south. I gobbled down a scrambled egg sandwich for breakfast with one hand while the other guided the ship. The salt air and the spray from the bow wave cleared my head. Today I was determined that I was not going to think about the loss of Donna Kay but instead appreciate the fun things we had done together. I would not forget our past, but I wouldn't regret it, either. There was a big lesson in all of it for me. I wanted to learn how to be a better communicator and how not to live my life in fear of relationships. I felt optimistic. From the wheel of the *Lucretia,* the future looked very promising indeed. I felt as if I had shed my victim skin back in that mud puddle only a morning ago and willed my way from the beach to this boat. I smiled the entire time at the idea that I was actually on the boat, not to mention driving it.

But the party was about to end. I turned the wheel to port a few degrees, at the command of Mr. Solomon, when Punta Allen came into sight.

Cleopatra sent word from the cockpit that she wanted to see me below. Solomon took the wheel, and I headed down the stairs. The smell of onions grilling and bacon frying wafted out of the galley as I passed through on the way to the ship's office.

Cleopatra was seated at her desk, beneath a painting of the USS *Maine.* She was writing in a thick journal.

I tapped on the open door. "You wanted to see me, Captain?"

"Come in, Mr. Mars. Have a seat." She turned to face me. "Well, I have some good news, sir. I contacted Dr. Walker. He was right where you said he would be on Half Moon Cay off Belize." Cleopatra laughed aloud as she lit up a Cuban cigar and took several long, satisfying puffs. "He couldn't believe we took the *Lucretia* out the Mayan cut."

"That makes two of us."

"It has simply been my experience to do things if they feel right, and this morning it all felt right. We have you to thank for that, Mr. Mars. That light trick was something," she said.

"I think we should thank those Mayan navigators who sailed to Egypt," I told her.

"Right you are, my boy. Right you are. Now to the business at hand. We are heading to Half Moon Cay ourselves. We are going to help Dr. Walker finish up his work on the light there, and then he will be joining us on board. We are headed to Panama. I am chasing a lead. There is a story that when the French first came to Panama to attempt to dig a canal across the isthmus, two Fresnel lenses were shipped to Colón among the tons of equipment they sent across the ocean. When their great adventure failed, the Froggies packed up and left twenty-two thousand of their countrymen dead in the jungle. They also left behind a lot of other stuff. There is a man in Colón who says he knows where the lenses are."

"That's great news," I said.

"Or bullshit," she snapped. "It's no secret in the back alleys and gin mills of the Caribbean that there is a rich hundred-year-old lady looking for a light and will pay anything for it. But it is worth a look, and besides, I haven't been to Panama for a while. It's a great little country, and it's not that far from Havana. I have to be back there by the first of next month for the Cuban all-star game."

"Sounds like your dance card is filling up," I said.

"Tully, did you kill anybody back there in Montana?" she asked abruptly.

"No, ma'am. I've never killed anyone, and it was Wyoming, not Montana. I busted a plate-glass window in my former employer's house. That's all I ever did. Honest."

"Oh, I believe you. You didn't look like the Pablo Escobar type. You have to be careful about who you hire in these waters, though."

"What do you mean?"

"I mean to be offering you a job as a crewman on the *Lucretia* if you want one — starting today. Our Peruvian guests will be leaving us in Panama, and so will some of our college swabbies. It is obvious you have a feel for the ocean, and this boat."

The cabin was silent. Cleopatra was waiting for my answer, and I was trying to come up with something to say. Here I was again, having to make one of those sudden decisions that needs to be acted upon immediately but will change your life forever.

"How much time do I have to think about it?"

"I'd say about twenty minutes."

"That'll be enough time," I said.

I went up to the rigging to think and sat there, watching the tip of Crocodile Rock become larger by the minute. The *Lucretia* was wasting no time in rounding the headland. I felt the power of the ship as it pulsed from the hull all the way up through the rigging to which I was clinging.

It wasn't long before we rounded the point, and directly in front of us, Punta Margarita glistened in the sun. I could see the skeletal frame of the tree house sitting atop the giant banyan that marked Lost Boys.

"Stand by to drop the staysails!" the mate shouted from below. The crew began to move along the deck, and I headed down. I had made my decision.

As we roared through the channel under a cloud of

canvas with a foamy wake trailing behind us for a quarter of a mile, I recalled a conversation I'd had at a bar a few years back with a Navy fighter pilot. It was a clear day, and we were watching the Blue Angels, who were practicing overhead. I was in awe of the spectacle of those rocket ships defying gravity.

The pilot just shrugged it off. "That's nothing," he said. "The big show happens at home."

I had asked him what he meant, and he told me that most air battles occur far away from the spectators, and no one sees the amazing life-and-death maneuvers of modern air combat. But once the battle is over, and the survivors head back to their ship, that is where they really show their stuff.

"Why?" I asked.

The wily pilot shrugged his shoulders, smiled, and looked back up at the looping jets. "Because that is where the audience is."

My ego got the best of me that morning as we sailed for home. Fully expecting to be met by a flotilla of skiffs, fishing guides, and staff with cameras flashing, I assumed an Errol Flynn stance atop the starboard rail. I held a pair of binoculars to my eyes, looking very salty.

"Stand by to drop da staysails!" Solomon shouted from below.

I repeated the command for effect.

I had been studying the action on the deck and in the rigging, and I hadn't even looked over at my audience. When I finally swung a glance sideways, I saw only the empty channel. All the flats skiffs were tied neatly in their places on the dock, and there wasn't a soul visible in the whole camp.

I couldn't quite process what was going on, but the

flurry of activity with sails, sheets, and halyards took precedence over my lack of a welcoming committee.

When I turned around, Cleopatra was watching me with an amused look on her face. "Well, Mr. Mars?"

I stood in silence below the luffing sails. Errol Flynn had left the bridge. "Looks like I might need a lift to the beach," I said timidly.

"I take it you are going ashore," she said.

"Yes, ma'am. Though this isn't the kind of welcome I was hoping for," I admitted, "I have a job here. And as much as I want to stay, and as thankful as I am for the offer, I have made a promise, and I have to keep it."

"I understand," Cleopatra said. "I have a feeling there will be more photo opportunities in your future. Now don't forget you have also made a promise to a certain Hendrix freak up the road."

"I gave you my word. I will get Hector to Sin City."

"I know you will, Tully," she replied. She paused as she gazed at the shoreline. The current was flowing swiftly seaward along the waterline of the ship. "Tully, there is something else I need. It is not a promise, just a favor. You have won the bet fair and square, but I am beginning to think I may never find my light. For more years than I care to remember, it has been my only crusade, but I am afraid I might be running out of time. That friend of yours, that Willie fellow, on his way to the Pacific — do you think you could ask him to keep an eye out for a light for an old lady?" The tone of her voice was something I hadn't yet heard. I knew it was hard for Captain Cleopatra Highbourne to ask for help.

"You bet," I answered.

Next thing I knew, she flung her arms around me and gave me a huge hug. Then, instantly, she became the captain again. "Mr. Solomon, Mr. Mars will be leaving the ship here. But he needs a lift to shore. Can't dally too long though. This tide is on the run."

As we watched the crew lower the dinghy and man the sweeps, I was having second thoughts about my decision. But the boat was in the water now, and the day was making its way west. I could feel the ship wanting to move.

"I am glad the winds blew us together. You will always have a place on the *Lucretia*."

"Thank you, Captain."

"No, thank *you* for an interesting day. But just remember, life does throw us some curveballs. So if anything changes in the next couple of weeks, we'll be out at Half Moon Cay. After that, you can leave a message at Highbourne Shipping in Miami." She handed me a card with the number.

Solomon announced the dinghy ready, and I went over the side and scrambled down the ladder. I took my place next to him at the tiller, and the men began to row.

"Don't be a stranger!" Cleopatra yelled out. "But most importantly, don't change. There are not many of you left."

When I reached the dock, I said good-bye to Solomon and the crew and watched their beautiful cadence as the dinghy swiftly returned to the mother ship. I walked up the dock and finally saw Gonzales, the gardener, busy in the tomato patch. He either didn't see my arrival or didn't think it was any big deal. What *was* the big deal was the news he relayed to me that Bucky, Sammy Raye, and all the guides had gone to Key West. The wind had come up, Gonzales said, and the fishing had dropped off. The fat man in the pink shorts took everyone in his plane to Florida for the weekend.

Willie was gone. I just knew it. My heart sank. He would be off on his world tour, and I would never reach him. The promise I had made to Cleopatra now seemed impossible.

I decided to climb the old banyan to sort things out. From the deck, I watched the *Lucretia* turn toward the wind and raise her sails. They snapped taut with a crack I could hear in the tree, and she heeled to starboard almost immediately. Several tacks later, she was around the point and shrinking in size, leaving me far behind, on the land. I headed for the hammock. It had been an eventful few days for this cowboy, and fatigue rolled across me like an approaching fog.

I woke up thirty minutes later from a restless dream in which Johnny Red Dust was asking me questions in a courtroom. The jury box was filled with raccoons in suits, and Thelma Barston was the judge. I could sense that something was definitely wrong, but I didn't know what it was. Suddenly the answer appeared like one of those messages in an old magic eight ball: "Hey, dumbass, you left your lucky shell on the boat."

I didn't have a chance to think about it because a voice boomed out from below. "Anybody home?"

My first thought was to jerk a large coconut from the overhanging branch of a nearby tree and start bombing the intruder. But that might result in death or injury to a stranger, which I really didn't want to add to my growing list of concerns. I thought about playing dead and hoping the stranger would go away, but something told me to make my presence known.

"Up here," I said and started back down the tree.

I hit the ground next to what I knew to be one of those late-model Jeeps that you could now rent up on the

Mayan Riviera. The fellow standing next to it held out his hand, and with a big smile, he introduced himself as Bonefish Bob, the owner of a fly shop in the States. He told me he had been down to Ascension Bay, fishing — and he had caught a near-world-record permit on his first-ever cast at the elusive, prized fish of the flats.

I immediately thought he was lying. Most fishermen do. Then he produced a photograph from his vest pocket of himself and a permit that would cover the hood of his yellow rent-a-Jeep. I couldn't help being jealous, but I forced the words out: "Nice fish."

Bonefish Bob then told me he had met Bucky at a fly-fishing exposition in Fort Lauderdale. Bucky had told him if he was in the area to come have a look around.

I wasn't exactly in the mood for giving a tour, but it was part of my job. I took Bonefish Bob on a quick circuit around the lodge. He told me he had a couple of hours to kill before catching his plane in Cancún to Miami.

"You're from Miami?" I asked him.

"No, Marathon."

"Jesus in a pair of Bermudas!" I blurted out.

Just then, I spotted a couple of tailing bonefish on the flats by the channel and pointed them out to Bonefish Bob — who predictably went nuts.

"Want to go for a quick run and catch a few fish?" I asked, knowing what the answer would be.

We rushed to the lodge, where I found him a rod and some wading boots for his size-eleven feet. Then I pointed the way to the channel.

With Bonefish Bob on his way, I ran back to the office, where I found the address of the hotel in Key West where Bucky and Willie were staying and left a message. Then I dashed off a note to Willie.

I met Bob back at his rent-a-Jeep and snapped his photo in front of the big tree.

"Bob," I said, "I need to get a message to a friend of mine in Key West. Is there any chance that you could —"

He interrupted me with a laugh. "Hell, after catching those two fish in thirty minutes, son, I'll swim your message anywhere you want it to go. But I'm meeting a friend in Key West for dinner, and I'd be happy to drop it off."

Bonefish Bob said good-bye and promised us lots of business.

"Watch out for potholes!" I shouted as he drove away.

Bucky would be happy with the news about future bookings, but more important, I had kept my promise to Cleopatra.

20

Hello from the Netherworld

To: Willie Singer
From: Tully Mars
Lost Boys Fishing Lodge

Dear Willie,
Well, as you can imagine things haven't changed
much since you flew away from Lost Boys. I am
sorry I missed you when you came back to get
Sammy Raye. I had some unfinished business in
Tulum. I got delivered back here on the schooner
of my dreams by Captain Cleopatra Highbourne. I
must say that it was one of the greatest days of my
life and couldn't have come at a better time. A
plane flies away taking one woman out of my life
and the same day a ship drops anchor off of an
ancient city and another woman drops into my
world. I'm no writer, but there might be a song
title in there somewhere that you could use.

I'm sure you've heard all the good news. There

are loads of permit on the flats and word is spreading. There is a guy from *Sports Illustrated* coming down here next week to fish and Bucky is all excited about the publicity. Looks like the lodge is a success. I am going to wrap up the season here as I had promised Bucky and then hopefully get my ducks in a row because I was offered a job on the schooner *Lucretia* by the captain herself. You don't get a chance like that very often and as you know from your own experiences, you got to go get it. Speaking of great vessels, how's *The Flying Pearl* doing?

I know you must be up to your elbows in working your way to China, so I will keep this short. I have an odd question, but I figured I would ask it anyway. I know you already saved my life at dinner but you seem to know something about lighthouses and I have kind of gotten interested in them myself after hearing Captain Highbourne's story. She is searching desperately for a bull's-eye lens, which is the original light source for a lighthouse in the Bahamas that she owns, on Cayo Loco. It is also called a Fresnel lens. They are very rare, and she is having a hard time finding one to buy.

I know it is an odd request, but you never know. If I hadn't boarded that shrimp boat in Alabama with my horse in tow and crossed the Gulf, we would have probably never met and I wouldn't be writing you this letter. I just thought that since you will be flying over the entire Pacific on your way to Hong Kong, if you see or hear about anything like that, could you just drop me a line at Lost

Boys? I would gladly trade you a few hours of fly-fishing in the lagoon if you ever get back this way. In the meantime, we will be right here. These fish aren't going anywhere for a while and neither am I. Fly safe.

Your friend,
Tully Mars

21

Quiet Time

Well, as one might guess, a few days in Key West often turns into a much longer stay than expected. That is what happened to the Five Fishermen of the Apocalypse — the name Sammy Raye gave to his entourage upon their sudden departure for America.

Bucky and Ix-Nay relayed this and other vignettes about the trip when they limped back to Lost Boys a week later. I heard the accounts of Sammy Raye dressing up like Liberace, singing with a salsa band; the incredible story of catching six sailfish on fly in the middle of the Gulf Stream one afternoon; and the sketchy remembrances of an evening in a strip joint with a bevy of Czechoslovakian dancers. None of these reports was more gratifying than the news that Bonefish Bob had found Bucky and had delivered my letter to Willie just before he departed for the West Coast. Willie said he would be more than happy to help Cleopatra with her search if the opportunity presented itself. Bucky also told me that Sammy Raye had taken a very keen interest in the whole idea. God only knows what that might entail.

The day after their return, due to the sad fact that we could never again get a pulse going on Bucky's drowned Jeep, Ix-Nay and I hitchhiked up to Tulum to take care of my obligation to Hector. I felt terrible about the Jeep, but Bucky told me to forget it, that it was on its last legs anyway.

Ix-Nay and I found Hector crouched in the ruins near the beach with a pair of binoculars trained on a group of Canadian girls in string bikinis, and I gave him his itinerary for his trip to Las Vegas. I also took advantage of the situation and dropped off my film from the day on the *Lucretia* at the one-hour photo shop at the Tulum gift shop and waited around for my prints. The Five Fishermen of the Apocalypse were not the only guides in town with stories to tell, but, like Bonefish Bob and his big fish, I knew I would need some proof of what I was going to tell my compadres that evening at dinner back at Lost Boys.

I was sitting on a bench in the shade near the souvenir shop when Ix-Nay reappeared with a big grin on his face.

"I have found an answer to your problem," he said.

"Which one?" I asked.

"You feel guilty about drowning Bucky's Jeep," he said.

"Yes, but I think I feel worse about my shell," I answered. I had not been without that shell since I'd dug it out of the snow in Wyoming.

"It's not as bad as you think," Ix-Nay said. "You did not abuse your charm. You just used it up. Anyway, how do you think those lamps with genies in them wind up on the beach? They get lost, and somebody else finds them.

You simply had your time. I wouldn't worry about it if I were you."

Of course his observation made perfect sense. He handed me a newspaper. It was in English, and I scanned the front page.

"Nothing worthwhile there," he said and took the paper from me. He folded it open, then in half, then in half again. He handed it back to me and pointed to a want ad in the auto section of the classifieds. "It's from Belize," he added.

I read the ad aloud: "Land Rover 110 4x4. Four-wheel drive with a vacuum-operated interaxle differential lock; built for military use; chassis modifications to 4x4 allow helicopter slinging, shipping tie-down, and vehicle recovery; 3.9-liter Isuzu 4-cylinder diesel with direct fuel injection, turbo charger, a heavy-duty four-speed gearbox with two-speed integral transfer case, and machine-gun mounts. Price: $11,000."

"Machine-gun mounts?" I asked. "Are we going to war?"

"You never know, but we have nearly a week before the next group is booked into the lodge, so we can go to Belize and check it out."

It all sounded good, but then I was still a little apprehensive about crossing borders with an outstanding warrant for my arrest. But Ix-Nay did know how to travel these parts without being noticed. Reading my mind, he said, "I know a little shortcut, off the beaten path. We'll be safe."

"I'll think about it and talk to Bucky tonight."

"Well, it looks like we just might have some urgent business in the South," Ix-Nay added.

My mouth dropped open. "What did you say?"

"I said it looks like we just might have some urgent business in the South."

"So you finally started to watch movies?"

"No. What is the big mystery?" Ix-Nay asked.

"Oh, there's no mystery. You just recited one of my favorite lines from one of my favorite movies — *The Man Who Would Be King*."

"What's it about?" Ix-Nay wanted to know.

"You're kidding, right?" I said.

"No. You know I don't watch movies. There are enough going on in my head."

"It's a classic," I told him.

"So is this civilization with which you find yourself surrounded today. What's it about?" Ix-Nay asked again.

"It's the story of two former British soldiers who decide that India isn't big enough for them."

"India is a very big country," Ix-Nay interjected.

"Not big enough for Peachy Carnahan and Daniel Dravot," I said with a laugh. "In the movie, they have actually been thrown out of the country. So they sign a contract between themselves, witnessed by Rudyard Kipling, the famous writer. Then they set out to find the lost treasure of Alexander the Great and become kings of Kafiristan in the process. They take a mule train full of guns and a few supplies, head off toward the Khyber Pass, traverse Afghanistan, and miraculously arrive at their destination. Their initial intentions are not noble. They simply want to loot the country and then flee to London and retire as rich men."

"A sadly familiar plot on the world stage," Ix-Nay said.

"That's true, but I think you might like it."

"Who's in it?"

"Michael Caine and Sean Connery."

"James Bond," Ix-Nay said.

"I thought you said you didn't watch movies."

"Ian Fleming created James Bond as a character in a book first. God, the twentieth century can be upsetting at times." Ix-Nay took the paper from my hand and put his nose close to the newspaper. He was silent for a moment, and then that netherworld look, as I called it, came across his face. "You say they went to Kafiristan to be kings?"

"Yes."

"Well, take a look at this." Ix-Nay handed me the newspaper and pointed to the bottom of the ad for the Land Rover. He read the address aloud: "Contact Sergeant Archibald Mercer (Retired)." Ix-Nay paused and slowly uttered the next phrase. "Kafiri Safaris, Cinnamon Bend."

We were lucky enough to catch a ride from Tulum all the way to the Punta Margarita ferry dock with a lobster fisherman from Punta Allen. All Ix-Nay talked about was the truck in Belize.

"They may have sold it," I told him.

"That is not the vibe I am getting," he answered.

As we crossed the channel on the ferry, we sat on the bow and watched the familiar land and seascape drift by.

"Remember that spot?" Ix-Nay said, looking to the south.

"Of course," I said. "Quiet Time."

Every good fishing spot had a nickname, and Quiet Time was properly named. Just off the beach, I spotted the tails of a small school of bonefish swimming lazily in a circle near a crescent-shaped sandbar. Not far from them, a medium-size barracuda lay motionless, his black eye on the fish. Normally this would spell trouble for the bonefish, but not at Quiet Time at this phase of the tide.

Ix-Nay had revealed the secret of the spot the day after he had saved me from the crocodile attack when we met. We had climbed into the branches of a tree to eat lunch. As we were propped up in the shade enjoying our ham-and-cheese sandwiches, I spotted two huge snook sitting motionless in the water. Right next to them, a six-foot shark inched his way along the edge. I thought for sure the shark would lunge instinctively at the fish and join us for lunch, but he just cruised by the snook and disappeared over the turtle grass.

"That's odd," I said, referring to the lack of predatory behavior in the ocean.

"Not really," Ix-Nay told me. "It always happens at the slack tide. Most of the time fish are swimming around either eating or avoiding being eaten."

"I know a lot of humans that do the same thing."

"But fish know they need a break from the cycle of the food chain, and that happens at slack tide."

"So it's kind of a universal time-out?"

"I call it Quiet Time," Ix-Nay said. "People would be better off if they did the same."

"How so?"

"You have to think more like a fish than a man and look for the slack tides and the pools and eddies in life so you can catch your breath and reflect on the good moments."

When we got back to Lost Boys, the boys minus Bucky were piled around the domino table, and the marine forecast was blaring in Spanish from the radio. A hint of daylight clung to the western sky while the stars in the east began to show themselves. I watched the game for a while and then took my horse for a little exercise up the beach. When I got back, I announced to all gathered that I had a little something to show them, but Bucky still was hunkered down in his office. I didn't want him to miss the dog and pony show of my ride home on the *Lucretia* and headed up to the office. I also needed to talk to him about the truck. As I climbed the steps to the porch, I heard the phone slam down, followed by a very loud "Fuck!"

I crept over to the office and poked my head in. "I guess a little business would be out of the question at this time, but I do need to ask you about something."

"Well, the septic-tank problems are the least of my concerns now," he said as he handed me a piece of paper he had crumpled into a ball. I uncrumpled the page and began to read. Across the letterhead were the names of at least twenty lawyers and twenty office locations from New York to Nairobi.

"My lease is up in six months, and they have a buyer for the property if I'm not able to exercise my option of first refusal."

"How much do they want?" I asked.

"Ten times what they paid for it. I should have somehow scraped the money together back then and just bought it instead."

"Surely they can see the improvements you've made that have added value to the property?"

"All Darcy Trumbo sees is dollar signs. Besides, I hear that Tex Sex has dropped more than several rungs down the ladder of hot country artists, and rumor has it that the Chinese are interested in the property. Well, that's enough time talking about my problems. Tully, what kind of business did you want to discuss?" He dumped out a drawer of fishing flies, sending hundreds of small feathers twirling into the wind.

"Buying a truck to replace the Jeep I sunk."

"Tully, I told you, it's no big deal."

"It is to me."

"Well, buying a truck ain't work. It's fun," Bucky said as he rose from the chair behind the desk. It was piled high with letters, envelopes, and fly-tying paraphernalia. "This shit can wait."

We took a seat on the porch, and I told him about Ix-Nay's discovery in the Belize paper and that we wanted to go take a look at it in the off days ahead. It didn't take long to work out a deal to split the cost of the Rover. He said that would be fair, and I didn't argue. He went back in the office, opened his safe, and counted out $5,500 in hundreds from a bank envelope and handed it to me. "There's my half," he said. "When do you leave?"

"As soon as we can contact the owner and make sure it's still there."

Bucky looked at his cluttered desk. "Be my guest," he said.

Well, business should always follow pleasure, and though I was dying to contact Sergeant Mercer in Belize, I had a show to do.

"You're not the only ones who had a little adventure recently," I began. Then I passed the photos around the campfire. My audience looked at the pictures by the light of the fire and flashlights, as I told the story of my lucky ride home.

After everyone had turned in, I went back to the office and spent nearly an hour attempting to contact Sergeant Mercer in Belize at the number in the ad. When I finally got through, I was told he was on safari. I asked about the truck, and the man on the phone said that it was still for sale. I left my message that we were coming to look at it. Then I checked on Mr. Twain and headed to my bunk.

That night, I was too excited to sleep, and I busied myself packing for the trip. Shortly after midnight, I heard the phone ringing in the office. I dashed to the lodge, startling Mr. Twain awake as I ran. Just as I got there and lunged for the receiver, the phone stopped ringing. "Shit!" I yelled, but then the whir of the fax machine began, and out came a letter. It was from Sergeant Mercer, a short, to-the-point set of instructions that spelled out the time and place to meet him three days from now.

As I walked back to my cottage, I was thinking that Belize was where I had promised to meet Donna Kay so long ago. Now I was going there to buy a truck. I hated to admit it, but I thought that said something about my priorities.

I sat at my little bamboo desk beneath my art collection, thinking about the tropical merry-go-round that I seemed to be sharing with a wandering pilot and a sea captain on a mission. I looked up at my art collection and smiled. Precious friends, unpredictable days, and colorful miles had put the right distance between me and the storms that had overtaken my emotions with the surprising arrival and sudden departure of Donna Kay Dunbar. I was fine with that, but I realized, as my gaze moved from one picture to the other, that it was the *Lucretia* and Captain Highbourne I missed.

I woke up the next morning with my head on the desk and the sound of Ix-Nay at the door.

"We're going," I said in a sleepy rasp.

"I know," he said.

"How do you know?"

"I dreamed it last night, but there was something strange in the dream."

"About the Land Rover?"

"No, it was about something else."

"Well, you won't know until you get there," I said.

"So I guess that means we have urgent business in the South," Ix-Nay said with a smile.

"That we do."

22

Any Place Named After the Holy Ghost Is Fine with Me

The way Ix-Nay had figured it, we could be down and back in four to five days, depending on the weather, and home a day before the next fishing party arrived. But buying a truck in the jungle ain't like going out to the Ford dealer on the interstate back home.

Our journey started on a bright day as we buzzed down the lagoon from Lost Boys to Punta Allen. There, we caught the coastal ferry that would take us to Ambergris Cay and the resort town of San Pedro, where we would catch a few hours of R&R and then take the day ferry to Belize City, our final destination.

Traveling as a fugitive in the banana republics is not as dangerous as doing so back up in the good old USA, but the incident with the Stiltons had left its mark. Ix-Nay laid out a circuitous route that would keep us away from the main border checkpoints that had computers and more inquisitive customs officials, though I did have a fake passport. He also brought along a disguise. He said I needed to look like either a tourist or a surfer — not a weathered expatriate. I opted for transient surfer. My disguise was an ugly rayon Hawaiian shirt, baggy Jams, Birkenstock sandals, and a ridiculous porkpie hat. Let's just say I was not happy with my traveling clothes, but I deferred to Ix-Nay's wisdom in these kinds of things.

The coastal freighter was named *L'Ostra Encantadora,* or "The Lovely Oyster." She may have been lovely at one point in her life, but she looked like she could use a shipyard face lift. Still, she appeared seaworthy enough. Of course Ix-Nay knew the captain, Claro, and introduced me as his friend.

With two blasts from the whistle, *L'Ostra Encantadora* slipped away from the dock, and Captain Claro pointed her south. Ix-Nay ran into a friend on board, and while they talked, I found a quiet corner and unpacked my little CD player, slipped in a Van Morrison disc, rolled up my towel for a pillow, and sang along to "Cleaning Windows" as we headed down the coast.

I dozed off and woke up to the sound of children laughing and shouting. As I slowly came to, I saw that a group of small Indian boys had turned the fantail of the ship into a soccer field, and they were kicking around a beat-up ball. Suddenly, a stray header veered left at an alarming speed. Though I instinctively raised my hands for protection, the ball was coming too fast, and it hit me right between the eyes. I was seeing spots and feeling the sting of the shot, which had made me angry.

"Kids one, Cowboy zero," Ix-Nay said as he sat down beside me. He said something to the players in Mayan, and they all laughed.

I didn't get the humor. The kid who had kicked the ball stood like a little statue in a dirty T-shirt and shorts, frightened of how the angry gringo might react. The look on his face reminded me instantly of myself many years earlier. He was just a kid having fun, and then suddenly something unexpected happened, and he was about to be punished. I knew. I had been there enough times.

"What's Spanish for 'good shot'?" I asked Ix-Nay.

"Forget Spanish," Ix-Nay said. "This is the perfect time to try your Mayan. It will make you less threatening."

The little Mayan soccer player who had scored the goal by hitting my head seemed puzzled as I started to laugh instead of scream at him.

I picked up the soccer ball and looked at the kid. *"Ba'as ka beetik?* [What's up?]" I asked.

"Ma'ya'ab [Not too much]," he mumbled.

I looked at Ix-Nay and he turned his hand slowly, signaling for me to continue.

"Bix a k'aaba? [What is your name?]"

"Carlos *in k'aaba,*" he told me.

"What's the word for 'foot'?" I whispered to Ix-Nay.

"Hatsutzi," he said.

"Carlos, *u yaan hun hatsutzti okkk.* [You have a very good foot.]"

That broke the ice. We smiled at each other, and I tossed him the ball. The game on the fantail instantly resumed.

"I am proud of you," Ix-Nay said.

"My Mayan was that good?"

"No, it was pretty lousy. But I love to see terror melted away by a smile."

Time passed slowly as we moved south, but the perfect day had begun to transform. The slate-gray curtain of a mackerel sky came out of the south, followed by a line of ragged clouds on the horizon, and the wind began to freshen. Also, the way Captain Claro addressed his young crew told me we might be in for a bit of a blow, but the passengers on the ferry didn't seem to notice.

Someone produced a guitar, and we sang the sun to sleep as it dipped down away behind the landscape, and the dinner hour arrived. Ix-Nay and I were invited to eat with the families of the soccer stars, and we dined on fish tacos and fresh avocados.

Then, sometime after midnight, the weather arrived with a vengeance. The sky opened up, and the wind rose to near gale force in a matter of minutes. Flashes of lightning illuminated the deck of the ship.

Captain Claro had his hands full, so we volunteered to help batten down the hatches and get a few of the people still wandering around the deck tied to something that would keep them on the ship.

In the process, a huge rogue wave appeared out of the dark, towering above the bow of the ship. That is when I said my quick prayer to St. Barbara. The wave broke at the foremast and cascaded down the whole deck, slamming into the wheelhouse.

After it passed, we circulated through the passengers huddled on the stern, and fortunately no one had been swept away. While we were lashing more people to the rail, I looked up and saw that the radar antenna had stopped in place. Seconds later, all the lights on the ship went out. This was not good.

Ix-Nay took the wheel, and I accompanied Captain Claro down into the engine room to try and sort out the problem.

We were able to jury-rig a power source and then

Captain Claro was able to fire up his GPS and determine our approximate position, which he showed us on the chart. From there, he somehow picked his way through the natural minefield of reefs and flats that lay between the fury of the storm and the shelter of the protected waters of Bahía Espíritu Santo. Somehow we made it and dropped our anchor.

Any shelter from that storm was fine with me, especially if it was named after the Holy Ghost. At first light, the storm had dissipated enough for us to get under way again, and Captain Claro steered *L'Ostra Encantadora* back out to sea. Even though we were still getting banged around, I couldn't help but feel awe when I looked out at the vast deserted beaches that we paralleled on our journey. The rain-soaked day and night passed without incident, and by first light, we could make out the channel entrance to Xcalak.

The choppy sea provided a wild ride through the cut, but we finally tied up at the ferry dock. Captain Claro informed us that he would not be sailing on to Ambergris Cay and San Pedro. He needed to make repairs, and he would do so at a small boatyard in the village of Sartaneja, just across Chetumal Bay in Belize. He asked us if we wanted to come along.

The change had me worried. Ix-Nay had planned for us to clear customs in San Pedro, where he knew the customs lady. He had a brief discussion with Captain Claro, and I could tell that my situation was the topic of conversation. After a few smiles and handshakes, they concluded the discussion, and Ix-Nay told me that everything was fine. The captain understood and had a friend at customs in the border town of Corozal. It shouldn't be a problem.

After he cleared us in, he would have his nephew take us to Belize City in the tender.

Back on board *L'Ostra Encantadora,* we used a combination of bilge pumps to noodle our way upstream through the channel. As we approached Sarteneja, a dugout canoe came toward us, and a small man climbed on board. He was the local pilot, and he directed us up the small channel to the village.

Ix-Nay told me that this part of Belize was more Mexican and Mayan than Belizean. It had been settled by refugees from the Caste War, a popular uprising against Spanish authority that tragically cut the Indian population by half. "It was one of the nasty wars that inspired no monuments," Ix-Nay said.

As we eased the leaky freighter next to the town dock, a small crowd of Indians watched us tie up. Captain Claro said it would be better if I stayed on board while he and Ix-Nay hopped in a cab and drove up to Corozal to deal with customs. I busied myself reading the week-old paper from Belize, then drifted off to sleep in the cabin.

I was awakened an hour later by the sound of Ix-Nay's voice. Before I could roll out of the bunk, he was through the door of the cabin.

"You're in," he said. He handed me my fake passport with the fresh stamp. "Just by chance, if a customs or immigration guy happens to come by the boat, act like you are blind and seasick. That is the reason the captain gave them that you had to stay on the boat."

"I can do blind and seasick extremely well," I said.

Ix-Nay had brought along the very precise fax from Sergeant Archibald Mercer that set the time and place of our rendezvous — 0900 at the City Market, south end of the swing bridge. It sounded like an appointment that you had better not miss. Even with the storms and the diversion from our original plan, we still were on schedule to make the rendezvous. Captain Claro's nephew would run us down to Belize City at first light, which would get us there in plenty of time.

The next morning, with barely a sliver of daylight in the eastern sky, we bid farewell to *L'Ostra Encantadora* and Captain Claro. Then it was over the side into the waiting Zodiac. The morning revealed itself free of the storm clouds of the past two days, and we continued down the channel through the offshore keys. Shortly before eight, we passed through the mangrove channels of the Drowned Cays and the weathered skyline of Belize City, accented by a large white lighthouse that marked the entrance to Haulover Creek.

For some strange reason, I felt right at home in Belizean waters. Maybe it was because I was a fugitive — this country had seen a few of those in its long and colorful history. Belize City was no cruise-ship port. It was one of the last real outposts of the Caribbean. It had thrived for nearly four hundred years through hurricanes, wars, and epidemics, and had been built and occupied by explorers, treasure hunters, slaves, convicts, criminals, missionaries, smugglers, pirates, colonial know-it-alls, Mayan gods, and, some even claim, space travelers. It felt alluring and dangerous at the same time.

We were immediately besieged by a swarm of street hustlers and cab drivers offering everything from crack cocaine to a four-hundred-pound stuffed blue marlin.

Fortunately, Ix-Nay took charge. He stood very quietly in the midst of twenty cab drivers, all yakking at once, and then he pointed at one face.

I followed Ix-Nay and the chosen driver to a weather-beaten old Mercedes and climbed in the backseat. We had an hour to kill before we had to be at the bridge.

"You fellas be needin' some breakfast?" the driver asked. He was a short, stocky black man, dressed in a lime-green jogging suit. His head was shaved, and he had about three pounds of gold chains around his neck. "My name is Hornblower, like da British admiral in da books," he said, extending his hand. "But I got da name 'cause I just love to do dis."

With that, Hornblower jumped in the driver's seat and leaned heavily on the half-moon-shaped metal part of the steering wheel.

"OOOOOGA-OOOOOGA!" blared out from under the hood of his car, and he drove away from the curb and down the street. "It's from a U.S. submarine. I bought it in a junkyard in Miami a couple a years back, and dat's where I got da name."

"And I guess you have a spot in mind where we can get a bite?" I asked.

"Oh, you bet I do. I am an ambassador for my country and everyting in it. Dis you first time to Belize?" I could almost see dollar signs rolling like a slot-machine window behind his reflector sunglasses.

"No, we know your country well," Ix-Nay told him.

"You just *tink* you know her well. But I *really* know her well and would be happy to take you on a little tour in dis cool, air-conditioned Mercedes for the bargain price of twenty U.S."

The decision wasn't hard — an hour on the already sweltering streets of the city or breakfast with Hornblower and a tour of town in air-conditioned comfort.

"Breakfast first, then the tour," I said.

"You are da boss."

Several minutes later, we were enjoying strong coffee and munching on sticky buns, scrambled eggs, and cheese grits, sitting at a plastic table under a pink umbrella alongside the busy thoroughfare at a place called Pete's Pastries. It was Saturday, which meant market day in the tropics. The wet streets were already crowded with trucks, pushcarts, bicycles, and a cacophony of wildly different musical styles coming from car radios and ghetto blasters. I bought a copy of the *Belize Times* and scanned the pages for anything interesting.

"All dat papuh be good far is wrappin' mullet," Hornblower snorted.

"Hornblower, you ever heard of a guy named Archibald Mercer?"

"Wooooo, he badass mon. One a dem trained limey killers from da jungle warfare school da Brits run here. He left da Army and has a safari business up da river, but he don't come to town much. Why you want to know?"

"We have business with Sergeant Mercer," Ix-Nay said.

"I can drive you up der afta da tour."

"We just need to meet him at the swing bridge at nine." I glanced at my watch. We still had a half hour left until our meeting, so we decided to take a tour of the town. We climbed back into the Mercedes as the electric windows slid shut and the air conditioner purred. Just as I began to relax, I heard the squeal of feedback coming through the speakers in the car, and I looked up to see Hornblower with a microphone.

"You have to tink of our country as a foot," Hornblower began. His right hand seemed to be welded to the horn switch on the steering column of his old Mercedes. He blew it at everybody and everything that passed his view. "Da heel starts near Guatemala, and da toes are da islands dat dip into da Caribbean."

Once he began his animated description of the sights of Belize City, there was no stopping him. The tour came with a sound track. Hornblower jammed a cassette into the tape deck of the car, and the blown-out speakers in the back window of the cab resonated with a calypso song called "Hot, Hot, Hot." As the music played, Hornblower went through his well-rehearsed description of the sights on the tour.

We passed a policeman sitting on a park bench sound asleep with his chin to his chest. Hornblower gave him a wake-up call. This time when he hit the button, the "William Tell Overture" filled the streets of Belize City.

"Yeah, Hornblower!" yelled a shirtless old man in front of a carpenter shop, who broadcast a toothless smile in our direction as he held up a half-empty pint of rum.

"Day say da city built on rum bottles and mahogany shavings. Could be fiction, could be fact." As we drove by several cruising yachts anchored in the bay, Hornblower sounded reveille.

Belize City was no day trip to the Grand Canyon. About twenty minutes after we started, Hornblower announced the tour was over, and we headed for the market. There was excitement in the streets as we made our way through throngs of people, cars, pushcarts, and trucks, all moving slowly in the same direction toward the old colonial market.

The traffic on Queen Street had come to a complete stop. Hornblower fired off every tone in his obnoxious arsenal, but we didn't move an inch. We decided to eject ourselves and walk the final stretch to the bridge. We paid Hornblower and gave him a nice tip.

The street hustlers were on us again as soon as we exited the car. I saw one pair of cold eyes locked on my backpack, where I had hidden the money for the truck. I shot him a return glance that could have bored a hole through kryptonite, and he quickly scanned the crowd for a less threatening target. I cinched my backpack tighter to my body, and we navigated through the sea of humanity the last hundred yards or so to the swing bridge, where a rusty, weather-beaten road sign identified the Old Colonial Market. From the height of the bridge, the scene below me struck a chord, and I started to laugh.

"What's so funny?" Ix-Nay asked.

"Well," I said, "if you put turbans on the heads of all these people below, you would have the opening scene of *The Man Who Would Be King.*"

"I must see this movie that has such an effect on you," Ix-Nay said. "It seems that movies, to gringos, are like myths to the Mayans. But this is not India, Tully. It is Belize."

As usual, Ix-Nay's point had been well taken. People of all colors were packed like fish in the aisles and alleys that ran between a long series of crowded market stalls, yelling in a variety of languages mixed in with Caribbean music, rap, and religious hymns being sung by a live choir. Cars honked, barkers yelled, monkeys and birds screeched, and several Hari Krishnas pranced around in orange diapers.

Suddenly I heard a scream, and when I looked around, a woman lost her balance and tumbled into me, almost launching me over the stairs. When I was finally able to turn my head, I was face-to-face with the skeletal head of one of two long, skinned, very dead animals that hung from her back.

"Jesus Christ!" I yelled at Ix-Nay. "What do you call that?" I instinctively recoiled.

"Lunch," he replied. The dead creatures were skinned iguanas. "Tastes just like chicken," Ix-Nay said.

It was precisely the time for our rendezvous with Sergeant Mercer, and as we turned back on the bridge, it didn't take me long to spot him.

His appearance shouldn't have surprised me, but it did. He was standing with that military posture on the dock, about a foot taller than everybody else, checking his pocket watch, which hung on a gold chain and was attached to his trousers with what looked to be a giant tiger claw dangling from the chain. Though it was already close to ninety degrees, he wore a safari jacket and sported a spotless white pith helmet. He had long, thick muttonchop sideburns that ran all the way down the sides of his face and connected to a bushy mustache. A bulge in his coat at his right hip made me think a pistol hung from his belt.

"He looks so English," Ix-Nay said.

"He looks like Daniel Dravot."

"Peachy's friend?"

"Yes," I said.

"Is there a Land Rover in the movie?"

"No, it took place before cars were invented."

"Do the good guys get killed?"

I didn't answer.

Sergeant Mercer had spotted us and lifted his pith helmet slightly. "I like people who are on time," he said. He snapped the cover of his watchcase closed and extended his large hand to me. "Archibald Mercer, retired gunnery sergeant of Her Majesty's Armed Forces. But you may call me Archie. And you must be Mr. Norman."

"No, he's my boss at the lodge. I'm just a guide. Name's Tully Mars, and this is Ix-Nay."

"Damn my eyes, he could be Billy Fish." He roared with laughter as he shook Ix-Nay's hand.

"Who?" Ix-Nay asked.

Archie never heard the question. "Come, come. I bet you boys have had a long journey and are anxious to see the truck. She is a beauty. We have about an hour's run up the river. Have you ever been to Belize before?"

"My first trip," I said.

"Many times," Ix-Nay told him. "To study with Attunaka."

"The great shaman?" Archie asked. "I know him well. A fine chap. So you are also a fishing guide, Ix-Nay?"

"Yes, but before that, when I was in Belize, I worked for the *National Geographic*."

"You don't say?"

"My cousin is an archaeologist in Mérida. He specializes in the late classic Mayan period from the seventh through the tenth centuries. I have worked for him at Altun Ha, Tecal, and Caracol," Ix-Nay said.

"An amazing civilization. As a jungle man, I admire what your ancestors carved out of the bush." Archie pivoted and began to walk. We instinctively followed him like a couple of fresh recruits. "Boat's down here," he barked. Then he led us to the dinghy dock, where we boarded a freshly painted Panga with the words KAFIRI SAFARI stenciled down the hull. The old, tired-looking outboard coughed, sputtered, and belched smoke, but it finally came to life.

"Ix-Nay, can you get the bowline for me, please?" Archie asked.

Ix-Nay untied us, and we slipped away from the dock.

"Now just settle back, and enjoy the ride." Archie steered the dinghy through a small fleet of sailboats anchored in midstream, waiting for the next opening of the bridge. "That bridge is perfectly balanced. Only takes four men to swing it. Built in Liverpool in 1923 . . . made to last."

As we passed near the end of the bridge, I saw Hornblower flashing me a peace sign from the window of his Mercedes in the stalled traffic. "Hundreds of hurricanes, but not one revolution like all the bloody hot-blooded countries that surround us," Archie said. "Some say Belize is so laid back, we are almost comatose, but you will have to be the judge of that." We passed through the shadow of the bridge on the water that momentarily cooled the air. "God's holy trousers!" Archie shouted, dropping the phrase on the tranquility of the moment like an incoming mortar round. "I damn near forgot." He pulled an envelope from his jacket. "This came to the lodge for you. Brought to my doorstep at dawn."

I had left a forwarding address with Bucky for Kafiri Safaris in case I heard from Willie while I was away. I had no idea how it had gotten to me so quickly, but I tore it open. The envelope was postmarked from Honolulu. I began to read.

23

Well, Hello, Cowboy

To: Tully Mars
From: Willie Singer
Honolulu, Hawaii

Well, hello, Cowboy,
It was nice to get your letter. I am sorry that we
didn't get to say good-bye in person, but the
circumstances at the time were, to say the least, a
bit awkward. Just so you know, I didn't know
Donna Kay was riding with me until she walked
out onto the dock that morning as I was leaving.

As for your question about a power source for
your friend's lighthouse, tell your captain I am on
the case. I happen to be kind of a lighthouse nut
myself. I used to spend summers on Nantucket
Island, where as kids we would go to an
abandoned structure off of Matamoy, which in the
old days marked the entrance to Nantucket Sound.
What a clubhouse that place was. I have flown

over most of those old lights in the Bahamas, but I am not familiar with Cayo Loco. It must be way down there. I am also one of the few people I know who has actually fired up the mantles of a bull's-eye lens at the Hopetown Light, so I know what you are talking about. Those are rare gems indeed.

Due to an unexpected turn of events, we are taking a new route to the Orient. It will take us in a roundabout way to Samoa, Tahiti, and then to New Caledonia, home of the largest lighthouse in the Pacific — it's called Amedee Light. I will make a point to check it out, ask a few questions, and see if they might have an extra bull's-eye lens lying around. I will drop you a line if anything comes up. I hope you don't mind that this is such a long letter, but I have been approached by a publisher in New York to do a book about my travels and I don't know a damn thing about writing a book. They suggested I start by sending long letters to somebody describing my travels. Since you are the only person who has written me a letter in over a year, I hoped I might be able to try out my writing skills on you. If they are too long or terrible, you have my permission to tell me so, and I will send postcards instead. Here goes.

I heard through the coconut telegraph that Sammy Raye is sending you a batch of the overreported news clippings of our unplanned takeoff from San Francisco.

Between you and me, the flight under the Golden Gate Bridge was always going to happen.

I simply did it as a tribute to Burt. He was
standing in the middle of the bridge as we flew
under, and I swear I could see the grin on his face.
It was worth the consequences.

By the time the air-traffic controller in San
Francisco figured out what had happened, we were
well on our way to the islands. I used my most
apologetic voice with the air controller to explain
that the problem was due to our excessive load of
fuel, lack of a headwind, and a litany of other
problems. The controller was too busy with the
stacked-up planes heading for a foggy approach at
San Francisco International and just handed me off
to the next guy, who told me that I would have to
check in with the authorities when I reached
Honolulu.

Well, when we reached Honolulu and put *The
Flying Pearl* down in Pearl Harbor, you would
have thought Lindbergh had come back from the
dead. We made every local newscast and one of
the networks as well. That, on top of the usual
Hawaiian welcome, kind of put us into a hero
category, and the under-the-bridge takeoff just
became part of the event.

I left the crew at the celebration and went to see
the local FAA chief at the airport. He was very
stern and quoted rules from the air manual about
the Golden Gate Bridge. He listed penalties that
ranged from license suspension to large fines. But
then he just told me not to do it again. He asked to
inspect the plane, which I happily agreed to. He
walked through the plane, and then we took a
couple of pictures in front of the plane with the

crew. He wished us good luck on the rest of the trip and went back to his office.

I had read Jack London's *The Cruise of the Snark* when I was a kid, and it was one of the big reasons I went wandering. I had bought a copy to reread the story of his voyage that paralleled mine, but in route only. The passages in the book about what he saw when he arrived in Honolulu were a far cry from what greeted us. I think Jack London would be shell-shocked by modern Hawaii, but then again he saw it all coming. That is why he went sailing. Old Jack was well aware of how quickly the world was changing.

Sammy Raye was also in Hawaii for our arrival and had surprised me by bringing Burt along. We were covered with leis, which of course Sammy Raye loved, and he toasted the completion of our journey with many bottles of champagne, long after the camera crews packed up and went home. Fortunately for us, the next morning, news from the mainland hit like a tidal wave and swept us off the front page of the *Star-Bulletin*. A woman from Maui had hit a $50 million jackpot slot in Las Vegas. So an old seaplane story quickly gave way to an instant local multimillionaire, though we still had our share of airplane nuts who came out and peered through the fence at our wonderful old plane. We were already at work preparing for the next leg of the flight with logistic planners from Pearl Harbor who oversaw operations at the U.S. naval base on Midway Island.

I know this is going to kill you after our conversation at Lost Boys about our influences and heroes, but Gardner McKay showed up to look at the plane. He was fantastic. I recognized him immediately as simply an older version of Captain Adam Troy. He and his wife took me to dinner at the Canoe Club, and he told me stories of his remembrances of flying the old Clippers from Europe to New York.

I invited them to ride with us around the harbor the next day on our test flight. If you haven't seen the tape yet of the "*Pearl*" over Pearl," as they are calling it over here, I will make sure that Sammy Raye gets you a copy. I must say, it brought a tear to my eye. So, after two days of basking in our own glory in the presidential suite of the Royal Hawaiian Hotel, several great Thai meals at Keo's, and a few surf sessions with the bathing beauties of Waikiki, we went back to work in preparation for the next leg of our journey to Midway. Just like the U.S. Navy in World War II, there was trouble waiting for us in that part of the Pacific.

We checked off Necker, Laysan, and Lisianski Islands on our chart. *The Flying Pearl* ran beautifully, and after leaving Honolulu, the green circle in the middle of the deep blue sea showed us the way to the atoll of Sand Island at Midway.

Midway had been one of the fueling stops along the original Pan Am route to China. They had built a hotel, which they had named the Gooneyville Lodge in honor of the birds that nested there. Juan Trippe, the owner and mastermind behind Pan Am, had transported all the creature comforts of home to Midway, including mahogany speedboats that carried passengers from the Clippers in the lagoon to the dock, where "woody" station wagons took them from the dock to the lodge.

Flying the Clippers across the Pacific was similar to flying the Concorde these days. Did you know that in 1935, the price of a ticket from San Francisco to Macao was twice the salary of the average American? It was the airline of the rich and famous. Ernest Hemingway and Captain Tony had stopped on Midway once. It seems those Key West boys did get around. Well, the war changed all that, and history was written when the Battle of Midway became the turning point of the war in the Pacific. It was also about to be the turning point of our adventure.

I was in the bombed-out remains of the old seaplane hangar when I got the news from the commander of the Navy base that our fuel barge had sunk in a storm off of Wake Island. The base itself would have been happy to give us fuel, but all they had was jet fuel. The only solution was to head back to Hawaii and try to arrange another delivery.

Problems in paradise are just not as disconcerting as problems in a different climate or environment. We took advantage of the Navy's hospitality and toured the battle monuments. I could really feel the history of the life-and-death struggle that took place on the island. It was as much a part of the atoll as the coral reefs, crabs, birds, people, and palm trees.

That evening we had dinner at the Officers Club. Though we had an invitation to stay on by our hosts, we decided to head back to Honolulu as soon as possible to tackle our problems. I walked the old runway to check the plane late that night. I stood under a blanket of stars and a full moon that reflected gouges in the concrete made by Japanese machine guns fifty years earlier. Staring at the old *Pearl,* I wondered how many places like this there are on this earth that have seen such conflict and now seem almost heavenly. As you might expect, that night I dreamed about seaplanes and battles.

Our return to Hawaii was not quite the event our first landing created. There were just a few observers who watched us taxi to the far side of the airport, where our team of problem solvers met us. The bottom-line consensus was that we simply had to wait for another barge to make its way to Midway, a delay of at least two weeks. I was not happy.

We settled into the routine maintenance to occupy the time, and the next afternoon, I was busy with a screwdriver and sullen thoughts when I heard someone calling my name. A young blond guy in shorts and a Hinano beer T-shirt was standing under the wing. "I think I can solve your fuel problem right now," he said, and I slid down the nose of the plane as fast as if it were a ride at a water park.

The guy's name was Ben Cooper. I recognized the accent as Texas immediately. Ben told me he had seen us on TV and heard about our problems at Midway. He said he had been in the Navy at Midway but had mustered out and now worked for

U.S. Fish and Wildlife and managed a private bird sanctuary on the island of Minola.

I tried to be polite but direct, and I told him I had never heard of Minola and asked him what that had to do with my problem.

"That's where the go juice is, Captain," he answered, and then in that rambling, Texas storytelling style, he proceeded to tell me a tale that was music to my ears.

It seemed that the Corps of Engineers was in the area doing some kind of surveys and had chartered an old piston engine DC-4 from New Zealand. They had begrudgingly been given permission to use the runway at Minola for their work despite protests about the effect it would have on the nesting birds. Well, as usual, something went sideways, and the whole project was suddenly diverted to Alaska. But what did show up was a barge with the fuel requisitions the engineers had asked for. It seems that some clerk in the General Accounting Office back in Washington must have fallen asleep at the keyboard of the computer, for instead of 6,000 gallons of aviation gas showing up, 26,000 gallons had arrived. I couldn't believe what I was hearing.

Ben Cooper told me there were still 19,000 gallons of 100-octane aviation gas sitting in a barge in the harbor at Minola. They had informed Washington about the mistake, and the response was the usual finger-pointing and a suggestion to use the extra fuel to run the lawn mower. Ben told me he could mow every lawn on the planet and still not dent his supply. "I can't think of a better use of it than to get you across the Pacific, but there's a catch," Ben told me. That is when I offered to buy him a beer on the beach and have further discussions.

Like any good remote island, Ben told me, Minola has a history. Stories of pirates, whalers, cannibals, treasures, and UFO crashes abound — and then there are the war stories. Minola was the site of a Navy air-and-seaplane base along the supply route from Hawaii to the Pacific theater. It is loosely and distantly attached to the state of Hawaii, but it is privately owned. If you have a globe, or an atlas, you will have to look hard to find it.

The island lies about a thousand miles south of Honolulu and about five degrees north of the equator in that tropical convergence zone known as the doldrums; thus light breezes, surf breaks, lots of birds, and — are you ready? — a lagoon full of giant bonefish. Well, six Hinanos later, Ben told me that the catch to getting the fuel was for him to be able to fly there in the *Pearl*. I immediately anointed him "fuel procurement officer" and gave him a hat and T-shirt to make it official. The one problem with the fuel at Minola was that it took us far from our original flight plan, so we got out the charts and redrew our course from Minola to Hong Kong. The weather is perfect, and we are leaving in the morning. I will let you know about the fish when I get there.

Meanwhile, keep your nose into the wind, and watch your six for bandits. Give my best to the boys, and I will say hi to Sammy Raye when I see him in Tahiti. Well, the supply plane is leaving for your neck of the woods in an hour, and I want to get this letter on board.

Your friend,
Willie Singer

24

Some Days There's Just Magic in the Air

The ride up the river was the perfect setting in which to read Willie's letter of his already amazing exploits, as we glided along under a canopy of red mangroves and a cacophony of shrieks and whistles by the local population of kingfishers, herons, and egrets. I would write to both him and Cleopatra when we got back to Lost Boys. I was glad he was on the case. I was jealous about the fish.

"News from home?" Archie asked.

"No, just a mission accomplished," I replied.

"Those always feel good." Pointing up at several small hawks banking in circles over the water, Archie commented, "I call this stretch of the creek Appetizer Alley. Those big holes in the mud are homes to the blue crabs of Belize — quite tasty little buggers."

We came out of the mangrove tunnel at an intersection in the waterway that Archie told us was Burdon Canal, a man-made, arrow-straight passage built in the 1920s as a safe inland route to market. Turkey vultures, pelicans, and frigate birds rode the thermals in the open sky above the jungle canopy. Archie pointed out monkeys and iguanas in the overhanging trees along the shore, and several crocodiles sunned themselves on the mud banks.

The creek gave way to the wider expanse of the Belize River, and at one point, the dinghy was surrounded by a giant squadron of brown butterflies with big orange spots. "They are called mangrove skippers," Archie informed us.

Ix-Nay listened attentively to Archie, as fascinated by his manner as by his tour.

"This is a fine little country, a fine little country," Archie pronounced as he guided the dinghy upstream. "There's rum, women, fertile soil, a pirate history, a Mayan past, mountains, and water aplenty. Kind of place a man can settle down in unless something better comes along."

"Covering the bases," I interjected.

Archie paused, seeming to ponder the metaphor. "Suppose you could call it that. It is just that I have seen heaven turn into hell more than once on these trips around the sun. A man has to be ready to go on a moment's notice, no matter how comfortable the moment might be."

"So how did you end up here?" Ix-Nay asked.

"Courtesy of Her Majesty, the Queen of England, by way of the Third Commando Brigade Royal Marines, son. After the Falklands War and a stint in Iraq and Pakistan, I was stationed here as an instructor at the jungle warfare training camp at Mountain Pine Ridge."

"I love the pine forest and the waterfalls up there," Ix-Nay said. "We have no pine trees or rivers in the Yucatán. Only cenotes."

"Ah, the pines." Archie sighed. "When it was time to re-up or re-tire, I'd had my fill of soldiering. I had seen the world, been shot at and missed, from Belfast to Kafiristan."

"I thought Kafiristan wasn't real," Ix-Nay said, interrupting.

"It's as real as you want it to be. Kind of like your netherworld," Archie added.

"Xibalba. I see your point," Ix-Nay said.

"Have you been to the Khyber Pass?" I asked.

"I have. I carved my name right up there with the best of them on those bloody cliffs. But, junior, you are interrupting the story of my life here."

"Sorry," I said. One of the things I've learned in my travels is never to interrupt a storyteller once he gets rolling. I put on my listening hat, and Archie continued. "So, after exploring some of the more interesting parts of the planet, I figured it was simply time to try my hand at something. People were starting to make a bundle with the ecotourism racket all over Belize, and I wanted to join the parade. I knew every jungle trail, waterfall, stalagmite, and stalactite in the bush, but I had no experience in the tourist trade. This country was created by pirates, and that still counts for a lot of how things are down here. It is a good place to fuck up and start over again. So I figured this: If you want to learn how to survive in the jungle, you train in Belize. If you want to learn how to survive in the tourist business, you train in Orlando. I wanted my own theme park. It's amazing what you can get people to buy if you package it right."

"Did you go to Disney World?" Ix-Nay asked.

"You can read the future, can't you?" Archie said in a strange voice. "I believe in visions myself. Disney World was where I had my vision of financial success. It was in Disney World where I determined how I would make my bloody fortune."

"And what was your vision?" Ix-Nay asked.

"The first time I went to the Magic Kingdom, I was shocked at the number of grumpy adults and crying children I saw coming out of the place. The children were overloaded with sugar and going off like Guatemalan volcanoes, and the parents were fifty pounds overweight. They were sweating and shouting like drill sergeants. It didn't look like any Magic Kingdom to me. And that's how I got the idea for Cat World."

"Cat World?" Ix-Nay and I repeated at the same time.

The words brought a roar of laughter from Archie. "Well, I got my hands on a piece of property just off Buena Vista Drive, and that is where I built Cat World. It was really pretty simple. We dressed little lab rats in tiny mouse sweaters and ears, and then we let our customers feed them to a pack of very hungry alley cats.

"We kept the cats in a jungle setting we constructed. It looked very authentic, I might say. Even had a couple of pythons wiggling around in the dirt and a talking toucan perched up on a mango bush.

"It worked. We had lines around the building. You should have seen the happy smiles on those faces that walked out of my place. I called it post-traumatic-theme-park-stress-release therapy. They did a feature in the local paper, and we even got on the cover of one of those grocery-store tabloids. We were making a bundle until a scum-sucking, spineless lawyer and a sheriff's deputy showed up with a cease and desist order from the county.

"They didn't just shut me down — they kicked me out of the bloody country. Booted out of the land of the free!

You don't fuck with that little rat in America, I can tell you. So, it was back to Belize I came, but my time in Orlando was time well spent. It got me thinking in another direction, and that's how I came up with the safari idea.

"My fortune was in my own backyard. I bought a couple of old Land Rovers from the training camp, fixed 'em up, painted 'em with leopard spots and tiger stripes. I spend my days in the bush; I still get to carry a gun, and nobody shoots back. It's adventure with a safety net. I take people around in the bush as they click away with their cameras at trees, snakes, and wildlife, and at the end of the day, I tell them war stories over a cool one at our tiki bar. You can't beat that."

"You certainly can't," Ix-Nay said.

"No, you can't, Danny," I added. I immediately tried to pull the words back into my mouth, but it was too late.

Archie was staring at me with an odd look on his face. He sat silent for a moment, and then he barked, "God's holy trousers! Tickets again?" and he burst out laughing.

"Is your name Dravot, sir? I'm to say that Peachy has gone south for the week," I spouted.

Ix-Nay studied us intensely as Archie and I looked at each other. As if on cue, we simultaneously said, "For the sake of the widow's son." Archie held out his hand, and I grasped it.

"But the raja is an independent ruler. He answers to nobody," I said. "How do you hope to put the screw on him?"

Again, we both answered jointly, "By telling him we're correspondents for the *Northern Star.*" At that point, Archie Mercer and I nearly tipped the dinghy over, belly laughing so hard.

"I have got to see this movie," Ix-Nay said dryly.

"That can be arranged," Archie told him. "I have a copy at the camp."

We all fell silent after that as the boat moved up the river. As I sat there, I had one of those moments where you just have to stop and look around at where you are and wonder how in the hell you got there. After having gone through this ritual a few times, my only answer to the question seems to be this: some days, there is just magic in the air.

25

Shackletons or Magellans They Are Not

I guess it is the isolation of living by yourself that makes it such an exciting thing when you find another human being who shares your interests. Archie and I had known each other for less than an hour, yet we were carrying on like a couple of amateurs at a vaudeville show.

"It's just around the bend," Archie finally said, and a few minutes later, he was tying the dinghy to the dock. I immediately wanted to take a swim. "Any large reptiles to worry about here?" I asked.

"Crocs don't hang out on this bank of the river for some strange reason."

I pulled off my T-shirt and fell backward, frogman style, into the refreshing waters of the river. I bobbed around like a manatee for a few minutes and then waded ashore near a red clay path that cut through a grassy hill on the riverbank. A young Indian wearing a Kafiri Safari T-shirt handed me a towel. Several bright yellow canoes rested on a small sand beach, and they bore the same logo as the boy's shirt.

"Welcome to the Kafiristan of Central America," Archie said as I walked into the main building. He held out a glass of fresh papaya juice, which went down easily in the heat.

"Why didn't you call it Cat World Deux?" I asked.

"Don't be ridiculous," Archie said. "I left all that behind me in Orlando. We don't sacrifice mice out here. Times have changed. Today, it's ecotourism. Here in Belize, everyone is fascinated with the bloomin' jaguar. Truth is, we rarely see them, but it doesn't matter a bit. Kafiri Safari conjures up a vision, and that sells just as well as the real thing. Do you think sane people would spend the kind of money your fishing clients do to trek to the jungle in search of fish that they catch and throw back?"

"I'm not sure I get the comparison," I said as we sat in a pair of wooden deck chairs on the porch.

"There is no comparison. It is just that the world is really not the cannibal-populated, yellow-fever-infested, lion-in-the-jungle place it once was. It's not that we have made the world a safer place — quite the contrary, in my opinion — but we have gained knowledge, and that separates myth from reality."

"You are starting to sound like a shaman," Ix-Nay said.

Archie laughed that laugh of his. "No, no, no. It's not that complicated. We simply learned that there are no sea monsters or dragons to contend with — just natural events like hurricanes and volcanoes. This lets the average Joe feel safer to venture out without *really* having to contend with getting squeezed to death by an anaconda or eaten by a lion. We have reduced the risks considerably. So some of the Joes go to catch your bonefish, and some come to my jungle in hopes of catching a glimpse of a jaguar. Our visitors aren't Shackletons or Magellans, except in their own minds, and that isn't such a bad thing for us, is it?"

"I get your point, Archie," Ix-Nay said with a slight smile.

Camp Kafiri had the look of a deserted Army outpost, which is exactly what it was. Archie told us he had bought it from the Brits when they began downsizing their presence in Central America. Several small cottages were perched on the hill above the river where overnight guests stayed, and an old Quonset hut stood next to a grass landing strip.

"So, gents, what'll it be? Lunch or shopping?" Archie asked as a small Mayan lady refilled our glasses of papaya juice.

Ix-Nay spoke to her in Mayan, and she smiled.

"I think we'd like to take a look at the truck," I said.

"Excellent."

We walked down the runway to the maintenance shed. "Do you have a plane?" I asked.

"I have a collection of used parts that appear to be a plane, but as you know, the jungle takes a heavy toll on flying machines — and just about everything else." He opened the hangar door. An old plane sat in the corner, along with a tractor and an assortment of canoes, old outboard motors, bicycles, and a Land Rover in a serious state of disrepair. The hood was up, and a collection of engine parts was stacked on the fender.

"God's holy trousers!" Archie barked. "It's gone. What the blazes?"

Before I could ask what was gone, Archie spun around on his heel and left us in the dust as he charged out of the shed.

A few minutes later, he reappeared. "Gents, the jungle

has struck again. It seems this truck took a mahogany log to the crankcase, and the boys had to put your truck into service. This all happened after I left to pick you up. Nobody told me anything about it, and I am terribly sorry."

"When will they get back?" I asked.

Archie let out a frustrated sigh. "Not until day after tomorrow."

This was not good news. We were due back at Lost Boys on Monday, and with no vehicle, we now found ourselves deep in the quicksand of third-world transportation.

"So what do we do?" Ix-Nay asked.

"What do you say to a nice lunch, and we can discuss options?" Archie asked.

The way I see it, you never, ever pass up a free meal. In my way of thinking, you eat before you attempt to solve a problem. But I did say a little prayer that the iguana lady I'd run into that morning hadn't made a delivery to Kafiri.

"Lunch sounds good," I said.

We sat on the porch and dined on grilled chicken, fresh frog legs, rice and beans, and sliced avocados. Archie offered us wine, and though it was the middle of the day, Ix-Nay and I joined him in a glass of cold rosé.

As we ate, a small ocelot came out from under the table and climbed on Archie's lap. "She's beautiful, isn't she? Except for that," he said as he lifted her back right leg, which was only half there. "Bloodly poachers. I tell you, I haven't killed any humans in quite a while, but if I were to run across one of these bloomin' cat poachers out here, I would stake 'em to an anthill, I would." The big cat took in every stroke of Archie's attention as she lay draped across his lap.

"What's her name?" I asked.

"Tripod."

Archie cruised along on the rosé, which fueled his stories as well as his salesmanship. At one point, he leaped up and ran inside the lodge, returning immediately with a stack of 8 x 10 color shots of the Land Rover. "Ain't she a beaut? And because of the inconvenience, I'm going to give you a significant discount," he said, beaming.

The Land Rover in the photo was all Archie. It had been painted mustard yellow with large black spots. The hood featured a very bad airbrushed jaguar head, fangs and all. It must have been painted by someone in a body shop who had inhaled way too many toxic fumes.

"Nice art, eh?" Archie asked. "I hate to part with her."

Ix-Nay pointed at the photo. "Why are the machine-gun mounts still there?"

"You never know when you might have to shoot your way out of a bad situation." Archie paused. Then he burst out laughing. "Just kidding, Billy Fish. The kids get a kick out of them, that's all."

The ceiling fans on the shaded porch and a cool breeze coming off the river were holding their own against the afternoon heat as the waiter brought coffee.

"Well, I think I have come up with a plan," Archie said. "Tully, I thought you sounded disappointed that you missed your visit to San Pedro. It just so happens that a party of folks is leaving us tomorrow for San Pedro. They have a charter flight picking them up first thing in the morning, and they have a couple of extra seats. I have a cozy little time-share bungalow at a local resort called Renaldo's. My bungalow is empty this weekend, and it's at your disposal, free of charge. Then you can catch the ferry to Belize City, and I will meet you in town with the

Rover. I'll take you for a test drive, and if you like her, you can be on your way home. What do you say?"

"Sounds too good to be true," I said, "but I have to call our boss to see if we can stay the extra days."

Archie bolted from the table and returned with a large satellite phone. He handed it to me and said, "Be my guest. Just point her at the sky and dial away."

Minutes later I was linked up from one jungle lodge to another. Bucky answered the phone. Captain Kirk had just pulled into port, and the two of them could cover for us until we got back. He also told us to have a good time in San Pedro. You couldn't ask for a better boss than that.

"We're in," I said, grinning.

Shortly after dinner, the paying guests returned from their safari, and we met our fellow passengers for the trip the next morning. It was a family from South Carolina whom Archie introduced as the Clemsons. Dad called himself Big C, Mom was Liz, and their three teenage children looked as if they actually enjoyed one another's company.

We turned in early. I was feeling a wine buzz, and I told Ix-Nay that I was going to have a look at the stars before coming to bed. Wrapped up in my blanket like a human taco, I fell under the spell of the night sky.

Somewhere in the middle of the night, I woke up to the sound of voices.

"Out of bloody ammo," I heard someone say and instantly recognized the voice. I unwrapped myself from the blanket and walked to the source, which was the game room in the main building of Kafiri. In the eerie blue glow of a television tube, Ix-Nay was perched in a chair about three feet away from the screen. *The Man Who Would Be King* had him spellbound.

I stood in the doorway and watched the scene that I knew like the back of my hand. It is near the end of the movie, and Daniel Dravot and Peachy Carnahan have been discovered not to be gods or kings, but simply greedy soldiers of fortune. A mob of pissed-off monks surrounds them, and there is no place to go. "I'm heartfully ashamed, for getting you killed instead of going home rich as you deserve, on account of me being so bleeding high and bloody mighty. Can you forgive me?"

I repeated the words with Peachy: "I do, Danny. That I do. Full and free." As Danny replied, "Everything's all right then," I said the words along with him.

"Shhhhh," Ix-Nay said, not taking his eyes off the scene. I took a seat and watched with him.

As the credits rolled, I was startled by Archie's deep voice singing the theme song: "The son of God goes off to war, not seeking wealth nor fame."

I sang back, "A glorious band the chosen few on whom the Spirit came."

As a duet, we continued:

> *Twelve valiant saints; their hope they knew*
> *And mocked the cross and flame.*

Soon we were singing at the tops of our voices:

> *They met the tyrant's brandished steel;*
> *The lion's gory mane.*
> *They bowed their necks the death to feel.*

We sang to the end, and we both held the last note. Then Archie closed his fists with a downward thrust, and the song ended.

Ix-Nay had watched this with his typical stoic attitude. Then he said, "We should call the Rover the Fishmobile — for Billy Fish, and because we fish for a living."

"You're the shaman," I said.

Ix-Nay started to laugh at what first seemed to be his own private joke, but then he said, "The gods sent you here for a reason."

"Lots of questions, and not very many answers," Archie said.

"If you want answers, that might require a trip to the netherworld."

"Can it wait until after we spend the weekend at Archie's beach house and get the Fishmobile home?" I asked.

"I think so," Ix-Nay said.

As I walked out of the game room and back toward the landing strip, the first sign of the new day was in the eastern sky, but the moon seemed to be defying gravity as it clung stubbornly to the dawn.

"The rabbit's in the moon," Ix-Nay said.

"What do you mean?" I asked.

He pointed at the yellow sphere. "Look at the shadows on the surface. It means friendship is in your life. Something significant is happening. It's a sign."

"No, that's the man in the moon," I told him, with the confidence of a child answering in science class. Ix-Nay laughed.

There wasn't much use in trying to go back to sleep, so I went to the cottage and packed the last of my things.

Soon the roar of airplane engines pummeled the sky no more than fifty feet above my head. It was followed by southern voices and laughter as the Clemsons waved to me from the back of an approaching truck. Archie was driving.

The clarity of the evening had been handed off like a cosmic baton to the morning, and there wasn't a cloud in the blue sky. The Clemsons loaded up in the Cessna Caravan, and Big C climbed into the copilot's seat. I was the last to board.

"Try and stay out of trouble," Archie said with a grin as I stood on the boarding ladder.

"I thought that's what we were going to find," I said.

"You know what I mean," he countered with a knowing look.

Though we hadn't discussed it, I knew he understood that I'd come into the country illegally. His warning was genuine and from the heart. "Just ask for Sandra at the desk at Renaldo's. She will take care of you."

Archie handed me a key attached to a wooden fish and said, "Suppose I was to tell you that I was a stranger going to the East to seek what is written about."

"Then I would answer, 'Where do you come from?'" I replied.

"From the West," Archie answered, "and I am hoping that you will advise me."

"For the sake of the widow's son," we said together.

"By the square, Peachy," Archie said as he shook my hand firmly and looked me in the eyes.

"By the square."

Archie handed me a card. "This is the satellite phone number. Call if you need me for anything." I stuffed the card into my wallet.

"Adios, Clemsons," Archie said. "Do come back and see us again. And as for you two, I will see you boys in the city with the Fishmobile." The engine began to spool up. "Take care of our boy, Billy Fish," Archie called out to Ix-Nay.

"I will try," Ix-Nay called back. And with that, we rolled down a carpet of grass. Then we left the earth behind and headed in the direction of the rising sun. We were going to the beach. What I would find there was more than a couple of conch shells and some driftwood.

26

Ground Zero

Mr. Mars? Time to strap in. We are just about to land in San Pedro."

I had dozed off. I looked at my watch. We had only been in the air for half an hour, but the open expanse of the arid highlands that surround Kafiri had given way to painted houses, clear water, and mangrove-lined shorelines.

We said good-bye to the Clemsons and headed into the busy little airport. Ix-Nay spotted an attractive local lady in a crisp uniform. Her nametag identified her as Consuelo, and she asked us if we were in San Pedro for spring break. Ix-Nay put an end to her assumptions by launching into the local Creole dialect. I was back in my "surfer" outfit, which blended in with the spring-break gringos, and I felt even more comfortable about San Pedro. There were no policemen or customs officials around. Of course I knew about the spring-break phenomenon and had seen TV footage of this modern-day rite of passage — where college students migrated like flocks of horny mating birds to the warmer latitudes, looking for any excuse to get drunk and screw.

Once again Ix-Nay acknowledged my presence and introduced me to Consuelo as he switched back to English. He said that he was fascinated with the idea of spring break, and he had actually witnessed the ritual once in Cancún. He described a wet T-shirt contest where skimpily clad coeds danced in circles while men in baggy bathing suits doused them with giant water guns. "And they call us pagans?"

That drew a big laugh from Consuelo. She told us that spring break in San Pedro was big business, and if we didn't have a reservation, it would be very hard to find a room this weekend.

"No problem. We have a condo at Renaldo's," I announced.

"Renaldo's?" she exclaimed, recoiling as if I had yelled "Cobra!" "That is ground zero for spring break."

"I can sleep through anything," I said.

"Then this will be a good test. By the way, if you are looking for a good meal, my aunt has the best Creole restaurant in town. It is just a couple of blocks up from Renaldo's, and don't forget to save room for the pineapple flan."

"Can you join us?" Ix-Nay asked.

"I would love to, but I have a meeting. If you need me, just call on channel sixteen."

I handed Ix-Nay the portable VHF radio. "I think you should be in charge of local communications."

I have to say that I am not a big-town person, but a town where the streets are all sand is a good sign. We walked in the direction of the hotel as a long dark cloud drifted in and the sky opened up. Even set against the dull gray backdrop of the morning squall, San Pedro sparked with life. The town was jumping with that Friday morning energy where you have to get everything done before the weekend begins. It seemed that spring break would provide a pumped-up, nocturnal crescendo.

We joined a throng of tourists, college kids, and locals seeking shelter from the storm in a coffee shop with an awning while the street vendors, in a rainbow assortment of waterproof gear, attempted to cover sidewalk stalls filled with T-shirts, postcards, black-coral jewelry, hair braids, and Guatemalan hammocks.

Fortunately the storm was over in a matter of minutes. We bought a Coco Frío and watched the vendor put on a show as he decapitated two large coconuts with the precision of a surgeon and dropped in a straw. "Mix dat wif your rum and der be no hangover, mon," he said as I paid for the drinks.

"Maybe later," I said.

Well, you couldn't have missed Renaldo's if you were blind. If a huge replica of Mayan hieroglyphics wasn't enough to get your attention, then the throng of kids coming and going from the entrance and Pink Floyd's *Dark Side of the Moon* blasting from speakers inside the mammoth resort told me that Renaldo's was happening. Suddenly, Ix-Nay and I both recognized the symbol above the entrance.

"It's the rabbit in the moon again!" I exclaimed.

"The goddess of friendship," Ix-Nay said.

"Let's check out their hospitality."

Sandra wasn't hard to spot. She was the oldest and whitest person behind the desk. She had that look of having once been drop-dead gorgeous.

"I've been expecting you boys. Archie is a dear, isn't he?"

I had a sudden mental picture of Sandra and Archie naked on a deserted beach, sharing a cold bottle of rosé, but then she caught me staring at her and returned the favor.

Sandra gave me a quick scan, and I felt that thing that women can do to you with just a glance. It is like having an emotional x-ray. Women can pass some kind of energy through a man's body using no high-tech, state-of-the-art gamma scanner but only their eyes. Sandra had correctly sized me up as an out-of-place cowboy in the jungle, trying to look like a surfer but not quite pulling it off. However, since Archie had sent us to Sandra, I felt relatively safe. It had started to rain again, and she grabbed a big umbrella and popped it open. "Come on, boys. I'll take you to the condo."

We passed the pool and bar, where a large group of waterlogged college kids was drinking, talking, and smoking cigarettes. The two-word lyric line "brick house" punched through the rain from large speakers hanging from the exposed rafters above the bar, and everybody sang along. Two very attractive blondes sat at the end of the bar sharing a cigarette and enjoying the attention they were getting from a cluster of college boys who had gathered around them like a court-jester convention. For a moment, the taller and more attractive of the two girls turned from her adoring fans, stared at me, smiled, and waved. Then she turned back to the crowd of men, executed a couple of well-coordinated pelvic thrusts, and drew a standing ovation.

"Do you know her?" Ix-Nay asked.

"I don't think so." Chicks who looked like that didn't hang out in cowboy bars.

We passed along a walkway lined with conch shells and hibiscus bushes. The palm trees along the walkway offered a bit of shelter from the rain as we made our way through the grounds, all decorated in a Mayan theme.

"What would my ancestors think?" Ix-Nay said.

We passed the end of the large, concrete, four-story hotel portion of the property, where more kids hung out on balconies, and the instantly recognizable smell of pot filled the air. "Hey, Sandra, show us your tits," a young pimple-faced boy called out.

"Careful, honey," Sandra said. "I remember my first beer."

Sandra pointed with the umbrella at a thatched hut bungalow next to the beach. *"Su casa,"* she said.

"Hey, *chico,* we are in a real resort!" Ix-Nay exclaimed.

"This is amazing," I added, staring at the bamboo structure. It looked as if it could adorn the cover of one of those in-flight magazines about tropical getaways.

Life is full of surprises, and that is what makes it so interesting. Twenty-four hours earlier, we were bailing seawater from a flooding cargo hold of a coastal freighter like the steerage passengers on the *Titanic,* and now we were dropping our backpacks on the porch of a beachside bungalow with ceiling fans, hammocks, fresh fruit, flowers, and a bottle of complimentary red wine sitting on a rattan table.

"Thank you, Archie Mercer," I said. "Do you think you have to grow up?" I asked Ix-Nay.

"Personally, I find it quite hard to break the habit of acting childish."

"Jesus, it seems like only yesterday I was shivering in a trailer in the snow, driving plastic flamingos on wooden stakes into the frozen ground. And yet at the same time, it feels like ancient history."

"That is because it is. Remember, you are in the land of ancient history."

We flipped for the shower and I lost, which suited me fine. "I think I will have a swim instead," I said.

"Is it the pool or the mermaids that are calling to you?" Ix-Nay asked.

"Both."

The pool was refreshing, but the frolicking girls in bikinis had changed venues. I ordered a cheeseburger and a beer and sat at the now-vacant bar. The bartender answered my questions about some construction I noticed on the beach. It seemed that every hotel on the island had a special party, and the next night was Renaldo's time to shine. When I asked him what that meant, he told me it was top secret. He said that Renaldo, the owner, was flying in from Miami with a planeload of celebrities, and it was going to be the premiere party of spring break. I shouldn't miss it.

The morning storms had passed, and the tropical sun was back in charge of the day. The heat returned. I ate my burger and drank my beer in the shade of an umbrella on the patio. It wasn't the most serene setting, with the sounds of hammers banging and saws buzzing from behind the giant tent hiding the surprise party. Added to that, out in the harbor, the girls I had seen earlier at the pool were now straddled across a pair of Jet Skis, spinning and swirling in a noisy, mindless, mechanical water ballet. A testosterone posse in a feeding frenzy carved wide circles around them.

I was focused on the girls on machines and fantasizing, so at first I didn't notice the stranger who walked up to my table. He was clean shaven, dressed in white pants and a neatly pressed Hawaiian shirt, and his hair was combed back.

"May I help you?" I asked.

Then I heard the familiar laugh and realized the stranger was a cleaned-up Ix-Nay. I was dumbfounded at his appearance.

"Your turn, amigo," he said.

I had never seen him in anything but shorts and T-shirts and flip-flops since we had met on the flats of Punta Margarita. "That *is* you," I said.

"Of course it is. I think we should use the time we have on this island to reacquaint ourselves with our respective cultures. We have been a long time in the jungle, my friend. I am having lunch with Consuelo. She got out of her appointment, and after that we will see."

"There's a big party tomorrow night down on the beach," I told him.

"Maybe I will see you there. Remember, if anybody asks, you are a surfer from Galveston."

With that, Ix-Nay walked over to the Mayan gates. I caught a glimpse of Consuelo, dressed in a halter top and a pair of tight-fitting jeans. She waved as they climbed into her golf cart and sped away.

"When in Rome," I thought. As I walked back to my room, I saw that the girls on Jet Skis were alongside each other and looking at me. They smiled and waved, and, having been raised a polite boy from the West, I waved back.

27

One Thousand One . . .
One Thousand Two

I don't know who came up with the idea of the siesta —
whether it was the Indians who were here first or the
Spaniards who realized that tromping around in the
tropics loaded down with armor, guns, swords, helmets,
and giant crucifixes would require a pit stop in the heat of
the day. Whoever they were, I must tip my cowboy hat to
them. Naps are really not a part of the West in the "sunup
to sundown" approach to how you spend your day. But
once I felt the humidity of the Gulf Coast for the first
time, it didn't take me long to understand the necessity of
sleeping away a small portion of the afternoon.

My siesta came with entertainment as I dreamed a
giant marlin was floating in the air with his head protrud-
ing through the window of the condo, talking in a soft
monotone voice like the computer Hal in *2001*. It told me
that if I didn't get up, I wouldn't be able to fish that afternoon. The soothing voice of the big marlin was suddenly replaced by the piercing sound of an electric guitar
that I instantly recognized as Eric Clapton's. Eric's guitar

wasn't actually in my dream — his music was alive and well on earth and was now blasting from the direction of the pool bar, acting as my wake-up call.

I verified my position on the planet. I was still on the four-poster mahogany bed in Archie Mercer's beachfront condo. I stared up at the slowly revolving ceiling fan, watching the blades try to keep pace with Clapton's guitar. I decided to give the fan a little help. A long braided line, with a brass ring at the end, hung down from the motor of the fan. I stuck my toe in the ring, gave it a yank, and the fan blades picked up speed. I pried myself to a sitting position and stared out at something blocking my view of the ocean.

Sometime during my nap, a large flatbed truck had rolled next to my bungalow, and a crew of workers were now very busy unloading generators, lights, a sound system, and an odd assortment of giant black objects that looked like Lego versions of a jet engine. Unfortunately, the proximity of Archie's condo to the construction site put us directly in the line of fire.

I walked out on the patio to see what was going on. A few feet away, a thin black man sporting long dreadlocks was whacking away at some palm fronds with his machete. "Looks like you got a ringside seat, mon."

"It looks that way," I said. Next to him a younger white man wearing a T-shirt that read BUBBLES 'R US — HOUSTON AND THE WORLD barked into a portable radio. With the other hand, he held a long yellow air hose that ran from a giant air compressor into an enormous cylindrical sheet of plastic.

"That sure as hell ain't no kiddie pool," I commented.

The man looked at me and smiled. "Hi, neighbor," he said with a Texas twang.

I took a seat in one of the chairs on the porch, and in about ten minutes, I saw the object start to take the form of one of those inflatable kid attractions I had seen when the carnival came to Heartache. "That's a bouncy castle," I said to the foreman.

"You could call it that."

I headed back into the bungalow to take a shower. I had been marinating for two days in seawater and felt as if I were turning into a giant pickle.

I don't know what it is about a hot shower that settles the nerves and wipes the slate clean, but it does. My eyes were shut, and I was completely covered in soapsuds. I was just about to rinse off when I felt a sudden, stabbing pain in the ball of my left foot. "SHHHHHHIIIIIITTTTT!" I screamed at the top of my lungs. In my soaped-up blindness, I had been nailed by a tarantula or a poisonous viper.

I instantly opened my eyes to a stinging twinge. I was blind and as slippery as an eel as I felt my way along the wall of the shower for the curtain. Then whatever it was hit again, this time on the heel.

"Goddamn!" I yelled. I wanted to dash away from the danger, but I had to go step-by-step from the confines of the shower stall. I had one foot out and one foot in when I heard noises coming from under my feet. It sounded like giggling voices. The giggles turned to loud laughter.

I was pissed. I felt my way to the towel rack, wiped my eyes, and grabbed the .38 revolver I kept in my backpack. I stormed out the door. My vision was slowly returning as I crouched down to look into the crawl space under the bungalow. I moved cautiously toward the rear of the building with my gun pointed in the direction of the laughter. "All right, you little fuckers, come out from under there," I growled.

The water was still running in the shower above me, and there was no drainpipe. The water just poured into a puddle in the sand. Then I heard a woman's voice say, "Don't shoot." Two figures ducked, crawling toward me until they could stand up straight. They held their hands high above their heads. It was the two girls from the pool. Like a perfectly placed piece of film scoring, "I Shot the Sheriff" blared from the jukebox at the bar as I held my gun on the girls.

They had looked pretty amazing at a distance, but up close, they were even more gorgeous. To say that they also possessed attitude would be an understatement. One was nearly six feet tall, and the other was just an inch or two shorter. One had short, curly blond hair, and the other's was straight and dropped almost to her waist. They wore matching cutoff sleeveless T-shirts, and with their hands stretched above their heads, I could see the tan lines between their abdomens and the white skin of their perfectly formed breasts. One shirt read FAKE, the other, REAL. At that distance I couldn't tell, nor did I really care.

The taller girl had a thin gold chain around her waist that attached to a small pouch. In her hand, she held the smoking gun, or should I say the smoking wire: a stretched-out coat hanger that had been jammed up through the drain and into the bottom of my foot.

"We give," the taller girl said.

"That wasn't funny."

"Yes, it was. I'm Dawn," she said, and the two of them began laughing.

"Of course you are," I replied sarcastically.

"And I'm Christmas. We're cousins," the other girl chimed in.

"I can't tell the family resemblance." I smirked. Christmas was a transmitting antenna with no channels set to receive. Dawn, it seemed, was the listener. Christmas broke the silence of the standoff. "My friends actually call me Noel-Christmas. It sounds like a long name, but it really isn't. I think it has a ring to it. . . . Get it? It's like saying Christmas without really saying it, you know?"

"It would be like being born on Easter and being named Bunny, but changing your name to Bonnet. Let's get back to the point here," I snapped, still fuming from the invasion of my privacy in the shower.

"Exactly!" Noel squealed. "You get it. See? Older guys are, like, so deep."

"Yeah, but deep down where it counts, I am still very shallow," I answered.

"We were just trying to have a little fun," Dawn said seductively. I was staring into her eyes mainly to avoid staring directly at her breasts — but then I saw her gaze move down my body.

"I was trying to take a shower," I said, suddenly nervous.

"Listen, Captain Testosterone, you better cool your jets," she hissed in a newly threatening tone. "The rain is trying to spoil our party, and then you showed up, threatening us. I suggest you put that thing back wherever it came from, because all we have to do is scream 'Rape' and those construction workers on the other side of your bungalow will come running, and I don't think they could help but figure out who's bothering who here."

"Nice tan," Noel-Christmas chimed in. That was when I realized that I was standing on a resort beach, butt naked, pointing a revolver and a hard-on at two gorgeous women. This was not what I would call keeping a low profile. I attempted in vain to cover myself with the gun and retreated to the porch.

"You can put the gun down, Tully. We are not here to rob you, and we are not going to run away."

"How did you know my name?" I asked.

"It's a small island."

I backed down the porch, and they followed in my footsteps.

"Where are you going?" I asked.

"To wait for you. Clean yourself up. We'll be out here."

Dawn and Noel-Christmas dropped into the patio furniture. I put the gun away, dashed back into the shower, and rinsed off.

"I believe in karma!" I yelled from the bathroom. "There is a payback in your future for this kind of behavior."

"I believe in karma too," Dawn called out.

As I was drying off, I could see through the small bathroom window that the work crew was in full swing, and a virtual plastic village now stood next to my bungalow. Along with the bouncy castle, there was a giant pool and a huge inflatable plastic "love doll." I slipped into a pair of dry shorts and a T-shirt. As I rounded the corner out onto the patio, I caught a whiff of very strong pot smoke. Of course it was coming from the direction of my porch.

I stood there, looking into the small dressing mirror tacked to the wall. I tried to warn myself away from these women and ask them to leave my patio and never come back, but that just wasn't working. I had never run into women like this in Wyoming. I hadn't laid eyes on a college campus since attending a Wyoming Cowboys homecoming two decades past, and I had been living on a boat and in a jungle hut for some time.

"That's enough solitude!" the imaginary devil on my left shoulder shouted in my ear.

"You're old enough to be their father!" the angel on my right shoulder yelled. Were they just using me for their spoiled amusement, or were they really interested?

"It doesn't matter" came the answer from the dark side.

"You don't have any protection," Obi-Wan warned.

Nothing was working. It is simply not in the genes of a heterosexual man in the tropics during spring break to throw two beautiful, barely dressed, very forward women in the possession of a joint of killer weed out of his life.

"You got anything to drink in there, Tully?" came the real and recognizable voice of Dawn from the porch. Without hesitating, I reached for the complimentary bottle of wine on the table and headed out the door. I had guests.

Noel-Christmas was lying in the hammock, rocking herself, and Dawn was draped across the wicker chair with her long, tan legs resting on the arm. She had a large cone-shaped spliff in one hand. I uncorked the wine with my Swiss Army knife and poured.

"Merci," she said with a smile.

"So how did you girls decide on Belize for your break?"

"It's like where everybody from UT comes," Noel-Christmas answered. "We go to school in Austin, but we are originally from LA — actually Beverly Hills."

"And what is your major?" I asked.

"Like, boys." Noel-Christmas let out a loud giggle.

"And you?" I asked, looking at Dawn.

"Geology. I like older things. What are you doing here, Tully?"

"I am, like, a victim of the weather," I answered.

It was obvious that Dawn picked up on my mocking valley phrase. Noel-Christmas did not.

"Like, we are all victims in this world, aren't we?" Noel-Christmas added.

"Ships in a storm," Dawn said philosophically. "So what do you do?"

"I surf," I said as I took the joint from her outstretched hand and sat down in the vacant chair. Two puffs later, I caught myself thinking that if I ever got the chance to experience an opium den in some back alley of an exotic seaport like Shanghai, Singapore, or Hong Kong, then Dawn would be the person I would most likely want to invite to join me. She looked like a young Catherine Deneuve as she took a long sip from the glass and made a circle on her lips with her tongue, took a toke on the joint, held her breath for a minute, then exhaled.

"Well, you look like a man of experience, Tully. What do your experiences tell you about being stranded in a storm?"

I rarely smoked pot, but these girls were in possession of what Chino and my island friends called *da kine*. I took the joint again. It had lipstick stains on the end and a slight scent of very nice perfume. I wasn't able to contain the large cloud of smoke in my lungs and convulsed into a short coughing fit.

"Careful there, kahuna. Better pace yourself," Dawn said.

I don't know if it was from the coughing or the pot, but my head certainly was lighter. "What was the question?" I asked.

Dawn laughed, lifted her long blond hair, and tied it quickly and efficiently into a knot on the back of her head. "I said, what do your experiences tell you about being stranded in a storm?"

"Oh, yeah," I said, remembering. "You keep the bow of the boat headed into the waves and try not to panic."

"Do you think you are in a bad situation, sitting here in this storm with us?"

"I wouldn't call it bad. I would call it interesting and almost prophetic."

"Heavy," Noel-Christmas said.

"In what way?" Dawn asked.

"Ix-Nay, that's my friend who is with me — he is a shaman and said we should reacquaint ourselves with our respective cultures."

"That's, like, a serious observation," Noel-Christmas said and sighed.

"If he is the little Indian guy I saw driving through town in a golf cart with one of the pretty local chicks, it sounds like he's trying to get laid to me," Dawn interjected. "I have it on good authority that when a man looks at a woman, he can't go more than five seconds without thinking about fucking her. Are you trying to fuck me, Tully?"

Well, those words detonated like an atomic bomb. I had never been asked that question by any woman that directly, and I was dumbfounded. It was the voice of Noel-Christmas counting that helped me gather my wits: "One thousand one . . . one thousand two . . ."

What came out of my mouth were the words "Are you?"

"Am I what?" Dawn shot back at me like a line drive.

"Trying to fuck me?" I asked.

"Not right now," Dawn said matter-of-factly. "We have plans this evening and have to go, but tomorrow is a new day, and you never know what the new day will bring." She stood up and stretched her whole body in a slow, wavy motion like a cat getting up from a nap. "Can we make up for our little attack and buy you dinner in town tomorrow night?" Dawn asked.

"I think I'm available."

"Belly of the Beast at eight, and don't be late," Dawn said. With that, the two of them strolled off, counting aloud: "One thousand one . . . one thousand two . . ."

28

A Little Family Fun

Sitting alone that night in Consuelo's aunt's restaurant, I replayed the afternoon again and again in my mind. Needless to say, after the pot party, I had quite an appetite and feasted on local paella with chunks of tuna, grouper, hot peppers, garlic, and roasted crab. I kept the fire on my tongue under control with several Belikins and the pineapple flan that Consuelo had recommended. Her aunt told me that Ix-Nay and her niece had been in earlier and had gone to see some ruins.

Though it was Friday night and San Pedro was shaking like a live wire, I'd had about as much fun as I could possibly have for one day. And then there were Dawn's closing comments to me about what lay ahead. I figured I might need the rest and steered clear of the loud music and jam-packed bars.

I was walking along the street when the Clemsons almost ran me down in a stretch golf cart.

"Tully, you got to try one of these cigars!" Big C exclaimed. "Hey, I chartered a seaplane to take us out to the

Blue Hole tomorrow. You know, the one Jacques Cousteau took the *Calypso* to? We're going to land right in the middle of the sucker and snorkel around. Why don't you and Billy Fish join us?"

Big C had been confused by Archie's nickname for Ix-Nay and had called him Billy on the whole plane ride. "It's just me," I said. "Billy's off exploring."

"We're leaving from the airport at eight. If you want to come, the invitation is there." And with that, Big C mashed the accelerator, beeped his horn, and rejoined the traffic procession.

The bar at Renaldo's was a zoo, and the pool was even wilder. The construction was illuminated like a Mardi Gras float with strings of lights. None of it bothered me. I fell asleep watching *The Magnificent Seven* on TV via satellite.

The next morning, I was up with the seagulls and feeling pretty good about having dodged the bullet of self-abuse. I noticed that Ix-Nay had not returned that evening. I went out to the beach for a swim, then had breakfast at a storefront café.

The airport was quiet, and I spotted the seaplane near a hangar at the east side of the field. It was different from Sammy Raye's plane; it was an amphibian, which was a regular airplane strapped to a pair of floats that raised it high above the taxiway. The pilot, Gerald, explained the advantage of being able to get to the Blue Hole long before any of the daily charter boats arrived. The Clemsons pulled up in their stretch golf cart a few minutes later.

The trip out over the pastel patterns of coral and sand was spectacular enough, but the Blue Hole, from a thousand feet, said it all. In the deep-blue water below us, a perfectly round, moonlike crater sat in the middle of a large shallow shelf. "Where are we landing?" Big C asked.

"In there," Gerald said. We spiraled down over the Blue Hole. Gerald expertly glided the floats a few feet over the exposed, antlerlike appendages of elkhorn coral and kissed the surface of the water. He carefully brought the plane to a halt halfway across the Hole.

"Sumbitch!" Big C hooted as we taxied to a mooring. "Now that's what I call sightseein'."

The Blue Hole was the first of several stops we made that day as Gerald guided us through the beauty of the offshore atolls. We dove for lobster, collected shells, explored an ancient Mayan fishing port, and swam at several postcard-perfect small islands. As we were returning to San Pedro, we flew along a sandy beach toward a lighthouse at the end of a small island. "That's Half Moon Cay," Gerald said.

The name instantly rang a bell, and as I was trying to figure out why I recognized the name, Gerald banked the plane sharply to the right. Directly below me was an old lighthouse. Several figures stood on scaffolding and waved up to the plane.

Now I knew where I'd heard of Half Moon Cay. I was thinking about Cleopatra when we buzzed over a stand of coconut trees and there was the *Lucretia,* sitting at anchor in the middle of the crescent-shaped harbor.

"Now *that's* what I call a big-ass sailboat!" Big C exclaimed. "I'd give a million bucks to ride on that baby."

I smiled to myself and remembered the ride I'd taken on her for free.

"Time to head home, folks," Gerald said and pointed the plane back to San Pedro.

I just sat quietly for a moment, thinking about the

strangeness of what had just happened. I didn't have the shaman powers of Ix-Nay, but I could see that things in my life were trying to connect; the sudden appearance of the *Lucretia* was a sign.

The sight of the boat set me wondering if I had made the right decision not to go with Cleopatra. Then, as we flew over the waves, I saw that the whole Clemson family had nodded out. They slept with smiles on their faces, wrapped in the invisible protection and comfort of family bonds. I probably would always be just an observer of such contentment; in truth, what I really wanted was to get back on that boat. I would finish my job of delivering the Fishmobile back to Lost Boys with Ix-Nay, make arrangements for Mr. Twain's retirement, and then somehow make my way back to the *Lucretia*.

Then I remembered the previous afternoon. This newly plotted course for my life could certainly wait until after I had dinner with Dawn.

The note pinned to the door of the bungalow just had the number "8" written on it. The paper was covered with a seashell print and smelled like marijuana and perfume. I was going on a date.

Two days earlier, I could not have imagined that I would be splashing on aftershave and heading out to dinner with a woman who was drop-dead gorgeous and who had indicated that we would probably be having sex at some point later in the evening if I behaved myself.

I didn't quite know what that meant. Back in Heartache, they have a name for that horrible moment when you have a willing partner yet your equipment is not responding. They call it "mean, sexy, and harmless." I did not want to be there.

I stood in front of the mirror and gazed at the dressed-up version of my surfer disguise. I had on a pair of jeans, a white Hawaiian shirt with little blue surfboards printed down the sleeves, and my "go to town" flip-flops. I had received a message from Ix-Nay via Sandra that he and Consuela had gone bird-watching on nearby Jumbo Cay and that he would be back in the morning. I had no idea if he had read my mind from a distance, but I had the bungalow to myself for the night. I turned out the light and headed for the bar.

The music was blaring, and the place was packed. I carved a path through the drunken college kids to the bar. They were all lined up, waiting for the doors to Renaldo's big party to open. The thing that struck me about the crowd was how young it was — teenagers blowing off a little steam by getting drunk and sometimes laid. I always had the feeling there was more "drunk" than "laid" in this kind of crowd.

I finally got the bartender's attention amid the whirring of blenders. He seemed relieved to simply pour me a shot of tequila and gave me directions to the restaurant. "You been to the Belly before?" he asked.

"No."

"It's a pretty wild place."

"How's the food?"

"Doesn't matter," he answered and went back to running the blender, which was fueling the extracurricular activities of the future leaders of our nation.

Over by the pool, a young coed was lying horizontal on the diving board while her sorority sisters were covering her with whipped cream, bananas, and chocolate sauce. At the other end of the pool, a quartet of jocks was swinging another coed by her limbs toward the pool. When she reached the top of the arc, the dental-floss-thin string that held her bikini top on parted, and the crowd let out a roar as the girl sailed through the air with her nipples aimed at the first evening star above.

29

Take Me to Your Blender

Donna Summer's "Hot Stuff" reverberated off the walls of the buildings that lined the streets of San Pedro, and I followed the music.

The entrance to the Belly of the Beast was not hard to spot. It was illuminated with a pulsating strobe light, and a twelve-foot head and teeth of a growling jaguar extended out over the street. The eyes were piercing red lights the size of channel markers, and occasionally hissing steam streamed out of the mouth. Enshrouded in a cloud of smoke, I allowed myself to be swallowed up by the beast. When the smoke cleared, I was in front of a lovely young girl dressed in a silk kimono. She held a handful of menus. She smiled and greeted me warmly. It was when she asked for the name of the party I was meeting that I realized I didn't know Dawn's or Noel-Christmas's last name. "They're from Texas, and they're gorgeous" is all I could come up with.

"Are you Tully?" she asked.

"That's me."

"They are at the bar with Renaldo," she said.

I made my way through the obstacle course of small, overcrowded tables. The place was as dark as one of Ix-Nay's cenotes, and black-light images of Mayan masks, snakes, crocodiles, and lots of jaguars covered the walls and ceilings. The bar was housed in a giant animal cage made of thick bamboo. Occasionally, several leggy girls in showgirl outfits swung by overhead on ropes disguised as vines that hung from the ceiling.

The bar was packed with every representative of island culture, from beach bums to debutantes. A dozen waitresses dressed in skimpy leopard-skin outfits buzzed around the crowd with trays of drinks and food. I was a long way from Lost Boys.

I was kind of swirling through the crowd, trying to spot my dates, and I got into the frenzied flow, smiling and saying hello to at least a dozen people I had never seen before in my life. Someone handed me a drink I didn't order, and I was suddenly part of someone's birthday celebration, singing and dancing, when I felt a hand on my arm. I turned to see Dawn.

She looked amazing. She wore a beige, ruffled miniskirt and a thick fringe belt, topped off by a see-through wrap shirt that was loosely tied with one string between her cleavage and her exposed belly button. She smelled like coconut oil, and her deeply tanned body was covered with specks of gold glitter.

"You sure do clean up good," she said.

All I could respond with was "One thousand one . . . one thousand two."

"Later, handsome—maybe," she replied, and she led me away from the birthday to the end of the bar where Noel-Christmas was entertaining two overly dressed men. She

wore a black bikini top and a pair of the lowest-cut jeans I
had ever seen in my life. She pulled me toward her. "Tully,
this is Edward and Rentzel. They're from New York."

Edward wore a pair of jeans similar to Noel-
Christmas's and a long-sleeved shirt tied calypso style.
Rentzel was in a dark black suit with no shirt.

"So this is your nature boy," Rentzel said. "What
brings you to San Pedro?"

Fortunately I didn't have to answer the question, for at
that moment, the volume of the sound system seemed to
double in intensity, and the voice of Donna Summer filled
the room. Everyone screamed and headed for the already
overcrowded dance floor. Noel-Christmas squealed,
grabbed Edward and Rentzel, and pulled them over to the
human pile.

"Eat first, dance later," Dawn said to me as she took
my hand and led me through the crowd.

We were intercepted outside the cage by the hostess,
who led us past the booths and tables on the floor to a
cavelike room, where she seated us on soft pillows and
closed the beaded curtains behind her as she left.

"What is this?" I asked.

"An apology with all the trimmings — provided, that
is, you didn't come packing heat."

"I don't go looking for trouble," I said. "Let's just say
that in my travels, I have been to some places where that
pistol came in handy."

"I'll bet you have." On the knee-high table were several small candles and a large bowl of gardenias. A champagne bucket held two bottles, snugly resting together
and covered with a white towel. "How's your foot?"
Dawn asked, as she slid her bare foot under the table and
over the toes of my right foot.

"Getting better by the minute."

"Champagne?" she asked.

"Of course."

I reached for one of the bottles, but Dawn pushed my hand away. "My treat," she said. As she reached over to lift a bottle out of the bucket, her half-buttoned blouse opened even further, exposing her breasts. I had stopped counting altogether.

She poured two glasses of champagne. "You make the toast," she said.

I picked up my glass. "To jungle encounters," I said, raising the glass to my lips. The menu back at the Fat Iguana was void of any champagne, and the ice-cold bubbles seemed to be in the right drink at the right time.

"Cristal eighty-eight. In St. Barts they call it Caribbean Kool-Aid."

"Well, I don't know where St. Barts is, but this sure as hell doesn't taste like any Kool-Aid I can remember."

Somewhere near the middle of the second bottle of Cristal, a waiter announced himself, slid back the curtain, and presented us with menus. Food was the farthest thing from my mind.

"You order for me," I told Dawn, and we went back to the champagne.

A plate of conch fritters arrived. I picked at them like an anorexic teenager. They were followed by what Dawn called tapas — little servings of grilled squid, roasted quail, and shrimp. Dawn ate with her fingers and occasionally offered me a tidbit, which I would nibble out of her hand.

A constant flow of guests came and went from the little cave. Noel-Christmas, Edward, and Rentzel brought along Renaldo, the owner of the hotel, and introduced him to me. He was very pumped up and could talk only of his party; it was less than an hour away, and it would be the best spring break ever.

We went back and forth to the dance floor several times, and it was packed with gyrating, sweat-soaked, hormone-hyped bodies.

Somewhere around midnight, a waitress in leopard skin danced from tabletop to tabletop, licking fire from her fingers as she delivered flaming bananas to anybody still interested in dessert.

The champagne was doing its thing, and I was high and happy. "Now that is an interesting way to deliver bananas," I said to Dawn.

"I have something more interesting for dessert if you are interested." We made our way back to the cave from the dance floor. Sitting on the table was a small bowl with one tiny scoop of ice cream and two spoons.

"That's it?" I asked.

Dawn closed the curtains behind me and then sat down at the table. She picked up a spoon, carved a small portion of the ice cream, and I watched it disappear between her lips. "Want some?" she asked.

"I'm not a big vanilla fan," I said.

"They say that presentation is ninety percent of the dining experience. Take this little scoop of vanilla ice cream. Not much to look at or taste, right?"

"Exactly."

"But if you give it an interesting name and a unique presentation, it's not just ice cream anymore."

I was having a hard time thinking about that peewee scoop of ice cream. I was more interested in the woman with the spoon. "I suppose," I mumbled.

"Well, let's see if we can make this dessert a little more

interesting." With that, Dawn placed our champagne glasses side by side and filled them. Then she slowly untied the string on her blouse, leaned over, and dipped her breasts into the champagne glasses. Then she covered her nipples with a spoon of ice cream.

I was waiting, speechless, staring. I figured that any minute I would be turned into a pillar of salt. Then Dawn leaned over and licked her left breast clean, looked at me, and said, "It's called a mother's milk, and the other one is for you."

My first instinct was to look around at the beaded curtains. It would be my luck to be in the act of licking champagne from the breast of an irresistibly sexy woman as the busboy arrived with coffee.

"I'll keep a lookout," Dawn said, and down I went.

Dawn kissed the back of my head as I twirled my tongue around and around her perfectly formed pink nipple until she pushed my head up, looked me in the eye, and said, "Now, Tully, see what you can do with a little imagination?"

I wanted to order a gallon of vanilla and more champagne, cover her in it, seal the curtain to the cave, and lick forever, but at that moment the curtains were flung open.

"There you two are," Noel-Christmas said without even acknowledging the compromising position she'd found us in.

I straightened up like a fence post, reached for a napkin, and started to wipe the milky liquid from my face. I adjusted my pants and made an abortive attempt at getting up while Noel-Christmas took her seat.

"It's nice to see good manners," Dawn said as she casually retied her blouse.

"Well, it's nearly time," Noel-Christmas announced.

"Time for what?" I asked.

"My party!" Renaldo exclaimed, poking his head in through the curtains and grabbing Noel-Christmas around her waist.

"Renaldo, tell me what the big surprise is," she begged.

"What's it worth?" Renaldo said in a lecherous voice.

"Me," Noel-Christmas answered as she licked the side of his face.

"It's a giant foam party," Renaldo blurted out.

"How totally awesome," Noel-Christmas squealed.

"What's a foam party?" I asked.

Noel-Christmas looked at me as if I had asked her for the formula for nuclear fission. "Tully," she said, "like, have you been living on another planet or something? Foam parties are *it*. Like, imagine a waterfall, okay?" She paused and looked at me.

"Got it," I said.

"Now imagine light, airy, luscious, slippery piña colada–scented foam flowing over your entire body while other bodies collide with yours."

"Kind of like being an ice cube in a blender."

"Tully, you're too much," Dawn said.

"Well, ladies," I replied, "take me to your blender."

30

A Cowboy Float

We all piled into Renaldo's red '58 Cadillac. Dawn had produced yet another spliff, this one the size of a tampon, and we smoked it down to a roach — to the delight of Renaldo's driver. He promptly shoved a Bob Marley tape into the cassette deck, and we sang along to "One Love" at the top of our very bad voices and laughed hysterically. I felt as if I were in a movie — because it was only in the movies that a guy like me could ever wind up with girls like Dawn and Noel-Christmas.

Renaldo was recognized immediately as he exited the Cadillac and was hoisted on the shoulders of a throng that carried him to the party like a welcoming liberator. The girls announced that they were going to their rooms to change for the party.

"You look great. Why would you change?"

"Because that's what girls do," Dawn said.

Edward and Rentzel took off to the beach. I politely declined their invitation to tag along and headed toward the party with a champagne and ganja buzz unlike anything I've ever experienced before. As I walked down the path, I saw a hand-painted sign that had recently been nailed to a coconut tree. It read: PEOPLE WITH EXTREMELY SENSITIVE SKIN OR SKIN DISORDERS SHOULD CONSULT A PHYSICIAN BEFORE PARTICIPATING IN A FOAM PARTY.

I had trouble locating Archie's bungalow. My sense of navigation had been seriously altered by pot and champagne, but I managed to get my bearings amid a sea of gyrating humanity. My neighborhood had changed dramatically since I had left for dinner. The bouncy castle that I had seen the day before looked to be ground zero for the evening. It was now flanked on both sides by two giant plastic pools, each with a twenty-foot penis sticking up out of the middle. The pools were packed with people drinking, dancing, and singing to the deafening music coming from the building-size speakers that framed the bouncy castle.

"Shake, shake, shake. Shake, shake, shake. Shake your booty," I sang along with KC.

Suddenly the girls were back. Noel-Christmas was wearing a camouflage bikini bottom not much larger than a giant Band-Aid and another cutoff top with the word BITCH written in rhinestone studs across her chest. When she pivoted, the word GODDESS was written across her back.

"This shirt totally encompasses my split personality — you know, like when I'm having my period at a party."

"Like tonight?" I asked.

Noel-Christmas blurted out a laugh and sprayed me with a mouthful of champagne, which she was guzzling from an open bottle. "No, silly, tonight I'm just ovulating."

"It's a chick thing," Dawn added.

"You look like Barbarella," I said, staring at Dawn's evening attire.

"Who's she?" Dawn asked.

"Never mind. I am dating myself. Let's just say that coming from a man my age, it is a supreme compliment."

"I'll take it."

"Does that mean we have bridged our generation gap?" I asked.

Squinting at her through the lizard slits that had replaced my eyes, I focused on the skintight pink bikini Dawn wore under a sheer piece of fabric draped across her shoulder. "That bathing suit looks like it was painted on," I said jokingly.

"It was," she replied as she rested her arm on my shoulder and leaned her hips against mine. Then she took my hand and slid it across what appeared to be the bikini top, but I was touching her skin.

"It is amazing what they can do with acrylics these days," I said.

There was a sudden acceleration in the energy level of the crowd as Renaldo, now dressed in Jams and a tuxedo jacket with a giant fin attached to the back, climbed up on the stage.

"Come on, kahuna," Dawn said, grabbing my hand.

"Do you girls do this every night?" I finally asked.

"No, just every weekend in Austin," Noel-Christmas said as she grabbed my other hand and led the way through the crowd.

I targeted the compass-rose tattoo that graced the small of her back just above her bikini bottom as my beacon through the madness.

"Have you ever heard of the patron saint of lightning?" I asked.

"No, but how did you know I was Catholic?"

"I guess it just shows."

We entered the bouncy castle and somehow managed to force our way forward to the stage where Renaldo stood next to the DJ booth. He started counting backward from ten, which the crowd immediately took up.

"Are you ready?" Dawn screamed into my ear.

"For what?" I asked.

"Three, two, one!" the crowd roared.

The unmistakable pounding intro of one of my favorite songs catapulted me into the moment. It was Warren Zevon's "Lawyers, Guns and Money." Needless to say, it set the mood, and the entire population of the bouncy castle all began to dance and sing at the same time.

> *Well, I went home with a waitress*
> *The way I always do*
> *How was I to know*
> *She was with the Russians too*

At first I thought by the noise and the shrieking sound around me that someone had actually fired a gun into the crowd, until I saw the starburst pattern above the trees and realized it was fireworks. I stared at the shell bursts and moved with the crowd and sang the anthem that had taken the night to another dimension.

> *Now I'm hiding in Honduras*
> *I'm a desperate man*
> *Send lawyers, guns and money*
> *The shit has hit the fan*

For a moment I reflected on those lyrics that had summed up my life on the run for some time, but the bouncy castle was not very conducive to thinking about my reckless behavior. I might be hiding, but the shit had not hit the fan.

At that point I rejoined the fantasy world as four men dressed like FBI agents appeared at each corner of the scaffolding that surrounded the castle. They each held a giant hose that they pointed at the crowd. "This is a long way from baby pools and Jell-O!" I screamed above the music.

"You're dating yourself again, Tully."

"I'm too old to date."

"Me too," Dawn said.

"Isn't it amazing how we Americans can turn a bubble bath into a foam party?" Noel-Christmas said.

"Yeah, it's right up there with landing a man on the moon."

Warren Zevon's tune was followed by what Dawn called a headbanger anthem — "Welcome to the Jungle" by Guns N' Roses. She danced like she did it for a living, adding that she had actually given a blow job to the guitar tech for Slash in the bathroom at the Santa Monica Pier.

Suddenly the hoses opened up, raining foam down on our heads. The place went nuts. In an instant, we were literally up to our asses in soapsuds, and that's when the clothes started to fly. Bikini tops and baggy shorts filled the air.

Dawn now pressed her whole body against mine, took my hands out of the air, and directed them down and around her thin waist. As the foam rose to chest-high level, she said, "I need to keep you close. There are some real bottom-feeders cruising through this stuff who might try to take advantage of a naive young college girl."

I laughed out loud. "I haven't seen any," I said.

"Perverts?" she asked.

"No. Young innocent college girls."

Suddenly I felt a leg between mine, and the next thing I knew, I was airborne and headed for the bottom. Dawn was covering me like a Secret Service agent thwarting an assassination attempt. "Better check the drain while we're down there," she said.

We surfaced again amid the frolicking, slipping, sliding, and ass-grabbing mass of humanity that had filled the bouncy castle.

Over at the giant foam machine, the main line had burst, and all the foam was shooting out of the machine, not the hoses. They obviously had a problem.

Dawn was now unbuttoning my shirt and nibbling on my stomach, but I couldn't really enjoy the titillating sensation because I could see that we all might be drowning in piña colada–scented foam in a few minutes.

Four more men were wrestling the machine and somehow pointed it away from the bouncy castle. I went back to enjoying being bitten on the belly by a beautiful girl, and I could have stayed in that trance forever, but I felt a sharp fingernail on my back.

"Like, check out your crib, Tully! Isn't that just bitchin'?" Noel-Christmas yelled.

The foam level was just below my chin, and I turned to see her topless and in the clutches of Renaldo, who wore that "died and gone to heaven" look. Behind them, the diverted foam machine was firing a steady stream of cascading bubbles into Archie's bungalow.

"I'm a navigator. Trust me," I said as I held Dawn's hand firmly and got my bearings.

"Where are we going?" she asked.

"To inspect the damage," I answered.

I took a deep breath, and we descended into the foam and wiggled our way through the maze of legs and bodies. We fended off probing, groping hands and fought our way against the sea of humanity moving in the opposite direction toward the stage. We came up a few yards from the porch, where I could see foam flowing out the windows.

"Well, there goes the damage deposit," I said.

We floated on the river of foam to the porch. Dawn emerged, and it was very apparent that the long journey through soapy water had taken its toll on her painted-on bikini. Small rivers of colored water now rolled down her legs. I stared at her naked body, which sported the smallest tan line I had ever seen.

"Well, if you are the navigator, then I am the cruise director. What kind of entertainment are you in the mood for, Mr. Mars? We've already had dinner."

"Let me think," I answered. "One thousand one . . . one thousand —"

She put two fingers to my lips and said, "You can stop counting now."

31

Belly to Belly

I knew the odds of having another evening like this would probably be slim to none for the rest of my life. So despite the large volume of champagne and THC that I had loaded into my bloodstream, I made a serious effort to try and remember the details of what would follow. I wanted to be able to tell the story in a bar when I turned eighty while an audience of young fishing guides and complete strangers looked at me with total disbelief. In the end, I knew my eyes would reveal it to be a true story from my misspent youth.

We started on the porch, worked our way to the bed, and ended an hour later in the shower — the scene of the original crime. At one point I wondered if I would just expire like a male salmon after spawning. But I survived the mating ritual with Dawn.

Afterward, a swim in the ocean was an absolute necessity. We had to cleanse our bodies and our souls. Amazingly, we were alone in the water.

The bouncy castle was still going full blast on the

beach, and it seemed that they had finally gotten the machine working normally and aimed back in the original direction. The party carried on. We dog-paddled side by side to the shore until our stomachs touched the turtle grass on the bottom. I was just blowing bubbles in the water and watching the moon and stars overhead when Dawn said, "God, I have been wanting to do this since the first day we met."

I laughed. "Yes, it is truly amazing the progress we have made in our relationship in a little more than twenty-four hours."

We floated next to each other as Bob Seger's gravelly voice rode the breeze from the party. Several small shrimp sprang from the turtle grass in front of me and skipped across the surface of the water as a small barracuda gave chase. I reached, and to my amazement, one of the shrimp landed in the palm of my hand. I looked down at his wriggling legs and phosphorescent eyes. "I know how you feel, buddy," I said and tossed him in the opposite direction from the predatory fish.

Then Dawn rolled over in the sea grass and clawed her way toward me seductively and settled on top of me like a stingray. "We've met before, Tully."

"Probably in another life," I answered with a laugh.

"Yeah, something like that."

Maybe it was a combination of the full moon, the champagne, the spliff, and the fact that I hadn't actually gotten laid in nearly a year; I had held a gun on this woman, stood in front of her naked with a hard-on, let her buy me dinner, licked vanilla ice cream from her breasts, went to a foam party with her, had sex with her four times, and only knew her as Dawn. I had forgotten my manners. I looked into her eyes and said, "What's your last name?"

"I think that names don't really matter in the tropics," she said as she inched her way up my body until we were belly to belly, as the old calypso song says.

"I think you've hit a reef," I said.

"I certainly hope so." She smiled. "I guess I'm stranded here until the tide can float me free."

Somewhere in the middle of the night, as the tide receded, the foam party began to wind down as well, and the crowds slowly drifted away in small groups. It was time to get out of the water.

"I need to check on Noel-Christmas," Dawn said as she walked toward the bungalow with no concern for her nakedness. I, in my puritan manner, made a mad dash behind her.

To my amazement, the bungalow had survived, though there were still patches of foam on the ceiling, and a putrid piña colada scent hung in the air.

"That is probably the best cleaning job this place has ever seen," Dawn said as she finished buttoning the top button of my other Hawaiian shirt, which she had taken out of the closet. "Can I borrow a pair of shorts too?"

I tossed her a pair from my backpack and grabbed a dry bathing suit for myself. "Where do we go from here?" I asked.

"I'm going back to my room to get a few hours of sleep. Why don't we see what the morning brings?" she said with a smile. She looked at her watch, kissed me, and hurried out the door.

"What's your room number?" I asked, realizing I didn't even know where to find her.

"Top floor, last door on the left," she called back and disappeared into the night.

I was tired, but sleep was out of the question. I was sitting on the bed trying to re-create the amazing evening when I suddenly realized that my wallet and money were in the shorts that I had lent to Dawn.

I jumped up and dashed out the door, heading for the main building.

My heart nearly stopped, and I sobered up in an instant at the sight of the large man standing under the floodlight near the office to Renaldo's. I ducked behind a coconut palm in the dark. The man looked around and then walked down the path toward me. Suddenly, without warning, a turd named Waldo Stilton had dropped into my punch bowl.

The pounding in my chest subsided a bit as Waldo veered over to the candy machine near the bar. Hiding in the shadows of the palm trees, I watched Waldo drop in some change and pull out a Butterfinger, which he munched with one hand while he spoke into the radio he held in the other.

People stumbled out of the party at a steady pace. As I stood there, helpless, I cursed myself for having let my guard down. Was Waldo alone, or was Wilton here too? Had they notified the police? When was Ix-Nay getting back? What should I do about my wallet? How the fuck was I supposed to get off the island with no money or fake ID?

Somehow I calmed myself down and began to force myself to think more clearly. I remembered that I had Archie's satellite phone number in my wallet. I did not want to involve Dawn in my problems, but I needed that wallet. Once I got the number, I could call Archie. I had no doubt that he would understand and help me out. Once I got in touch with him, I could lay low until help arrived.

My salvation appeared in the bushes in the form of the face of the fortieth president of the United States. It was a discarded disguise from the party. I put the Reagan latex mask on and tried my best to look like a drunken reveler leaving the party. Other people stumbling out of the hotel passed me and waved. "Great party, Mr. President," someone shouted, and I waved back.

Once clear of the courtyard and in the corridor of the building, I dashed for Dawn's door.

"Tully," she said in a surprised voice, as she cracked open the door. "You look like you've seen a ghost."

"I'm sorry to bother you, but my wallet is in those shorts, and I kind of need it." I tried to control the anxiety in my voice.

"Is anything the matter?" she asked.

"No, but I need to call Ix-Nay, and his number is in my wallet."

"Tully, it's four-thirty in the morning."

"He's an early riser." Panic was returning, and if Dawn invited me in or started to ask more questions, I was afraid I would begin babbling like an idiot.

"Just a sec," she said and left me at the latched door. She returned seconds later and slipped my wallet through the crack. "Get some rest," she said as she leaned through and kissed me on the forehead. The door closed, and I stood there for a minute thinking how odd the whole thing was. I'd spent four hours performing porn-movie-style sex in the foam, on the floor, in the shower, and underwater — and now it seemed that my romance with Dawn had ended with a first-date peck on the cheek. Cinderella was gone, and my coach was quickly turning into a pumpkin again.

I made a mad run down the hall, snuck across the courtyard, and made my way into the bungalow. I dialed the number and waited.

"Hello," the voice from space said.

I sighed with relief. I had made contact. "Archie?" I called out.

"You have reached my sat phone," the voice continued.

"Shit!" I yelled and hung up the phone. I frantically stuffed my belongings into my backpack while I mentally went over my escape plan. I tried Archie again and got the same message. "Goddamn it!" I yelled and threw the phone against the wall. "Fucking sat phone!" I zipped up my backpack. I was about to heave it on my shoulder when I realized that my gun was missing. I felt the hidden pocket on the side panel, but the gun wasn't there.

"Looking for this?" a voice behind me whispered.

I spun around to see the unwelcome and familiar face of Wilton, the other Stilton brother, standing six feet from me. He was spinning my pistol on the index finger of his left hand while aiming some kind of weird-looking gun at me with his right.

"Hello, asshole," Wilton snarled.

Before I could get a word out, I saw a bolt of blue light coming at me. I followed its path to my bare chest — and the lights went out.

32

Somebody Call
a Witch Doctor

In my cowboy days I had used cattle prods and had been hunting with folks who used shock collars on pointers and retrievers who roamed too far from the man with the gun. The point of these devices was to remind a living, breathing creature that electricity is an instant attention getter. The stun gun is a human version of the shock collar, and that is what Wilton had fired at my chest. It got more than my attention. It knocked me unconscious for half a day.

When I finally came to, I was greeted by a twangy, high-pitched voice that yelled out, "Waldo, he ain't dead!" I was lying on my stomach, and my hands were fastened tightly behind my back. The inside of my mouth felt as if someone had poured a bag of chalk down my throat. My brain was a wreck. It had taken a direct hit from an electrical torpedo. I took a deep breath and gasped, "Water."

"Still or flat?" I heard Waldo Stilton ask, and then he burst out laughing at his own joke.

Red dots and little bubbles floated across my vision as

I was rolled over and shoved up against a cool rock. Somebody poured water on my head.

"Well, haven't we been living the lifestyle of the rich and famous, Mr. Mars? You caused me and my brother a fat lot of trouble back in Alabama, but your ass is ours now. You ain't goin' nowhere 'cept back to a jail cell in Wyoming."

I could have cared less. All I wanted was water.

"Well, we sure as hell don't want him to die before Barston gets here. We best feed him. Check the system," Wilton said to Waldo.

I could finally see both of them. They were dressed in some kind of khaki uniforms with green baseball caps.

"Where am I?" I croaked like a frog.

"You're in a *Star Trek* episode, butt head. You're in the transporter room, and we are the Klingons, and we captured your ship. We're transporting your sorry ass somewhere far away. Cut him loose so's he can eat, but check the system first."

Waldo came up behind me and wrapped something around my neck. Then I heard a snap at the back of my head, and I felt the weight of some kind of collar.

"You even move an inch and I will put the juice to you, hear?" Waldo said and untied my hands.

"I'm not going anywhere." My wrists came free, and I rubbed my hands together and stretched my arms. My feet were chained to a large stone in what appeared to be a cave. That told me that I wasn't in San Pedro — or on any of the offshore islands; they were all flat and made of sand.

Waldo laid a couple of packages of cheese crackers and a bottle of water within reaching distance and stepped back. He kept his eyes on me and his thumb on the control button of the shock collar.

As I gobbled the crackers, I began to remember bits and

pieces of recent events, but I couldn't put them in order. I remembered boat noises, confusing voices, and pain — lots of pain.

My only hope was that Ix-Nay had come back and found me missing — and that either he or Sandra had been able to contact Archie. It was obvious that the Stiltons weren't going to the authorities. They had hidden me and were doing the extradition job themselves. I only hoped that Ix-Nay had his mojo working as I put out an urgent cosmic call for any shamans who might be tuned in to the psychic disturbance I was trying to cause.

"Get him up," Wilton said as he came back into the cave. "That was the plane. Barston will be landing in two minutes."

They jerked me to my feet and tied my hands behind my back. Then they pushed me forward.

"If it was up to me, ass breath, I would ship your butt across the border in a two-hundred-degree cargo container or cut you up for crab bait. But Thelma Barston has chartered a prison plane to take you home, complete with a cell and two guards. It's time to meet your traveling partners."

They shoved me through the cave entrance, and the full sunlight blinded me. Waldo shouted a string of commands. I had to fight back the urge to turn around and kick him in the balls and just take the zap from the shock collar. He pushed me over to a hardwood tree and fastened me to the trunk. My eyes finally adjusted to the light. We were next to a deserted dirt strip surrounded by miles of nothing but scrub brush and weed patches. I figured I was back on the mainland in some remote corner of Belize, and I knew I wouldn't be there long when I saw the twin-engine plane and two uniformed guards.

Overhead, the eggbeater thump of helicopter blades announced the arrival of more visitors. The chopper circled the field, then set down in a cloud of red dust behind the prison plane.

The pilot cut the engines and walked around to open the passenger-side door.

"We got the slimeball, Ms. Barston!" Waldo yelled out.

Well, this was it. Crazy-as-a-loon Thelma had finally tracked me down. I hadn't seen her since that day I shattered her living room window.

Sitting in the tropical heat, shackled to a tree, I wondered if I should have quit in a calmer fashion, but if a frog had wings, his ass wouldn't hit the ground, and no "shoulda woulda" mattered. I had done what I had done. Now Thelma the Terrible had come for her revenge.

Her arm reached out from inside the plane, and the pilot took her hand.

A dust devil swirled across the runway, kicking up debris that made me turn my head from the wind. When it passed, I looked back at the helicopter.

"Here's your boy, Ms. Barston," Waldo said proudly as he walked over to the chopper.

But it was not Thelma Barston who had stepped out. It was Dawn.

If Waldo Stilton had pressed the button of the shock-collar controller, I don't know that I could have been any more stunned than I was by the sight of Dawn. First of all, the tight jeans and halter top tied just above her naval was more clothing than I had ever seen on her body.

She walked toward me with an air of authority. She glanced at her watch from behind a pair of wraparound sunglasses and then ordered the Stiltons to fall in behind her, which they did. "That's far enough, boys," she said, halting her bodyguards. "I need to talk to my soul mate alone."

The Stiltons walked back to the pilot and prison guards at the plane while Dawn eased herself to the ground next to me and gave me a peck on the cheek.

"It's amazing how our relationship has gone from 'Strangers in the Night' to 'Ball and Chain' in just forty-eight hours," I said.

Dawn picked up a stick and started drawing in the dirt. "Oh, Tully," she said with a laugh, "we *have* met before. You don't remember, do you?" She poked me in the knee with her finger and resumed her flirtatious manner.

Some kind of pattern was forming in the sticky heat of the Belize scrub, but I couldn't get a handle on it. "You mean before the pool?" I asked.

I tried to do a rapid search of my memory — rodeos, stock pens, cowboy bars, topless clubs, beach bars, and even a couple of Japanese bathhouses, but I couldn't match up anything.

"I'll give you a clue." Dawn paused and then leaned over and whispered in my ear, "Annie Oakley in Polo," she said.

I rolled the phrase over in my mind like a Ping-Pong ball in the lottery machine, and then it popped up. "Good God!" I yelled. "Thelma Barston is your mother, isn't she?"

"My wicked stepmother," Dawn replied with a casual air.

"Pipe down, creep," Waldo barked at me.

Dawn shot him an angry glance, and then, with the accuracy and speed of a circus knife thrower, she launched a stick at Waldo. She hit him squarely in the crotch.

Waldo grabbed his balls and slumped to the ground, moaning in obvious pain.

"Waldo!" Dawn snapped in a dominatrix voice. "When I need your opinion, I will ask for it."

Dawn nudged me gently on the shoulder. "Remember? It was just after my asshole stepmother and my father bought the poodle ranch and moved to Wyoming. My cousin and I were ordered out from California by Thelma, the ranch Nazi, to 'work with my hands for a living.'" Dawn spat those last three words out as if she had eaten a bad oyster.

"Well, Heartache, Wyoming, isn't Beverly Hills, is it?" I said.

Dawn laughed. "We had seen you working fences and thought you were cute. We'd heard you were crazy. We wanted a closer look, so we rode up one day to your trailer, hoping to run into you. I can still see those pink flamingos standing in the snow. We were cruising around your trailer when you surprised us by riding up. You looked at us and said —"

"Well, if it ain't two little Annie Oakleys in Polo," I interrupted. I could see it as clearly as the morning it happened. There they stood, against the backdrop of clear-blue sky and snow-covered mountains — two spoiled-brat, early-teen products of a broken home in perfectly matching Polo ranch outfits, trying to flirt with me during one of the worst days of my life. Until now.

"Jesus Christ, you were twelve years old."

"Actually, sixteen. I was a late bloomer," she replied in an almost childish voice.

"That was how long ago?" I asked.

"Tully," Dawn said in that casual manner of hers, "you don't have to do the math. I just turned eighteen."

"I need to see some ID," I said.

"Tully, I have had a crush on you since that day at the ranch, and when I heard you had been fired for tearing up Thelma's house, I was so sad and pissed off at her."

"I wasn't fired. I quit."

"I know. She is such a bitch."

"So you two don't get along?" I asked.

"When it comes to Thelma, my inner child is a mean little fucker," Dawn said, steely eyed.

"Well then, could you please explain to me why it is that you are sitting there, free as a bird, and me — your teenage heartthrob — has been shocked, beat up, and chained?"

"I think I can," Dawn said, glancing down at her watch. "But it will have to be the short version."

So Dawn told me the story of how she and her step-mother had continued their hateful relationship through high school graduation, which was two weeks before her father died. "He dropped dead of a heart attack, and I swear she drove him to his grave," she said bitterly. "Of course Thelma was the one with all the money. My father tried to talk to her about her obsession with you. And so did I," Dawn added. But she could only go so far because of "the money thing," as she put it. As a by-product of Thelma's poodle ventures, the ranch land was discovered to hold huge reserves of natural gas. So Thelma was now worth a staggering fortune, and Dawn was the only heir.

Dawn had been due a huge trust-fund payment in six months, but she had really angered Thelma five months earlier. She and her cousin, Noel-Christmas, had been thrown in jail in Austin when they were photographed naked, riding a couple of bull riders on the bar.

Thelma had threatened to cut off her allowance and disinherit Dawn, which presented the horrible reality that Dawn might have to actually get a job. Dawn laid low the last quarter of school and actually studied and made the dean's list. It was all a ploy to get Thelma to reward her by letting her go to spring break in Belize. Her stepmother had agreed, but only on the condition that the Stilton brothers, Thelma's own private posse, would go and keep an eye on her.

Dawn despised the Stiltons. They had been sent to bail her out of jail after the bare-assed bull-rider incident, and she had been forced to ride home with them in a plane. Those three hours with Wilton and Waldo had been worse than jail to her, but if that was the only way she could get to the beach, then she agreed.

So Dawn and Noel-Christmas had come to Belize with the Stiltons seated four rows back on the jet from Houston to Belize City. It had been Dawn's plan all along to divert the Stiltons to Cancún with bribes of money and hookers when they got there. Once out of the country, the Stiltons gladly took the deal.

"Waldo and Wilton were on their way to Cancún when you walked by the pool," she said. "At first, I couldn't believe my eyes." She took a deep breath and looked me in the eye. "Tully, that was the hardest decision I ever made in my life. I had to turn you in. Thelma has been obsessed with your capture beyond anything rational. I hate to say it, but to her, you are the Charles Manson of exercise equipment and picture windows. I caught the Stiltons just as they were about to board the plane for Cancún. I have to say they're not your biggest

fans since the pay cut they took when you got away
from them in Alabama. Of course those morons wanted
to bust into your room like a SWAT team, but I told
them you were too smart for that. And that's when Noel-
Christmas and I came up with the plan to flush you out
of the shower." She laughed and looked at me. "You
have to admit, that was a good one. And then I got to
have my cake and eat it too."

"I don't follow that concept," I said.

"It meant that I could make my teenage fantasy come
true at last and then turn you in to Thelma. And that is
what happened."

We sat next to each other in silence for a moment, and
then Dawn put her hand on mine. "At least we had a good
time at the foam party," she said in a naive, almost baby-
like voice.

"Well, I guess that will have to last me through
prison," I said flatly.

"Oh, you'll be out in no time, Tully. Once you're in
jail, I plan on getting you into one of those cushy Club
Fed places where all the politicians and corporate crooks
go. They say it's like a country club." She beamed.

"With bars," I added. "Dawn?"

"What, Cowboy?"

"Do me a favor?"

"Anything but let you go."

"Just don't do me any favors."

"Something tells me you're not thrilled with my plan.
Oh well." She sighed. "Tully, I really had no choice."

The silence of the morning was broken by the click of
the igniters and the high-pitched engine of the prison
plane as it roared to life.

"Most of us don't!" I hollered back above the noise.

Waldo ran to us in a limping gait. "Ms. Dawn, if we are going to meet Mrs. Barston, then we best be movin'."

"Call Thelma and tell her you are on the way. I'm going back to the beach for the afternoon," Dawn said. With that, she leaned over, gave me a kiss on the lips, and put her sunglasses back on.

It is a sick feeling to lose your freedom, and that was the way I felt as I sat there helplessly. I had tempted fate and had gotten myself into this trouble. The scrub brush and weeds that surrounded me were as bleak as my future.

Then, out of the corner of my eye, I saw something move against the stationary landscape. A small, spotted wildcat was zigzagging with a strange hopping gait through the brush.

"What the hell kind of animal is that?" Waldo guffawed.

"You don't see them too often," Dawn said, gazing at the animal.

But I *had* seen it before. There are not that many three-legged ocelots running around Belize. It was Tripod, Archie's pet cat. He stopped dead in his tracks and looked directly at me.

I had spent too many times like this with Mr. Twain to know that animals can communicate with humans. Tripod's eyes told the story. He was not on a casual walk-about from Kafiri. He was there for a reason.

"Well, it makes him an easier target," Waldo said as he raised his pistol.

Once again, Dawn jerked his chain. This time her weapon of choice was a huge dirt clod that she picked up and hurled at Waldo's head, striking him on the side of the face. Waldo let out a howl, and the cat darted for cover.

"Waldo, what is it about what we are doing here that you don't get? If this air force sitting in front of us isn't enough to draw attention our way, then let's just start shooting the local handicapped wildlife as a way to alert the general population to our whereabouts. You idiot! We are kidnapping an American citizen and transporting him illegally back to Wyoming."

Dawn got up and went over to have a word with Wilton, but I wasn't paying much attention to what they were saying. For coming in our direction, from the other side of the runway, was a rapidly moving cloud of dust.

"Jesus, it's the game warden! Thank God Waldo didn't shoot that cat!" Wilton said.

But it wasn't the game warden. As the Rover emerged from the dust, there was no mistaking the paint job. Tripod had been right, and now one thing was certain: I was not on the prison plane yet, and the Fishmobile was a hundred yards away — bearing down on my captors at a rapid pace.

33

Put on Your Sailin' Shoes

All around me, people scrambled in different directions. Standing in chains, I began to tap my foot in the dust, quietly singing the words of Fontella Bass, with one slight lyric change:

Come on, Archie, and rescue me
Come on, Archie, and rescue me

As the Land Rover neared the tree, I saw that Archie was not alone. A head bobbed up out of the sunroof and aimed a video camera straight at us. Bucky and Captain Kirk stood in the rear, shooting off their flash cameras in rapid, paparazzi style. Suddenly, I realized the cameraman was Ix-Nay dressed as an Englishman. They had come to rescue me.

Right then and there, I knew I was not going back to Wyoming. The Rover skidded to a halt directly in front of the airplane, and Archie popped his head out the window.

"Pardon us," he said to no one in particular, "but have

you seen a three-legged ocelot running about? We are filming him for the BBC, and we seem to have lost the little bugger."

The arrival of the Land Rover had totally confused Dawn, the Stiltons, and the crew. I just bit my tongue and watched, waiting to see how this was going to play out. Archie had blocked the plane's path back to the runway.

"Listen, your highness, you gotta move that truck right now. We're taking off," Waldo commanded.

"Name's Archie. Archie Mercer." He was grinning broadly.

"Whoever. And you," Waldo snapped, pointing a finger at Ix-Nay, "put down that fucking camera."

"Well, you certainly don't have to be rude about it, Jocko."

"Name's Waldo. Waldo Stilton."

"That's just great, shit-for-brains," I heard Dawn hiss as she walked over to the truck.

"Well, Waldo, what brings you to our little country?" Archie inquired, his voice getting more serious.

"We are having a picnic," Waldo replied.

"And I suppose the bloke wrapped in chains over there is being punished for not bringing the potato salad."

"That's right, sport, but none of this is any of your business. I am only gonna ask you nicely one more time to move that truck."

Suddenly Tripod walked out of the bush and stood between the Stiltons and the plane.

"There he is!" I heard Ix-Nay shout.

"We must get this shot, if you don't mind," Archie explained.

"Don't touch those goddamn cameras!" Waldo ordered.

Dawn, sensing Waldo's loose screws, interrupted. "Mr.

Mercer, please take your pictures. But it would be so helpful if you could move the truck, as we do have to be on our way shortly."

"Is he going with you?" Archie asked, pointing at me. He flashed me a quick wink.

"That's none of your fucking business," Waldo growled.

"Mr. Stilton, such language!" Dawn gasped. She was trying to act cool, but I could see that she wanted to claw Waldo's eyes out.

"Shut up, bitch! I have had enough of your spoiled rich ass," Waldo barked as he pulled the pistol out from under his shirt. He walked over to the Rover and pointed the gun at Archie. "Now drop those cameras, and get your tree-hugging asses out of here."

Archie and the boys put away their cameras.

"That's better," Waldo said with a smile. "Now move that truck."

"Waldo, you need to get a grip," Wilton said cautiously, walking over to Waldo.

"You stay right where you are, ass wipe. All my fucking life you've told me what to do. Not anymore. This is my collar. I am taking Mars to Wyoming. You are off the case."

Dawn lunged at Waldo, who wheeled around and aimed the gun at her. As he did, everyone in the truck disappeared from sight.

"Stay right there!" Waldo yelled at Dawn. "You are no longer in charge of this!"

"You are absolutely right about that," Archie said. As Waldo turned to point the gun back at the Rover, the rear door snapped open, caught him squarely in the face, and sent him flying. His gun sailed off in the other direction.

Archie, Ix-Nay, Bucky, and Captain Kirk were no longer holding cameras. Instead they were pointing a variety of assault rifles at Dawn, Waldo, and the prison-plane crew.

It was over in a matter of seconds. Wilton and the prison guards surrendered without a word. Dawn just dropped to the ground and began sobbing uncontrollably. Her perfect breasts heaved up and down as she shrieked, "There goes my fucking money! I am going to have to get a job waiting *tables*."

Ix-Nay and Kirk went to work on the collar and my chains. "How in God's name did you find me?" I asked.

"Your cry for help was heard by the Mayan gods," Ix-Nay said as he freed my hands and feet.

"It might have been the gods, but it was also the phone message that saved your ass. Good thinking," Archie said.

"I didn't leave a message."

"I know. But Waldo shit-for-brains didn't have the sense to jerk the phone out of the wall. After he zapped you with the stun gun, he and his pals described exactly where they were going — and all of it was recorded on my sat phone. I called Sandra, and she found Ix-Nay. Once he tracked down Bucky, Kirk, and me, all we had to do was come up with a plan. Worked quite well, that photo-safari thing — don't you think?"

"Where are we?"

"Not in Marwar Junction, brother. We're up in the Corozal district. We'd best be sending this pack of vultures on their way and worry more about where you're going."

Bucky and Kirk marched Wilton, the prison guards, and the pilot onto the airplane, and then Archie helped the debilitated Waldo aboard. His nose looked as if it were made of putty, and blood streamed out of his nostrils.

I walked Dawn to the helicopter and helped her put her seat belt on. She said nothing. I went back over to the plane. I was having mixed feelings about the whole thing, and there was no ready advice about what to do. Archie had just tied Waldo to his seat, and he exited the plane.

"I'm thinking about turning myself in — not to Thelma but to the police in Wyoming. I have to stop running sometime. I don't want to always have to rely on you guys to bail me out."

"Tully, prison is not the place to ponder your future," Archie said. "The windows are very small."

"So what's my other option?"

"Follow our little plan that will safely get you out of the country to a place where you can live in peace until the statute of limitations runs out. Then you can be a free man again," Archie said. "But first we really must get rid of these rotten eggs."

The passengers were tied and duct taped to their seats. Waldo was trying to speak, but with blood dripping from his nose and his brain scrambled from the sudden impact with the Rover door, he sounded as if he were mumbling into a megaphone.

Archie walked to the front of the plane. "Captain, I don't care where you guys go as long as it is north and you don't attempt to free these buggers until you are five hundred miles from the Belize border. Just so you know, if you attempt to come back here, the local authorities will be informed of your exact whereabouts and that you are carrying a kilo of cocaine on board your plane."

The pilot's navy-blue shirt turned three shades darker from the sweat that flooded from his armpits.

"What you do with it when you get to the States is your business — that is, if you can find it."

"You have got to be kidding!" the frantic pilot called out.

"Afraid not. Either fly or get ready to die," Archie said. "It will just be another dope deal gone bad." The engines fired.

In the helicopter Dawn sat in the front seat with a pout on her face. "I suppose you're happy now," she said as I walked over with Archie.

"I would say I'm more relieved than happy."

"Tully, I would have taken care of you. Even now. We could still do it. You could come with me. Eventually —"

Archie began digging at the pockets of her jeans. "Let go of me, you limey pig!" she screamed.

It was in her sock that Archie found the hidden cell phone. He pulled it out, dropped it on the ground, and stomped on it. "That takes care of that. Now what to do with you?"

"I am going to the beach," Dawn said smugly, settling into the seat.

"Not in this machine, and not today," Archie said. With lightning speed, he pulled her from the helicopter and shoved her to the ground. He whistled loudly, and another Land Rover burst out of the bushes. It was driven by some of the workers from Kafiri, who were also carrying guns. They gagged Dawn, and the last I saw of her was her lovely golden hair as she was loaded into the back of the Rover. It disappeared into the bush, and Archie came back to the helicopter.

"Winston," he said to the helicopter pilot, "the less said about this, the better, if you know what I mean? They are going to hold her until we can get clear of this area, and then she will be released, unharmed."

"No problem," the pilot replied as he started the engine.

"I never got to say good-bye," I said to Archie.

"I said it for you," he replied.

We watched the chopper take off and head south. In a few minutes, the sound faded, and only the wind and the birds could be heard. Then the Fishmobile roared up to us with Ix-Nay at the wheel. "It is a great truck."

"Great truck," Bucky added.

"I guess it goes without saying that we bought it."

"We did," Bucky said.

"But I doubt I will be making the trip back to Lost Boys with you guys," I said.

"Tully," Captain Kirk told me, "if I were you, I think I would be putting on my sailing shoes."

34

On the Case

Before Ix-Nay stepped on the gas, Bucky handed me an envelope. "This came while you were gone. You sure know how to pick your pen pals, Tully," he said.

From the handwriting, I could see it was another letter from Willie Singer. I was going to write him back last time, but the events of the past few days put a monkey wrench in that plan. I promised myself I would sit down and write to him the first chance I got.

I tore open the envelope and read it as we bumped along the road. Not only had my rescuers snatched me from the Wicked Witch and her flying monkeys but they had also devised a plan to hide me in a safe harbor somewhere. I could sense that this ride in the Fishmobile was going to be a long one. That was good, for it was a long letter.

To: Tully Mars
From: Willie Singer
Nouméa, New Caledonia
French Polynesia

Dear Tully,

Please inform Captain Highbourne that as her South Pacific representative in the search for the soul of the light for Cayo Loco, I have made progress, as you will see — but I have to start where I left off.

After we blasted off from Minola, I began stocking up on lighthouse reading material wherever I could find it, and I have made some progress, I think. Getting to New Caledonia was quite an adventure, and there were times I said a few prayers to your patron saint of lightning.

The leg to Tahiti started off without a hitch, and the *Pearl* ran like a Swiss watch. But the weather reared its very ugly head as we crossed the equator. We wound up zigzagging like a bottle rocket and going nearly to the Cook Islands to get around the storms. Let me just say one other thing about squalls on the equator: they take rain to another level. At times we were flying through such a thick downpour that I thought I was driving a submarine. At other times, we had to scud run only a few feet above thirty- to forty-foot waves because it was the only place where we could make out any kind of a horizon. I don't think I was ever so glad to see the sun as when it finally broke through the clouds north of Bora-Bora. After that, the run to Papeete was uneventful.

No mode of transportation elicits as much interest as making a water landing in an old flying boat. The harbormaster who came out to greet us in the pilot boat told me over the radio that we were the first flying boat to set down in Papeete

Harbor in more than thirty years. The French don't need a lot of encouragement to declare a celebration, and I guess we were a big two-engine excuse. I have taken off and landed from a lot of tropical ports, but I never saw any greeting like this. There were flags, bands, a boat parade, hundreds of hula girls blowing us kisses from the shore, and a small barge loaded with leis that were tossed by children into the water as a means of guiding us up the channel to our anchorage.

Tom Prophet, an old friend and promoter on the island who had brought me here to sing the first time, was riding the lead boat, surrounded by a bevy of hula girls and a man I didn't recognize. Once we had the plane secure and went ashore, the party began. That is where Tom introduced me to his partner, Philippe Parfait, who is the cultural attaché for French Polynesia.

Any country, territory, or island larger than a postage stamp has a minister of culture or a cultural attaché. Their job seems to be having drinks with visitors and getting their picture in the local papers and on TV with visiting celebrities.

Boy, did Philippe Parfait fit the part. He stood about six feet tall, with a head of curly silver hair and obvious Polynesian features along with his "Frenchness." He wore tailored blue slacks and a white silk shirt, and a lei of fresh jasmine blossoms hung around his neck. As I was about to shake his hand, a beautiful girl, dressed in traditional dance attire, stepped forward and lowered a similar lei around my neck and kissed me on both cheeks.

Parfait spoke perfect English as he gently took my arm and walked me toward a podium where I was welcomed by the mayor, did several interviews with the local paper, exchanged a multitude of champagne toasts, and topped it off with platters of fresh oysters flown in from New Zealand. Add ten hours of hard-weather flying to that, and you are a tired puppy by the time you get your head on a pillow. I slept an entire day, which is unheard of for me.

The next morning the phone rang early. It was Philippe. "I am taking you to breakfast. There will be a few press people around afterward to ask you about your film."

"What film?" I asked.

"The one you told me you were making," he answered.

"Oh, you mean my homemade video of the trip?"

"No, the documentary you are producing and directing about your epic flight across the Pacific. The film that will provide you easy transit through the islands."

"I don't quite understand."

"You will once you wake up," he told me. "I'll be waiting in the lobby with some strong coffee."

Philippe greeted me with a huge mug and a morning paper. There was a giant photo of *The Flying Pearl* landing in the bay on the front page of *Le Peche*. "You are a very popular man on this island today, Willie," he said with an air of self-satisfaction. Over breakfast, Philippe explained the reason for the dog-and-pony-show approach to our visit. Between recent rebel activity in New

Caledonia and nuclear testing in French Polynesia, the military was suspicious of any oddball traveling through the islands and could give us problems. We did not appear to be your typical tourists. "I have created a cover story for you, and it will hopefully help you to avoid any unpleasant confrontations with these paranoid paratroopers. For the next few days, it would help if you acted like a movie star."

"Why?" I asked.

"To deal with bureaucracy. You see, we French invented bureaucracy as well as diplomacy. 'No' is the easiest and safest answer for any government employee to say. But everything changes if you are in the movie business. Hollywood is the detour around any bureaucratic logjam. Movie stars get more attention than diplomats or presidents. Nothing greases wheels anywhere in the world faster than the thought of a movie coming to town, and you, my friend, are now a movie star. That is, if you want to get to New Caledonia."

"I do."

"Then finish your breakfast. We are late."

"For what?" I asked.

Well, it didn't take long to find out. We walked out of the restaurant and were instantly greeted by a crowd of reporters that suddenly surrounded us at the corner. I guess Philippe thought I might run, because with one hand he gripped me like an osprey holding a fish while he waved with the other. I waved and smiled as well.

"How long will you be shooting in Tahiti?" a reporter shouted from the crowd.

"I always do."

The crowd looked confused but wrote down my answer. I just smiled like a movie star as Philippe pulled me into a waiting car.

We soaked up our few days of celebrity status. The piece in the paper made it sound as if we were going to film the Polynesian remake of *Gone with the Wind*. But it worked. Strangers waved and offered to buy me drinks. Women smiled as they passed me on the streets. Gendarmes along the boulevard called me by my name. Then it was time to leave. We bid farewell to our friends in Tahiti and headed for New Caledonia, expecting the same kind of warm greeting. Boy, were we in for a surprise.

I hate to think of any time spent in the *Pearl* over the Pacific as routine, but things were just humming along, and we enjoyed the view. We were greeted in Pago Pago by a classic third-world screwup when the fuel truck parked in front of the plane ran out of gas. A gang fight nearly erupted among the very large Samoans on the ramp. Somehow we assumed the role of UN peacekeepers and managed to get fueled and get going to New Caledonia. Eight and a half uneventful hours later, I was sitting in the cockpit rereading our headlines in the Tahiti newspaper when Hollis, my copilot, yelled, "Jesus, look at that!" I dropped the paper immediately when I spotted a lighthouse that looked as if it reached all the way to the floor of heaven.

Here are a few lighthouse-junkie facts: Amedee Light is about 185 feet tall. It sits on the edge of the Passe de Boulari, which carves through the largest lagoon in the world — about ten miles from Nouméa, the capital of New Caledonia. It was built in 1862 under the reign of Napoléon III, and it has been working ever since.

I let Hollis fly the plane and went to the rear and poked my video camera out the hatch into the wind and recorded our circles around the light. After all, we were supposed to be making a movie. Below us, tour boats and a couple dinghies were tied to the pier by the light. People on the beach and in the light tower were waving frantically at us as we dropped down to two hundred feet and did a tight circle around the light itself. I am sure they weren't expecting an air show that day, but they sure as hell got one.

We headed off for the airport and readied ourselves for another celebratory arrival, but our welcoming committee was not a crowd of flower-laden hula girls. Instead we were boarded, searched, and interrogated by some not-too-friendly Frenchmen, who it turns out were members of the DGSE — the French equivalent of the CIA. They are the guys who blew up the Greenpeace ship *Rainbow Warrior* in Auckland back in 1985, as it was getting ready to sail to Moruroa in the Tuamotu Islands where the French still explode nuclear weapons. These guys were serious.

There we were, dressed in shorts, T-shirts, and flip-flops, doing our best to look like movie stars as Parfait had instructed. At first, I knew this had to be a practical joke, after all the press and

assurances from Parfait that we could go anywhere
and do anything we wanted on French soil. But
when I saw the automatic rifles hanging from the
shoulders of our camouflage-covered greeting
committee, I knew they were not big readers of the
local-living section of the papers. I guess we fit
the profile of troublemakers, so that was how we
were being treated. We were detained in a small
room for four hours before a very short, chain-
smoking officer came in, dismissing us like bad
cheese. He told us we could not enter the country.

I then explained that there must be some kind
of misunderstanding — that Philippe Parfait . . .

At the mention of Parfait, the muscles in the
man's neck began to quiver. "That oyster," the man
snapped.

Just as he said it, the door opened, and I heard
a voice say, *"Belons, Capitaine. Je prefer les
belons. Et vous?"*

The chain-smoking officer's face turned scarlet.

The last time I had seen Philippe Parfait, he
was singing Frank Sinatra karaoke with the local
band at our farewell party. Today he was all
business, and I watched in glee as the cultural
attaché trumped the hard-assed officer. He
presented the officer with several documents and
excused him out of our lives with a scolding that
was felt by all the gun-toting soldiers in the room.
They all filed out as he pointed at the door.
Simultaneously, smiles returned to the faces of the
customs agents who stamped our passports and
now welcomed us to Nouméa. That night, Philippe
arranged our hotel accommodations and bought us

an apologetic dinner, where he told me he had arranged everything at the lighthouse. "Amedee will make a great opening shot for your film, no?" he said with a wink.

Philippe was unable to go to the island with us the next morning. The message came as we exited our cab at the Club Med dock for the half-hour ride out to the light. A small government boat was waiting for us. The captain greeted us, gave us life jackets, and once we were away from the dock, he became an instant tour guide as well. I asked if a Fresnel lens powered the light. The question seemed to startle him. "Why, yes, of course," he answered.

When we docked, the light keeper and his staff were standing in perfectly starched uniforms and greeted us warmly and ushered us up the tower. I was more interested in getting information about a bull's-eye lens, but they were on another page and brought us quickly up to the light. Tully, all I can tell you is that the lens in that light room looked like a small glass cathedral, and I knew then something good was about to happen. Our tour was concluded, and we were ushered back down the steps, where we posed for photos with the light keepers. I still tried to ask about the bull's-eye lens, but the light keeper ignored my questions and just said, "Monsieur Parfait."

Philippe greeted us at the dock. "Well, you are now famous in New Caledonia," he said as he handed me a copy of the paper with a collage of pictures from our dinner party. A story had been fabricated around the suggestion that we would be back to film a movie on the island. It was then that he mentioned the local TV station would like to film our departure and flyby of the lighthouse.

I knew my answer was yes before I said it. It was part of the game.

"Come, I have a van," he said and led us down to the dock.

We all rode in the van behind the police car, into which Philippe had climbed. I wanted information about the bull's-eye lens, but I suddenly found myself being whisked to the airport where God-knows-what awaited. It suddenly dawned on me that we would probably be in the air on the way to Vanuatu in a few minutes without ever having discovered anything about the lens. My worst fears were realized as we passed through the airport security gate.

The press had all gathered around the *Pearl*. Next to it a helicopter stood by, with the engines whining. We were cleared through customs faster than a waiter making a table change at Joe's Stone Crab, and Philippe handed me our paperwork and passports. I was trying to ask Parfait a question about the lighthouse when he hugged me and kissed me on both cheeks. The video cameras whirred, and the flashbulbs popped. "By the way," he said quietly as we walked to the door of the plane, "when you get to Luganville, if you draw as much attention there as you did here with your plane, ask around the airport for someone who can get you to my friend Waltham. I think he might be able to help you with your bull's-eye. Smile at the cameras, and don't ask any questions."

It was the way he said it that made me realize this was not another one of his publicity stunts. He was serious.

So, as the boys are preflighting the plane, I am rushing to finish this letter so I can drop it through the window to Parfait before we taxi out. He already promised me that he would have it delivered to you. Now I am off to find this Waltham character. I have a strange feeling I am on to something.

Willie

PS: Do you have any of these at Lost Boys? The photo I've included is three-quarters of the largest bonefish that I have ever had on the end of a line. I caught him on Minola. I thought he was a fucking barracuda. He ran three hundred yards, backing off my reel twice, and as you can tell by the missing last third of his body, the sharks got him before I could reel him in. As a whole fish, he was probably well over twenty pounds, but I will let you and Ix-Nay be the judges of that.

35

Trying to Catch a Little Neutral

I find that laughter can cure just about anything, and boy, that long letter of Willie's tickled my funny bone. I studied the pictures of the giant, half-eaten, world-record bonefish and then put the letter in my pocket. I was jealous about the fish. But when I went back to looking at the scenery, the bumpy road woke up my nervous system, and I could feel the lingering pain. Still, all I could do was laugh at what had just happened to me, and to Willie, halfway around the world. We had both escaped bad situations with the help of friends. I can never quite figure out how things work out, but they always happen for a reason.

As the flat cane fields rolled by, I have to admit I was still thinking about Dawn. I couldn't believe that I was actually feeling sorry for a femme fatale who had come so close to sending me to prison as if it were part of her spring-break agenda. I realized that any woman who could come up with such a scheme was going to find her way in the world. I would probably see her again, on the arm of a Dallas Cowboy quarterback or as the trophy wife of some obscenely rich mogul. A woman like Dawn, as young as she was, always had a plan B. I was pretty sure I wasn't the only key that could unlock her mother's treasure box.

Archie was now at the wheel, and Ix-Nay was up front with him, inspecting all the gadgets, buttons, and switches on the dashboard. In their haste to rescue me, he hadn't taken a proper test ride. He read the owner's manual aloud at times and asked Archie endless questions about the truck. Archie happily answered all of them. Bucky was stretched out on the rear seat, asleep after the all-night race from Lost Boys to Kafiri. I was bone tired as well, but I wasn't closing my eyes until I knew we had put a fair bit of distance between my pursuers and me. Captain Kirk sat next to me with his headphones on, listening to his Joni Mitchell.

Of course I was interested in what the next stage of my escape plan was. I suspected that the *Caribbean Soul* was moored at the village of Sartaneja, where Ix-Nay and I had come ashore with Captain Claro. I figured Kirk had come down with Bucky by land and had had the boat moved.

We kept to the unpaved back roads and headed northeast toward the shore. As we did, the scenery turned from scrub brush to cane fields to marshes and bayous, not unlike the scenery of lower Alabama. There were few vehicles traveling these roads, just the intermittent westbound pickup truck.

I stared out the window at cornfields and banana plantations set against the pink, tropical evening sky. Though I was determined to stay on guard, I dozed off. When I woke about half an hour later, we had stopped on a sand

road that came to a dead end at the water. A huge yellow
cloud of butterflies drifted between the land and the sea.

"Looks like they've come to see you off, Tully."

"Where are we going?" I asked Captain Kirk.

"We aren't going anywhere," he replied.

I was confused. I had figured that the *Caribbean Soul*
would be waiting for us to board up with Mr. Twain
standing on the bow, just like it was when we had left Alabama. Instead, all I saw was a cloud of butterflies and a
large bay with no boat in sight.

"Kirk's going back with me to the lodge," Bucky said.
"You and Ix-Nay are going to meet Cleopatra."

Just then, the butterflies began to fly rapidly in a big,
counter-clockwise circle, and then they peeled off like a
fighter squadron for the trees at the shore. Seconds later,
the sound of an airplane engine could be heard.

My initial thought was that the Stiltons had returned,
but then I recognized the deep thump that came out of the
sky. I had heard it first back at Lost Boys.

"There they are," Ix-Nay said, pointing a few inches
above the horizon where the biggest flamingo in the world
banked out over the bay in a slow descent. It was Sammy
Raye in his seaplane.

"Is there anybody I know who is not involved in this?"
I asked.

"Thelma Barston," Bucky said.

As Sammy Raye's plane touched down and taxied to
the shore, Bucky told me that one of the Stiltons' other
bounty hunters had shown up at the Fat Iguana. He'd
been asking a lot of nasty questions about me shortly
after Ix-Nay and I had left for Belize. Bucky and Kirk
couldn't get through to Renaldo's, so they had made a
plan with Archie and headed for Belize to find us and

warn me. So when my frantic call had come in to Archie, they were already in Belize. Archie had then contacted Cleopatra at Half Moon Cay and filled her in. She had said to bring me to the *Lucretia,* and that was where I was going.

"What about Mr. Twain?" I asked.

"We will take good care of him until you get all this shit sorted out. Sammy Raye has connections out in Wyoming and is going to work on it. In the meantime, we thought it best that you go sailing."

My first thought was to protest and get all defensive about this being my decision, but then I thought it would be bad manners to argue with the people who saved me from going to prison. "Whatever." I sighed. I said goodbye to Bucky and Captain Kirk and couldn't find the words to thank them — they knew I would do the same for them if the roles had been reversed.

"Hello there, Peter Pan," Sammy Raye said. "You seem to be up to your ass in crocodiles." He was seated in the copilot's seat, and Drake was at the controls.

Ix-Nay and I loaded up on the seaplane, and I thanked Sammy Raye for getting involved.

"I may be an old queen, but I hate poodles as much as you do," he said with a grin.

Ix-Nay and I sat in the back and waved to our friends as the plane lunged forward and spray covered the windows. When it cleared, we were airborne, and I could see that we had taken off from a small estuary that emptied into Chetumal Bay. Minutes later, the pilot banked right, and we left the shoreline of Belize behind.

"So how did you make out with Consuelo?" I asked.

"Better than you did with Mrs. Barston's stepdaughter. While you were lost in that sea of bubbles, we camped out on the beach and watched sea turtle hatchlings as they struggled out of their shells and ran immediately for the ocean. It was strange, for as I looked at the predators who awaited them — frigate birds in the air and barracudas in the water — I had a vision that you were in danger."

"I was."

"But you are not anymore."

"Which means?" I asked.

"Which means that you didn't get eaten up by the frigate birds and barracudas. Congratulations. I believe your journey is just beginning."

"Well, if you ask me, these last few days have felt like ten years," I said.

The pitch of the engines changed, and I felt the plane slowly start to lose altitude. "Five minutes!" Sammy Raye yelled from the copilot's seat.

I looked out the window at the partially submerged coral heads below us. It looked as if we were following the reef south.

"You know," Ix-Nay said in what I had learned to recognize as his prophetic voice, "life, when you get right down to it, is no more complicated than the gears on the Fishmobile. But there is one big exception."

"Which is?"

"Which is that the Fishmobile has three basic gears — forward, neutral, and reverse. We have only two. There is no reverse on the road of life, Tully. You just keep moving forward, and every now and then you try to catch a little neutral."

"There's your ticket out of here, Tully!" Sammy Raye yelled to the rear cabin.

I looked down below, where an endless panorama of shallow green water suddenly gave way to a cluster of mangrove islands. They were sitting atop pillars of sub-merged coral, surrounded by a deep blue inner harbor that was protected from all points of the wind. There at an-chor, in the middle, was the *Lucretia,* her green hull glis-tening in the sun like a floating emerald. She wasn't the only boat in the anchorage. A number of small fishing skiffs and dugout canoes were tied alongside the port and starboard rails.

I tapped Drake on the shoulder. "Where are we?" I asked.

"They are called the Dragonfly Cays," he responded and went back to his landing checklist.

We swung around to the south and lined up the chan-nel, where everyone in the tender — Benjamin, the oars-men, and Solomon — looked skyward and waved.

Drake made a perfect landing, then water taxied down the channel to within a hundred yards of the *Lucretia.* He cut the power, scrambled up to the bow hatch, and dropped the anchor. The tender paralleled our course off the left wing, and when the anchor was secure, it nudged carefully alongside.

"I kind of wish I were going with you, kid," Sammy Raye said as he walked down the aisle and opened the rear hatch.

"I kind of wish I knew where I was going," I replied.

"Well, I guess it's time to find out," Ix-Nay said.

"You don't know?"

"Your destination was never discussed. Cleopatra just told us to bring you to the *Lucretia* and gave us this loca-tion. I'm kind of anxious to find out your new zip code myself."

We climbed out of the plane and into the dinghy. Sol-omon grabbed my hand, pulled me toward him, and gave me a big hug. "It be nice to have you back on board, Mista Tully," he said. "How long you goin' to be wit us?"

"That, Solomon, is the question of the day."

I introduced Sammy Raye, Drake, and Ix-Nay to Solomon and the crew. I shook hands with all the oarsmen, who greeted me warmly, and then, at Solomon's command, they took up their familiar task at the sweeps.

"We have a little surprise for you," Solomon said. The young boy in the bow produced his turtle shell and began to tap out a rhythm. The boat once again caught the beat of the song, and then the crew began to sing the chorus from "The Wind Cries Mary." It was quite a welcome back.

We rowed past the dolphin figurehead. Ix-Nay and Sammy Raye hadn't said a word since we had boarded the dinghy, but both of them just looked at the tall ship in wonder as we circled her. Now dwarfed by the towering masts and huge green hull, Ix-Nay said, "I can see why my ancestors thought these ships came out of the clouds."

"I think I gotta get me one of these," Sammy Raye added.

"What are all these boats doing way out here?" I asked Solomon.

"It be a farewell party," he answered.

"For him?" Ix-Nay asked, pointing at me.

"No, for us, mon," Roberto said with a laugh. "We loaded all da provisions for dis voyage in Belize City. Den da captain always come down here to Pelican Cay so as for us to see our families and friends. Day all come out here from Dangriga. We leave tonight on da tide, and we won't see dem again for six months."

We eased along the starboard side of the boat as Solomon conversed rapid-fire with men on the small boats.

They were moving away from the ship to facilitate our coming alongside. Solomon looked to the bow of the boat where the drummer boy tossed a line to a crewman on the gangway.

"Mr. Mars." It was the unmistakable voice of Cleopatra Highbourne. She was standing at the companionway. "I guess we have been delegated as the means of transportation to put a little distance between your recent causes and effects."

"I appreciate the ride, Captain," I replied. "Permission to come aboard, Captain?"

"Permission granted, Mr. Mars," she said with a smile.

36

Not a Bad-Looking Piece of Driftwood

Cleopatra looked at me and then sniffed the air. "Mr. Mars," she said, "you look like a shipwrecked castaway and smell worse than a shrimper on a three-day binge."

"Permission to jump overboard?" I asked.

"Permission granted — as long as you take a bar of soap with you. After that, Solomon will get you squared away in your quarters and into a proper uniform — since you are now the research consultant on the *Lucretia*."

I tore off what was left of my shirt, climbed the spreaders, and did a swan dive into the indigo waters of Dragonfly Lagoon. I am not a religious person, but as I scrubbed away in the salt water from head to toe, I felt about as baptized as I am probably ever going to get.

Meanwhile, Sammy Raye's plane was being towed by the rubber dinghy. Drake was straddling the bow, waving at me. When they got to the *Lucretia*, they passed a line to the stern, and the plane drifted back on the current aft of the transom.

As I climbed back on board, Cleopatra was giving

Sammy Raye and Ix-Nay a tour of the ship. Solomon was there to greet me, and I followed him below. I smiled as we went down the companionway and passed the cabin where I had spent my first night on the *Lucretia*. I was a guest no more.

He took me forward to the crew's quarters to a much smaller cabin. "Da captain said dat after da big problem you be havin', you might be wantin' to have a good night's sleep. Dis will be your cabin for da trip."

"Mr. Solomon, I would rather stand watch. I really do feel fine."

"Den you can join our section for da second dogwatch dis evenin'."

He told me we would sail on the tide just before sunset. Since he was now my boss, I asked where we were headed.

"Cayo Loco."

Solomon left me in my cabin. On the bunk was a pair of clean khaki shorts and a blue crew shirt. I shaved, showered, and stopped by the galley and whiffed down two huge ham sandwiches. Then I presented myself for inspection.

The bon voyage party was under way. I stared in disbelief as I walked toward the bow and saw Sammy Raye and Cleopatra dancing a merengue around the foremast — and they were not alone. Even the *Lucretia* seemed to sway back and forth on her anchor to the beat of the music. "You look pretty good, Cowboy," Cleopatra said as I stood at the rail.

The entire forward section of the ship was alive with gyrating bodies. It was a foam party without foam, but something was very different. This was not some meaningless, drunken beach orgy. This was a celebration of life, and it had been done this way for hundreds of years when a ship was about to sail. It was about laughter and tears, good-byes and good-luck wishes to sailors from the families they would be leaving behind.

Someone grabbed my hand from out of the crowd. It was Ix-Nay, and he dragged me to the limbo line. I followed him under the bar that was two feet off the deck as my new shipmates applauded.

That famous group of musicians from Dangriga called the Turtle Shell Band had set up in the forepeak. Two guitar players and three drummers were draped in elaborately rigged harnesses, and from them hung a variety of turtle shells in different shapes and sizes. With some signal known only to the rhythm section, the drummers began beating on the shells in that syncopated groove that immediately said "Africa" without a lyric being sung. Benjamin, the drummer boy from the dinghy, joined in with his little shell, and that seemed to put the party into high gear. Those who knew the song sang along. Those who didn't faked it, and everybody danced.

"Mr. Coconuts?" Drake said, nervously walking into the crowd and tapping Sammy Raye on the shoulder.

Sammy Raye, still dancing in place, turned and faced Drake.

"If we are going to make it back to Punta Margarita by sunset, we had best be gettin' a move on."

Sammy Raye suddenly looked like a kid at the fair who had just dropped his foot-long chili dog in the dirt.

"Well, I guess this is good-bye," Ix-Nay said, and I realized what he meant.

With the sounds of the party in our ears, Ix-Nay and Sammy Raye boarded the rubber boat, and I cast off the bowline as Roberto steered for the plane. "You have a very worried look on your face," Ix-Nay added.

"It's all happening so fast."

"The world spins at one thousand miles an hour. This is nothing," Ix-Nay said and smiled.

"I was worried about Mr. Twain too," I told him.

"Don't worry, Tully. If we sprung you from a plane ride to prison, we can certainly look after your horse and your artwork. And when you get settled on Cayo Loco, we will bring them to you."

"How did you know where I was going?" I asked.

"I am a shaman, remember? Besides, Cleopatra told me. It sounds like an interesting place."

"I guess I'm about to find out."

The dinghy pulled alongside the rear hatch of the seaplane, and Drake vaulted aboard. We helped Sammy through the hatch, and Ix-Nay and I stood there, bobbing in the ocean together.

"Thanks for everything, Ix-Nay," I said as I grabbed his hand. "I never really got to thank Archie, Bucky, and Captain Kirk. Tell them —"

"You don't have to tell any of us anything. That's what friends are for."

The chain clanked as Drake pulled the anchor aboard through the bow hatch.

"Sammy Raye, please give Donna Kay and Clark my best, and tell them I'm sorry I can't make the wedding!" I called into the cabin.

"I will do that," Sammy Raye said with a laugh. "You are always welcome at Pinkland, and I'm going to look into this Thelma thing for you."

"I would appreciate that."

"Take care of yourself out there. I'd stay away from any future foam parties, if I were you," Ix-Nay said.

"For my penance, I'm giving you my skiff," I told him.

"What?" he gasped.

"You heard me. She's yours, and don't try to refuse. The ocean gods would be angry."

With that, the starboard propeller started to turn, and the engine sputtered to life. I let go of the wing, and the plane began to move away.

Roberto steered the rubber boat out of the middle of the channel where we would watch the flying boat take off. I could tell by the disappearing flats at the edge of the channel that the tide was coming on pretty strong. I stuck my bare foot in the ocean and felt the current push against my leg. Looking at the lagoon, the ship, and the plane, I thought back to the day I had loaded Mr. Twain in my horse trailer and had decided to take him to the shore. Never in my wildest dreams did I ever imagine that I would be where I now was.

In the distance, the engine noise rose in volume, and the plane threw up a sheet of white water as she clawed her way to the surface. Then she glided elegantly on top of the waves, moved down the channel, and lifted off. She did a beautiful, slow climbing turn that cleared the masts of the *Lucretia* by more than ten feet, and we rode the current back to the ship.

As we brought the dinghy up on deck, the sun hung in the western sky just above the faint outline of the mainland, and the tide rushed at river speed into the lagoon. The party was winding down, and people had broken off into smaller groups for their final good-byes. Then came an eerie yet familiar sound as Solomon stood on the bowsprit and blew into a large conch shell. It was the song of the ocean.

"The tide is right," Mr. Solomon called out. "Lucretians, prepare to weigh anchor."

In an orderly and quiet procession, the locals going ashore moved back to the gangway and into the boats. They knew better than anyone that the tide would not wait.

The anchor was stowed, the sails were hung out, and the *Lucretia* rode the land breeze and the current out of Dragonfly Lagoon and into the open sea. As the sun dropped behind the horizon, I watched the shoreline shrink. The watches changed, and Mr. Solomon was at the wheel when Cleopatra came on deck.

"I haven't danced like that in years," she said. Her smile was followed by a long period of silence. Then she added, "You are wondering if you made the right decision, aren't you?"

"Kind of."

"It's called being between Scylla and Charybdis," she said.

"Sounds like Greek to me," I joked.

"It is. Homer."

"The Odyssey?"

"You think you had a tough time in San Pedro. That was nothing compared to poor Odysseus."

"I don't remember Scylla and Charybdis."

"At one point during his epic voyage, Odysseus had to make a very difficult passage between two equally dangerous perils." Cleopatra studied the sail configuration as she talked. "I think we can run up the fisherman, Mr. Solomon."

"Aye, Captain," Solomon said from behind the wheel. He called to his watch to set the big sail.

"Anyway," Cleopatra continued, "Scylla was a beautiful maiden loved by Poseidon, god of the sea, but her rival, Amphitrite, fed her magic herbs that turned her into a monster. She was horrible to behold, with six heads, and each head had three sets of teeth."

"That would be Thelma Barston in my world," I said.

"I have found that dragons come in many shapes and sizes. To say the least, Scylla was not dealing with her fate very well. She was pissed off at the world, and she went to dwell on a mountain in a high cave overlooking the sea. When ships passed by, each of her terrible mouths would snake down out of the cave and have a sailor for lunch."

"Sounds familiar," I said.

Cleopatra kept one eye on the sail as it was raised. "That's not all," she went on. "On the other side of the narrow channel, beneath an immense wild fig tree, lay a huge and dangerous whirlpool called Charybdis. Three times a day, it sucked in and spit out the sea. The fate of Odysseus was to sail between Scylla and Charybdis."

"Is there something like that where we're headed?" I asked.

"You can never be certain." Cleopatra looked off into the distance. "There could be a whirlpool or two ahead — like the one that just sucked you into all that foam and spit you out in the Dragonfly Cays."

"I did feel like I was going under for the third time out there in the bush. But that was my own stupidity," I said.

"I am not sure it was stupidity. You men have that inherent problem when the little head thinks for the big one. Or maybe it was because you forgot this," she said and pulled the Lister's conch shell out of her shirt pocket. "Whatever it was, the point is this: Like Odysseus, you made it through. You are still here," Cleopatra said in a kind, counseling tone.

"That I am." My fingers tingled when I wrapped them around the shell.

"Try and hang on to this conch, will you?" she added.

We watched the twilight sky and the first stars of the night pop through the dark, mysterious curtain of the universe. "Take up a bit on the staysail, Roberto," she called out. Instantly there was a definite increase in our speed across the water. "Looks good, Mr. Solomon," she said. Then she turned and looked me in the eye. "It seems like luck is on your side again, Mr. Mars."

"Looks that way, Captain."

"Son, I have been around a long time, and I can tell you that in saving one's self from his own devices, there is luck involved. But it is more about friends. You better thank your lucky stars and that shell of yours that you have a few. They came to your rescue because you were worth saving."

"Thanks." It was about the only word I could say.

"We weren't just socializing here, you know. We are going to get Thelma out of your life. Sammy Raye seems to think there are a few skeletons in her closet that she might not want to share with the public." I didn't even ask what they were up to. I just wanted to do my job on the boat, whatever that was. Cleopatra continued, "So now it's my job to keep you out of sight and out of trouble for a while. I figure with all of your expert knowledge about lighthouses, you can help me find the soul of the light."

"Sounds good to me."

"Mr. Solomon!" she called out. "Let's take a look at the chart for a second. I am thinking of stopping at Port Antonio. Mr. Mars can take her." Solomon gave me the course to steer and moved from behind the wheel. I stepped in.

"You are heading for the Windward Passage. Cuba is on one side and Jamaica is on the other. Try not to hit either of them," Cleopatra added.

"Aye-aye, Captain," I answered with a smile.

My hands again welcomed the feel of the spoked wheel.

I scanned the whole ship from the bowsprit to the stern. There was just enough daylight left in the west to make out an object in the water just outside the wake. I grabbed a pair of binoculars and focused on the object. It was a long, dark tree trunk covered with barnacles and knots. Sticking up at one end of the log was a branch about two feet tall; it looked like a tiny mast. At the tip, a small green cluster of new-growth leaves swayed in the wind.

I ran my fingers over the little wooden gecko hanging around my neck. Johnny's words came instantly to mind. He had told me to become a seed and ride the winds and the tides — to follow the song of the ocean to my appointed shore. Johnny's prophesy had come true.

I had thought that Lost Boys was the beach where I was to take root, but the weeds of my past had grown larger and more threatening than I had realized. That little branch sitting atop that water-soaked old log told me that I was exactly where I was supposed to be — floating along on the winds of time a little bit longer.

I was not yet quite ready to come ashore, but the *Lucretia* was not a bad-looking piece of driftwood to be floating on.

37

The Spare Bulb

To: Tully Mars
Cayo Loco
From: Willie Singer
Vanuatu

Dear Tully,
If you thought my practice letters were long
before, you haven't read anything yet. Hold your
breath and stretch out under a palm tree. Do I have
a tale for you.

Somebody once told me that you don't have to
go looking for stories. The good ones will come to
you. I think that just happened to me.

But let me back up.

It all started with our departure from New
Caledonia, which of course Monsieur Parfait
orchestrated.

To sum it up, our departure from French
Polynesia was not subtle. We circled the

lighthouse at Amedee in the company of not one
but three helicopters and several private planes.
When I talked via radio to Parfait, who was in one
of the helicopters, and asked him what in the hell
was going on, he just smiled, waved at me across
the sky, and said, "Willie, Willie. By now haven't
you learned that we French don't do anything
simply?"

That was an understatement.

Well, with the day starting like that, I should
have known it probably wouldn't end any
differently. Parfait had mentioned a contact in
Vanuatu. It does get my curiosity up when a
Frenchman tells me to go and look up someone
named Waltham.

We plotted a direct course for the most northern
island of the chain, Espíritu Santo, and the town of
Luganville. That's where my search for Waltham
would begin. A look at the chart showed that the
chain of islands that make up Vanuatu resemble
the Windward Islands of the Caribbean. The
difference is there are a lot more bigger, active
volcanoes on this side of the world.

The weather remained beautiful for the whole
trip, and we actually had a slight tailwind, so we
stayed at about three thousand feet, where the air
was cool. In a couple of hours, the peaks of the
highest mountains began to rise above the horizon,
and we went down on deck for a better look.

The island was easily identifiable from the air; I
had read about it in my pilot's guide, and it truly
did look like a small dog sitting on its hind legs.
We ran a systems check as we neared the coast,

which was prompted in part by Parfait's parting words: "You'll love Vanuatu. They haven't eaten anybody there since 1969."

All systems were go, and it looked as if our risk of falling out of the sky and into a boiling cauldron was quite remote. I pulled the power back, and we descended to slightly above treetop level, which revealed rain forest canopies, driftwood-littered beaches, and a multitude of palms bent by the trade winds. From the cockpit window, I could see that the string of islands gave way to the open waters of the Bougainville Strait, and puffy cumulus clouds signaled a large landmass beyond the horizon. That would be Espíritu Santo.

These were historic seaplane waters we were flying over. After the surprise attack on Pearl Harbor and the rapid conquest of the Philippines, the real-life chess game for Japanese control of this part of the world went into full swing. The battle for Australia and New Zealand was on, and that is when the pawnlike Solomon Islands — and the amphibious aircraft that flew in and around them — suddenly took on enormous strategic importance. As a result of the ensuing conflict, the natural harbors and bays of Espíritu Santo had been transformed overnight from sleepy backwater ports to major staging-and-support areas for the pivotal battles on the islands of Guadalcanal, Tulagi, and Savo. At one time, eight Navy and Marine airfields and several PBY squadrons were based on Espíritu Santo alone. After all these years, I wondered if there was any trace of that

seaplane legacy still left. It did not take long for
my question to be answered.

Espíritu Santo is a bit too Catholic a name for the
locals, who refer to both the island and the main
town of Luganville as simply "Santo."

"November 928WS, this is Santo Tower.
Welcome. Welcome" came the excited voice of the
controller who fed us our landing instructions,
interspersed with compliments about our plane.

After landing, we were directed to a remote
corner of the airport, where we were met by a
customs officer, a policeman, and a film crew from
the local TV station. A large crowd of curious
bystanders aimed their video cameras at the plane.
Unlike the welcoming committee from our initial
arrival at New Caledonia, where it looked as if we
might be deported before Parfait saved the day, the
Vanuatu officials were quite pleasant. They asked
questions about the plane and wanted to have their
pictures taken in front of *The Flying Pearl,* which
of course I happily agreed to.

When they asked what we were doing, I just
said, "Passing through on the way to Hong
Kong." It never raised an eyebrow from the
official. He stamped our inbound docs and
passports. I paid the landing fee, and we all
smiled for the camera.

Things were so friendly that, at one point, I was
tempted to inquire about Waltham, but my
instincts told me to hold my questions.

Like everything else in these islands, the heat has a way of shortening the time it takes to do anything that isn't protected by shade or air conditioners, so our jubilant welcome was over in about five minutes. I had told the crew that we would stay the night, and if I wasn't able to contact Mr. Waltham, we would follow our original flight plan to the Solomons and the Philippines, and on to Hong Kong.

I called in our fuel order to the tower, and they replied that the truck would be right there. I just crossed my fingers and then ducked under the wing of *The Flying Pearl,* away from the sweltering heat of the tarmac, praying that the truck would actually come. To our astonishment, it appeared within minutes of our call.

"I am Jetfuel Joe!" a jolly man shouted from the open window of the fuel truck. It came to a halt in front of the left wing. "Welcome to Vanuatu. Dis is a beautiful plane you have here. We don't see many like dis no mo." He was a small man with no front teeth and a bushy Afro under his grease-stained Dodgers baseball hat. He wore surf Jams and a Bob Marley T-shirt. I liked him already. "Can I help you?" he asked.

"Well, Jetfuel Joe, I am Captain Will, and we are happy to be here. You think you can come up with about a thousand gallons of avgas for this old girl?"

"No problem, mon. I am way ahead of you. Dis

here is da avgas truck," he said with a huge, gapped smile.

"Well, let's fill 'er up," I said, and I climbed up on the wing.

Looking around the airport, I could see that the presence of more than half a million U.S. soldiers, sailors, and Marines sixty years ago had left a lasting impression on the town.

As we fueled the plane, Joe showed no more than the usual curiosity that *The Flying Pearl* always creates, but when we finished, and after I had paid the bill, I invited him inside. I know a plane freak when I see one. We walked through the aft cabin where all our gear — from life rafts to fishing gear to surfboards — was bundled up and cinched down. Then we passed through the small galley — the bunk beds and the gallery of photos attached to the bulkhead — to the flight deck. Taking it all in, Jetfuel Joe said, "You have come a long way."

"You're right," I told him.

We made our way to the flight deck, and Jetfuel Joe let out a whistle when he saw the instruments and gauges. "Go ahead. Sit up there," I said and pointed at the pilot's seat.

He cautiously wiggled his small body up into the seat and put his hands on the wooden yoke. Then he stared straight ahead and immediately became silent — as if he had gone into a trance. Suddenly he looked up at me and said, "You from Florida in the U.S. — Pensacola."

"I am from Mississippi," I said.

"But in dat pitcha out der you in Pensacola," he said with a strain of confusion in his voice.

"This plane has been to Pensacola many times."

"Florida a good place."

"You ever been?" I asked him.

"No," he said. Then he paused before adding, "But I do know about it."

There was something about the way he said those words that rang a bell. It's that sixth-sense thing you develop if you spend a lot of time in not-so-populated corners of the world where one thing actually means another. It is the code of the road, a way of saying "All is not what you think it appears to be here, and we probably ought to have a beer and discuss it." So that is exactly what we did.

The crew grabbed a cab and followed us into town. I rode through Luganville on the back of Jetfuel Joe's moped. The waterfront looked like an aging World War II movie set, with numerous rusting Quonset huts, steel walls, and the remnants of a different time scattered along the road.

I had traveled eight thousand perilous miles across the Pacific without ever feeling the kind of danger I felt on the back of Jetfuel Joe's moped as he weaved his way through trucks, cars, and tour buses. Finally we pulled up to a place called the Coolidge Bar.

The bar was not a tribute to the thirtieth president of the United States. I don't think it was the kind of place Mr. Coolidge would have frequented. It was named for the old passenger liner that bore the boring former president's name and had been converted to a troopship in the war. The ship had been sunk entering the harbor after it hit a couple of friendly mines and was now a big attraction for scuba divers.

The Coolidge Bar was a little of the Complete Angler in Bimini and Le Select in St. Bart's, one of those waterfront bars that serves as a gathering place for sailors, pilots, travelers, and the occasional reprobate. All of the above seemed to be present in the Coolidge Bar that afternoon.

Jetfuel Joe disappeared, and almost instantly he reappeared with a couple of Tusker beers wedged between his fingers. He pointed to a table away from the bar. We sipped our beers, and then the crew took off on a tour of the town. I agreed to meet them later for dinner.

I still had to try to contact Waltham, and I knew from our short time together that Joe would be the right guy to ask.

We ordered another beer. Joe's father, like most everyone on the island, had worked for the U.S. Navy during the war. He asked me where I had been, and I told him. "You should land in da harba in da plane. Make an air show for everybody. People here love seaplanes. Most people, dat is."

The way his sentence trailed off from happiness to anger aroused my curiosity. "What people?" I asked.

With that, Jetfuel Joe looked around the bar and then stood up. "Captain Will, let's please take a walk," he said.

To anyone with good sense, this request for a

A Salty Piece of Land 369

"walk" should have been politely turned down, but it bounced off me like a Ping-Pong ball. Off I went with Joe, pushing the envelope one more time.

It took us about fifteen minutes to walk back through town. We passed Chinese stores, kava bars, dive shops, and government buildings on our way to a small park near the river. I followed Joe to a corner of the park behind a giant ficus tree, and when he was sure we hadn't been followed, he turned and said, "You bring a message from Captain Keed?"

"Who?" I asked.

"Captain Keed from Pensacola."

"The only Captain Kidd I know was a pirate from New York who was hung by the British three hundred years ago," I said.

Jetfuel Joe didn't see the humor in my answer. "Der annuda Captain Keed, and he is a god." There was reverence in Joe's voice. He continued, "Captain Keed was a seaplane pilot from Florida. *You* are a seaplane pilot from Florida. You come from Captain Keed."

"I told you. I'm from Mississippi."

"But da plane from Pensacola."

Joe was expecting me to understand something, but I didn't quite get it. I figured this was the perfect place and time to ask my question. "Joe, have you ever heard of somebody in Santo named Waltham?" The smile instantly returned to Joe's face, and he waved a finger at me. "You pilots. You very much smart."

"You know him?" I asked.

"I know him, and he know you. But he not in Santo. He on Dalvalo."

"Where's that?"

"South, much south."

"Can we fly there?" I asked.

That question started Jetfuel Joe laughing loudly and shaking his head. "You could, but you can't," he answered.

That one threw me for a momentary loop.

"Tings on Dalvalo are different from Santo. Waltam, he not so liked by da gubment people. It not be wise to take da plane der. Could be trouble for you. But if you really want to meet him, der is annuda way," he said with a smile.

My initial hunch to keep quiet at the airport about Waltham had proved to be right. He seemed to be some kind of dope dealer or conspirator, but why would someone with a pedigree like Philippe Parfait tell me I should contact him?

The easiest choices in life just aren't that fun or interesting. The practical voice in my ear was saying I should let the whole Waltham thing go. He was probably a smuggler or a revolutionary and somebody who could cause me problems simply by my mentioning his name to the wrong people. This was clearly another wild-goose chase — it was time to go crank up the *Pearl*, forget about lighthouse hunting, get back on course, and move on to our original destination of Hong Kong. But that other voice in my head, the mischievous, reckless, romantic one, kept saying, "Things don't add up here, and you need to find this Waltham guy. He has a big answer to some kind of big question. And if the route to his whereabouts takes you down a back alley in the middle of an island with a long history of cannibalism, then right on, man. That is the way you are supposed to go."

I guess you don't have to be a rocket scientist to figure out which voice I listened to.

Somehow I had the foresight to make a call to my crew at the hotel. I told them I was going south for a day, and they should enjoy themselves until I got back. If anybody asked about my whereabouts, I told them, they should say that I had met an old sailing buddy in the Coolidge Bar and that I went off with him to dive on some old war-relic wrecks up in the Torres Islands. I would be back in a couple of days. That was my last lucid thought for a very long time.

Joe told me we needed to see a man about a freighter, and off we went down the backstreets of Santo to his neighborhood kava bar.

How I got from the kava bar to one of the most remote islands in one of the most remote countries in the South Pacific on a tramp steamer is just one of those events you chalk up to the roller-coaster theory of life: You buy a ticket willingly and let yourself be strapped into a seat. The ride starts out slow, like the little train being pulled to the top of the roller-coaster track, and that's when gravity takes over. After that, you hang on for dear life.

This was not my first experience with strange

brews. About fifteen years ago, I took off on a wild hair for Rio at the urging of a friend who was there. Somewhere in the middle of the Rio Carnival, I was taken by a drummer friend of mine from Brazil to the rehearsal of one of the main dance groups. They were named Beja Flora. Though the women and their costumes — or lack of them — were enough to hold my attention, I was also intrigued by the drummers, who sat in a tight circle behind the dancers and pounded out rhythms all night. I started to fade at about four in the morning, and the drummers were still going strong. I asked my friend what they were on, assuming it was cocaine, speed, or some other stimulant, and he handed me a cup. "It's called hoodlum drink, and it's only given to the drummers."

"What's in it?" I asked.

"Nobody really knows. It's a mystery."

That was good enough for me. I guzzled my hoodlum drink, danced until dawn, and the last thing I remember was serenading a couple of Brazilian models as we stretched on a launchpad in the mountains above Rio while hang gliders leaped into the morning sky.

After that, you would think I would have steered clear of any similar situations. But I didn't.

Above the kava bar was a sign that read THE BLACK HOLE. That should have been a warning, but through the doors I went. I followed Jetfuel Joe down the rabbit hole, continuing to listen to the more adventurous voice of my inner child.

As I walked through the door of the Black

Hole, music was blaring from the jukebox. Joe told me the singer was Don Tiki. The song was called "The Natives Are Restless." I immediately noticed the lack of haoles in the joint, but the owner acted as if I were some kind of long-lost relative. The next thing I knew, a big bowl of muddy-looking liquid was carried out to a table in the corner, and the owner escorted me there. Joe told me it was kava.

After those beers back at the Coolidge, I was game for anything, and it was important for me to be the not-so-ugly American. Joe told me that being asked to drink kava with the owner was an honor. To refuse it would be to refuse friendship. I wasn't there to make enemies.

Joe said the small coconut-shell cup was called a low tide and the big cassava bowl next to it was called a high tide. Either was fine. I watched the owner gulp his down, lick his lips, and smile. He clearly enjoyed the experience.

As a sailor, I had learned that the more water under you, the better — so I downed the high tide. Unlike the *fufu* cocktails that you might see on a brightly colored plastic drink menu in a tiki bar on Waikiki Beach, with cute names like Kava Kocktails or Krakatau Killers, real kava tastes like shit — a mixture of mud-puddle water and diesel fuel.

The good news is this: after gulping it down, I didn't throw up like you do if you eat a peyote button or two. But kava, I can now tell you, will make you see God with one eye and those flying monkeys from *The Wizard of Oz* with the other.

My lips immediately went numb, and my speech sounded like a record on a turntable being played at the wrong speed. Let's just say, for comparison's sake, that if the Brazilian hoodlum drink was a hang glider, then a bowl of kava was like being launched from the deck of a carrier in an F-14.

Joe showed me a picture of an old tramp steamer, and I remember some vague reference to me being on it. The only thing was, when I went to look at the picture, I saw two boats. A few minutes later, my legs quit working, and then I felt as if I were trying to watch a 3-D movie without glasses. I had hazy recollections of being carried, of pointing out the Southern Cross in the sky, and of ascending a gangplank of some sort as if I were making an assault on the final steps to the summit of Mount Everest without oxygen. When I woke up the next morning — don't ask me how — something told me I was on the deck of a rolling ship.

I had memories of singing and dancing, meteor showers, and the sky lit up with orange streaks of fire, but when my brain returned to this dimension and this planet, I was informed by Jetfuel Joe that seventeen of the nineteen hours required to reach Dalvalo had gone by. Somehow I had wound up in a hammock strung from the cargo crane, and I had wrapped myself up in my own little cocoon.

The strangest thing was that when I pulled myself up to the smell of coffee brewing and bread baking, I felt as if I had spent a week at a five-star spa. I can't tell you why, but I felt no residual effect from the kava — no headache, no flashback. The numbness had left my body, and my eyes were clear. I felt as if my batteries were fully charged for the first time in years. When I thought back on it, I realized that before my first bowl of kava in Santo, what little sleep I had been getting was in the form of combat naps on the planes or pit stops in bad hotel beds. There's a favorite song of mine with a line that says, "I must confess, I could use some rest." Well, I got it. And since I had missed the first seventeen of the nineteen hours of the trip, I was in the perfect frame of mind to enjoy the last two hours as the world went by at eight knots.

The ship was a very old island trader that reminded me of those boats you see up the Miami River. She was called the *Copra Queen*. Her rusty decks were crowded with an assortment of humans, animals, fruits, vegetables, and a variety of transportation vehicles that ranged from skateboards to mopeds to a large diesel generator that was lashed to the superstructure and bound for one of the southern islands of Vanuatu.

Joe seemed to know most of the passengers and made sure I did too. "Dees all Keedos," he said.

"What are Keedos?" I asked.

"We believe in Captain Keed's return. Dat whay we all going to Dalvalo for da big day, and we here to protect da messenger."

"And that would be who?" I asked.

"Dat would be you," Joe said.

Somehow I had become an important piece of some bizarre puzzle created by a cargo cult in the

South Pacific. I didn't think that the deck of the ship that morning was the place to explain to Joe, once and for all, that I came with no message from a long-dead Navy pilot from Pensacola. I didn't want to disappoint them, but I was thinking that history as a whole hadn't been too kind to messengers. Also that lingering cannibal thing was running through my kava-sharpened brain.

As the sun peeked above the gray horizon, the Keedos were gathered around a little portable barbecue grill where an old man was opening cans of Spam and dropping the thick slices onto the hot fire. I had sworn off Spam since my cafeteria days in high school, but the hunger from no dinner the previous evening, the salt air of the morning, and the smell of sizzling meat made my stomach start growling.

Jetfuel Joe handed me a cup of coffee and motioned for me to sit at the fire. Then he encouraged me to attempt a few basic phrases in Bislama, the local pidgin dialect. The crowd seemed very pleased with my efforts and began patting me on the back and calling out my name. I figured that because I was the only white man on the boat, it was just natural curiosity that made both the people and the animals stare at me with such intensity.

The old man at the grill shouted something in Bislama, and everybody around the fire got excited as he began to remove the charred Spam from the grill and distribute it to outreached hands. The old man pointed a piece of the meat at me, and I grabbed it and began to chew.

"Tastes a lot better than I remember it," I said.

Joe chomped on a slice of Spam and licked the hot grease from his fingers. "Da old fellas say Spam taste lots like long pie, and dat why it so popular."

"What's long pie?" I asked.

"Roast leg of missionary," he said without skipping a beat, and he kept smiling as the gathering of Keedos feasted and laughed in the morning light.

I had no choice but to swallow the Spam. An old lady nearby sensed my reaction to the story and offered me half a sliced mango, which I gulped down.

The *Copra Queen* pushed on through fairly calm seas and light wind. After breakfast, I picked up a little more information about my "high tide" passage on the ship. I was told that I had indeed seen the sky on fire. It was the volcano on Tanna Island named Mount Yasur, and it had been going off as we passed. The boat was still covered with fine volcanic ash, which the crew was busy washing away. Jetfuel Joe told me that the English explorer Captain James Cook had called Mount Yasur the largest lighthouse in the Pacific because it was constantly erupting and could be seen from a distance of fifty miles. As for the dancing ocean, Joe explained that during the night, the boat was surrounded by a large school of playful dolphins that put on an acrobatic demonstration. Everyone, except me, had leaned over the port rail to get a closer look.

Shortly after breakfast, we rounded the southern point of Atofrum Island, and there, directly ahead, was what I somehow knew to be the island of Dalvalo. Immediately, the picture of the mythical Bali Hai, home of Bloody Mary, came to mind.

At first I thought I was still feeling the effect of the kava, but soon I realized that I wasn't seeing double. Dalvalo rose up out of the sea as a pair of perfectly shaped volcanic cones with a low, flat land bridge between them. A long black plume of smoke rose up into the pastel dawn sky from the easternmost summit.

"Da shortest, dat be Kami, and da big one be Poodi," Jetfuel Joe said. "Dat where we all come from, and dat be where we all go."

"So heaven is a pair of volcanoes?" I asked.

"No, no, no," Joe said. "It go like dis. Keedos believe dat at one time Dalvalo was da onliest land in da universe, and dat volcano der, Poodi, was and still is da originator of all tings.

"According to legend, in dat time der were many wild animals on Dalvalo — lions, tigers, elephants, and sharks as big as dis boat. Deez were very dangerous creatures, and human people are what dey had for breakfast, lunch, and suppa. Well, da first chief of Dalvalo, named Huakelle, come up wif a plan to distribute some of dis danger elsewhere in da universe. So he took fiery lava dat squirt off da volcano, and he trows it in all directions and creates Europe, Asia, Africa, Australia, and America. Some of da small drops of hot lava got caught and was scatted by da wind, and dis what made da rest of da islands of Vanuatu and all Melanesia.

"Da chief den ordered giant canoes to be built. Not only was der too many dangerous animals on Dalvalo, der was too many people, so he sent a bunch of animals and people off in da giant canoe to da new land. Most a da canoes went to Africa, but some got caught up in storms and wrecked on da reef. People was tossed into da sea, and when dey finally got to land again, dey noticed dat da salt wattah had bleached dem white. Dat is how you got here.

"After dat, da people of Dalvalo lived to demselves and to der customs till da Protestants show up and say, 'No more kava drinking, no more magic, no more wife swapping, no more, read dis Bible.' It was den dat Captain Keed show up and make everyting all right."

Standing on the deck of that freighter, staring at the volcano, I realized that Joe's description of the creation of the world made perfect sense to me.

Thirty minutes later, the distant, almost miragelike image of the island dissolved into a shoreline, a river mouth, and a small village. Jetfuel Joe said it was called Huakelle, just like the first chief, and it was the village where he was born and raised. I asked if this was where we would find Waltham, and he just smiled. "You no need to go looking for Waltam. He find you."

A fleet of primitive outrigger canoes lined the black-sand beach in the distance, and what looked to be an old Navy landing craft was anchored offshore. A flurry of activity commenced the moment we dropped anchor inside the reef. Drums were played, children poured out of the grass huts

and lined the shore waving, and near-naked men
dragged the outriggers into the ocean, climbed
aboard, and began racing toward us. But the most
bizarre greeting came from what appeared to be a
group of men dressed like American soldiers, who
rolled a 40mm howitzer out to the beach and fired
several salutes, which were answered from the
bridge of the freighter with the air horn.

As I watched all this, I thought to myself,
"Where in the hell am I?"

As if answering my silent question, Jetfuel Joe
said, "We home now, Willie. Time to practice your
pidgin. It a very big time now on Dalvalo, and you
bring de good luck to da peoples. Wait and see."

As the first canoe reached our ship, the people
on the boat waved and shouted, and the paddlers
of the canoes returned the greeting. Some on the
ship dove into the water and swam toward the
approaching canoes.

The landing craft followed the small armada
and came alongside, and a large cargo net was
draped down the hull. The crew busied themselves
with loading and unloading cargo, unaffected by
the party going on around them. The ship itself
instantly became a high-diving platform for the
barely dressed young men and a few women in the
canoes. Music played on deck, flower leis were
exchanged, and the sky was filled with an aerial
bombardment of flips, somersaults, and swan dives
into the crystal clear waters of the protected
lagoon.

I watched Jetfuel Joe climb a ladder up to the
top of the ship, and I followed his trail. How many

times in your life do you get to experience being welcomed as a messenger from the gods on a small ship on the shores of a remote South Pacific island? When in Polynesia, do as the Polynesians. So off the boat I leaped.

Maybe it was the remnants of the kava, or a flashback to my high-school diving days, but I executed a front flip and plunged deep into the water. When I surfaced, the paddlers in the canoes were clapping wildly and chanting, *"Keed bok, Keed bok, Keed bok."* It would take a couple of days to figure out what they were so happy about.

As I swam to a nearby canoe, a beautiful young girl in the bow of the boat took a flowered lei from around her neck, revealing a pair of perfect breasts that mirrored the twin volcanic peaks of Dalvalo. She dropped the lei around my neck as I was hoisted aboard.

I was welcomed ashore with more hugs and flowers, and then Jetfuel Joe spoke in pidgin to the crowd. When he was finished, they all cheered and guided me through the village to one of the Quonset huts. Joe and I were followed by a big man carrying a bamboo copy of an M1 rifle. He wore nothing but a pair of ammo belts across his chest and a piece of decorated fabric wrapped around his penis. He and Joe led me into the hut.

Inside, it looked like a time capsule from 1942: a gray-painted concrete floor, government-issue desks, bunk beds, and ceiling fans. On the wall hung an assortment of old black-and-white photos of U.S. Navy sailors, airplanes, and local warriors.

In the center of the wall was an enlarged photo that showed an old Catalina PBY flying boat on a beach. Stretched across the wing was a long line of natives, and in the middle one lone white man stood in a Navy uniform.

I pointed to the photo. "Captain Keed?" I asked Joe.

With great solemnity, he stared at the picture and smiled. "Dat Captain Keed," he said. "Dat is why we are here." Joe stood for a moment like a pilgrim at Lourdes, and then he clapped his hands together. "Dis Berkeley. He speak good English. He your man till I come back." Joe then said something to Berkeley in pidgin.

"Me you man," Berkeley said with a smile.

"Deez you quatahs," Joe told me. "Rest up. Big day tomorrow. I go see family. Check you lattah. You need someting, tell Berkeley." With that, Jetfuel Joe saluted and disappeared out the door into the bright sunlight.

I took a walk around the village with Berkeley. It was immediately apparent that Huakelle bore the visible signs of several cultural clashes. Quonset huts and thatched-roof huts sat side by side, and an American flag flew on a tall bamboo pole next to the artillery that had been dragged down to the beach for our arrival.

Back when we were en route to Espíritu Santo in the *Pearl,* I had read a few chapters about these islands, briefly preparing for my voyage. I knew that in the heyday of whaling in the Pacific, there had been a settlement of whalers and loggers on Dalvalo. As usual, the sailors brought along the diseases of the times and had infected the island. The locals did the logical thing in those days and wiped out the settlement.

Across the river from Huakelle, the charred remnants of those times still stood — the decaying wooden pilings of the pier, several burned-out stone buildings, and a tombstone on a hill. I crossed the shallow river for a closer look and found a collection of whale bones on the beach that had been assembled into a makeshift monument.

As I wandered through the graveyard, I spotted several English surnames with military titles and the letters USN carved on a row of bamboo crosses. The graves were lined with pink conch shells and covered with fresh flowers. I asked Berkeley about this, but he didn't answer my question. "Wal-tam explain it all," he told me.

My tour of the ruins was cut short by the sound of laughter; a group of children had followed me across the river. They led me down to the beach and into the ocean for what I thought would be a quick swim. Instead, it turned into a scene from a water park back in the States.

All the children began imitating airplanes, using their arms as wings and making motor sounds with their mouths. They buzzed around haphazardly in the shallow water until one of them yelled something. Then they immediately lined up into an attack-fighter wing formation and took up a course for the whale bones. It was infectious behavior. I too turned myself into a plane and joined the squadron for the bombing run. We chased one another around the shallow water to the delight of a group of onlookers who had gathered on the beach, and once again they began chanting, *"Keed bok, Keed bok."* Something told me this was all leading somewhere, but I had no idea what I would find when I got there.

After the aquatic dogfight, I asked Berkeley about getting something to eat, and from out of nowhere, grilled lobsters, poi, slices of fresh pineapple, and a bucket of cold beer were brought to the beach by a procession of young girls.

After lunch, I decided to heed Jetfuel Joe's advice and returned to my hut for a nap. Before I closed my eyes, I thought that if the world all went to hell, Dalvalo wouldn't be a bad place to be stuck.

I don't know how long I slept, but I was awakened by a loud rumble and realized that my bunk bed was moving. I flashed back to a time when I was laid up in a swanky hospital in Los Angeles with a broken leg when an earthquake hit. Instead of caring for their patient — me — the nurses in the room completely panicked and ran out into the hallway to seek shelter. They left me dangling in traction to ride out the tremor.

I am a swamp creature. Heat, mosquitoes, and hurricanes are things I grew up with, so they seem natural. The ground moving does not.

I sprang up in my bunk bed and looked around. The walls of the hut were moving as well, and the rumbling began to get louder. Then it suddenly stopped.

"It's just the volcano doing its thing," a voice said from the shadows. And it wasn't Jetfuel Joe or Berkeley speaking, unless they had attended accelerated English classes during my nap.

"Like everybody and everything on this island, the volcanic activity comes, and it goes. Welcome to Dalvalo, Captain Singer. I am Waltham. I hear you are looking for me."

The next thing I knew, I was seated in the passenger seat of an ancient military Jeep as Waltham, the leader of the Captain Keed cargo cult, drove down a deserted grass road lined with sandalwood trees. We had two very modern long boards strapped across the roll bar of the Jeep.

"I know you surf. I have seen your music videos and thought you might enjoy this break after your long trip from Santo. It's kind of like a miniature Waikiki without two million tourists and a skyscraper shoreline."

The invitation to go surfing and the news that Waltham had been to Hawaii just added to the mystery surrounding my visit. The one thing I knew at that point was not to ask a lot of questions, so I just listened.

Waltham apologized for not meeting me upon my arrival and said that there was much to do, as the following day was Captain Keed Day. When I asked him about the American gravestones, he, like Berkeley, avoided the question.

"It all must seem quite confusing, I am sure,

but I promise I will explain everything. I am much better at conversation when I'm on a beach or sitting outside a surf break. How about you?"

As we buzzed down the road, I noted that Waltham certainly did not fit the image of a model on a surf-magazine cover. He was more a cross between an aging lifeguard and a sumo wrestler. He looked to be around six feet tall, and his skin was the color of coffee with a slight splash of cream. Blond ringlets surrounded a perfectly circular bald spot on the back of his scalp, and he wore camouflage board shorts and a tank top. From his neck to his ankles, every visible inch of skin was covered with tattoos.

His forearms and shoulders carried the firm muscle tone that a life of paddling will produce, but he sported a rather large beer gut and held a big, cone-shaped spliff in his right hand, almost like an extra appendage. He viewed life from behind a pair of reflector Ray-Bans. A string of shark's teeth and black pearls hung around his neck, and he had a .45 automatic stuck in his shorts below his potbelly.

Whatever he was, he was obviously in charge, and I was strictly following orders. I didn't really know what I was doing on Dalvalo, but for the moment, surfing wasn't a bad option.

As we broke out of the hardwood canopy, the ocean appeared instantly, and the road paralleled an endless stretch of white-sand beach along the leeward shore to a point in the distance.

Waltham sang along with a Polynesian singer on the radio. I had a thousand questions, but I was trying not to act like a white man in a hurry, so I just enjoyed the view.

"Your arrival has caused much excitement in the village — do you know?"

"I know, but I don't quite understand," I said.

"I would say you came to the right place at the right time. I don't think your visit is a coincidence."

"I know. I was sent here with a message from Captain Keed."

"I didn't say that," Waltham told me with a laugh.

"But you are the leader of the Keedos?" I asked.

"That is true, but you have to understand. You came from Florida on the eve of Captain Keed Day in a giant seaplane from the past. On Dalvalo, that is seen as much more than a coincidence. Would you not agree?"

"Well, maybe you could explain to them that I am just a visitor and not a messenger from their god," I said.

"Oh, no!" Waltham laughed. "I told them exactly the opposite. I told them that you *do* bring a message from Captain Keed."

"Why would you do that?" I asked.

"Because whether it is true or not, they need to hear it. And as their leader, I have to do what I think is best for them."

For the first time in the very brief time I had known him, the smile disappeared from Waltham's face. He crushed the spliff out on a rock. "Things have not been good here lately. The government hassles us constantly. We are like the Rastafarians of the Pacific. We are an easy target — crazy people on a distant island who worship airplanes and a dead aviator. The outsiders blame all their inadequacies on us, but we are still safe for the time being here. They don't come to Dalvalo because they know they won't go home in one piece. The rest of these islands are worshipping the tourist dollar. I ask you, Captain Singer, why can't we worship our airplanes and be left alone?"

"First of all," I said, "my friends in the islands back home call me Singa Mon. Second, I would say that your freedom is a threat to them."

"Spoken like a true messenger from the gods. See? I knew I had the right man."

"So you invented me?"

"How could *I* invent you, Singa Mon? You exist. You are on the radio all over the world, and today you are right here, riding in my Jeep."

"I can't argue that point," I said with a laugh.

Waltham lit another huge joint, took a big hit, exhaled, and continued. "We are all supposed to be certain places at certain times, and right now you and me are supposed to be out there."

Just then, we rounded the rocky point, and Waltham stopped the Jeep. Below us was a crescent-shaped bay, ringed in primitive beauty. Long lines of perfect, glassy waves cascaded down the reef line nearly all the way across the bay to the deep channel just below where we had stopped.

"We call this spot the Chinese Restaurant because you can order up just about any kind of surf you want. We've got gaping barrels, long, perfect lefts, and beach breaks for the kiddies. Looks like the special of the day is a mile-long, chest-high left break."

In the distance, I could see what looked to be a weathered, carved pyramid midway down the beach. "Was this a holy spot in the old days?" I asked.

"You mean that pyramid? That's Chinese, the other origin of the name of the bay."

"It looks ancient," I said.

"It is," Waltham told me. "The Chinese knew these waters long before Magellan or Captain Cook. They sent a treasure fleet out in 1421 to explore the world and discovered most of it, including America, long before Columbus set out to sea. Columbus actually used their maps. The Chinese fleet stopped here on its way back from Antarctica, where they went to find Canopus, their steering star for the southern hemisphere."

"How do you know all this?"

"The Chicken Man," Waltham answered. "It seems that all up and down the West Coast of North and South America and into the Pacific Islands, Asiatic chickens were discovered by the Spanish when they got there. The Chicken Man is Professor Whit from England, who came here to do some research. He was pretty convincing, and then he showed me how the pyramid was aligned with the stars of the Southern Cross. He said the Chinese put them all over the world."

"Did they surf?" I asked.

"No, they didn't surf," Waltham said, "but we do."

We drove to the bottom of the hill where the sand road ended, and then we kept going, directly out onto the beach.

When we reached the pyramid, we stopped. There was power on that spot for sure, and I imagined a Chinese fleet anchored out in the bay. "Does anybody else know about this place?" I asked.

Waltham began laughing as we unloaded the boards and leaned them against the pyramid. "Let's just say that it's a private spot. A few years back, a group of Brazilian surf Nazis arrived one day on the mail boat with boards, camping gear, and video cameras. They were all set to claim the Chinese Restaurant as theirs. Berkeley and I met them at the beach. We had chosen to dress in traditional cannibal costumes, complete with shrunken-head belts, spears, and bones through our noses, not to mention a couple of old Thompson submachine guns in our hands.

"The surf dudes fled to the whaling village and stayed there until the boat returned a week later. They scrambled aboard and headed north. A month later, our little episode showed up in a surf magazine, and of course it was blown out of proportion, but nobody has been here since."

We paddled out from the beach, and I followed Waltham through a small channel that led through the reef. If any remnants from my kava night in Santo were still lodged in my brain, they were certainly cleaned out by the succession of head-high lefts that broke all afternoon.

Between rides, we flopped on our boards, and there I learned a little more about Waltham. He told me he was born and raised on Dalvalo. His father had been a member of a local group of coast watchers and guerrillas that had been organized by Captain Keed and had raided Japanese installations in the Solomon Islands during the war. Having been exposed in a unique and indirect way to American culture, he wanted to see it firsthand.

Waltham had been sent by his father to America with a mission to explore the country and go to Pensacola, Florida, and see if Captain Keed was ever coming back. Waltham told me that Pensacola had not turned out to be heaven, even though he had seen the Blue Angels flying down the beach. No one there remembered Captain Keed.

Waltham stayed on in Florida and wound up in Orlando, but he didn't last long there. He drifted down to Fort Lauderdale, where he spent another couple of years working at the Mai-Kai before heading to California and then home to Dalvalo.

Shortly after he returned, his father passed away, and it wasn't long before Waltham had been elected chief. "After seeing America, I couldn't tell my people that it was heaven." Waltham said that since his trip, all he was trying to do was prevent his people from becoming victims of a materialistic tidal wave.

We got out of the water shortly before sunset.

Waltham came ashore with a large red snapper and produced a grill and utensils from his Jeep. I managed to knock a few papayas free from a tree at the edge of the jungle, and we devoured the fish and washed it down with cold beer from Waltham's cooler. He told me that normally we could camp out on the pyramid, and he would show me how to line up the stars from the top of it, but tomorrow was the biggest day of the year on Dalvalo, and we had to get home.

We drove back to Huakelle under a purple sky. Several rain clouds swept down the side of the volcano, and we stopped and stood in the rain for a few minutes to wash the salt from our bodies. When we made it back to the village, it was strangely deserted. The flag had been taken from the bamboo pole, and a smoldering fire sent a plume of wood smoke skyward.

Waltham told me that everybody was resting for the big day, which would start very early. He suggested I do the same. He stopped at the entrance to my hut. "You will be my guest of honor tomorrow for the march," he said. "There is something up on the mountain that I think might be of interest to you. Work on your speech before you go to bed."

"What speech?" I asked.

"The one you bring from Captain Keed and will deliver tomorrow night at the celebration."

It is not often in life that you fall asleep to the rumbling of a distant volcano, but on that night, I was so worn out from my journey to Dalvalo, and my afternoon at the Chinese Restaurant, that when

my head hit the pillow, I really didn't care if the
mountain exploded and blew us all sky-high.

***

*O*bviously, that did not happen. I was awakened
out of my coma by several nudges from a firm
hand, and I turned to see the face of Berkeley
illuminated by a torch. "Captain, it is time to go."

I was in the middle of brushing my teeth when
I remembered that I had forgotten about the
speech.

Shortly before dawn, what sounded like a
symphony of conch shells began an eerie tune.
The villagers of Huakelle began to assemble
around the flagpole. I was munching on a piece of
pineapple and sipping a cup of coffee that
Berkeley had brought me when I saw Waltham
walk out of his hut. He was wearing a khaki flight
suit, and an old helmet and goggles were propped
on his forehead. He completed his naval officer's
uniform with a white ammo belt and holster that
now housed his pistol.

As Waltham walked to the flagpole, a column
of twenty men fell in behind him. They wore
green khaki shorts and had the words U.S. NAVY
painted in blue across their bare chests. They were
soldiering bamboo replicas of M1 rifles and
submachine guns. He and his little army marched
to the flagpole, where, in English, he ordered the
detachment to halt.

At this point, another group of men came
forward and ran the American flag up the pole. As

it flapped away in the tropical breeze, Waltham
pulled his gold-plated .45 out of the white holster
and fired one shot into the sky. The flag was
immediately lowered and folded by the honor
guard into a perfect triangle and handed to
Waltham, who made a short speech in pidgin.
Then he put his gun back in his holster and turned
to face the men with the bamboo rifles.

The villagers fell in behind the little army, and
Waltham motioned for me to join him at the front
of the parade. A small band of drummers gathered
at the end of the formation and began to beat out a
cadence. Waltham turned to me and whispered,
"How do you like our religion so far?"

Before I could answer, he shouted a command
and pointed at the volcano that had begun to
materialize on the edges of the gray dawn. The
procession began to move. As we went forward
through the jungle, the drummers kept playing,
and the villagers sang.

"What are they singing about?" I asked
Waltham as we walked.

"It is the story of Captain Keed and how he
arrived here. Would you like to hear it?"

Somewhere between Waltham's first shot and
the rhythm of the jungle, I had forgotten any
logical reason why I was on the island. I had
become caught up in the moment. I could feel the
excitement of the marchers. "Yes," I told him,
"please tell me."

"Very well," Waltham said. "Our book of
Genesis starts back with those damn missionaries.
We couldn't eat them all. They were like the big

moray eels on the reef — once they wrapped their tails around a piece of coral, it was almost impossible to shake them loose. Next thing you know, the Bible started to take the place of the religion of our ancestors, and pretty soon the missionaries were telling the people that kava was evil, dancing was sinful, and wife swapping would send you to hell. It was not a good time. But everyone knew the gods would send us help. Then came the war, and our shamans told us of visions of a warrior who would come out of the sky. It would be the sign to throw the Bibles into the sea and go back to the traditional ways. And that is exactly what happened."

"What do you mean?" I asked.

The path we were following opened into a clearing where a small waterfall poured down a volcanic ledge. This created a deep pool that then spilled over the edge in a long, misty cascade to the sea below. The villagers broke rank and dashed for the water and began splashing and playing around in the idyllic spot.

Waltham waded into the water up to his knees. "This is called Bible Falls, and this is where it happened. One moonless night, my father and the other elders of the village secretly collected all the Bibles from the village. They brought them up here and tossed them into the ocean. Then they told everybody in the village it was a sign from the gods. About a year after that, the missionaries left the island, and the people were happy.

"This is a sacred pool for the Keedos. It is where the whole thing started, and it also happens

to be the perfect resting spot before the big climb.
I love it when spirituality and practicality
merge — which isn't very often, you know."

I found a spot in the shade and sat on a big
boulder. I gulped water from my canteen and
thought again about the speech I was supposed to
give.

"We will rest here for fifteen minutes, and then
we will continue the climb. We must reach our
destination by sunset," Waltham said.

"Where are we going?" I asked.

Waltham took a drink from the canteen and
then pointed up to the rim of the southernmost
volcano. "Up there," he said. Then he lit a spliff,
and in the serene surroundings of Bible Falls, he
continued telling the story of Captain Keed.

"The prophecy came true," he told me. "A PBY
patrol plane based at Espíritu Santo was returning
from a night mission. It was passing over Dalvalo
when there was an eruption from the volcano.
Rocks and lava were propelled skyward like
surface-to-air missiles. The plane was hit by
volcanic debris and was forced to make a crash
landing in the jungle of Dalvalo. All on board the
plane were killed except the pilot."

Waltham stopped the story and unbuckled the
watch he was wearing on his left wrist. He handed
it to me. It was obviously an old spring-wound
wristwatch, and I couldn't help but notice that the
manufacturer's name was printed on the face with
a pair of aviator's wings etched beneath it.

"Waltham Watch Company," I said.

"Turn it over," Waltham said.

On the back, etched in the metal, were these words: TO LT. J. D. KEED — PENSACOLA, 1940.

Goosebumps ran up my arms to the back of my neck. Since I had first heard Keed's name spoken by Jetfuel Joe back on Vanuatu in the Coolidge Bar, it hadn't really occurred to me that the story might actually be true. Holding that watch, I immediately felt the connection. "Jesus," I said.

"No, Keed," Waltham replied. "That was given to my father by Captain Keed. That is how I got my name. But I am getting ahead of the story here, and we need to move on."

Waltham shouted an order to Berkeley, who passed the word on to the villagers still frolicking in the waterfall. Instantly the little parade reformed. Soon the terrain became much steeper, and the trail ahead took the form of a switchback, snaking its way up into the low-hanging clouds.

As we walked, Waltham continued the story. "My father and the men of the village pulled Lieutenant Keed from the wreckage. They knew his name and where he came from because of the inscription on his watch. They buried the dead crew members in the cemetery. Those were the tombstones you were asking about. The spirits of the dead crew are our angels.

"Captain Keed was taken to Huakelle and nursed slowly back to health by the shamans and healers. Word had spread among the villagers that a messenger from the gods had fallen from the sky. It was quite a shock to the folks on Espíritu Santo when Lieutenant Keed, who was presumed dead, was delivered back to his base in an outrigger canoe parade.

"When he was put ashore at the Navy base, he gave my father the watch and thanked the people for saving his life. He promised he would never forget them. It was also the beginning of the special relationship between the U.S. Navy and the villagers of Huakelle. Captain Keed convinced the commanders at the base that my father and his men were excellent fighters, fearless in combat, and versed in all the island dialects. That was when the guerrilla unit was formed.

"When he wasn't on missions, Captain Keed would always make a run down to Huakelle and drop off supplies. These were dangerous times for an island even as remote as Dalvalo. The Japanese had occupied parts of the Solomon Islands, and the Vanuatu chain was a logical next target as they attempted to control the sea-lanes to Australia. Lieutenant Keed was promoted to captain and squadron leader, and he organized a special force — a combination of guerrillas from Dalvalo and Navy frogmen. They constantly harassed the Japanese ship installations in the Solomon Islands. You will see more of the story when we reach the top.

"After the war, Captain Keed did not return to Pensacola, Florida. He came back to Huakelle to live. He bought one of the old PBYs and eventually a tramp steamer. The guerrilla force he had organized went from fighting a war to running an island freight business. They bought huge amounts of war surplus that the Americans left behind and supplied the villages and outposts throughout the Pacific with goods. Then one day, Captain Keed took off from the bay on a routine flight to Pentecost Island and was never heard from again. My father and his men searched all over the ocean for years, but nothing was ever found — no wreckage, no life preservers — nothing. And that is why we know that he flew back to Pensacola, Florida. And that is why we pray for his return. And that is why, on this night, we light the lamp once again to show him the way home."

The climb to the top of the volcano continued for the rest of the day. Fortunately, as we gained altitude, the heat dissipated. We were rained on occasionally, but it did not dampen the spirits of Waltham and the villagers. The energy and excitement of the climbers seemed to intensify the closer we got to the rim of the volcano.

Luckily the followers of Captain Keed had picked the extinct volcano as the destination for their march, but the rumbles and steam clouds that came from the sister peak, Poodi, only five miles away, could be felt and seen by all of us.

The final segment of the climb took us through a very thick jungle canopy. It was like being inside a wet sponge for about thirty minutes, but finally the rim of the crater came into view. A strange object angled up toward the sky, and it obviously did not fit the surrounding landscape.

"Wait here!" Waltham commanded as he headed up the trail. I stood in place as directed while the villagers passed me and fanned out in a semicircle along the rim and around the strange object.

Prayers, chants, and wild drumbeats filled the air when Waltham motioned for me to move up the trail. As I topped the mountain, the noisy crowd parted in front of me, and I stood, motionless, staring at what I knew to be the tail section of a PBY.

It didn't take more than a second to figure out that it was the remains of the plane that brought Captain Keed to Dalvalo. Although the wreckage was more than sixty years old, the tail sported a fresh coat of black-and-white alternating stripes. Just below the horizontal stabilizer, perfectly blocked letters formed the world SACOLA.

"Welcome to Sacola," the villagers all said in unison.

The spot where the tail section had been erected commanded a stunning view of the island to the west. The sun was suspended out over a stretch of the horizon that was framed between the two volcanoes.

For a moment, as I stood near the monument, I thought we had come an awfully long way to see the wreckage of an old seaplane. What a task it must have been to drag it up the mountain. I figured we were there to pay our respects, and some kind of ceremony would transpire at the setting of the sun. Then Waltham would make a speech, introduce me, and I would say something that hopefully the villagers would appreciate. After that, we would head back down the hill for the long walk back to Huakelle.

Boy, was I wrong. The blinding light from the angle of the sun slowly melted into the ocean, and the floor of the crater became visible. The sun continued its time-tested disappearance, and when it was no longer visible, the crowd roared.

I just stood there in shock at what lay below me on the floor of the crater. Carved out of the lush green foliage was a perfectly manicured grass runway that looked to be three thousand feet long. Along the edges, flaming tiki torches outlined the long rectangle, and a line of guards in uniforms surrounded the airfield. Near the center of the runway to the left, a bamboo control tower stood above several other small buildings.

As I stared down with my mouth open, a rumble came out of the jungle, but it was not a tremor from Poodi. It was a power of a different kind. The muffled rumble of a diesel generator purred in the distance, and lights popped on like flashbulbs in the tower and the small buildings below it.

A voice echoed from a set of loudspeakers that hung from the tower. "Testing, one, two, three. Testing, one, two, three." With that, the villagers danced their way down the path to the runway, and the party began.

I walked with Waltham, and we were greeted by a strange group of aviators. They all wore headphones made out of coconut shells that were covered with wire and wooden antennas. Waltham

told me these were the high priests of Keed and
the keepers of Sacola. The priests each held a
carved wooden replica of a tower microphone into
which they chanted collectively, "Cleared for
takeoff, cleared for takeoff." They split into two
groups, each taking one of my arms. Then they led
me to the runway.

I was anxious at first, but they seemed happy,
not hungry. When we got to the runway, all the
villagers lined up in two rows. They were making
loud engine noises and flapping their arms. The
priests joined in the acrobatics but were even
louder.

"Are you ready for takeoff?" Waltham asked
me. "I will lead the first group. You take the
second squadron."

"What are we doing?" I asked above the hum of
human engine noise.

"Captain Singer, you are a pilot, aren't you?"

"Yes."

"Well, we are going flying." Waltham held his
arms out behind his body in a winglike fashion.

"Squadron is cleared for takeoff," the voice from
the PA speaker blared out. With that, the priests
roared down the runway like sprinters at the
Olympics. Waltham and his squadron followed the
priests.

"Squadron Two, you are cleared for takeoff,"
the voice echoed across the floor of the crater.

I never hesitated. I ran the imaginary throttle
forward, and my verbal engine roared to life. I
took off.

Who is to say that some of the human planes

did not defy gravity? Surrounded by the places
and the circumstances, I sure as hell thought I left
the ground on a few occasions.

Somehow we all finished our flights. I was
looking up at the first stars of the night sky that
were perched on the last of the orange rays of the
setting sun when I noticed something else was in
the sky. It was closer to us, and it was moving.
The crowd on the runway saw it too. From
somewhere, the chords of a guitar sounded, and
soon all the fliers were looking at the object and
singing in perfect English:

> *You are cleared for landing, Captain Keed.*
> *Can you see your loyal crew?*
> *We can touch your heart and feel your speed.*
> *Dalvalo waits for you.*

The Mormon Tabernacle Choir never sounded
any better, and as the melodic voices of the
praying congregation echoed off the walls of the
crater, the object took shape. I knew immediately
that it was a hang glider, and the pilot maneuvering
it knew his stuff. He made wide, beautiful figure
eights above the runway. As he did, small
parachutes began trailing down from the glider,
and the people plucked them out of the air.

One floated within my range, and I grabbed it.
Attached to the parachute were pieces of beach
glass on which were painted the words YOU ARE
CLEARED FOR LANDING, CAPTAIN KEED.

When he was through with his drop, the hang-
glider pilot banked left over the field and came

around on the east side. He returned to the earth, stepping from the air like a ballet dancer. As he touched down, the singing stopped, and a huge cheer went up from the crowd.

Waltham made his way over to me. "And those Bible-thumpers call us a primitive, archaic cult. I picked the hang glider up from a haole over on Villa who had come here to try and do a tourist thing, but it never got off the ground — pardon the pun. I thought it would add a little flair to our yearly celebration. Those TV evangelists up in America have corporate jets that their congregations rarely see. At least our people get to see our aircraft as part of the ceremony. The pilot is Jetfuel Joe. He flies well, no?"

"He flies well," I said.

Tully, I have to tell you, I was brought up a child of the Mardi Gras. I was taught to believe in the magic of carnival since the days my dad held me high on his shoulders so I would have a better chance to catch the boxes of Cracker Jacks being thrown by grown men dressed as pirates, gods, devils, and cartoon characters. I was an ex-Jesuit-trained altar boy who was force-fed Catholicism for a third of my life. I had been taught to believe in things like Jesus raising the dead and turning water into wine — and, my favorite miracle, the loaves-and-fishes picnic — along with resurrections, ascensions, and the Last Judgment. So it wasn't a big stretch for me to believe that

Captain Keed might actually zoom in from heaven on a hang glider and drop gifts that floated to the earth on little baby parachutes. Tully, I have to say, I was getting quite fond of a religion that worshipped pilots.

"Well, I have to go and get ready for tonight," Waltham said. "I will see you later in the tower. Berkeley will bring you. Watch out for that high tide out there. Remember, you are the messenger from our god." His words suddenly reminded me of the speech I hadn't written. What was I supposed to say?

As Waltham had predicted, the kava bowl got a big workout. The villagers partied like combat pilots, sang and danced all night, and then there was the food and sex. All in all, it was some kind of an evening. Just before midnight, as I was enjoying the festivities and dancing away at the luau, Berkeley came up to me and said, "It is time to go to the tower."

Waltham's little army stood guard with carved bamboo machine guns and mortars, all of which sat atop sandbagged bunkers at the base of the tower. As I began climbing, I noticed that the noise level at the party below me dropped a few decibels as the generator sputtered to a halt, and the revelers began to walk to the runway. They all carried torches that at first looked like big fireflies dancing on the breeze.

As I climbed, I passed a gaggle of hissing pipes, valves, and several large pressure tanks. I stopped to catch my breath at the top of the tower, and when I looked down, the torches outlined the full rectangular border of the grass strip. I was nearly knocked from the tower by the sudden, deafening voice from the loudspeaker. It was now three feet from my ear.

"We have a visitor with a message from Captain Keed."

A roar came from the crowd below as I reached the door to the control tower. Berkeley guided me inside. I looked at my watch. It was four minutes before midnight. The tower room was bathed in an eerie red light — like the night-lights in our plane.

Waltham was standing on a set of winding stairs about three feet above six of his men. They stood their duty stations in front of fake radios and radar screens. Waltham held a hurricane lantern that illuminated the dress-white Navy captain's uniform he now wore. There were scores of medals on his chest and gold-braided epaulets on his shoulders, and a silver parade sword hung by his side. He looked up at the hands of the old military clock. The minute hand was inching toward the hour hand at the twelve o'clock position. He smiled and said, "Welcome to the tower. It is time for the message." Then he walked up the stairs and motioned for me to follow.

At the top of the stairs was a small, round room where a real radio transmitter sat on a desk. A canvas cover concealed a very large object in the middle of the room, but I was not admiring the furniture. Tully, I was panicking. There I was, a messenger from a god with no message, and there was no burning bush or parting of the seas to cover my ass. It was like that dream I sometimes have when I am on the stage doing a show, but something is not quite right. I don't have any pants on, or the seats are empty, or the band is playing a different tune.

Through the clutter of my own brain, I heard Waltham say, "Captain Singer, I know that you were not sent by Captain Keed, and I know you didn't write a speech. You were actually sent here by Parfait as a favor to me."

If my thoughts weren't confused enough, this revelation came as a shock. "I don't quite understand?" was all I could say.

"Singa Mon, paradise as we have lived it and known it is disappearing fast. All we are trying to do here is hang on to our ancestral beliefs as long as we can. They may be whacked-out beliefs according to the standards of governments and missionaries who try to modernize us, but we were here first. I know that kind of rationalization didn't work too well for the native people in your country, and they struggled for hundreds of years until their gods came to them with the idea of Indian casinos. Now they are gathering the money to control their own destiny. That is all Parfait and I are looking for here."

Parfait was working on this? I didn't quite follow Waltham's logic, but I was in no position to analyze this problem. I had a speech to make.

"Parfait?" I asked, surprised.

Waltham chuckled. "He may look like a phony-baloney French PR man, but he is originally from this island — our village. He made it out, but he keeps close ties to his family here and does what he can to help us survive. That is how you got here."

I was finally starting to connect the dots.

"When you arrived in New Caledonia in the plane, and the gods allowed him to rescue you from the authorities at the airport, he knew you had been sent for a reason, and he contacted me. Since it was so close to Captain Keed Day, and spirits have been a bit down, we thought it would be a good thing for the village to receive a message from Captain Keed."

I smiled back. "So you two pirates lured me here for what?"

"To show the people that the gods still care about them."

"So the whole story about you knowing something about the soul of the light was just a scam to get me here?"

"No, that part is true."

"Well, if you don't mind, I would like a little proof," I told him.

"I will make you a deal," Waltham snapped back. "You give a speech of hope to my people, and I will show you what you came for. But we have to hurry. It is almost midnight." Waltham picked up the microphone and handed it to me.

"What do I say?" I asked.

"Hell, you are a performer. Do what you do when you forget the words to your own song. I saw it happen back in Orlando. I went to one of your shows, and you know what? The audience sang the song for you. Think about your journey here, where you have been and what you have seen. And now that you know what is at stake, think of something that will uplift them and make them believe in the future."

I took the microphone from Waltham and made my way out onto the catwalk, dragging the cord behind me.

"Remember, keep it short too!" he yelled out the open door.

I pressed the talk switch on the mike, and the words came. I said a few words of welcome and thanks in the little pidgin I knew, and then it all came gushing out. "Friends," I began, "like Hank Williams said, I saw the light."

Boy, did those words shortly become prophetic. I don't remember much about what came next. I just did as Waltham had advised. I thought about how I got here and how it had affected me. Below, the lines of villagers holding their torches stood silent and still as the breeze blew their flames back and forth. I don't really know how long I talked, but when I finished, the crowd roared with approval and began to sing the Keed song.

I put the mike back to my mouth and joined in the chorus. At that moment, the sky was ignited by a blinding flash of light. "Oh, shit," I thought. "All of this is true."

Another beam of light cut a bright silver hole in the sky, briefly illuminating the top of the crater and the summit of Poodi in the distance. Immediately I turned to see that the light was coming from the tower room. I knew at first sight that the source, which had been concealed earlier beneath the canvas cover, was a Fresnel lens.

Waltham walked out next to me and waved to
the crowd. I followed his lead and waved too.
"Excellent speech, Mr. Messenger. Look how
happy they are."

"That is a Fresnel lens!" I shouted.

"Yes, I told you that part was true. Wave to the
crowd." I was still waving, but my mind was elsewhere. I was very confused. I had found the soul
of the light, but I hadn't found anything I could
take home.

"But it is *your* light. Not mine," I said
somewhat accusingly to Waltham. "I could never
take that lens from you for Cayo Loco."

"And I could never let you have our sacred
beacon," Waltham calmly replied.

"So what's the fucking point?" I blurted out.

Waltham gave me a serious look, and then that
devilish smile spread across his face. "There is a
spare bulb," he said.

>━━━

Well, my message seemed to have worked. The
party continued into the wee hours, but I had
turned in my dance card. As strange as it may
seem, I was actually back on the track of my self-
appointed mission of scouring the Pacific for a
Fresnel lens.

Waltham and I walked out of the crater, and as
we topped the hill, I could hear the strains of Artie
Shaw's "Begin the Beguine" blaring from the
speakers at the base. Small silhouettes and shadows
of dancers jitterbugged up and down the grass strip.

As we made our way down the mountain trail, Waltham filled in the blanks of the story for me. Somewhere around the end of the winter of 1942, after several weeks of delivering mail, transporting military big shots to R & R locations, and doing goodwill trips for local island chiefs, Captain Keed had received new orders. He was to enlist the aid of his guerrilla fighters on Dalvalo, who were to join a Navy frogman team. All of them, under Keed's direction, were flown up to the Santa Cruz Islands, where they were to capture and incapacitate a pair of lighthouses that marked the channel through the islands. They had specific orders not to destroy the lights themselves but to dismantle them and load them aboard a waiting transport, which would take them back to Espíritu Santo.

The mission started out badly, as weather had moved in, and Keed was forced to make a dangerous night landing in the ocean. But the landing and the mission were successful. Both lighthouses were secured with a minimum of casualties, and the first lens was loaded aboard a waiting PT boat that sped away to the safety of Espíritu Santo.

However, as the second light was being loaded onto a much slower transport, a Japanese patrol boat spotted them. Keed again took off at night and circled the ship as the gunners tried to cover the transport's escape. The Japanese eventually gave up the chase, but the transport had been hit badly. Keed and his crew managed to rendezvous with the transport in the Torres Islands, where they beached the sinking ship. Somehow the guerrillas got the lens off the ship and hid it in an island cave.

In the meantime, things were heating up in the Solomons as the battle for Guadalcanal began, and the missing lens fell off the radar screen of the Allied forces. At the end of the war, the lens that had made it back to Espíritu Santo was just another item among tons of planes, tanks, vehicles, guns, ammo, and other war surplus that was simply left behind when the Americans took off for the land of the free.

Captain Keed found the Santo Fresnel lens in a warehouse full of surplus he had bought. His original idea was to go back to Torres and find the missing lens and then construct a pair of matching lighthouses at the entrance to the lagoon at Huakelle, but then he and his plane disappeared. Waltham's father, who had spent every minute of the rescue mission looking for his friend without any results, took it upon himself to use the one lens to build a monument to Keed, and that is how the Keed cult came into existence. The light at Sacola was intended to guide Captain Keed home.

As Waltham finished the story, we arrived at the trailhead, where Waltham's Jeep was parked. I stopped, turned around, and looked back up at the mountain path as I thought about what had transpired up there. It had been off the radar screen of just about everybody on earth. Dawn had broken, beautiful and clear, and the twin volcanic peaks of Poodi and Kami framed the morning view perfectly.

"So the other light that was hidden in the Torres Islands is the spare bulb," I said.

"Exactly!" Waltham told me.

"And is it still there?"

"Not exactly," he said. "But I think I can lead you to it. You did fulfill your part of the deal. Now it is time for me to do the same. Let's take a ride."

We drove through the silent morning back to the deserted village of Huakelle. Waltham stopped the Jeep in front of the main Quonset hut and went inside. He came back with the folded American flag and two bowls filled with Cap'n Crunch cereal. He and I raised the flag on the bamboo pole and then had breakfast.

"I have arranged for you to get back to your plane. A friend of mine has a small amphibian he operates out of Villa. He is due here in an hour, and he will take you back to Santo. It would be good for you and us if you kept this visit a secret."

"Roger that," I said.

We finished our cereal as the parrots squawked and flew between the palm fronds above our heads. "Now let's find that spare bulb," Waltham said, and we walked back to the hut.

Once inside, Waltham went immediately to the storage racks at the rear of the building and rummaged through stacks of boxes, crates, and trunks. He had disappeared into the clutter, but I finally heard him call out, "Give me a hand with this, Captain."

We wrestled a rusty old government-issue file cabinet down from the shelf and placed it on the table in front of the photo of Captain Keed. There, Waltham produced a key ring with several hundred keys attached, and somehow he instantly found the one that opened the padlock. Both his hands went into the open drawer, and he thumbed through the file folders. Then he extracted an old, mildew-covered manila folder and handed it to me.

"I think this might interest you."

Inside the file was a stack of yellowed papers that looked like shipping bills of lading and several photographs with the words TORRES ISLANDS, '42 scribbled on the back. The photos on top were of a group of islanders and soldiers in frogmen gear, all armed but smiling. They were holding captured swords and guns. The rest of the pictures had no date, but they were from a different, and later, time period. They showed a group of men moving an unmistakable Fresnel lens out of a cave and onto a flatbed truck. The final shot showed the lens being hoisted into a crate at a dock with a ship in the background.

"It's the spare bulb," I said excitedly.

I stared at the photos, still not believing that I had stumbled upon not one bull's-eye lens but two. I noticed that one of the white men who appeared in several of the loading photos was standing on the bridge of the ship with the captain.

"See the man next to the captain on the bridge?" Waltham asked.

"Yes," I said.

"His name is — or was — Ian Saxon. He was an ex-Aussie Navy man who ran coastal freighters out of Melbourne. He's the one who finally recovered the lens from Torres Island. Only thing is, the day before the ship sailed, old Ian choked on an egg roll in a Chinese restaurant and went toes up at dinner. The ship and the lens sailed for Melbourne the next day without him, and that is the last I ever heard of it."

"Well, that is not quite like having a spare bulb!"

"Hold on, junior. Those pictures are nice, but I think the pages will be more — pardon the pun — enlightening," Waltham said with that now-familiar sly smile of his.

I dropped the photos and pulled the papers out of the file folder.

"Check out that shipping invoice from the steamship company, and look at the signature of the captain at the bottom."

"Holy shit!" I yelled.

"Name ring a bell?"

"Singer!" I shouted in total amazement. "His name was Singer! Captain Stanley Singer!"

"Looks like lighthouses are in your family blood."

Half an hour later, the familiar sound of an airplane engine came from the north. It was my ride. The Cessna 185 on floats made an arcing turn to parallel the shore and touched down out of the swell at the mouth of the river. It was obvious he had done the landing a few times before.

I smiled as I watched the landing. I don't get to see many of my own, and I thought to myself, "This is why we fly these things, because they can get to places like Dalvalo."

Waltham rowed me out to where the pilot anchored the plane. It had been a hell of a couple of days. I remembered that opening line from *Star Trek:* "To boldly go where no one has gone before." I thought I had just done that.

Waltham greeted the pilot and introduced me. Then we ferried my gear from the dugout to the aft compartment of the plane.

"The flight is on me and the happy citizens of Dalvalo, who were inspired by your message. We will be praying that you find your light. I expect an invitation to the lighting up of that lighthouse of yours, and I warn you, so will Parfait."

"If I find the other Mr. Singer and the light, I will send you a ticket," I said.

"Be careful about promises like that. We Keedos can turn anything into religion," he said. "Seriously, though, I thank you on behalf of my people for your understanding of our struggle to hang on. I know our way of life doesn't scratch the surface in this high-tech world, but I believe it is worth saving. I would rather we believe in Captain Keed and his return than see them all turn into a generation of fry cooks for expanding fast-food restaurants."

With that, he pulled a weathered old baseball cap out of his knapsack. It was sealed in a plastic bag. On the front of the cap was written VP 23, and there was a patch of a PBY sewn above the bill.

"It belonged to Captain Keed," Waltham said. "It is a gift from all your friends on Dalvalo. Think of us when you wear it, and if you run into our leader in your travels, tell him to get his ass back here. We are still waiting." Waltham gave me a huge hug and stepped back into the dugout.

"Permission for a fly over Sacola," I said as I changed hats and put on my new prized possession. I snapped my right hand up to the brim.

"Permission granted," Waltham said and returned the salute.

We taxied down the shore, turned back, and took off above Waltham. I watched him wave from his dugout as we climbed toward the volcano. The morning clouds were just beginning to form, but the rim of the crater was clearly visible, as was the procession of villagers walking, antlike, down the path and back to Huakelle. They all stopped and waved as we flew over.

At the top of the mountain, the pilot lined up the runway and made a low approach about twenty feet off the ground until he was abeam of the tower. Then he pulled back on the stick and climbed. As I looked out the window of the plane, I saw the bull's-eye lens in the tower had been covered up with the canvas again. The high priests patrolled the catwalk, and I thought to myself, "One down, and one to go."

Well, Tully, by the time you finish this epic, I will be in Australia. Don't worry about my dream of getting *The Flying Pearl* to Hong Kong. That city isn't going anywhere for a while. No, I am headed to Melbourne, where I know a man named Captain Stanley Singer brought a bull's-eye lens ashore. I intend to find him or his family and the soul of Cleopatra's light. It looks like you just might get a light in that tower of yours.

Your man in the Pacific,
Willie

38

From a Distance

From a distance, things appear to be what they are not. Our planet looks to be a calm, blue jewel floating in space, but on the surface, there are wars, riots, and rock concerts. A splash in the ocean becomes the tail of a giant sperm whale. The reflection of the sun on a desert sandpile looks like a pristine lake. From a distance, a tiny speck of coral becomes a 150-foot lighthouse tower with a short-wave antenna stretched across the top. Cayo Loco is a good place to be these days, considering everything else.

Tango music spills out of my old Hallicrafter and echoes across the sand dunes, as the sea oats seem to sway to the beat. I don't think it's a coincidence that the singer is Carlos Gardel, coming to me from a station in Ecuador, the land of volcanoes and Grandma Ghost. I am sitting atop a sand dune, staring at the nearly completed renovation of the Cayo Loco Light. We are in the cleanup stage now, and when I look at the piles of debris that will soon be removed, I think of my memories that have also piled up.

It is a beautiful day here in the southern Bahamas and hard to believe that it is the middle of winter. A gentle breeze blows from the southeast. There is not a cloud in the sky, and it is so clear that I can almost make out the coastline of Great Inagua, thirty miles to the south. I watch the silhouette of a sail slip over the horizon, which reminds me of one of the countless adventures I have had since I left Belize.

It seems like yesterday that Diver Pinder and I were standing in knee-deep water, completing the final wall of our conch-and-grouper pen that Diver had named the Cayo Loco Fish Market. Diver is Solomon's son. He had been working as a flats guide and a teacher over on Crooked Island, but when his father told him about what we were doing at Cayo Loco, he arrived one morning with a boatload of friends and a pile of tools. He told me his real name was Solomon Pinder III, but that got too confusing. So since he had started swimming underwater at the age of two months, his mother had changed his name to Diver. It made sense to me.

"Looks like you could use a little help," Diver had said as he viewed the work site. "This was my grandfather's light, you know." And that is how we became friends. With Diver's help, I was finally starting to make a dent in the monumental task ahead of me. Meanwhile, Cleopatra and Solomon had taken the *Lucretia* to Corpus Christi, Texas, to check out stories of a lens that had been hidden on a cattle ranch during the Civil War. I was finally feeling comfortable in my new surroundings, safe from Thelma and the Stiltons, and I was happy as a clam just working my ass off, organizing a workforce with the help of Diver.

We were putting the finishing touches on the Cayo

Loco Fish Market and were just about to stop for lunch when the unmistakable sound of radial engines and the unforgettable pink fuselage announced the arrival of Sammy Raye to Cayo Loco.

It turned out that Sammy Raye wasn't on board, but Drake, the pilot, delivered the news to me: Thelma Barston was dead. My first thought was that I would be a suspect in her murder, but then Drake added a sentence that nearly flattened me like a tidal wave. "All the charges against you have been dropped."

He went on to explain the bizarre series of events that had followed my disappearance. It seems that after the Stiltons returned to Wyoming without me, Thelma came unglued. The way Drake told it, Thelma had decided to run as a born-again, right-wing conservative for the seat in Congress left vacant when Zachary Scott Stilton, the corrupt uncle of Waldo and Wilton, decided to retire. Sammy Raye's investigation of the not-so-public side of Thelma had turned up the news that she had a very kinky S and M thing going on with a Lithuanian movie director in Miami. It seems her choice of entertainment was to be saddled and ridden like a pony by her boyfriend. There were videos. They included scenes of Thelma prancing around with a bit in her mouth wearing leather gear and being urged on with a few swats from a riding crop. That was a little much for a congressional candidate. Sammy Raye subtly got word to Thelma that if she didn't drop the charges against me, the video would find its way into the hands of a reporter he knew at the *Miami Herald*. I guess that message sent Thelma into a complete hysterical rage, and apparently she jumped on her snowmobile and roared off into the mountains. A few of my pink flamingos were still up there where my Airstream used to be, and I guess she let loose with the double-barreled shotgun she had taken with her.

Drake told me that the park ranger who found her said the gunshots triggered a small avalanche, and it roared down the mountain and turned Thelma Barston into an instant Popsicle. Dawn got her inheritance and called Bucky at the lodge to let him know that I was a free man.

Drake handed me an envelope that Sammy Raye had told him to deliver to me. Inside was all the paperwork that concerned my case, with a big rubber stamp across each page that read CASE DISMISSED. It felt wonderful not to have to live under the constant legal radar, but the funny thing was this: I didn't want to go anywhere. Cayo Loco was now my home, and restoring the lighthouse was my job.

Not long after word of my freedom arrived, so did my horse and Ix-Nay with a new version of the *Bariellete*. Captain Kirk had provided transport for horse and boat along with my art collection, my wardrobe (a box of shorts, flip-flops, and T-shirts), and my trusty Hallicrafter radio. The new skiff was amazing. It was a perfect replica of the original, right down to the Mayan gods on the bow. Ix-Nay told me he had let Sammy Raye make a mold of the boat, and then Sammy Raye made one copy for himself and one for me at a boatyard in Key West. Mr. Twain seemed to rediscover his life as a horse on the island — I just let him run wild for a few weeks after his arrival before I built him a corral and stall under the lighthouse. Ix-Nay liked the place and the purpose of our work so much that he wanted to stay awhile. Six months after I had first set foot on Cayo Loco, things were shaping up.

And that was the way it was for a good number of months. Willie Singer was on the case in Australia, and we all had our fingers crossed that he was going to get lucky and come through with the lens if Cleopatra didn't find another one first.

I spent my time between the solitude of Cayo Loco and the deck of the *Lucretia*. On the island, I watched the pieces of our giant puzzle start to take shape as first the light keeper's quarters, then the dock, and then the marine railway were rebuilt. Finally, the tower itself began to resemble its original stature.

Cleopatra came and went from Cayo Loco as she continued her search with no results. She never got discouraged. We always knew that the light would one day come our way. She reminded me countless times of others who had faced what seemed to be overwhelming odds. She told me stories of treasure hunters she had known. They had a blind resolve that I couldn't fathom at the time. It didn't matter whether they dug two days or twenty years for a ship they hoped they would find. We never doubted that Cleopatra would succeed. We just kept on working.

Then one morning, it hit me. I looked up at the lighthouse and realized that we were almost done. The thought rekindled a memory that brought the whole thing into perspective. I was aboard the *Lucretia,* halfway up the Amazon River at an outpost called Macapá, where the equator crossed the river. Just out of town on a bluff above the road, there was a monument that marked the equator — a piece of granite with the words MARCO DE CERO etched across its face. I stood next to the monument while Cleopatra snapped my picture. It was my birthday.

They call photos still shots, but Cleopatra reminded me I wasn't still at all. She pointed out that in fact we were both doing at least a thousand miles an hour as the earth rotated on its axis.

As we drove back to Macapá to board the boat, she looked out the window at the green blur of jungle and said, "I think the reason the years seem to fly by is because they really do."

It had been months since we had gotten Willie Singer's letter telling us of the news about the lens in Australia. I had taught Cleopatra how to use a satellite phone, and she strapped it to her waist wherever she went. She never tried to call Australia; she just waited for the news to come to her.

In the meantime, we now sailed to Havana, where Cleopatra took me for a shave and a haircut. Our destination was a barbershop in the middle of Old Havana, near the Plaza de Armas on Avenida Obispo. Cleopatra said it was the oldest one in the New World, and the condition of the building seemed to confirm that. I have to admit I was a little nervous, lying in a chair with a towel over my eyes while a communist barber with rum on his breath held a straight razor blade to my neck.

Cleopatra sat and chatted with the idle barbers and shared a glass of rum. Then she dropped the bombshell that she had actually been born in the chair in which I was now lying with a hot towel on my face.

"Look up," she said.

I opened my eyes to see a faded mural that I had failed to notice earlier on the wall of the shop. It was a painting of pyramids and ancient boats carrying what appeared to be Egyptian royalty.

"I guess I better start at the beginning," she said. It was then that she told me the story of the *Lucretia,* her family, and her birth in the barbershop.

Like Cleopatra, the *Lucretia* wore her age well. The ship had been built originally as a pilot schooner in the Netherlands in 1887, and she was christened the *Neptunia* by her builder and owner. She ran the trade routes from Europe to the Cape Verde Islands, and later she was put into service moving illegal immigrants from Africa to the rubber plantations up the Amazon River near Manaus. Eventually the *Neptunia* settled into a routine of hauling bananas from Martinique to San Juan and the U.S. Virgin Islands.

While the *Neptunia* plied her predictable routes between the islands, not far away, the world stage was about to be graced with a new historical eruption. In the spring of 1895, Captain Anderson Meador stepped onto the embarcadero in Havana. He was there to assume the job of naval attaché to the U.S. Embassy in Havana. He had brought his young wife with him. It was a hot time in Havana. Just two months later, the revolutionary leader José Martí was killed in his first battle at Dos Ríos. His death ignited the revolutionary cause, and a year later, there was fighting in the streets of Havana, which gave the U.S. government the excuse to send in the battleship USS *Maine* to protect American citizens there.

On the evening of February 15, 1898, Captain Meador kissed his eight-months-pregnant wife good-bye and headed off to dinner with the commander of the USS *Maine,* which sat at anchor in Havana Harbor.

As fate would have it, that evening, the *Neptunia* was berthed near the embarcadero no more than half a mile away from the battleship. While the whole city danced through the streets in celebration of Mardi Gras, revolutionaries in the hold of the *Neptunia* were secretly off-loading crates of weapons that had been smuggled from France.

In the early-morning hours, the USS *Maine* was rocked by a horrific explosion and sank in Havana Harbor. Hearing that the *Maine* had exploded, Lucretia Cannon Meador immediately rushed out of the house and into the embassy carriage in an attempt to find her husband. The trip was cut short, for the shock of the explosion sent her into labor.

Between the Mardi Gras crowd and the panic of the explosion, the streets were packed. There was no possibility of getting her to a hospital. The driver carried Lucretia into the barbershop on Avenida Obispo, where the owner of the shop delivered the baby. Amid the chaos, when the little girl was handed to her mother in the barber chair, they asked what her name was to be. Lucretia looked up at the Egyptian mural on the wall of the shop. "Cleopatra," Lucretia answered. "Call her Cleopatra. She already looks like she is in charge."

When Lucretia and her baby daughter were loaded back into the carriage, the owner of the shop gave the driver a wooden chest the size of a beer case. It was decorated with carved scenes of palm trees, shells, and fishing boats. He said it was a toy box for the baby.

Cleopatra had come into the world the day her father, Captain Anderson Meador, died. Sometime around dawn,

Spanish authorities seized the *Neptunia* as she tried to make her way out of the harbor on the morning tide. The boat and the baby would meet again.

After the tragedy, Lucretia Cannon Meador shocked her family back in Annapolis by not fleeing Havana at the outbreak of the Spanish-American War. Instead she boarded a ferryboat for Key West. Lucretia had fallen in love with the tropics and saw no reason to return to the chilly shores of Chesapeake Bay. Her plan was to wait out the war in Key West.

Lucretia attended the dedication of the memorial to the men of the *Maine* in Key West Cemetery and was informed by the Navy that she was entitled to housing on the Navy base. She gracefully declined. Instead, she found a small conch house off Fleming Street on a little alley called Nassau Lane. It was here she would begin the task, like many Navy widows before her, of raising her infant daughter — and hopefully finding a new husband.

Meanwhile, a local sailor and cavalry officer named Patrick Highbourne had left his family shipping business in Key West at the outbreak of hostilities and had charged up San Juan Hill with Teddy Roosevelt. His actions in the battle had earned him the Silver Star for bravery. When Patrick returned home, he was honored with a parade on Duval Street, where admirers threw confetti from the windows and blew conch-shell salutes to their native son.

Patrick Highbourne humbly accepted the gratitude, but his attention was suddenly diverted to the beautiful young widow who was introduced to him by the commanding officer of the Key West naval station. By the end of the ball, the embers of mutual attraction had already turned to hot sparks. The next morning, Captain Patrick Highbourne called on Mrs. Meador, where he met Cleopatra for the first time. They took advantage of the picture-perfect day and sailed out to the Marquesas Keys, where they picnicked under the palms. Tiny Cleopatra chased minnows and made a sailboat out of coconut husks and palm branches.

It wasn't long after that first meeting that Cleopatra's life changed forever. The new century had brought a new father.

The Highbournes of Key West were descended from a clan of loyalists who had wanted no part of the American Revolution, and after the British defeat at Yorktown, they had decided to get out of Dodge. In the late summer of 1783, they had sailed for the island of Abaco in the Bahamas.

Life in the islands was directly connected to the elements, and times of prosperity and despair rose and fell like the ever-present tides. In 1821, a late-season hurricane roared up through the lower latitudes and swept across Abaco. As it approached, young Augustus Highbourne, a boat builder, made preparations. He had moved his small schooner, the *Queen Conch,* up into the protection of a deep tidal creek surrounded by mangroves. Then he emptied the cistern below his house and climbed down into the cool dark pit with a lantern, food, and water to ride out the storm.

After hours of screeching winds and driving rain, he was suddenly staring up into a blue sky. Not to be deceived, Augustus assumed it was only the eye of the storm. But what finally filtered through his weather-beaten brain was this: he was suddenly seeing the sky above because the house he had built upon the rock foundation of the cistern was no longer there.

When he came out and looked around, he saw his

house sitting perfectly intact, but it was a hundred feet away from where he had built it.

Augustus took this as a sign from heaven. Several days later, he hoisted his house onto the deck of the *Queen Conch,* said good-bye to friends and family, and set a course for Key West.

Augustus had decided it was time to change latitudes. Like his ancestors before him, he went chasing the dream of a better, safer life. But for Augustus, the dream came true. Key West had risen from the mysterious beginnings of an Indian village covered with so many skeletons that it had been named Cayo Hueso (Bone Key) by the Spanish. Seven miles offshore along the edge of the Gulf Stream lay one of the most treacherous reef systems in the world, which since the days of Columbus and the conquistadores had laid claim to hundreds of ships, mixing the bones of sailors and passengers with those of the original Indians.

No sooner had Augustus Highbourne dropped his house onto the island than a ship hit the reef, and he raced ahead of the other boats in the speedy *Queen Conch* and laid claim to the first of many a wreck. He immediately used his shipbuilding talents and went right to work designing faster boats that would beat out the competition. But he was also building freight-carrying schooners that connected Key West to Havana.

The Highbourne shipyard blossomed, and a cargo company was added, moving people and provisions from their home base at Key West to Havana and the islands to the south.

Augustus passed on at the age of seventy-six, and he left a legacy and a fortune to his eleven children. It was his youngest son, Patrick, who would eventually wind up running the family shipping business with the style and flair of his father.

Patrick had protected and enlarged the family business and answered the call of his country, and now, in the spring of 1900, he had a family. That required a home.

It didn't take Lucretia long to find what she wanted. By the first Christmas of the new century, the Highbournes celebrated the holidays in their new house at the end of Spoonbill Lane, one of the highest pieces of land on the island — six feet above sea level. They named it Highbourne Hill.

Though the house and the tropical garden that surrounded it were meant to be an anchor for the family, Cleopatra, like her stepfather, was in love with the sea. It was soon discovered that Lucretia was unable to bear any more children, so Cleopatra became the center of attention and the pride and joy of her parents. Though her mother attempted every possible enticement to stay ashore at Highbourne Hill, Cleopatra saw the house as the place where she ate and slept when she wasn't on the *Queen Conch*.

By the time she was five, Cleopatra was traveling — whenever allowed — with her stepfather on his schooner, picking up the knowledge that would serve her well for nearly a century. She learned Spanish from the housekeepers at Highbourne Hill and French patois from the stevedores on the docks of distant ports such as Fort-de-France and Port of Spain. Patrick Highbourne taught his daughter to bait a hook, plot a course, read a map, and steer by the stars — to the chagrin of her mother, who constantly battled to keep Cleopatra ashore and interested in school and the social world of Key West.

Cleopatra's life changed course radically in the summer of her seventeenth year, when her mother became ill.

Despite Patrick's heroic attempts to find a cure, Lucretia Cannon Meador Highbourne succumbed to the rigors of tuberculosis. She was laid to rest in the Key West Cemetery in the family plot adjacent to the *Maine* memorial.

Patrick Highbourne kept his word to his dying wife despite his daughter's cries of opposition, and Cleopatra was forced to go to boarding school in France. As her luck would have it, she returned to Key West only six months later, fleeing the conflict in Europe that led to World War I.

Cleopatra took up her old life where she had left it, and she went back to sea. For several years, she worked as first mate to her father on the *Queen Conch*. It was an odd sight in the ports of the Caribbean to see a beautiful young girl handling the duties of running a ship, but Cleopatra Highbourne quickly gained the respect of the sailors who reported to her.

The morning of Cleopatra's eighteenth birthday, the *Queen Conch* rested gently at anchor in the little harbor of Les Trois-Îlets across the bay from Fort-de-France. When Cleopatra leaped out of the bunk in her tiny cabin and went topside to have her coffee, she was greeted by the sight of her father sitting on the rail of a beautiful old schooner moored next to them. Cleopatra stared in amazement at the lovely ship, which smelled of fresh varnish, paint, and pine. She jumped from the deck of the *Queen Conch* and strode across the small finger pier to where her father sat.

"She was called *Neptunia*, but I haven't nailed her name boards on," Cleopatra's father said. "That's the job of the captain. It is an old tradition that when a boat changes hands, the captain can keep the original name or change it. Happy birthday."

Then he told her the story of how the *Neptunia* had

been in Havana Harbor on the night of her birth. "What do you want to call her?" her father asked.

Tears streamed down Cleopatra's face as she ran into her father's arms. "*Lucretia,* Daddy. I want to name her for Mama."

The next morning, they were saluted by a cannon as both the *Lucretia* and the *Queen Conch* sailed out of Fort-de-France, racing to America, fifteen hundred miles to the north. They made the run in an astonishing eight days, and when they sighted the Cape Florida lighthouse at the south end of Key Biscayne, only thirty seconds separated them at the finish line.

"I won, but I am sure Daddy let me. And that's the story of how I got the boat," Cleopatra told me. "After that, the years just seemed to roll by like so many waves and so many storms. Somewhere along the line, I realized that I had forgotten to settle down, marry, and have a family — but by then it was too late. Besides, I was married to the sea. Though I sometimes wonder what my life would have been like if I had stayed ashore in Key West, that was not my destiny, and I wouldn't trade my experiences for the world. I may be an old woman, but I still feel like a young girl on a long voyage."

There was silence in the barbershop; then the wet towel was unwrapped from my face, and the chair was suddenly cranked to a sitting position. A cloud of white powder enshrouded my head as the barber brushed me off with a broom.

Cleopatra was standing next to me, smiling. "Mind if I take a ride in that chair now that you are finished?"

"Of course," I answered and helped her up.

She sat there and stared at the faded mural for a few moments. "It is fading with time, just like me."

She looked around the shop one more time and then back at the painting. "I'm just glad it wasn't Helen of Troy on that wall. I couldn't think of being named Helen. Now let's go do the town, Tully."

At sunset, we had *mojitos* and tapas at the bar at the Angleterre Hotel, then headed out to the ballpark and the real reason we had come — the ultimate battle without bullets in postrevolutionary Cuba.

El Cohete, the man Cleopatra lived to see pitch, was taking the mound for the Havana Industriales. The opponents were not Columbus and the Spanish conquistadores like in my dream, but the much-hated Santiago de Cuba. Millions of Yankee dollars called El Cohete from the other side of the Gulf Stream, hoping he would defect and play what the Cuban press called *pelota esclava* (slave baseball). But El Cohete stayed home. Thousands of newspaper articles had been written about his decision, but nobody in the press really knew why he stayed in Cuba.

"He doesn't need to go" is all Cleopatra said about it when I asked her. We inched along through the throng of fans pouring into the stadium. "Besides, El Cohete can't swim."

The game was a classic battle. Sixty thousand fans were in the stands two hours before the first pitch was thrown. The screaming, air horns, drums, and timbals never stopped. In fact, they only got louder; El Cohete had his magic working.

After each strikeout, the crowd would collectively count all of them off. That night, they were hoarse by the end of the game as El Cohete fanned sixteen batters and shut out Santiago.

The Industriales were up two games to none, and the series would now go to Santiago. As much as Cleopatra wanted to follow the team, the overland trip by car or train was too much for her. We were heading back to Cayo Loco.

After the game, Cleopatra and I caught up with El Cohete. He invited us to an open-air block party not far from the stadium, where he hung out in the neighborhood. Nobody asked for an autograph, and there were no agents, managers, lawyers, sponsors, or groupies screaming behind police barricades. El Cohete visited with people on their porch stoops and in their *cocina,* and then he and Cleopatra sat and talked family together. When the streets emptied and the party was put to bed, he walked with us in his uniform, and his cleats hung over the high handlebars of his bicycle.

We stopped at a street vendor and shared an ice cream, and he told Cleopatra he would try to get by the boat tomorrow morning before the team left for Santiago. He gave her a ball from the game and wrote something on it for her to keep. She put it in her pocket. Then the best pitcher in Cuban baseball (and 15 million Cuban fans would argue he was the best in the world) got on his bike and pedaled home.

It was just around midnight when we arrived in Cojimar. Our cab made the turn around the statue of Ernest Hemingway at the end of the road and stopped at the stairs leading down to the dock. There, under a Cuban moon, the satellite phone rang. Cleopatra handed it to me.

"It's in Miami!" Willie's echoing voice yelled out from the phone.

"No, we are in Havana," I said.

"Not you! It's in Miami. The bulb! The soul of the light! It's in a junkyard on the Miami River."

Well, you can imagine what kind of commotion that caused as we rode back to the ship. Cleopatra wanted to leave immediately, but we had to wait until morning to clear customs. We called Willie Singer back, and he told her the story three more times until she was finally able to believe that the object of her quest was sitting up the Miami River about a mile from the Highbourne Shipping Company dock.

Willie Singer had managed to track down his long-lost relative, Captain Stanley Singer, in Holland, Michigan. He indeed had a paper trail of clippings and shipping receipts for the lens. It had made its way to Australia, where it had been sold to a developer in Cuba in 1957. It seems the bull's-eye had been shipped to Havana back in the days of gambling, and it had been bought to be used as a prop in a casino. Then Fidel Castro came along, and somehow the lens was smuggled out of the country. It wound up in a warehouse in Nassau and had finally been bought by a marine junk dealer in Miami, who had written to Captain Stanley Singer for information about the light.

Willie had called the junkyard in Miami, and the original owner had died, but his son knew exactly where the lens was stored. Willie didn't even try to bargain with the junk dealer, just asked the price, wired the money, and told the man someone would pick it up. Talk about the season to be jolly. Two days after the call, the *Lucretia* sailed under the Christmas decorations on the Brickell Causeway and up to the Highbourne docks, where we were met by Diver in a U-Haul truck. He had flown in ahead of us. Cleopatra, Diver, and I headed up River Road to the junkyard. I was listening to directions from Cleopatra and keeping my eyes peeled as Diver wound through trailer courts, boatyards, and shotgun houses that made up the backwater world of the Miami River.

"Stop!" Cleopatra suddenly screamed from the passenger seat.

Diver slammed on the brakes, and I nearly launched through the windshield. I expected to see a body rolling across the hood or hear the howl of a wounded potcake dog under the wheel of the truck. My heart was pounding.

"Look," Cleopatra said in a whisper. Her lucid green eyes were wide open, and her lower jaw had dropped. There, in the corner of a junkyard, camouflaged by a collection of lobster traps, cable drums, cargo containers, and rusted cruise-ship lifeboats, was a light tower.

"It's got to be a prop," I said, "for a movie or a theme park or something." But Cleopatra knew better. She was 101 years old and had been on the trail of the soul of the light for the last decade of her life.

"No," Cleopatra said, shaking her head. "It's real."

"I would call dat a helluva Christmas ornament," Diver said.

"And I know just the tree to top it with," Cleopatra said.

A decade of searching had ironically brought Cleopatra right to her own backyard. It took the rest of the day to carefully transport the lens from the junkyard to the hold of the *Lucretia,* but we did it. As we all just stood around the lens staring at it, with a collective sense of disbelief that we had actually found it, Cleopatra said, "I think we were meant to bring in the new millennium with this light." Our job was obviously far from over.

Cleopatra's desire to bring in the New Year with the soul of the light gave us less than three weeks to get it done. Needless to say, we were busy little beavers. Solomon knew more about lighthouses than just about anybody alive. He quickly did an inventory of the parts we had and the other things we needed to make the light work. Before we set sail, I called Sammy Raye and Captain Kirk with the news and gave them our "shopping list." They immediately got to work.

While we rode an uncharacteristic southwest wind to Cayo Loco, Sammy Raye and Kirk had spread the word throughout the world of lighthouse freaks. They had located a petroleum burner, hand pumps, piping fittings, and pressure tanks. Sammy Raye commandeered a young engineer from MIT, who designed and manufactured the missing hardware out of titanium. We now had a space-age lighthouse on our hands.

Drawing upon his childhood memories, Solomon sewed the mantle material into "big socks" like the ones he had helped his mother make.

Upon our arrival at Cayo Loco, Cleopatra learned that the tug pulling the crane she had contracted had broken down and was stuck in Georgetown. It did not faze her. She and Solomon quickly came up with an ingenious rig that used the masts and rigging of the *Lucretia* to hoist the seven-hundred-pound light from the deck of the ship to the light tower.

Finally, barrels of mercury that Sammy Raye had ordered from West Palm Beach arrived on a chartered supply boat.

We celebrated Christmas quickly under a palm tree near the dock that the kids had decorated, and then on Boxing Day, we exchanged presents and had a wonderful lunch on the beach, but then it was back to work. Progress was rapidly being made. The various rooms and passage-ways of the giant steel tower were filled with an array of pipes, lines, and tanks that supported the soon-to-be-illu-minated bull's-eye lens above. Sammy Raye added his own personal touch by bringing in a paint contractor to re-create the original paint job on the tower. Cleopatra granted him permission to also spray one of the storage rooms bright pink. Problems presented themselves, and problems were quickly solved. Somewhere in the middle of all this wild activity, on a perfectly clear day, the sound of large airplane engines buzzed in the distance. Out of the sky descended a large silver flying boat.

"Come in, Cowboy," the voice on the radio crackled.

Willie Singer had finally arrived at Cayo Loco. He was not alone. Off the plane stepped a wild-looking man in Navy dress whites and a perfectly groomed, middle-aged man in a tropical tan suit. I didn't need a passenger man-ifest to know I was looking at Waltham and Philippe Par-fait. Of course Cleopatra and Willie hit it right off when she told him about meeting Lindbergh and Juan Trippe in Trinidad one carnival, and Parfait was his usual charming self, but there was no time to socialize. Even my promise to finally bring Willie bonefishing had to be put on hold. Willie and Waltham and even Parfait joined in the work-force. Only on the morning of New Year's Eve, when the final touches of red paint were dabbed on the huge rings that candy striped the light tower, did we stop. With work pronounced finished by Solomon and Diver, Willie loaded us all up in the *Pearl,* and Cleopatra got to see Cayo Loco from the air, which had her talking a blue streak.

And so it was that shortly before midnight on the last day

of the twentieth century, on a salty piece of land south of the Crooked Island Passage, a bucket brigade of lighthouse nuts with flashlights strapped to their heads wound themselves around the freshly varnished steps of the Cayo Loco Light like a string of Christmas-tree lights. Ix-Nay, Willie, Captain Kirk, Solomon, and Diver, the crew of the *Lucretia,* local villagers, Sammy Raye, Waltham, Parfait, and I passed jugs of fossil fuel up the stairs to fill the tanks for the first time in nearly fifty years.

Cleopatra Highbourne followed us up along with friends and crew. Everyone crowded into the light room, out on the catwalk, and down the ladder to witness this moment, when the sun slowly dipped below the western horizon.

"Ready, Captain?" Solomon asked.

Cleopatra let out a big sigh, and it was the first time I had ever seen her the slightest bit nervous. "Aye-aye," she answered.

With that, Solomon gave the signal to start pumping kerosene. He then dropped the sun curtain from around the bull's-eye lens, and a shower of tiny rainbows caused by the reflection of the setting sun on the glass prisms lit up the lighthouse walls like a kaleidoscope.

Solomon leaned over the huge tub of mercury in which the bull's-eye floated. He inched the light left and right with the tip of his index finger.

"Standing by, Captain," he said. This meant that all that was left was for Cleopatra to strike a match and light the mantles. Solomon handed her a long-stem wooden match and a flint striker.

"I feel as if I am about to light the biggest goddamn firecracker in the world," Cleopatra said as she struck the match and moved her aging hand toward the mantles.

There was a small pop as the kerosene ignited. The little blue flame transformed into a piercing white glow that was instantly magnified by the beautiful lens.

Solomon released the lock on the winding clock. The cables tightened and groaned as the seven-hundred-pound counterweights began their descent through the light tower, and the light beam shot from the lens out over the open ocean like a meteor streaking across the sky. The soul of the light was sending out its signal, and the Cayo Loco Light was back in business.

The realization that we had pulled off something close to a miracle seemed to temper our emotions, and there was not the usual jubilation of an island party to ring in the New Year, not to mention the new century. We just sat on the beach and built a fire, and Willie strummed his guitar while Diver and Ix-Nay joined in on congas. It was the perfect background music to watch the smooth sweep of the five swords of light cut constantly through the darkness.

"Electricity cannot hold a candle to it," Cleopatra said.

Through the night, we took turns climbing the tower every two hours to wind up the lens clock until the first signs of the new day arrived from the east.

On the last trip up to the light tower, Cleopatra came with me. She extinguished the light, and I pulled the lens curtains back around the bull's-eye to keep the sun away. We put the light to bed.

We walked out onto the catwalk and surveyed the scene below us. The panorama of salt, sea, sand, and sky had in effect been our own little planet, which had once again discovered its sun.

It was apparent that the New Year would be ushered in with a perfect tropical day of clear skies and gentle breezes. Below us, the *Lucretia* sat at anchor amid a fleet of boats that included the *Caribbean Soul,* an array of smack boats and skiffs, Sammy Raye's pink plane, and Willie Singer's *Flying Pearl.* The dock was deserted except for a few pelicans perched on the pilings, preparing to make their breakfast dives into the schools of pilchers moving along the shore. Cleopatra stood there, surveying things. Then she said, "I was just thinking back to that afternoon when I saw you on the beach for the first time in Tulum. Do you remember?"

"Yes, I do."

"Do you remember what you said to me that made the difference between me having a polite conversation with what appeared to be a gringo beach bum and inviting you aboard for dinner?"

I had a clear memory of that conversation. It had changed my life forever. "I asked what you were looking for," I said.

"Did you ever think we wouldn't find it?"

"Not really," I answered.

As we talked, a tiny hummingbird banked around the corner of the rail. It rapidly changed directions like a ricocheting bullet, and then it slammed on its air brakes and hovered in place, its small wings a blur of motion not more than two feet from our heads.

"I'll be damned," Cleopatra said. "It's a ruby-throated hummingbird. What are you doing way out here?" she asked the little bird.

With that, the tiny bird accelerated at a right angle and flew through the open hatch into the light room. Discovering that it was trapped behind glass, the little bird began to panic.

I rushed inside and approached the bird, hoping I

could gently trap it and take it back outside. Then the most amazing thing happened. It flew directly for me and landed on my arm. It sat there as I walked back outside.

"You know, those little fellas fly all the way from Cape Breton Island in Nova Scotia across the Gulf to winter in your old neck of the woods. It is way off course," said Cleopatra.

The hummingbird on my arm sat as still as a piece of Chinese porcelain, and I could see its small, intense eyes were locked on mine. "I can identify with that feeling," I said.

"So can I." And as suddenly as the hummingbird had buzzed into our life, it buzzed out, circling the light tower as if it were collecting its bearings. Then it picked up a heading that we both recognized to be the course to its winter nesting grounds somewhere in Central America.

"He should see the lights of Havana by sunset, and after that, he will steer by the stars," she said as I imagined such a small but determined creature winging its way over the expanse of the Caribbean Sea, following the only course it knew.

"I wonder if he knows his final destination," I said.

"Few of us do," Cleopatra replied. "Few of us do."

39

Catching the Tail of the Comet

I had done what I had come to do. The Cayo Loco Light and light keeper's quarters were back to their original — if not better — condition.

Now that it was once again in service, the light had to be tended. To my pleasant surprise, Ix-Nay asked to stay on for a year and join Diver as a light tender. They would train a couple of the local boys who had expressed interest in helping them. Mr. Twain had also become an islander. Since his arrival on Cayo Loco, he had defied the odds of horse aging and looked better at twenty-three than he did at ten. I have heard of some quarter horses living to forty, and that looked to be where he was headed. He seemed to know the island even better than I did. Speaking of me, I was looking like the odd man out. Though I would always have my little cabin and my horse to come back to, I was beginning to feel the urge to move along again. I was not alone.

A week after the light had been rebirthed, all of our friends and guests had left, and Cayo Loco went back to being a quiet place. The light ran as smoothly as a Swiss watch, and my captain gave orders to sail. Cleopatra and I watched the beam disappear in the wake of the *Lucretia* as we headed for the Old Bahamas Channel. I was returning to Key West.

I was a bit confused at her insistence that we sail to Key West so soon because I thought that we had rebuilt Cayo Loco as her place to retire and watch the light. She said nothing to Solomon or me about the trip other than that she had some things to do.

When we arrived, we anchored off Christmas Tree Island and rowed to the old Singleton Shrimp Company docks, in the heart of town. From there, we walked through the crowds that now made Lower Duval Street seem like a mall, but a few blocks away, old Key West could still be found.

We were met at a dock by an old Cuban man who stood about four feet five inches in a red guayabera shirt and a weathered panama hat. He looked to be damn near as old as Cleopatra. She introduced him as Lupe Cadiz and told me that he was the caretaker for her property.

We climbed into an old wood-paneled station wagon that looked as if it had just come from an antique show.

"I don't get back here much anymore," she said.

"When was the last time you were here?" I asked.

"Nineteen eighty-eight," she told me, as if it had been last week.

We drove the few blocks down Simonton Street, where the laid-back aura of Key West revealed itself by the number of odd characters who made their way down the street on bicycle and on foot. I was taking in the scenery, looking at a row of restored old captain's mansions that lined Southard Street, when Lupe hung a right into a tiny alley named Spoonbill Lane. It was barely wide enough for the car. The street came to a dead end at what appeared to be a small rain forest. Then I saw the rectangular shape of a widow's walk perched above the thick hedge of bamboo and bougainvillea.

"Welcome to Highbourne Hill," Cleopatra said as Lupe got out of the car and swung open a hidden iron gate.

We had only driven a couple of yards down the conch-shell-lined driveway when a house came into view that made the other mansions seem like minor-league architecture.

The house appeared to be ancient, but like the *Lucretia,* it was perfectly intact. It was obviously designed to combat the heat, salt, and sun, as it was protected by a canopy of palms and banyan trees. It sat behind a massive manicured lawn of Saint Augustine grass. A pathway of slab coral stones led to the expansive front porch, where two giant ship's anchors were partially sunken into the ground. The house itself looked as if it had been freshly painted yesterday.

Both levels were wrapped with porches and carved railings that were accentuated by a pair of large green pineapples at each corner of the house. Dark green Bahamian top-hung shutters lined the front of the house on both stories, and a squadron of ceiling fans stabbed at the still air.

"This is what I wanted to show you. This is the house I grew up in," Cleopatra told me. "This is as close to a real home as I ever had, Tully. I am going to stay here a few weeks and gather up the things I want to take back to Cayo Loco, and I would like you to help me."

That was her first mention of going back to Cayo Loco. Of course I agreed.

Over the next few weeks, I took up residence in the garden cottage near the rear of the property under a sprawling mahogany tree. It was certainly a different introduction to the island than the one I'd had when I came here as a deckhand on a shrimp boat. I liked this version better.

Lupe, his wife, Carmen, and I helped Cleopatra catalog a collection of keepsakes, photos, clippings, letters, and small treasures about her family and her travels. Mostly we boxed them up and hauled them over to the Key West library, where they were added to the archives of the Highbourne family.

In the process, Cleopatra kept me in a state of both sheer awe and hysterical laughter as she made me tape-record stories about her family every evening over several rum drinks. It was such an amazing and simple thing to do, and I wished I had thought of doing the same with Johnny Red Dust. So many people live such dull, predictable lives these days that the real adventurers are becoming a thing of the past — but their stories are like channel markers for the stormy waters of the future.

Besides my oral-history project, I was given a thorough discourse on the architecture of the house and the botanical makeup of the garden. I felt as if I were in school again and fully expected a pop quiz at any moment, but it never came. Meanwhile, Cleopatra packed her keepsakes into wooden trunks that were loaded onto the *Lucretia*.

While winter raged from the frozen iron mountains of the Upper Peninsula in Michigan down to the orange groves of Central Florida, Key West stayed unseasonably warm, and I took advantage of the weather. When I wasn't working for Cleopatra, I actually got in some fishing.

Sammy Raye had put me in touch with Garnett Woolsey, the builder who had made the copy of my boat. He also ran a guide service in Key West and Belize and played in a local calypso band. Garnett was in the process of designing his own brand of flats skiffs, and I figured Sammy Raye had something to do with it, as he was in Key West a lot during this time. I spent many an enjoyable afternoon on the flats west of Key West and also in the shop watching the new boat come to life. I even bought a used bicycle. I explored the island from my red bike, weaving through traffic on the main streets as I went looking for the out-of-the-way parts of the island. Granted Key West was a small island, but it was the size of a country compared to Cayo Loco.

We stayed on into February, and the day before our scheduled departure for Cayo Loco, I heard a knock on the door of my cottage.

"I want to show you something before it gets too hot," Cleopatra said as she clipped three climbing roses from the garden.

We strolled down Spoonbill Lane onto Angela Street and were driven to the sidewalk by a swarm of mopeds that sped down Passover Lane. When we got to the cemetery gate, Cleopatra motioned to the right. The street inside the cemetery was named Magnolia Avenue, but it was lined with palm trees. We passed among the elevated crypts and mausoleums covered with bouquets of real and plastic flowers.

"I figured I owed them all a visit."

"Who?" I asked.

"The good angels and the bad angels. I guess we'll start with the worst."

I stared at the huge black obelisk that looked so out of

place compared to the surrounding plots. "What's that?"
I asked.

"It's not what, it's who," she commented. "Those are
the Diamond boys."

"They seem to think a lot of themselves," I said, staring up at the grotesque monument.

"The Highbournes had money, but we didn't flaunt.
My father taught us that. But it all changed when the Diamonds invaded our family," Cleopatra said.

"So these are the ancestors of Donald H. Diamond the
Third?"

"Yup. Donald and Ronald, my no-good, nouveau-riche
stepbrothers, their trophy wives, and several of their
ne'er-do-well offspring, legitimate and not. My stepmother wasn't so bad, but I seldom saw her since I was at
sea most of the time. Still, she came with some major
baggage in the form of Ronald and Donald. Just look at
that piece of shit," Cleopatra blurted out as she stared
with contempt at the tall obelisk. "They wanted everybody
to know who they were — alive or dead." On the left side
of the giant black obelisk, three large granite tombstones
backed up to the fence. They were overshadowed by a
pair of marble angels with ten-foot wingspans. "Just goes
to show you, money never does buy good taste," Cleopatra said. "Now for the good angels."

We walked past the monument to a rusty gate next to
the Diamond plot. A bronze anchor with the word HIGH-
BOURNE hung above the gate. She opened it and went in.
I followed.

She walked to the shadow beneath a tree and placed the
first rose on the gravestone of Lucretia Meador Highbourne, her mother. The second, she placed on the crypt of
her stepfather, Patrick Highbourne. We left the plot and sat

on a bench in the shade. "Donald was such an ass kisser," she said. "And that goes for Ronald, as well. I love the fact that I outlived both the greedy bastards. Teddy and I had figured them out, but it was already too late."

"Who's Teddy?" I asked.

"The youngest and most decent Diamond in the bunch. Shortly after my father's death, while Teddy and I were both out at sea, the Trojan horse popped open. Ronald and Donald and some venomous lawyers concocted a way to take over the company. That is when they left Key West and moved to Miami. This is way too boring to discuss further," she said and sighed.

"Not at all," I protested.

Cleopatra fell silent for a moment as she stood in front of a simple headstone with the words THEODORE DIAMOND on the face. "Notice it is in the Highbourne, not the Diamond, plot."

"Now you get to meet my dad." Her voice was filled with excitement, like a teenage daughter on her first date. We exited the family plot, crossed a sand road, and walked over to an American flag. Under it, surrounded by a painted iron fence, were buried victims of the USS *Maine*. We walked among the small headstones that lined the perimeter of the plot to an area where the officers were buried.

"Nothing like a little closure."

"How so?" I asked.

"I came to say good-bye and hello — like in that Beatles song."

"That was my favorite song on *Magical Mystery Tour*," I told her, thinking how odd it was to be discussing sixties music with a 101-year-old woman in a cemetery.

Suddenly Cleopatra began to cry. "I always have the

same feeling when I come here." She wiped tears from her face with her hand. "I knew my stepfather and loved him dearly, but I never knew my father." She was sobbing now. "I hope I turned out the way he wanted me to be."

I put my arm around her shoulder. It was the first time since I had known her that she looked and felt frail. I held on to her as she continued.

"I wonder what might have happened if I had just stayed here with my poor mother and had been the kind of daughter she wanted me to be."

"Well," I said slowly, "all I can say is it certainly wouldn't have been as much fun for me."

"And why is that?"

"Because I wouldn't have met you, and my life would have been far less interesting."

Cleopatra wiped her eyes and her composure returned with a laugh, which made me feel better. "You know, you're right. Who else would have gotten your ass out of the clutches of those pole dancers in Belize?"

"Do we have to bring that up here?" I asked.

"Just messing with you, kid," she said with a smile.

Intensity returned to her eyes as she stared at a dangling ficus vine overhead. Then, with catlike speed, she swept her hand across the branch. "Look," she said, opening her hand to reveal a small brown tree lizard. It was in the process of turning from the green of the vine to a more undetectable shade. Cleopatra lifted the little lizard by the nape of its neck and placed it up next to her face, where it clamped its jaws around her left earlobe and dangled in the breeze. "It doesn't hurt," she said with a childish laugh. "We had a maid once who came from Martinique and showed me this little trick. She called it the dancing earring. Try it."

Before I knew it, Cleopatra had gently pulled the lizard from her ear, and it had latched on to mine. A shiver went up my spine as I felt the little jaws hanging on for dear life.

"It's kind of a Highbourne tradition to go around with lizards dangling from our ears. It is one of the many things that separated us from the Diamonds. They worshipped money. We were taught to love the natural world." The little lizard hung in the air for a few more seconds and then dropped off. Cleopatra caught it and placed it back on the vine.

We walked past a few more military headstones, and then Cleopatra dropped to her knees and placed the last rose next to a headstone that read CAPTAIN ANDERSON MEADOR — SAILOR, FATHER, AND PATRIOT. She then stood at attention and saluted the grave.

Cleopatra again reached for my steadying hand, and we walked back down Magnolia Avenue. "Well, I have gathered my belongings, and I have paid my respects to my parents. That leaves just one final thing I have to take care of before we sail, and that will be best done over a couple of rum-and-coconut waters."

"Okay."

"I am going back to the house, but I need for you to pick up some ice at the Waterfront Market, if you would."

I watched her walk slowly toward the gate of the cemetery. She seemed to lean a little more than usual on her cane.

"Are you okay? I can go get the car," I said.

"Don't be silly."

I came back to Highbourne Hill with the melting ice, but Cleopatra wasn't there. Lupe and Carmen were also gone. The phone rang as I was walking through the house to the kitchen. The voice on the phone sounded very official, and the man identified himself as Dr. Malta. He told me that Cleopatra had suffered a heart attack and was in intensive care at the Florida Keys Memorial Hospital.

Hospital waiting is a strange state of existence. You're filled with your own concerns for your loved ones, but you are also suddenly part of a community of people who are dealing with the comings and goings from this world that our mortality presents. I hadn't been in a hospital since I saw Johnny Red Dust for the last time. But what happens in a waiting room is that time slows way down, even more so than on Cayo Loco or at sea. All you can do is wait. You read a story in the paper or in a magazine.

Usually when you read, you think for a minute, and then you go about your business. But when you're sitting in a waiting room, about to get a life-or-death announcement, you reflect. I was doing just that as I waited for news about Cleopatra. I had spent the past hour mulling over an article about idiots in Northern Florida who had gone out and shot hundreds of pelicans and herons in a wildlife refuge. Then they had drunkenly bragged about it to the people in line at Dunkin' Donuts, where they were arrested. In my mind, I had devised more than a dozen methods of punishment — from burying them in the sand so other birds could peck their eyeballs out to public flogging at halftime during the Florida-Florida State game.

I was deep in thought when a young man in a white coat approached me and said, "Mr. Mars, I am Dr. Malta. She wants to see you."

I walked in the room not knowing what to expect, and I was shocked to see Cleopatra fully dressed in her khakis, sitting on the bed and staring out the window at the ocean.

"I am not going to die in a goddamn hospital," she barked.

Three hours later, we were riding the Gulf Stream east. A cold front had finally draped across the Straits of Florida, and the temperature dropped twenty degrees in twenty minutes. The wind blew a steady twenty knots on the beam, and the *Lucretia* seemed to know that time was of the essence as she slapped aside the rolling waves along the Cuban coastline. Cleopatra called it the Mardi Gras wind.

She had been rolled out of the hospital in a mandatory wheelchair, but at the curb, she sprang up and walked to the waiting station wagon. Lupe had driven us to the dock. I had called Solomon with the news that we were heading to Cayo Loco at full speed, and when we reached the dock, the boat had been ready to sail.

The wind never stopped blowing, and we ran every stitch of sail up the masts, daring the cold front to tear at the rigging. Amazingly, nothing broke. We never saw the log drop below seventeen knots, and we covered the five hundred miles from Key West to Cayo Loco in just under twenty-nine hours, half the time it had taken us to come up.

Cleopatra had settled into her cabin with the help of Dr. Malta, the young doctor whom she had somehow enlisted into her scheme to get to Cayo Loco. Dr. Malta was from Pakistan and was an avid sailor with four days off. I knew from my own experience the lure of the ship and the adventure she represented. Dr. Malta had come with a boxful of supplies and had Cleopatra stable and resting comfortably.

I had heard Cleopatra's orders to him as she came on board. She simply told him to keep her alive until we reached Cayo Loco.

40

The Seconds Between Light and Dark

The power of weather still never ceases to amaze me. A storm that is born in the frozen, sun-starved Arctic ten thousand miles to the north can cover that distance at twice the speed of the *Lucretia* and still chill you to the bone in the seventy-degree waters of the Gulf Stream.

Just south of the Cay Sal Banks, waters well known to be shallow and dangerous, Solomon and I were taking sextant readings of the evening stars to verify our position. I have always thought of star sights as moving the heavens — which is exactly what you do with the help of a mirror and some tricky math. You move the reflection of a star on your mirror down the arch of the sextant and sit it on a visible horizon, which gives you an angle you can measure.

Solomon and I were busy working the sight, which indeed confirmed our remarkable speed and our estimated time of arrival. We were due in Cayo Loco the next morning just before sunrise.

I went down into the cabin to report the news to

Cleopatra, but she was asleep and had suddenly begun to look her age. Dr. Malta followed me out of the cabin.

"What's the story?" I asked.

"We are racing death," he said in a somber but compassionate tone.

"Then let's see if we can win."

Back on deck, I reported my conversation to Solomon. He didn't say anything but merely stared up at the rigging. The look on his face told me he meant to get Cleopatra home. It was confirmed when he called all hands on deck and ordered the fisherman hoisted. "If she blows, she blows," he said.

When my watch was over, I did not go below but curled up on the pilot berth in the doghouse, closed my eyes, and said a prayer for Cleopatra.

I wasn't sure how long I had been asleep on the doghouse bunk when I was awakened by the sound of somebody singing. As I clawed my way back to consciousness, I saw through the portholes that it was still pitch-black outside. The wind was blowing, and we were moving at a fast clip. It was freezing. I bundled up in my wool crew sweater and foul-weather gear, then climbed into my harness. The ship was heeled over about twenty degrees to starboard, and I clipped onto the life rail and worked my way steadily and carefully back to the cockpit to join the party behind the wheel.

I wedged my body into the cockpit, using my legs to brace me against the wind, waves, and gravity. To tell the truth, I didn't know whether I was shivering because I was freezing or because I was afraid of what might have happened to Cleopatra. As I climbed out of the confined space of the doghouse, I was shocked to see Cleopatra wrapped in a cocoon of blankets, sitting beside Solomon at the wheel. She had a large string of purple-and-gold beads around her neck, and she was singing to Dr. Malta in Spanish as he took her blood pressure.

"Happy Mardi Gras!" she exalted, trying to put on her best happy face. "I'm still here — not quite a neighbor of Grandma Ghost yet," she added. "That was a song my mother used to sing to me when she was trying to raise me properly and distract me from boats. It didn't work. Poor thing. I just had a dream about her." Dr. Malta finished his work and tucked her arm back under the blanket. "Come sit with us, Tully," she said as she patted the wooden seat at her side. "I have a present for you." She pulled another strand of beads out from under the blanket and slid them over the hood of my foul-weather jacket.

"Happy birthday," I said.

"Oh, that birthday thing." She let out a sigh and then laughed. "Just one more trip around the sun for this old fart."

I pulled out the small box I had wrapped back in Key West when I had expected we would be celebrating her one-hundred-second birthday on Cayo Loco. But as we huddled together in the cockpit of the *Lucretia,* this seemed somehow a much more appropriate place to give her my gift.

"Can you open it for me, Tully? And Dr. Malta, I think I might have a medicinal nip while I am waiting."

Dr. Malta pulled a pint of rum out of his black bag and poured a healthy portion into the coffee mug Cleopatra was clutching. "Care for a snort, swab?" Cleopatra asked me.

"Not right now, Captain," I answered. I unwrapped the box and handed it to her. She lifted the lid.

"Tully, that's your lucky shell," she said.

"It's yours now. Johnny Red Dust told me that it was to remind me of where I was going. It's been bouncing all over the place with me for a long time. I think it needs to rest for a while, and the mantel of your cottage on Cayo Loco seems like a good spot to me. Besides, what do you get a woman who has everything?"

Cleopatra held the Lister's conch up close to her eyes, examining it as if she were a child. "It's a lovely thought, Tully, but I can't accept it. My luck has just about run out, but I am sure you will find someone who will need it more than me."

With that, she leaned forward, gave me a weak hug, and gently pressed the shell back into the palm of my hand.

Roberto came out of the doghouse. "We are making incredible time. I put us a little less than an hour from Cayo Loco." He clipped into the lifeline, bent his body to the wind, and moved forward along the windward rail toward the mast, pointing a spotlight up into the rigging.

"Well," Cleopatra said, "I appreciate all of your gifts and what you all have done for me, but I think I better say what I have to say right now."

"Don't be silly," I said with a laugh. "We're just under an hour away."

"And what do you think I am going to do when I get there? Jump from the rigging and swim ashore as the first leg of a goddamn triathlon? Oh, Jesus, I am sorry about that. This close to my day of judgment, I probably should watch my language. Anyway, son, I am dying. It's not that I am giving up on you, I am just giving out. So no more interruptions until I am finished saying what I have to.

"Solomon, when I am gone, the *Lucretia* is yours, and I mean as the owner, not just a captain. Hell, she's really been yours all these years anyway. There is a trust fund set up to pay for the operation and maintenance costs. There is a bonus program for the crew and money to build a new school in Dangriga. I also want you to start a program for island kids all over the Bahamas to teach them to be sailors and preserve the tradition of sailing in these islands. It seems to me that if we saved the lighthouse, then we certainly have to have beautiful ships to sail by it. Don't we?"

"Aye-aye, Captain," Solomon answered as tears ran down his cheeks.

"Dr. Malta, you haven't been with us long, but you did keep me breathing and got me out of that damn hospital. That clinic you want to build in your village in Pakistan? You have it."

The young doctor bowed his head to Cleopatra and then looked at us, asking with his eyes if what he just heard was true. We nodded our heads.

"Tully, that leaves you, and of course your situation is a little more difficult than the rest. You have done the task I brought you here to do. The soul of the light shines on and my final resting place is built. I am trusting you and Solomon to see to it that Cayo Loco never gets into that state of disrepair again."

"Yes, ma'am," I answered as I tried to control the trembling that swept over my body.

"There's one more thing. You are also fired," she said as she sipped at her rum. In an instant, Solomon went from crying to laughing at her sense of humor.

"It's no joke."

At first I thought she had just gone delusional in her last hours, or it was the rum talking, but then I looked in those eyes I had come to know so well, and I could see she was serious as a heart attack.

I had no idea how to respond. At that moment, the *Lucretia* carved into a huge rogue wave that jolted the hull and sent a forty-foot cascade of spray flying across the deck, drenching the cockpit. Solomon held the wheel steady as the cockpit, which now looked like a swimming pool, quickly drained.

Cleopatra laughed. "We are all survivors — even you, Dr. Malta; you have survived your first real storm. But the trouble with being a survivor is that you find yourself dancing alone a lot. It is a tricky seesaw on which the survivor has to sit. On the one side is your ability to be comfortable in a world inhabited only by yourself. And on the other side is your desire to share your time with others. How do you balance? Being a survivor is not a bad thing, but you do run the risk of being the last one at the party when the punch bowl is empty and the confetti has turned to dust — like me."

Cleopatra closed her eyes and was silent. At first, I thought she had gone. But her breath frosted in the cold air, and she popped her eyes open again and picked up where she had left off. "Tully, I don't want that to happen to you. That is why I am firing you from Cayo Loco and giving you Highbourne Hill as a place to plant yourself for a while. You have done more for me than you will ever know, and this is a small way to pay you back. Have parties, find a woman, raise some children, and fish a lot. Key West ain't the cultural center of the universe, but it will do for starters."

"Light ahead two points off the starboard bow," Roberto called from the foredeck.

Cleopatra twisted her head but couldn't see the light. Solomon let the boat fall off to starboard and brought the light to her.

"There," I said and pointed.

"It's the darkness that brings out what is sacred," Cleopatra said. Then she added with a smile, "That would be the Cayo Loco Light."

The whole crew stared out into the darkness, and when the piercing white light cut through the night, cheers, howls, and whistles reverberated across the deck.

I counted the seconds between light and dark. "Four flashes at four-second intervals," I said, turning to Cleopatra. "You're right, as usual, Captain. It's Cayo Loco. We're home."

Suddenly we were distracted from our celebration as the wind, which had hauled steady out of the north-northeast since we had departed from Key West, started to back off. Then it veered every which way, as if it couldn't make up its mind what to do. The sails began to luff, and the rigging chattered loudly as Solomon held the ship steady, expecting some kind of sudden blow.

The opposite happened. The wind dropped to nothing, the howling stopped instantly, and the *Lucretia* righted herself. Then in the sky to the east, a falling star, with a fiery tail that stretched halfway across the sky, tumbled through the dark and then disappeared.

I was watching the path it had taken when I heard the sound of something shatter on deck. It was as loud as a broadside from a ship off the line. When I turned and looked at Cleopatra, her eyes were closed. There was a smile frozen on her face, and the coffee mug lay in pieces at her feet. I knew she had stood her last watch aboard the *Lucretia*.

41

On the Back of
a Crocodile

When a queen died in ancient Egypt, it was said that her soul sailed down the Nile on a golden ship to the afterlife, where she would hook up with Ra, the sun god. The supplies for her heavenly journey would have been prepared here on earth years in advance of her departure. The funeral barge, a wooden ship 150 feet long and painted with gold dust, was packed with coins, jewels, food, royal flip-flops, books, musical instruments, a few unsuspecting loyal servants, favorite cats, and star maps etched on sheets of papyrus. The Egyptians seemed to believe that in fact you *could* take it with you.

I am not saying that a woman who had been named for a mural in a Cuban barbershop was in some way related to the ancient rulers of Egypt, or that the *Lucretia* was her royal barge, but like the Egyptians, she sure as hell knew how she wanted to leave this world. Riding in the hold of the *Lucretia* was a mahogany coffin that Cleopatra had commissioned in Key West. There were also bags of conch shells and earth from the Malecon in Havana, the wooden toy box from the barbershop, and the baseball that El Cohete had signed for her the night we had spent with him in Cuba; and of course there were instructions as to how it would all be utilized in the celebration of her life and departure from this earth.

True to her pragmatic view of things, it was short and simple. The shock of seeing her motionless behind the wheel never really had a chance to register.

Dr. Malta and Solomon carried her gently back to her cabin. We had no time to cry or grieve or reflect on what had just happened. The winds had returned, the beacon on the horizon was getting larger, and the business of getting the ship safely to Cayo Loco took precedence over our emotions. Life moved on, even as we dealt with death.

Once the anchor was dropped at Cayo Loco, with the exception of the oarsmen for the dinghy and Roberto, the crew set about putting the *Lucretia* back in order after the harrowing run before the cold front from Key West. Roberto supervised the lowering of the dory over the side, then he and his crew loaded all the keepsakes and cargo and finally the coffin aboard, and the oarsmen took their places at their sweeps. Solomon and I piled in the packed dinghy and found standing room near the tiller. Roberto gave the order to cast off, and we took our captain ashore.

Once clear of the boat, Benjamin, the young drummer, tapped out a cadence on his turtle shell, and the oarsmen began to sing the song Cleopatra had requested.

> *Well, she sailed away on a bright and sunny day*
> *On the back of a crocodile.*
> *Can't you see, said she, he's as tame as can be;*
> *I'll ride him down the Nile.*

Well, the croc winked his eye as she waved a sad good-bye,
Wearing a happy smile.
At the end of the ride, Cleopatra was inside,
And the smile was on the crocodile.

When they finished, Roberto shouted out, "Dead stroke on the mark — now." The oarsmen pulled in perfect cadence as the blades of the sweeps took the dory toward the shore. The oars were then feathered, and on the second stroke, they glided in unison through the air just above the surface of the sea. Once again they were feathered, and the following stroke bit at the water. The alternating pattern was continued all the way to the beach.

I asked Roberto if the choreography of the sweeps was something Cleopatra had asked for. He told me no, that it was an ancient Garifuna custom that was reserved for chiefs and shamans — it transported both the body and the spirit of the special person to their burying place. It was a send-off from the crew to Cleopatra.

We were met at the shore by Diver, Ix-Nay, and a small group of local families who had already gotten the word. Solomon had radioed his son with the news of Cleopatra's death and instructions to gather a large pile of driftwood and stack it near the salt pond at Osprey Point. Per her instructions, Cleopatra would be cremated there, and her ashes were to be put in the toy box she had received from the barber in Havana. Then the toy box was to be buried under a palm tree on Osprey Point with a view to the southwest toward the shores of her not-so-distant birthplace — Cuba.

As if by design, Mardi Gras Day had fallen on the day she was born — and the day she died. We loaded up a wagon with the coffin, the toy box, and the other items

Cleopatra wanted buried with her, and we harnessed up Mr. Twain. The crew laid piles of red, pink, and white hibiscus on the coffin, and Solomon climbed aboard to steady the load. On his signal, I gave Mr. Twain a slight tug on the reins, and we walked along a spiderweb of footpaths to the one that led to Osprey Point.

The winds of the cold front still glazed the morning with a slight chill, but once we descended to the shoreline behind the protection of the dunes, the warmth returned. The outgoing tide had exposed the flats, and that pungent smell of the shallows mixed with the perfume of night-blooming jasmine and the pine-needle scent from our five-tree forest. At the edge of the water, inch-high waves unfolded onto the beach as if they were trying to sneak ashore. The reflection of the sun on a scattering of tails gave the location of a school of bonefish traveling in the same direction as the funeral entourage. The usually skittish fish were not spooked by the noise of the wagon or the song that the crew sang as they followed along.

At the end of the beach, the school of fish became clearly visible as we climbed the path to Osprey Point. As we watched, the bonefish slowly banked around to the left like a fighter-jet squadron, then made a complete circle before disappearing into the blue water offshore. Circles were being completed all around me, I thought as I walked with my horse. It seemed like only yesterday that I had waded ashore with Cleopatra.

Roberto set a ghetto blaster on the wagon and pushed the power button as we all gathered around the grave site. The now-familiar voice of Carlos Gardel could be heard above the waves lapping against the shore. The mahogany coffin was placed on the stack of driftwood, and Solomon lit the fire.

So it was, on a clear, crisp morning on a salty piece of land in a hidden corner of the world, the orange-and-yellow flames of Cleopatra's funeral pyre burned brightly on Mardi Gras Day. A flock of pink flamingos that had not been seen on the island for several months suddenly returned and flew in several circles around the flame, then repeated the maneuver around the red-and-white tower of Cayo Loco.

Cleopatra Highbourne had not only found the soul of the light. She had become a part of it.

42

Gone Fishing

I don't want to sound superficial about losing my friend and mentor, but when I finally stopped running at full speed after dealing with the details of death, it was time to take a quiet, thoughtful ride across the island on my horse. I experienced a bit of long-overdue silence, and what came to me was this: Life is, and always has been, a struggle. The fishing pole bends heavier for some than others, and nobody has yet to figure out why — just as you never know, when you make a cast, if what attacks your fly is a finger-size baby snapper or a tiger shark that can turn you into bait. Still, we struggle with the rod just the same. Life to me is like a fish on the line. When it is there, you feel it. You fight it. You gain line. You lose line. But if that line suddenly snaps, or the pole breaks, or a thousand other problems occur that fishermen use as excuses when the tension is gone, you feel it even more.

I was looking out at the ocean when the annoying sound of a cigarette boat interrupted my thoughts. It took me back to a day when I had met the not-so-delightful present-day patriarch of the Diamond branch of her family. I had accompanied Cleopatra to Miami, to the Highbourne Shipping Company slip and dockside facilities that Cleopatra's father had built to maintain her boat.

"My father, God bless his soul, was wise enough to protect the things he loved most — me and my boat. If it was up to that moneygrubbing, social-climbing, luckysperm-club extended family of mine, run by Donald the Turd, this dockside would have been turned into luxury condominiums long ago."

I burst out laughing at the name. "Sounds like a royal shithead," I added.

"Exactly," Cleopatra said. "His real name is Donald H. Diamond the Third, but 'Turd' seemed more appropriate than 'Third.' He is the kind of man who makes you instantly think that public flogging should be reinstated into the penal code of South Florida and carried out during happy hour at any of a dozen sidewalk cafés on Collins Avenue."

We were about to leave Miami for Cayo Loco when a big Mercedes pulled up to the dock and out stepped Donald the Turd. I could tell by the serious look on his calculated face that he was not there for a "bon voyage" party. Decked out in a blue blazer, white pants, and velvet loafers, Donald carefully crossed the grimy concrete wharf as if he were navigating a pile of poisonous vipers.

"I heard you were here and wanted to know if you could take a moment to chat about the last of your stock options I mentioned in my recent letter," he called out. Cleopatra ignored him and was in the middle of commanding Solomon to cast off when her voice was drowned out by the deafening roar of the straight-pipe exhaust stacks of an approaching cigarette boat.

"I hate those fuckers," Cleopatra hissed. "They've been glamorized by TV shows, but there's only one reason they came into existence, and that's to get large amounts of cocaine from Colombia to Florida as fast as possible."

So around the bend in the river comes this penile extension–looking thing loaded down with several overweight, bare-chested males with obvious testosterone imbalances. The boat was painted bright yellow with the words PAR-T-ANIMAL scrolled down the side in metallic orange letters. The men, surrounded by a bevy of what appeared to be aspiring porn queens in small bikinis, were passing a bottle of champagne.

The boat sped by our mooring, throwing a huge wake that seconds later hit the *Lucretia* broadside and sent the hull crashing into the dock and the crew scurrying for fenders. Several of the teak planks of our deck were splintered, and naked bolts sat where the big cleat used to be. At that point I turned to look at the culprits, and that's when I saw Donald wave to the driver of the boat, who grinned, then turned around and shot us a moon.

Cleopatra was not amused. She waited until the *Par-T-Animal* had moved about a hundred yards downriver, and she watched as three men climbed onto the stern of the boat and peed into the river, shaking their flabby asses out of time to the blasts of heavy-metal music, while one of the women shouted at the trio to pee in the direction of the lens of her video camera.

That's when Cleopatra asked Roberto for her gun. He appeared instantly with her M16. From the dock, Donald the Turd screamed, "No, no, Aunt Cleo! I don't think we should be firing off semiautomatic rounds on Sunday!"

She shot Donald the bird, snapped the clip into the

gun, walked to the bow, knelt down out of sight between two large sail bags, took aim at her target, and fired.

Next, we heard the sound of a seriously badly running engine rev up as the driver of the boat tried to speed up with no success. Smoke billowed out of the lower units of all three engines. And as if that weren't satisfying enough, a two-ton freighter and several tugboats suddenly filled the narrow river as the party monsters abandoned the *Par-T-Animal* and swam for their lives through the grimy water before their boat was crushed by the freighter.

In all the commotion that followed, we slipped by the scene relatively unnoticed, which is something for a 142-foot boat.

As we sailed off, Cleopatra turned to me and sighed. "Tully, this is not the same city I knew as a teenager, when my father and I raced from Martinique. Hell, there were rapids on the river not far from where we sit. Miami was just a trading post then, where the Seminoles would bring their fish, fur, and gator hides down to market. Tully, I am damn near as old as this city. Age is like an opium dream. I'm not quite sure what is real and what is not anymore. I find myself rambling more, and I think I talk to as many ghosts as I do humans."

It is that kind of wisdom that I already miss. I hope my memories will help to fill that empty hole in my life now that Captain Cleopatra Highbourne has boarded her golden barge and sailed off to eternity.

Sitting on the beach last night, I twirled the Lister's conch shell in the palm of my hand and pondered Cleopatra's words. As the boys cranked up the light, I watched the beams sweep the horizon. In the west, Venus appeared hot and bright, just south of the setting sun, and it seemed that our light was connected to it. Call it a cosmic moment or a simple sunset, but it was at that instant that I understood why Cleopatra had fired me. She knew that if she didn't, I would never leave the island.

She was right. I needed to.

43

A Gang of Lady Pirates

If being fired by Cleopatra on her deathbed was not enough to get my ass in gear, then being fired by my horse could not help but get me moving.

My greatest concern about leaving Cayo Loco had been my horse. Though he seemed to thrive on the island, and the kids from the neighboring islands kept him pretty well occupied, I often saw Mr. Twain standing alone at the fence at night, staring back toward the west and Punta Margarita. I worried about him.

One night I dreamed I discovered a machine that could shrink him to the size of a golden retriever. He could climb up on my lap, sleep on the porch of the cottage, and hop in the skiff with me. I had even thought of contacting Donna Kay and Clark Gable to see if I could send him back up to their farm in Alabama, but something better happened.

Of course the locals say that the filly that suddenly appeared one day in the channel, swimming for the shores of Cabin Boy Bay, was a gift sent from Cleopatra. Maybe

that was the case, or more likely, she'd been washed overboard from a passing ship, or perhaps she'd even swum
from Cuba or Haiti. Wherever she came from, it did not
matter to Mr. Twain. We named her Ocean, and from the
instant she saw him, she was constantly at Mr. Twain's
side — whether in the corral or when we were riding
around the island.

With my worries about Mr. Twain suddenly disappearing, I found myself out of excuses to stay. I set a deadline
for the end of the month. I would pack up all my things,
and Solomon would take me to Key West on the *Lucretia*. But first I would spend a few days with Ix-Nay and
Diver enjoying what we had created. We sped over to
Crooked Island to see Sammy Raye's new boat and fish
with the boys. It was quite a toy.

When I first came to Cayo Loco, I was shocked at how
long the days in the hot sun seemed to last. Now, suddenly, they seemed to pass at alarming speed. There I
was, on my last official day as the lighthouse restorer of
Cayo Loco. All there was left for me to do was fire up the
soul of the light one more time before I left.

I climbed up into the tower with Solomon, Ix-Nay, and
Diver that last night, and we went through the familiar
routine of priming the fuel tanks, winding the weights,
and lighting the light. Then we sat there for the whole
night in silence, watching the light. With each revolution
of the bull's-eye lens, a story or a memory came into my
mind as I replayed the events since I left Wyoming behind and set off to take another road.

In the morning, we doused the flame, covered the lens,
and wound our way down the stairway. Nothing else
needed to be said. Solomon headed for the ship, and
Diver went to his cottage. I couldn't sleep and asked Ix-

Nay to take a ride with me. We made for the corral, where we saddled up Mr. Twain and Ocean and took them for a final ride around Cayo Loco.

I am not good at long good-byes or farewell parties where everybody gets all rummed up and sentimental. That kind of behavior makes tough decisions even harder for me. More than anyone, Ix-Nay understood this. Hell, he had taught me whatever patience I had found. We rode around the island in silence. Ix-Nay had never been a man of many words; he did not possess that gringo flaw of sharing and embellishing his adventures. As we rode up to Osprey Point and looked over Cleopatra's grave to the ocean beyond, his wisdom once again worked its magic. As had happened often over the last month, I was suddenly overwhelmed by the loss of my dear friend, and I began to cry. It only lasted a minute, and then I wiped my eyes, blew my nose, and recovered my composure with a few deep breaths.

"Old friend," Ix-Nay said, "grief is like the wake behind a boat. It starts out as a huge wave that follows close behind you and is big enough to swamp and drown you if you suddenly stop moving forward. But if you do keep moving, the big wake will eventually dissipate. And after a long enough time, the waters of your life get calm again, and that is when the memories of those who have left begin to shine as bright and as enduring as the stars above."

Somewhere between the waves of grief and the heaven full of shining memories, my life suddenly made sense. I said farewell to my old friend and turned my pony toward the shore.

I had opted to spend my last morning fishing alone on Fortune Island at a spot that Diver and I had found and kept secret, where a large school of tarpon had decided to vacation for the winter. I would fish the morning, then rendezvous with the *Lucretia,* and after we hoisted my new little skiff on board, I would head out for my new home in Key West.

The ocean was flat as a pancake, and the trip across to Acklins Bight took a little under two hours. As I passed by the Fish Cays, I spotted what I at first thought was an oil slick. It might have been the glare of the morning sun or my lack of sleep the night before, but to my amazement, as I got closer, the slick turned out to be a huge school of bonefish at the mouth of the channel. They were literally being herded toward the shallow water by a school of lemon sharks, whose pointed dorsal fins showed they had the school completely surrounded. As they were driving the bonefish along, a pair of dolphins picked off the disoriented and frightened stragglers with sudden, swift charges. In all my time on the water, I had never seen sharks and dolphins in a coordinated attack. It was a sign that this was to be no ordinary day.

It had been a long time since I had slept on the beach in the light of day, but I was feeling the effects of my sleepless night. It was time for a nap, and the tide wouldn't be right for fishing anyway until just before eleven. I found a campsite beneath a stand of Norfolk pines that cast a blanket of shade across the sand.

I gathered a pile of driftwood and coconut husks and lit a small fire upwind from where I had strung my hammock between two pines. There was just enough of a breeze to push the smoke over my camp and keep the horseflies and no-see-ums at bay. My rods were rigged, and the boat was secure.

Before settling in for my nap, I grabbed my mask and

snorkel and swam out to the channel to see what I could find. The shallow water over the flats gave way to the channel just past a large bed of turtle grass, where I grabbed two conches for lunch.

I floated in the still water of the slack tide of the channel. In food-chain terms, this was like one of those great diners off the beaten path. The outgoing tide was a liquid conveyor belt that served up the weaker swimmers to a host of creatures lying in wait at the mouth of the channel. It took me only a few minutes to make out the long, dark shapes eight feet under me, cruising on the bottom.

I counted twenty fish, some well over a hundred pounds. They would come to the surface once the current got rolling. I figured I had two hours. I swam back to the beach, dried off, and dropped into the hammock.

I looked up from the hammock and saw the crescent of the waxing moon still very visible in the bright blue sky overhead. Watching the moon above me, I had a sudden sense of my place amid the mysterious inner workings of the universal clock. As I rocked in my hammock, the earth was spinning like a giant gyroscope as it orbited the sun. Out there beyond the blue, the distant invisible planets and the Milky Way moved with us.

It never seemed so grand and mysterious in a classroom. Maybe teachers ought to approach astronomy from a hammock on a deserted beach as well as from the lenses of giant telescopes. The earlier in life we know we are part of something magical and mysterious, the better off we are.

At that point, the inertia of the hammock overcame the rotation of the earth, and the spinning of our galaxy and everything else drifted away as I slept.

I was awakened a few hours later, not by the alarm I

had set on my watch but by people speaking in tongues. It took me a few minutes to realize that they were not coming from my dream but from out on the open ocean, and the language I was hearing was French. When I turned in my hammock, I saw the most beautiful little ketch under sail coming up the channel. She looked to be about thirty-five feet long and towed a small tender astern. Her sails were perfectly trimmed and drove the dark-green hull steadily through the calm water. She had a raised cabin sole just aft of the main mast that sported two portholes, and the sides of the cabin were painted white to match her waistcoat. At the helm, a single sailor in yellow foul-weather gear sat on the weather rail of the small cockpit and gingerly worked the boat upstream.

I was impressed with the beauty of the boat and the sailing job that I was witnessing. At the same time, I was ever so appreciative of the fact that whoever was driving the boat was sailing rather than motoring to anchor in my secret fishing hole. The noise from an engine would be tantamount to a cherry-bomb explosion as far as those big tarpon I had discovered earlier were concerned.

I climbed out of the hammock, got my binoculars out of my bag, and scanned the water ahead of the boat. The fish were still rolling happily. I swept the glasses back to the sailboat. I could make out a small French flag flapping from the backstay above the helm, and the helmsman was no man. She wore that familiar look in her eyes of an all-night passage, but it only added to her natural beauty.

The long, sun-streaked ponytail that hung down over her jacket was held in place with what I knew to be a sail tie. She looked to be in her late thirties, very tan and very confident, and she was all business at the wheel. Her eyes flashed between the approaching shallow water off her bow and the set of mainsail.

As I watched, she slowly and quietly rounded the little boat up into the wind, lowered and furled her main, and then sprang forward and eased the anchor over the side. She remained there until she got it set, and the boat corrected course and settled back on the line.

I broke out in solitary applause. The clapping sound echoed across the flat and stunned her for a moment, as she saw me for the first time. She paused and then waved. It is amazing how a smile from a beautiful woman who drops anchor on top of the fishing hole you have been dreaming about for days can completely make you forget about fishing.

I busied myself with untying the skiff, and I headed for the channel. The sun, which had dropped behind a cloud, suddenly reappeared and blinded me momentarily. I angled off, and when my sight returned, I saw the woman on the sailboat perched naked on the stern. It was a lovely sight indeed.

In the old days, I had read stories about marooned survivors or sailors too long at sea mistaking everything from manatees to maidenheads for mermaids. As the naked captain stood on the stern of her vessel, motionless for a moment, and then did a perfect dive into the water, I knew this was no vision. The splash of her entry spooked several big fish that had been floating behind the boat, but fishing had taken a backseat to the woman in the water.

"Good morning," I said, hailing her from about twenty yards.

"Good morning," she answered in English laced with an unmistakable French accent. She had a pleasant smile.

I was trying to act nonchalant as she bobbed on the surface, completely comfortable with her nakedness. There were no tan lines on her thin but firm frame. Her hair was slicked back close to her scalp as she did a lazy backstroke toward her boat, where I read the name that was painted on the stern: RÊVE BLEU — CALVI.

"You are a long way from Corsica," I said.

"You know Corsica?" she asked as she continued to kick.

"No, but I've heard it's beautiful."

"It is. You are a fly fisherman?" she asked.

I was startled by her accurate assessment. "Yes, I am."

"I've always wanted to try it. I like the idea of fishing quietly, and it is beautiful to watch."

"My name is Tully Mars," I said.

"And I am Sophie Diamant."

"It's a pleasure to make your acquaintance. You certainly have a beautiful boat."

"Thank you." She paused and studied the *Bariellete* from her viewpoint below the bow. "That is a very interesting skiff. What does the face on the bow represent?"

"It's a Mayan god of the sea." I used the pole to hold the skiff steady against the tugging current.

"You are a long way from Mexico," she said with a smile.

"Punta Margarita." I laughed, thinking how long it had been since I had left those shores.

"What are you fishing for?"

Just then, a big fish rolled within casting distance off the starboard bow of the skiff. "Excuse me a second," I said. I secured the pole to the platform, stepped down lightly, and tiptoed quickly and quietly to the bow, where I had my rod laid out. I grabbed it, checked my line for tangles, made one false cast, and then dropped the fly between the naked Sophie and the wake left by the rolling fish.

I saw the dark shadow appear behind the moving fly and felt the familiar powerful tug on the thin line. The fly line went taut, and the rod bent in half. It was only seconds before the water show would begin.

I stood there in the hot sun, sweating in anticipation. I didn't have to wait long. The big fish rose out of the water in a vertical leap. He was well over a hundred pounds and bent my rod as if it were made of rubber. He shook his body so violently that the gill plates behind his head rattled, and he landed on his back, sending up an explosion of water.

"My God!" Sophie yelled. "It's a tarpon!" She then began speaking rapidly in French, calling to the boat.

As the fish jumped the second time, the head of a young girl popped out of the companionway. "*Regarde,* Montana!" Sophie said, pointing at the fish. The little girl was the spitting image of the woman in the water except that her hair was completely blond and curled in ringlets. She wore a bright red dress. In one hand she was munching what appeared to be a large, golden-brown croissant, and blue jam was smeared around her mouth.

The big fish made a series of acrobatic leaps, and the final one saw him completely rotate his five-foot length in the air and do a backflip, which freed the barbless hook from his rock-hard jaw. He made a final defiant jump and disappeared below the surface.

The little girl on the boat began to clap.

"Do you do that for all the girls you meet, Mr. Mars?" Sophie asked.

"Who are you?" the little girl called out to me. Her directness took me by surprise, but before I could answer, her mother interrupted, speaking sternly to her in French. The little girl listened intently to her mother, then said in perfect English, "My name is Montana. I am pleased to meet you, Mr. Mars."

"You can call me Tully, Montana."

"Where did that big fish go?" she asked.

I was trying to come up with the answer, but I was feeling extremely awkward. There I was, explaining the natural world to a little girl while her gorgeous mother casually climbed naked from the sea, grabbed a towel from the lifeline, and wrapped up.

"Do you just play with them, or do you try to catch them?" Montana asked.

"Both," I said.

"Do you see that one?" she asked.

"Where?"

"Behind you, silly," she said with a giggle.

"Montana," her mother said.

I looked to where Montana had pointed, and the large, expanding ripples on the surface indicated that a fish had indeed just rolled up there. I did not cast again, and Montana disappeared back in the cabin.

"She speaks very good English," I said.

"Her father was American," Sophie told me as she ran her hands through her hair. "It seems as if I dropped my anchor on your fishing spot. For that I am very sorry."

"It's a big channel. Besides, they wouldn't have even been here if you had motored in."

"My grandfather always taught me that they called the engines auxiliary because they were only to be used if the wind wouldn't get you where you wanted to go. But still, I disturbed your spot."

"The fish won't go far," I said.

"Well, if you don't find them again, at least we could make you breakfast for ruining your fishing spot."

Montana reappeared with a fresh croissant and extended her arm out over the transom toward me. "Want one?" she asked.

I put down my fly rod and picked up my pole. "Breakfast sounds wonderful."

"Then throw me a line," Sophie said.

As I secured the *Bariellete* to one of the stern cleats on *Rêve Bleu,* a wonderful bakery aroma came from the galley below.

"Just drop your shoes and come down," Sophie called out from below.

"I don't wear shoes," I said.

"Then you are closer to eating than you think."

I descended into the cabin of the boat. I immediately felt a strange sense of familiarity that I couldn't quite figure out. Having been used to the spacious but dark quarters of the *Lucretia* for so long, I found Sophie's ship to be tiny but bright, and more of a home. There were colorful Moroccan throw rugs on the cabin sole, and the bulkheads were covered with photographs. Two small paintings were hung on each side of the forward bulkhead. Sophie was wedged into the small galley, studying the omelet pan on the burner of the gimballed stove and whisking eggs in a small wooden bowl. Nets drooped from brass hooks above her head and were filled with fruits and vegetables. Montana was seated at the table coloring in a book.

"Hello, Mr. Mars," she said.

"Hello, Montana. What are you drawing?"

"You," she answered.

Sophie went about the almost second-nature, effortless process of cooking. Bacon now sizzled in a pan as she surgically diced an onion with a piece of French bread clenched between her teeth. "I hope you like onions," she managed to say.

"I eat everything."

My stomach began to growl. I remembered that I hadn't eaten since dawn, when I'd had a peanut-butter sandwich for a snack.

"The bread is an old trick to keep you from crying when you cut onions," Sophie mumbled. She finished chopping, dropped the pile of diced onions in the pan with the bacon, and tossed the piece of bread through the open porthole above her head. "I am still thinking about that fish jumping. That was amazing to see," Sophie said as she poured the eggs into the hot pan and concentrated on creating an omelet. "I have fished all my life, but there are so few fish in the Mediterranean." She dropped the bacon-and-onion mixture into the eggs and artfully flipped the omelet. "I have read about tarpon and seen videos and pictures, but like most things, it never comes close to the actual experience. I never really thought that a fish so big could jump so high." Sophie gently eased the omelet onto a plate that was garnished with sliced mangoes and watermelon.

"Where did you find watermelon out here?" I asked.

"In the Dominican Republic. Please sit," she said.

I eased by the galley and accidentally collided with Sophie's shoulder as she turned to reach for a dish towel to wipe her brow. I caught a whiff of jasmine. I took a seat on the opposite side of the table from Montana.

"Well," I said, "there is still a lot of morning left, and a few more hours on this tide. That school should be settled back down. Want to give it a try after breakfast?"

"You are kidding?"

"No, I am not. I don't have anything to do until my friends arrive later this afternoon."

"That would be wonderful." With a sheet of butter, she glazed the croissants she had taken out of the oven. I glanced quickly at the bulkhead on the starboard side, which was covered with a collage of photos of both Sophie and Montana at younger ages against a variety of backdrops. Some were familiar, and others were not. One showed a man suspended from a harness, hanging in the air from a mountain.

Montana continued to draw intensely with her brow furrowed, and her little pink tongue poked out of the side of her mouth. "How do they jump so high?" she asked in a practical voice.

"Who?" I asked.

"The fish. They have no legs or feet."

"They use the muscles in their body and tail," I answered.

She started to giggle as she continued to draw, and then she said, "My daddy loves to fish. I fish with him in my dreams."

"Really?" I answered, suddenly feeling a little bit uncomfortable.

"Yes, we catch lots of different colored fish, but I do not like to touch them. They're slippery, you know." She continued to sketch and then looked up and pointed to the picture of the man hanging from the mountain. "That's him. My papa fell off of a mountain before I was born. He lives in the sky now. He is a star, and I can see him at night. He is very close, but I cannot touch him. Sometimes that makes me sad."

Not knowing how to respond, I looked again at the photos above us.

Sophie sensed my discomfort immediately. She had obviously dealt with this before. She spoke to Montana in French, and the young artist put away her pencils and pad and slid off the seat.

"It will be fun to catch a real fish with a real person," Montana said to me. From the companionway, she gave me an impish look, then held up the drawing for me to see. It was a picture of a stick man on a small boat with a line connected to a giant fish that had legs. At the end of the legs she had drawn tennis shoes with springs on the bottom. "I gave your fish feet," she said with a giggle. I was about to comment on her drawing when she turned and disappeared into her cabin.

Sophie arrived with two plates and set them down. "*Mon Dieu,* I haven't set the table!" she exclaimed. "Please excuse me." With that, she produced two place mats, silverware, and cloth napkins from a drawer in the galley. In a matter of seconds the table was set, and the omelets were still piping hot.

So it was over breakfast on a solitary sailboat anchored off a deserted island that Sophie Diamant told me her story.

She had been born on the island of Corsica and grew up there in a small coastal village called Calvi. Her grandfather was an American PT boat captain from Key West, Florida, who had been stationed there during World War II. He had fallen in love with Corsica and the daughter of a hotelier and did not return to the States. He married and took over the hotel, then started a diving business and raised a family. Sophie was an only child, and when her father died in a diving accident, it was her grandfather who filled the hole in her life. It is said that adventure is second nature to Corsicans, and Sophie was no exception. Early on she had dealt with her overprotective mother by spending as much time as she could on the beach, until she was old enough to go to school in Paris, where she studied photography. Through her grandfather's friendship with the legendary Jacques Cousteau, she landed a job on the *Calypso*. By the time she was twenty-five, she had circumnavigated the world twice. During the last voyage, both her mother and grandfather had passed away while she was halfway around the world in Tasmania. Her mother was buried next to her father in Calvi, but, according to his wishes, her grandfather was laid to rest in Key West, his original home. Sophie Diamant was left to grieve as an orphan on the high seas. She dealt with it by losing herself in her work.

Through her position with Cousteau, she had gained a reputation with other filmmakers and had established her own career as a top nature photographer. That is what took her to the remote and barren landscape of Mali, the former realm of the Sahara known as French West Africa. She had gone on assignment for a French magazine to shoot a story about a tribe that inhabited the Bandiagara Cliffs. They were called the Dogon, and they guarded the place of their ancestors, a mysterious tribe called the Tellem, who, thousands of years ago, used their magical powers to fly about the cliffs. The Dogon had sidestepped the organized efforts of Islam and Christianity and still held on to their ancient mythology — where desert foxes foretold the future, and spirits roamed at large, and rocks and trees guarded the elevated burial chambers of their Tellem ancestors in the overhanging sheer cliffs.

While they were there shooting pictures, she had met Montana's father, a mountain-climbing guide named Larry Moore. Although he lived in Montana, like her grandfather he was originally from Florida. "It was amusing to me," she said, "that such a great climbing guide like Larry would come from a place as flat as Florida."

Larry had come to Mali to lead an expedition up the sheer sandstone faces of the Bandiagara Cliffs for a client. They were a thousand miles from any hotel, and the huts in the local village were full, so Sophie, the orphan from Corsica, shared a tent with a climber from Florida. Sophie discovered that Larry had actually grown up in the Florida Keys and had worked in Key West. She told him of her family connection to the island — through her grandfather — and that she was bound to travel there to visit his grave. Sophie told him the stories she had heard all her life from her grandfather about alligators, Indians, trips to Havana, and the beauty of the Florida Keys.

Larry's own tales intensified her longing to see this almost mythical island city for herself. Traveling there became a necessity for Sophie Diamant.

It is amazing how things unfold. I had come to Fortune Island to be alone with my thoughts, to fish in solitude, and then make the giant leap into the new chapter of my life. The next thing I knew, I was being served breakfast on a picture-book ketch by an enchantress from Corsica who was going to the same place I was. When Sophie told me of her longing to go to Key West, my first instinct was to inject my own agenda and tell her I was traveling to the same destination; of course I would be happy to be her guide. But I sensed there was more to the story of Sophie and Montana, so I waited and kept the information to myself. I am glad I held my tongue.

Sophie and Larry had fallen immediately in love in one of the most remote and inhospitable places on the planet. They spent a week with the Dogon, and then Larry went with her to Dakar. There they spent a romantic weekend by the sea in the exotic city. The night before Sophie had to catch a flight to Paris, they stood on the African shore and watched the sun set over the vast Atlantic. When it had disappeared, Larry had promised her that they would see the sun do the same thing from Mallory Square when he finished his expedition. He would build a boat and take her to Key West.

Sophie flew off to Paris, and Larry went back to Mali to meet his clients. He was to join her a month later in France. Larry never arrived. He was killed in a fall, and that was all she had been told by a voice on the line from the U.S. Embassy in Paris.

It was later, through friends, that she learned he was killed by Dogon guards when he tried to protect his client, who had accidentally stumbled upon an ancient Tellem burial chamber. As far as French and American officials were concerned, Larry Moore was just another crazy climber who had stumbled into the wrong place at the wrong time.

A staffer from the U.S. Embassy in Timbuktu had claimed the ashes of his cremated body and shipped them to his relatives in Florida, where they were scattered out at sea. The story of his death was no page-one account in the *New York Times* or *Le Monde*. It was only mentioned in the local Montana papers and the *Key West Citizen* in a two-paragraph story, but to a young woman waiting in Paris, it rocked her world.

The news of Larry's death arrived the day Sophie discovered she was pregnant. She went back to Corsica to have the baby and try to get some perspective on her life in sage and familiar surroundings. She named the baby Montana as a tribute to Larry. Word had come to her that days before his death, Larry had arranged to make her the benefactor of his estate, and she was surprised to receive a large check, accompanied by a letter from Larry. In it, he wrote that he was worried about the dangers of his upcoming trip and that he had made an adjustment to his will in case of an accident. He told her to use the money to fulfill their mutual dream to build a boat and take the trip. Sophie fulfilled Larry's last wish with fiery purpose.

She set about the task of finding the right boat for her mission, which was to sail to Key West with her daughter and visit the final resting place of Montana's father and Sophie's grandfather. Along with raising her young daughter, she supervised the construction of the *Rêve Bleu*, learned to be a navigator, and trained herself for the rigors of an Atlantic crossing. Once Montana was old enough, Sophie turned her into a little sailor as well, and when the boat was finally launched, they sailed away.

"You're not eating," Sophie said.

I had been so fascinated by her story that I hadn't paid attention to my breakfast, which is not a good thing to do to a French chef. I attacked the eggs as she laughed at my absentmindedness.

Finally, I could hold my excitement no more. "I am going to Key West too," I said.

"You are kidding. In that boat?" she gasped.

"No, no, no. I have a friend who has a much larger boat. He's picking me up here. I'm kind of starting a new chapter of my own life," I added.

"Do you know Key West?" she asked. "Have you ever been to the cemetery?"

"Strangely enough, I was just there."

"That is where my grandfather is buried," she said.

Sophie stepped into the galley and picked up another croissant. She placed it on my plate. As I took a bite, she said, "You must come with us."

I deflected the seriousness of her statement with a question. "Does this mean I've been taken prisoner by a gang of lady pirates?"

"If that is what you wish to believe," she said with a smile.

Breakfast was over. I helped Sophie move the dirty dishes from the table to the tiny sink in the galley.

"You must take us to the cemetery," she said. "I want to hear your Key West story. I will feed you and teach you to sail."

"I already know how to sail," I told her. I was about to describe my time at sea when Montana dropped down the ladder.

"Look what I found," she said excitedly as she gently opened her hands and revealed a small green lizard.

"Now where did that come from?" Sophie said as she picked up the lizard and attached it to Montana's ear. The little girl giggled and ran back up the stairs.

I stood there with my mouth open. "The dancing earring," I whispered.

"What did you say?" Sophie asked.

"Mama!" Montana yelled down through the companionway. "It's the big boat! The one from my dreams. It's right out there!"

Sophie looked out the porthole. *"Mon Dieu!"* she screamed as her coffee mug slipped from her hand and shattered on the table. Déjà vu.

"It's Aunt Cleopatra's boat!" I heard Sophie shout. She leaped over the mug fragments and quickly climbed up the stairs to the deck.

I was suddenly totally disoriented. Then, as I stood there beside the shattered pieces of the mug, an old photo on the bulkhead caught my eye. There, mixed in with the rest of the pictures, was a three-by-five faded color print of the unmistakable wheel of the ship that had rescued me and changed my world. Seated behind it was a much younger version of Cleopatra Highbourne in her familiar foul-weather gear. On her lap sat a young girl in a blue sailor suit who looked exactly like Montana, but I knew it was Sophie.

Sophie's voice cut through my thoughts. She was yelling for me to join them up on the deck. I followed her orders and climbed through the gangway. Montana was there to greet me with the lizard still dangling from her ear.

"Why are you crying?" Montana asked.

I couldn't answer. I felt her take my hand, and she led me over to Sophie, who stood with a pair of binoculars trained on the ship.

We watched the *Lucretia* under full sail, knifing her way through the waves as she approached. Cleopatra

Highbourne had not only sent a girlfriend for my horse but also made sure that, unlike the statue of Carlos Gardel in Buenos Aires, I would not be dancing alone.

I pulled the Lister's conch out of my pocket and placed it in Montana's small hand. She looked down at the shell and then up into my moist eyes. "Montana, I believe this is for you," I said and closed her fist around her new good-luck shell.

44

Boats to Build

Diamant means *Diamond* in French. Sophie Diamant was the only granddaughter of Teddy Diamond, Cleopatra Highbourne's beloved younger stepbrother. Yes, it is true: her grandniece had sailed into my life that day on Fortune Island.

I think that Sophie and her daughter were more shocked to learn that Cleopatra had lived to be 102 than they were of the news I had the sad duty to tell them. Their welcome aboard the *Lucretia* was greeted first with joy and then tears, as the news spread as to the identity of Sophie and Montana. But the ship herself served as the perfect floating funeral parlor as we sat in the cockpit with all sails stretched above us and set a course for Cayo Loco. Montana wasted no time in befriending Solomon, who harnessed her up and took her to the top of the spreaders.

"Aunt Cleopatra taught me to do that," Sophie said from the deck. I took her hand and placed it on the rail, and we followed Montana and Solomon up to the crow's nest, the way Cleopatra had trained us all.

We left several crew members behind on the *Rêve Bleu* while we headed back to Cayo Loco. Sophie wanted to see the light. As we sailed for the island, I led Sophie and Montana out to the tip of the bowsprit, where we rode with the boat behind us and the ocean below. It was perched there that I told them the whole story of the search and discovery of the soul of the light.

Needless to say, our unscheduled return to Cayo Loco with living relatives of Cleopatra was greeted by the lighthouse crew with shock and jubilation, in that order. Sophie and Montana were treated like mythical sea goddesses who had sailed in to put the proper ending to a wonderful story. And that is just what they did. They, in turn, fell instantly in love with Cayo Loco and spent several hours examining all the treasured possessions from Highbourne Hill that Cleopatra had deposited in her small cottage.

The light was attended like a church, and then we rode Mr. Twain and Ocean along the beach. Our final stop was Osprey Point.

It was there that Montana produced a conch shell she had been carrying in her little backpack, and she placed it below the tree. "I think I will bring her a new shell from someplace different every time I come to visit Aunt Cleopatra," she said.

No more words were needed from the adults in attendance. Montana saw the island the way Cleopatra had truly intended it to be.

A day later, we returned to Fortune Island, where we were greeted by the persistent school of tarpon rolling in the channel. They seemed to be waiting to be caught. We happily obliged, and before I loaded my skiff onto the deck of the *Lucretia,* I took Sophie and Montana fishing. Each of them hooked and released her first tarpon.

The *Bariellete* then went on board the schooner, but I did not. Instead, I had accepted the captain's invitation and signed on as the first male crew member of the *Rêve Bleu*. As the sun was setting, we sailed for Key West.

The day we dropped anchor behind Christmas Tree Island, I took Sophie and Montana back to what was now familiar territory for me: the Key West Cemetery. It was very emotional, standing there at the grave sites of a collection of lost relatives. I pointed out the family plots and Teddy's headstone, then waited, as I had done for Cleopatra, while Montana played with the tree lizards. Then she finally broke the silence, saying simply, "I would like to see your house now."

Walking together down Spoonbill Lane and up the driveway to Highbourne Hill, I think we collectively sensed that it was time for us all to finally come ashore. A few days later, I drove Sophie and Montana up to Marathon. Sophie had asked me to help her make contact with Larry's father. She wanted Montana to meet her grandfather. He was a crusty old retired Navy pilot who had outlived his wife and resided alone aboard an ancient catamaran anchored in the harbor. He was thrilled to meet the granddaughter he had only heard rumors of.

Sophie and I volunteered as crew members, and Montana and her grandfather handled the wheel as we sailed out to the edge of the Gulf Stream past Sombrero Light, where Montana dropped a small bouquet of hibiscus into the water where Larry's ashes had been scattered. Sophie and Montana decided to stay and visit for a few days. I headed back to Spoonbill Lane and Highbourne Hill.

When they returned from Marathon, I was helping

Lupe trim the bougainvillea hedges along the driveway. They walked up the driveway, surprising me from behind. The first thing I noticed was the small gold chain Montana now wore around her neck. From it dangled her new lucky conch shell. "If it is okay," Sophie said, "we would like to accept your invitation to stay here for a while."

It was and still is. Sophie and Montana have brought a sweetness to my life that I still find hard to describe.

One day, while I was sanding and varnishing the cap rails of the *Rêve Bleu,* Sophie rowed out in the dinghy. She climbed aboard, kissed me, and then hung a FOR SALE sign on the lifeline. "I have some good news," she said. It seemed that in a devious attempt to exclude the High- bournes from the family holdings, Donald Diamond the Turd had made direct descendants of his branch of the family the sole heirs of most of the shipping fortune. Guess who he didn't count on showing up in this life? My Corsican wife.

Yes, we were married in Haiti, and now I, too, have a beautiful stepdaughter I am helping to raise at High- bourne Hill and teaching how to fish.

Needless to say, the sudden arrival of Willie Singer's plane one afternoon was a welcome surprise. In the skies over Key West Harbor, he made his presence known to me as I was fishing with a client on the flats west of the ship channel. He flew the *Pearl* no more than ten feet above the water and passed my skiff to port. This took a bit of explaining to the shell-shocked angler on the bow of my boat, who was obviously not used to friends stopping by to visit in such an abrupt manner.

At dinner that night, Willie told us he had received the news of Cleopatra's death as he was backtracking home, and ironically, he had been in Vanuatu. He told me that he had passed the news on to Waltham and Parfait. To his surprise, both men appeared the next day in Santo at the airport with a sacred tree that they asked to have taken to Cayo Loco and planted beside Cleopatra's grave. It was a gift and an everlasting connection to the Keed people of Dalvalo.

The next morning, we all loaded up on Willie's plane, took off from Key West Harbor, and landed in Cabin Boy Bay three hours later. Ix-Nay, Diver, the locals, and a few passing sailboat families watched the air show. Diver told us Solomon had taken the *Lucretia* to Nassau to pick up a load of kids who were in his sailing school. After a big impromptu lunch on the beach, we hiked up to Osprey Point and planted the sacred tree from Dalvalo next to the lone palm that marked Cleopatra's grave. Montana brought a conch shell from Key West and put it next to her initial offering.

We had come for a day, but we wound up staying a week. That happens in the Bahamas when the weather is good. Montana and I rode Mr. Twain and Ocean every day. Sophie had found something magical, she said, in the barren landscape of Cayo Loco, and she started taking pictures with her new digital camera. We had slide shows in the cottage on her computer every night, to the amazement of the locals. I could tell she was happy to be behind the camera again.

Willie and I finally got to fish together, but he was more infatuated with the soul of the light and how it operated. Diver took him under his wing, and Willie gladly stood a watch every night of his stay. By the end of the week, he sat us all down around a fire on the beach and played us a song he had written for Cleopatra. It was called "A

498   *Jimmy Buffett*

Salty Piece of Land." We asked him to take his guitar up to Osprey Point so he could play it for her.

One day, we hooked and released a bonefish that he said was bigger than any he had seen in his travels to the Pacific. Willie got a call from Sammy Raye to meet him down in Grand Turk, where they had a treasure-salvage operation in progress, but he flew us home first. Before we departed for Key West, I sat in the copilot's seat and watched him enter the coordinates of Osprey Point into his GPS. He anointed the spot with the abbreviated title ASPL (A Salty Piece of Land).

Our takeoff from Cayo Loco included a low-level turn around the lighthouse — where all were gathered below on the catwalk, waving up at us — and a low pass and a dipped wing over Osprey Point. As Montana looked out the big porthole at the island disappearing behind her, she turned to Sophie and me, seated across the aisle, and said, "It's great here, but I am ready to go home." So was I.

It is a beautiful night in Key West, not just because I have Sophie and Montana, but also because I have been lucky enough to have been rescued from myself. Sure there are scars, but no regrets. My lovely wife is sitting at a desk working on a new book of incredible photos. My stepdaughter lies in my arms after correcting my accent as I read to her from a children's book in French.

This whole adventure roared into my life on a storm, but tonight it rides on a breeze not strong enough to lift one page of my story. Many things pass through my mind as I sit here with a great sense of peace and satisfaction, but there is one thing that suddenly crystallizes everything, as the words of a great song should. I look down at Montana, pick up my guitar, and play. Together we sing those haunting words from Mr. Hendrix:

Will the wind ever remember
The names it has blown in the past,
And with this crutch, its old age and its wisdom
It whispers, "No, this will be the last."

But the wind does remember — everything.

Epilogue

survivors

finally have a real job. I am designing boats for Sammy
Raye's company on Stock Island. The business is called
Los Barcos, and we are building the finest flats skiffs
around. Yes, I still do a little bit of guiding when friends
and a few old clients come to town.

Sophie's photography book was bought by a top
French publisher and became a bestselling book in
France. Along with her work, she has taken up her aunt's
torch, so to speak, and is busy with the lighthouse
keeper's foundation and camp for kids on Cayo Loco
with Solomon and Diver.

When "El Cohete" Torres received word of Cleopatra's death, he was on his way to the stadium in Havana.
He had the team manager sew a black armband on his jersey. He publicly dedicated the game to her and went out
and pitched a no-hitter.

Solomon didn't last much longer than I did on the *Lucretia* by himself. He had spent too many years with
Cleopatra in his life, and now that the light had been re-

stored, he was finally ready to come ashore. The day after he unloaded us in Key West, he told me that he was going to retire, give command of the *Lucretia* to Roberto, and move back to Cayo Loco. He was done with traveling the world. He just wanted to see his grandchildren, work for his son as a light keeper, and start the school Cleopatra wanted on the island where he had grown up. And that is what he did. He visits with Cleopatra every day, bringing flowers from the garden.

Diver became the head light keeper. He and his father immediately started building several more cottages for relatives and friends, and there were plans for a small school and a library as well. Cayo Loco was coming back to life.

Ix-Nay simply fell in love with the Bahamas. He has stayed put on Cayo Loco, and I gave him my cottage. One day, a weird wayward sailor named Chap Chap dropped anchor in Cabin Boy Bay on a weather-beaten sloop named *Mantequilla Suave*. He and Ix-Nay became instant friends. A week later, I got a letter from Ix-Nay telling of his new friend who was taking up temporary residence on the island. Chap Chap was going to help Ix-Nay build a boat that he could sail around the world. It came as kind of startling news to us, but hell, after what happened with the soul of the light, I have steered clear of using words like impossible, ridiculous, or unfeasible. Already several old boatbuilders from Acklins and Mayaguana have showed up to lend a hand, and the keel has been laid. Sammy Raye, in his new position as a kingpin in the marine industry, is backing the venture. Ix-Nay has already chosen a name for his boat: *Cleopatra.*

Roberto keeps the *Lucretia* busy with the usual cargo business but sticks to a route that traverses the Bahamas chain of islands, Key West, and Belize. He and Solomon take a yearly cruise through the islands, teaching local kids about sailing and lighthouses as part of Cleopatra's school programs. I think nothing would have made her happier than to see wide-eyed kids discovering how to tie knots, read the constellations, and scramble like monkeys up the tall rig of the ship as it moved from island to island.

We often see the crew from the Lost Boys Fishing Lodge here and in the Bahamas. Once Sammy Raye was bitten with the fishing bug, he left Alabama for Key West and bought an island called Ballast Key, where he built a hideaway estate. He also financed Bucky's purchase of the Lost Boys property from Tex Sex and Darcy Trumbo. It is still one of the top fishing lodges in the world and is now managed by Archie Mercer, who left Belize to the jaguars and moved to Punta Margarita. Sammy and Bucky basically travel around on a two-hundred-foot converted Canadian icebreaker named *Nomad* that Sammy Raye bought to explore remote fishing spots. It is run by Captain Kirk and carries all the toys any group of adult children need to go global flats fishing — helicopters, onboard seaplane hangars, two auxiliary sportfishing boats, and lots of wine. They now have built Lost Boys lodges in Tahiti, the Seychelles, and Zanzibar, and one on nearby Crooked Island, just within range of Cayo Loco.

Dawn Barston blew the family gas fortune in just two years, but she had a good time. After several trips to rehab, she landed on her feet and married a car dealer in Las Vegas. Noel-Christmas is a born-again missionary in Africa.

Speaking of fortunes, Hector the guard made it to Vegas and hit a $3 million slot jackpot at the Flamingo

Hotel. He retired as a security guard and opened a bar on the beach at Tulum called Kiss the Sky.

Donna Kay and Clark continue to live in Alabama with their three kids. Clark still trains cutting horses, but only his own. A few years after they got married, Donna Kay sold a new idea for a cooking channel on cable TV to the Superstation in Atlanta. Now she is worth nearly as much as Sammy Raye, and when Sammy moved to Florida, Donna Kay and Clark bought Pinkland. Of course they repainted it.

The tree from Dalvalo inspired a ritual. People who came by boat to see the Cayo Loco Light and hear the story of how it came back to life began bringing trees to plant. There is now a grove of trees on Osprey Point, and Cayo Loco is not quite as salty a piece of land as it used to be.

Afterword

May 10, 2004
Bird Rock, Bahamas

The novel is done, except for dotting some i's and crossing some t's. There have been thousands of words, added and crossed off, chapters lost and found and gone through the black hole of computer hell to some parallel writer's universe. The world also changed forever in the middle of this literary journal after 9/11, which made me realize that now, more than ever, we don't just enjoy our escapism — we NEED it. I lost parents and friends, not to mention a multitude of bonefish and permit flies, sunglasses and space pens, yet I found Cayo Loco.

The idea began not far from where I stood this morning after rowing my kayak across from Pittstown to the Bird Rock Light. It began rather predictably during a night at the bar, where the

conversation was dominated by the topics of flying
and fly-fishing. That evening, I was introduced to a
fellow who was down restoring the light. His
name was Chris Owens, and he hailed from
somewhere up in New England. He had stumbled
through here like the rest of us, on a boat, but he
had actually restored the Rose Island Light in
Newport, Rhode Island. The locals on Crooked
Island had anointed him Lighthouse Mon.

I had always had a fascination with the old
lights of the Bahamas that I had flown over, and I
had visited several, so talking about lighthouses
and his work of bringing one back immediately
got my attention. I left the fishing and aviation
world to the experts who were gathered around the
platter of conch fritters, and I began to ask Chris
questions. In my world of making things up for a
living, I feel that you have to find the story. It
rarely finds you. In the thirty minutes before
dinner, what I heard from the lighthouse restorer
would change my life for the next five years.

I had planned to paddle out to Bird Rock the
next day to meet Chris and see what his plans
were, but as usual down here, the weather stepped
in and stayed. I went home, and the next time I
came back, Chris was gone, and I never saw him
again. The hotel was changing management, and
the project had been abandoned — another dream
dead on the beach. I climbed silently up the spiral
steps to the light, careful to avoid the rusted-out
bolts and rotten boards that Chris had identified
with strands of duct tape. Then I pried the hatch
open, walked out on the catwalk, and took in the

view. "Not so fast," I thought to myself. The dream of restoring this light might be on the rocks in the real world, but not in my mind.

Nearly thirty years ago, on an island further south of here, I had arrived on my dream boat to that one particular harbor, where I sat one morning talking to a group of young gypsy sailing-boat children as we ate croissants and drank tea. One of them was talking about an amazing car that he said he drove around the island. The description of the vehicle was a cross between a *Star Wars* spaceship and a Jet Ski, and when I asked him where he kept his car, he looked at me with a mischievous grin and pointed to his head. "In my mind," he said.

It was Chris who pointed me to Dave Gale up in Abaco. Dave runs the Bahamas Lighthouse Preservation Society, and I flew over to visit him one afternoon. I told him I was thinking of writing a book about an abandoned lighthouse. He was working on a book himself and opened his files to me. I took the rest of the afternoon to sit quietly in his office on Parrot Cay and read the stories of the people and places that occupied the world of lighthouses in their heyday — the beacons that guided the commerce of the planet past dangerous shores.

I left Parrot Cay knowing where I was going. It was Chris Owens's tales that inspired me, Dave Gale's notes that directed me, and my own imagination that created the mythical island of Cayo Loco, which I hope you will come to love as much as I have.

Bird Rock is still abandoned, and the breathtaking panorama as seen from the catwalk hasn't changed a bit, except for the remains of a small boat that foundered on the north shore. Maybe one day, the dream of restoring the lighthouse will be realized; then again, we all may fade away, and the light will be left as it is, a deserted landmark on a conch-shell-lined island. But at least there will be a story.

I'm done. Time to go fishing.

— *JB*

about the author

After more than two decades of recording and performing music, popular singer-songwriter Jimmy Buffett splashed down into the world of books in 1988, when he cowrote *The Jolly Mon*, a children's book, with his daughter Savannah Jane Buffett, who was then six. In 1989 he published his first stories for adults in *Tales from Margaritaville: Fictional Facts and Factual Fictions,* which was the longest-running *New York Times* and *Publishers Weekly* bestseller of that entire year. His next book, the novel *Where Is Joe Merchant?*, immediately hit #1 on the *New York Times* bestseller list, and in 1998, when his autobiographical book *A Pirate Looks at Fifty* was published, he became one of only six writers to have held the #1 position in the categories of both fiction and nonfiction on the *New York Times* bestseller list.

Jimmy Buffett was born in Mississippi and raised in Mobile, Alabama. He is a fourth-generation sailor, a rabid fisherman, a pilot, a surfer, and a frequent traveler to the remote and exotic places of the world, having become addicted to *National Geographic* magazine as a child. Among his many professional accomplishments, he has recorded nearly forty albums, most of which have been certified gold, platinum, or multiplatinum. On July 13, 2004, Jimmy's *License to Chill* album was released and immediately entered the *Billboard* Top 200 and Top Country charts at #1. It is his first #1 album. He and his wife, Jane, and their three children live in Florida.